He was too close, too powerful . . .

"Do you care for me?" Sullivan asked.

Whirling away, Chelsea sought some measure of control. *"Care* for you?" she answered in what she thought was a teasing tone. "I don't know you. I know . . . I know a gentle savage. A vulnerable heathen." What she had intended as playful repartee quickly melted into bare fact. Her need for reassurance hung naked between them.

He held her shoulders softly, caressingly. "I am that man, Chelsea."

She abandoned all pretense, responding to him with the fears she harbored in her heart. "No. You're not. The man I thought I knew doesn't exist. You . . . you're . . ."

"I'm what, Chelsea? A gentleman? A titled lord? Is that what has your heart pounding so erratically? That I have become the very man you wanted me to become? My, aren't we the little hypocrite. Wanting a prim and proper Englishman for appearance's sake, but longing for a barbarian between the sheets, where it counts. . . ."

Books by Lisa Bingham

Silken Dreams
Eden Creek
Distant Thunder
Temptation's Kiss

Published by POCKET BOOKS

TEMPTATION'S KISS

LISA BINGHAM

POCKET BOOKS

New York   London   Toronto   Sydney   Tokyo   Singapore

An *Original* Publication of POCKET BOOKS

POCKET BOOKS, a division of Simon & Schuster Inc.
1230 Avenue of the Americas, New York, NY 10020

ISBN: 1-4165-0700-0

This Pocket Books paperback printing September 2004

10 9 8 7 6 5 4 3 2 1

POCKET and colophon are registered trademarks of Simon & Schuster Inc.

Cover art by Donald Case

Printed in the U.S.A.

To Susan and Marnie,
all night pinochle games and fantasies.
Theora, LaVera, LaRee, Taryn, Ladies of the League,
and all the rest of you who lend me
your undying support on those days I need it most.
You know who you are.

TEMPTATION'S KISS

Chapter

1

Isla Santiago
April 1835

Sullivan Cane's mount thundered through the night, responding to the imperceptible touch of rein that urged the steed to abandon the beach for the tangle of underbrush beyond. Bending low over the animal's neck, Sullivan dodged the branches that whipped at his head and snagged in the streaming waves of his hair. Squinting his eyes against the darkness, he ignored the destruction caused by his horse as the animal's hooves trampled flowers and foliage, pummeling the greenery into the moist earth beneath.

Keeping a close watch for vines and pockmarked surfaces, Sullivan prayed that his headlong flight into darkness would not be met with disaster. He knew he should slow the stallion and pay heed to the shadows that bled like tripping fingers across the narrow path. But there wasn't time. His innate caution had been shattered by a haste born of desperation.

After several minutes of hard riding, he saw his goal. Behind the main road, tucked amongst the trees, stood a small thatched cottage. The scent of exotic orchids thickened the tropical breeze, but the unusual dwelling brought to mind visions of bleaker climes—rolling moors and heather. Imported timber supports had been interspersed with pale clay that seemed blurred in the moonlight. A spindly white rosebush struggled to climb up to the eaves; a split rock path led from the front gate to the threshold.

"Rupert?" Drawing his animal to a halt, Sullivan swung his leg over the horse's bare back, then dropped to the ground. "Rupert!"

The huge shape of his brother loomed in one of the windows, then reappeared in the doorway. "Great bloody hell, man! What's the rush?"

"I've just come from the beach." Sullivan's hazel eyes gleamed as he stepped into the wedge of candleshine spilling out of the house. His hair fell thick and dark to a point past his shoulders. This, combined with the scowl creasing his features, gave him the appearance of an avenging privateer.

"Where's Gregory?" he asked.

Rupert shrugged. "Who knows? Since Lydia's death . . ." He didn't finish the statement. There was no need.

Sullivan stifled his impatience at Gregory's disappearance. Right now, there were more important issues to consider than their other brother's whereabouts. "A small clipper dropped anchor in the cove an hour ago. A pair of sailors brought two men ashore in a skiff. I heard them talking amongst themselves. They are looking for Richard Sutherland IV, seventh Earl of Lindon."

Rupert limped backward to let him enter, and Sullivan walked past, his expression growing even more fierce. "This time, I think they are determined enough to find him."

"Damn."

Wasting no more time, Sullivan strode to the far side of the low-ceilinged room and flung open the lid to a tin trunk. Inside lay a pile of carefully folded shirts and breeches. "We haven't got time to carry all of our belongings. Pack a few of Richard's things, and take him to another island—Isla Santa Maria or Nossa Senhora should be far enough away. Leave a message for Gregory. I'll see if I can't keep the two English bloodhounds occupied while you make your escape."

When Rupert didn't reply immediately, Sullivan glanced up. "Well?"

Rupert's jaw hardened into a stubborn line. "No."

Dropping the items he'd begun to gather, Sullivan frowned. "What do you mean, no?"

"Damn it, man, look at him!"

For the first time, Sullivan noted the strident breathing coming from the cot in the corner. He straightened, then couldn't seem to move toward the bed, dreading what he might find there. Two weeks had passed since he'd last visited the tiny island which was completely uninhabited save for a few dozen natives and Sullivan's family. Richard had been so ill then; evidently he had not improved in the intervening time. His raspy respiration was not a good sign.

"I've kept him covered and spoon-fed him broth, but he hasn't improved." Rupert's impressive size became so over-shadowed by his concern that the gentle giant appeared to shrink within himself. "The fire's been roaring all day, but I can't chase the chill from his skin."

It wasn't until Rupert spoke that Sullivan realized the air in the common room was stifling. The monsoon season had come and with it the rains and cool winds. Normally, the fireplace would have been considered an oddity here on the island—a cause for good-natured jesting on the part of the architect. Presently, a driftwood blaze filled the confines of the dwelling with a cloying warmth.

Forcing himself to move forward, Sullivan resolutely pushed images of another invalid from his mind. His father had died in this room, this cot. He'd died cursing his enemies. Richard's enemies.

Sullivan tried to tell himself that Richard was young—that he couldn't possibly die—but his hopes sank when he saw how gaunt Richard had grown. "He's so pale." This was the only thing he could manage to say as a very real fear began to twine around his heart.

"Yes."

"I'd hoped he would have grown stronger in the last fortnight." Disappointment lay bare in the tone of his voice.

"The damp steals his strength."

Sullivan lifted his gaze to meet that of his older brother. "He's not well enough to travel." It was not a question.

"Nor well enough to hide."

The crackling of the flames merely underscored the worried silence that followed.

Sullivan was the first to break the stillness. "I heard the Englishmen telling their escorts that they mean to find Richard and take him home. To his legacy." His words held a bitter cast that left no doubt that Sullivan thought an English title worth little to a man accustomed to the freedom of the islands. "They will not be content with half-baked tales and misinformation. They *will* find him eventually."

Richard moaned and stirred.

"What if these strangers were to . . . disappear?" Rupert queried with an apparently idle interest, but Sullivan absorbed the way his brother's thumb stroked the knife sheathed against his side.

"They seem most adamant. I have no doubt that they're being handsomely rewarded to uncover the truth. If they were to . . . *disappear,* as you say, more of their kind would come in their place."

Rupert's brows creased in thought. Hesitantly, he offered, "Perhaps it's time we finished the game."

Finally. For years, Sullivan had been trying to persuade Rupert into facing their enemies instead of dodging them. His eyes sparkled with cool green shards as he measured Rupert's acceptance of the inevitable. Then he took two slender tapers from a tarnished ale mug resting on the center of the hearth. "You know what needs to be done?"

"Aye."

"One of us will have to draw the English bastards away from the area before they catch sight of the cottage. After adopting Richard's identity, he must then unearth the names of those who mean to harm him."

"As well as his allies," Rupert reminded him.

Sullivan ignored the automatic protest. They spoke guardedly of their predicament, but the words they exchanged were not the result of some half-formed idea. Gregory, Rupert, and Sullivan had discussed their options over and over in the past few years—after the Sutherland clipper,

The Seeker, had first been sighted in the cove nearly three years ago. They had eluded those bloodhounds as well as those that followed. But with each year that passed, those who sought them grew more cunning, coming closer and closer to the truth.

After breaking one of the candles, Sullivan held the pieces partially hidden in his fist. "Choose."

Rather than studying the waxy nubs, Rupert measured Sullivan. His brother gave no hint of his thoughts as Rupert made his selection and drew the taper free.

"Then it's settled." Sullivan tossed the stub he held into the fire. Offering no explanation, he unbuttoned his shirt and stripped the bright red-orange garment from his shoulders, quickly following with his trousers.

Rupert displayed little more than mild surprise. When Sullivan proceeded to tear a strip of fabric from his shirttail and wind it about his hips as a makeshift loincloth, Rupert raised one brow slightly. "What do you intend to do?"

"Play the savage." Sullivan's lips tilted in a grin that was at once infectious and bone-chilling. "If those who seek us have managed to track us here, they must believe that Richard has spent most of his time with the natives and has therefore adopted their customs. I'll ride past the cove on my way to Sutherland's Roost. The shack where Mama and Papa first lived is in such disrepair that it should add credence to my masquerade. I'm hoping that seeing a white man dressed in such an unconventional manner will attract their attention and keep them off-guard until we have a chance to . . . chat."

"To what end?"

"If they've been sent by the old woman in an attempt to bring Richard back to reclaim his titles, the entire situation will prove harmless enough. I'll speak with them and convince them to tell dear Grandmama Sutherland that I'm a heathen and a savage—a man ill fit for any claim to the holdings and titles given to the Earl of Lindon. In an hour or two, they'll leave this place in a fit of disgust."

When Sullivan began to walk away, Rupert touched his arm, forcing him to acknowledge his concern. "What if these men have been sent by Nigel Sutherland? He went to great lengths to betray our father and ruin his name. Since the rumors began, he has hunted a legitimate Sutherland heir in every corner. He won't take kindly to finally finding one alive, heathen or otherwise."

Sullivan's expression grew icy. "Nigel Sutherland can rot in hell for what he's done. I swear to you by all that's holy, if these men are his employees, I'll send the bastards to perdition."

"Wait for Gregory first. He'll—"

"He'll what? He's been so numbed with grief since his wife died, he doesn't even know where he is most of the time. If we delay, Richard could be harmed."

The muggy atmosphere of the tiny cottage pulsed with Sullivan's threat. Rupert grew more glum.

Attempting to lighten the mood and allay his brother's fears, Sullivan cuffed him affectionately on the shoulder. "All will be well, Rupert. You'll see. With luck, I should return by dawn."

Rupert wasn't convinced. The natives of the island had once accused him of having "the inner eye," of seeing events before they actually occurred, but if half-digested impressions flitted through his mind, he made no attempt to dissuade Sullivan from his task. "You will be careful."

"Aye, Rupert. I promise."

Rupert scrutinized him long and hard. A note of warning feathered his words as he said, "These men may try to seduce you into considering the numerous pleasures to be found in England, Sully."

"England has already betrayed me and my family. It can offer no enticements to tempt me away from what I already have. All we need are some answers. Who sent these trackers? How much do they know? Then we can decide how to deal with the situation."

Sullivan cast one last look at the figure on the cot, enduring the pang he felt at Richard's ill health. He had to be protected, at all costs. But Sullivan was not stupid. He might reassure Rupert that the task he intended to perform was a simple one, but he knew he would be walking straight into a den of wolves.

Nigel Sutherland had gone to great lengths to extinguish all blood ties to the Lindon titles except those of his own lineage. He had trapped their father in a web of lies and treason which had all of England afire with the scandal. The nation had become divided over whether or not Richard Albert Sutherland's guilt had been adequately proven or merely conveniently arranged. Then, amid an inferno of controversy—before even the king himself was completely convinced of the legitimacy of the trial—Nigel had arranged for Richard Albert's exile to a penal colony in Australia.

As the only surviving male heir to the sixth Earl of Lindon, Nigel had thought his position secure—until word returned that Richard Albert, his wife, Julie, and a fellow prisoner had jumped ship during a storm. Their bodies had never been found, and no other solid evidence could determine whether or not they had actually died.

London had been in a furor of speculation for a decade—especially after the old earl died and Nigel took his titles. Nigel had fought to stop the whispers of slander that accused him of supplanting the earldom before his true ascension had been ensured. Meanwhile, he tried to waylay the stories that intermittently spread through England like wildfire when, every year or so, a seaman would return swearing that he had sighted the elusive long-lost Sutherland heir in Rio or Cairo or Milan.

Sullivan's lips thinned. Nigel Sutherland had been correct to grow cautious, because Richard Albert *had* survived. For two decades, he'd safely hidden himself, his wife, and their fellow escapee, Lyle Morton, on Isla Santiago. He had carved a life for himself, under the name of John Cane, begot sons who could prove to be his heirs. But he had vowed never to go back to the world that had forsaken him in his innocence. Even when the means to travel home to England had become available, he'd refused to advertise his existence and throw his fledgling family into a kettle of danger and deceit. He had kept his true identity a secret for years—until those last few days of his life, when, in the shadow of death, he had drawn his sons about him and begun a detailed series of confessions pertaining to his heritage. He had not wanted to die while trapped in a lie of omission.

Before his sons could comprehend the significance of his tales, Lyle Morton disappeared from Isla Santiago. It was not until a month later that their father admitted he had sent Lyle to England with a packet of letters, small gifts, and miniature portraits of his family he himself had fashioned during his exile. His mother still lived, and he wanted Beatrice Sutherland to know the fate of her son as well as the existence of her heirs.

But Lyle had not reached England alive. During his voyage, he had suffered a stroke. The packet of papers he had so carefully guarded had been pilfered for valuables. The ransacking had been so complete that one elderly seaman, upon entering the room mere hours after Lyle's death, had discovered nothing more than a single portrait and the final page of Richard Albert's letter of introduction. The seaman had been about to cast the trinkets to the seagulls when he caught sight of a name more famous in England than that of the prince royal. *Sutherland.* Within days of reaching port, he had gone to Beatrice Sutherland, holding the proof in his hands that her son had survived and had left an heir of his own. Richard.

Sullivan grimaced. It had taken years for the brothers to piece together such information. At the time, they had been unaware of the storm of anticipation that had erupted in the British Isles. Or that the seaman who had gone to their grandmother, disappointed at not being rewarded amply for his efforts, had then gone to Nigel Sutherland.

Forewarned by their father, and knowing that the world might soon learn of their existence, the brothers awaited the arrival of some type of envoy from England. What they were not prepared for was the violent nature of the chase that would ensue—and the fact that those who sought them were looking not for all of the Sutherland clan but only for one. Richard.

In the intervening years, both Sullivan and Rupert had infiltrated enough of the taverns frequented by English sailors to understand how such a mess could have occurred. In hindsight, he supposed such a muddle of affairs could have been prevented. But at the time, they had been working blind, wondering why those who came from England to find them were so intent upon seeing Richard dead.

During the past few years, the Sutherland brothers had lived on the brink of discovery, knowing that at any moment their life-style could be shattered and their future endangered. Not wanting any part of the deceit that had ultimately killed their parents, they had struggled to retain their anonymity. But of late, the search for the long-lost heir had intensified threefold. The brothers had been forced to dodge from one place to the next—from the tangled seaports of Jamaica, to the remote outposts of the Jesuit missions on the Brazilian coast.

For a time, the fervor of the hunt had dwindled. Thinking they had succeeded in shaking their pursuers, the brothers had come full circle and returned to the place of their birth. But the men Sullivan had seen at the wharf had proven that the results of their subterfuge had been transitory. Rather than shaking their pursuers, they had inadvertently led them to their home.

Their current dilemma demanded more aggressive measures, and Sullivan was the only one in a position to help. He knew the seriousness of his predicament. He knew that one wrong step could lead the English bloodhounds straight to this cottage, to Richard. Even if he managed to draw the Englishmen safely away from this place, a single careless mistake could cause him to forfeit the game with his own life.

Sullivan bent to tuck the sheets more tightly around Richard's shoulders. "The two of you are vulnerable here. The natives are aware that we sometimes stay at this cottage. They are loyal to us, but I'm not sure if the Englishmen have brought a translator and what lies they might employ to force a confession. Take care of him."

"I will guard him with my life, if necessary."

Rupert's voice was slightly husky, and the evident emotion gripped Sullivan's own throat, but he swallowed past the tightness and straightened. Unsure of what else to say, he hesitated, then finally held out his hand. "Take care of yourself as well."

Ignoring Sullivan's outstretched palm, Rupert hauled him close for a bone-crushing embrace. "You know I will."

Sullivan walked determinedly from the cottage. At that one instant when his powerful figure was framed in the narrow arch and juxtaposed against the blackness beyond, Rupert believed him to be the savage he intended to play. His long hair, golden bare skin, and brief attire somehow gave him an air of invincibility.

Then he was gone, leaving the house bereft of his vibrant energy. Sighing, Rupert limped toward the hearth and sank into the only chair. He rubbed the ache that lingered deep in his twisted knee and angled a little closer toward the heat of the fire.

Noting the puddle of wax being greedily consumed by the flames, he ruefully admitted to himself that Sullivan had destroyed his taper before the two halves could be compared. Rupert doubted Sullivan's piece had been shorter than his own, but he'd made no effort to challenge Sully's decision. Rupert had long since accepted that his younger brother would go to great lengths to protect his family— whether it meant deflecting Gregory's anger, saving Rupert's pride, or challenging Richard's foes. And now . . .

As of this evening, Sullivan had another, more serious objective to attain. He was about to confront their enemies and demand recompense for three decades of wrongs. His success could mean the life—or death—of the Sutherland heir. It could mean the destruction of the happiness they'd managed to find, or it could be the first seeds of a lasting peace.

A trickle of fear slithered down Rupert's spine. He didn't like the fact that Sullivan would be confronting the English bloodhounds without his help. But it was the only option available. Richard was far too ill to be left alone even for a short while. The day had come to discover who chased them.

There was no one better to accomplish the feat than Sullivan. A rage had been burning in him since their father had admitted he was not John Sullivan Cane, but Richard Albert Sutherland III, sixth Earl of Lindon.

Lindon . . .

Closing his eyes, Rupert tried to sweep his own demons aside. But even Richard's mumbled groans could not drown out the memories. As clearly as if it were yesterday, Rupert could see his father's haggard face. He'd drawn his sons near with gnarled, work-worn hands and sighed in remembrance of happier times. When he'd spoken, his last words had carried the sharp sting of warning.

"Richard is heir to the Sutherland estates. Guard him well . . . guard him well. Treachery has carried me to this island. Although I've found a measure of joy, my enemies will not rest . . .

"Until they find him, too."

Chapter

2

Firth on Forth, Scotland
June 1835

Whoever had argued that revenge could never be sweet had obviously not tasted it upon his own tongue.

The braid-covered slit of Chelsea Wickersham's cape flapped beneath a taunting burst of cool, salty wind, and she caught the restless flutter of cloth with a gloved hand. When the gust of ocean air shifted, calmed, she released her grip and tucked a stray strand of red-gold hair away from her cheek. She stood motionless upon the beach, staring seaward into the gloom.

A few yards away, waves bashed and slithered against the shore, their white, effervescent foam teasing the edges of wet sand like a coy maiden's flounce. Chelsea remained quiet beneath their beckoning rhythm, feeling certain that if she kept still enough, silent enough, she could melt into the darkness. Then no one would ever know she'd been there. Or that Richard Sutherland had arrived.

The heavy night wrapped around her shoulders like a woolen shroud, and she squinted against the mist caused by the crashing breakers to the left. Some hundred yards out to sea, she managed to pinpoint the towering masts of *The Seeker* as the ship tugged at its anchor. The craft gleamed in the moonlight, obviously as well cared for as it had been when Biddy's husband had owned it.

Less than a week had passed since Chelsea had been notified of the clipper's imminent arrival. Less than a day had passed since she'd journeyed to Firth on Forth. Less than an hour had passed since the vessel had struggled against the tide and taken position ten miles north of the actual wharf. But to Chelsea, each second had stretched into an eternity.

"Shall I go and retrieve him, mum?" The hushed, worried tones melted from the blackness.

Chelsea's lips softened into a hint of a smile as she acknowledged the portly, balding man who waited next to the battered skiff. "As soon as they signal, Mr. Smee."

"Yes, mum."

The curve of her mouth faltered, then faded. A knot of expectancy settled in her chest. Chelsea searched the water, fear and hope warring for supremacy in her breast.

To think that for months she had been dreaming of this night. It seemed like only yesterday she'd begun to believe in the impossible. She clearly remembered the afternoon when Dowager Lady Beatrice Sutherland had appeared to disrupt the tedious rote of habit Chelsea had begun to call life.

Chelsea had been walking with the Barrinshrop children in Hyde Park when her elderly friend had stepped from behind the gnarled vines of a wisteria plant that wound about an arbor support. It had been more than a year since they'd visited last, but so much had changed in the interim. Chelsea's heart ached when she saw the gentlewoman wearing a threadbare gown that was so patched and faded that the stamp of haute couture had long since disappeared into obscurity. Her hair—which had once been the luxurious color of gold and as thick as the pelt of a fox—had grown snow white, its texture fine and thin. Despite the definite nip to the prewinter day, she'd worn no hat, no coat, merely a wisp of a knitted shawl clutched tightly around her neck. The inappropriate covering had underscored a once-beautiful face lined with worry and regret.

Beatrice hadn't approached Chelsea directly. Beckoning

to the younger woman, she had waited, her expression haunted, until Chelsea found some diversion for her charges. Offering the twins a bag of bread scraps from a nearby peddler, she'd sent the children in search of ducks to feed. Then, making her way beneath the frost-withered vines covering the pergola, she settled on the worn bench beside the dowager.

So small, so frail, Beatrice Sutherland should have been unable to inspire anything more than pity, compassion, and an overwhelming sense of gratitude. But leaning close, Beatrice had whispered one word in Chelsea's ear and thereby instinctively touched the embers of a long-buried need.

Justice.

The event had occurred more than three years ago. Since then, the two women had plotted and fretted and dreamed— until this very night, when all of those machinations were about to come to fruition.

"Look, mum! I see something!"

Chelsea noted the arc of a lamp being swung back and forth from the deck of the distant ship, and her pulse beat a little more quickly.

"That's our signal, Mr. Smee," she concurred, her own voice ringing with excitement. "Be as swift as you can. We must be at the inn before midnight."

"Yes, mum."

Smee hurried toward the boat and pushed it into the surf, leaving Chelsea to wait. Alone.

The sea breeze that skimmed her cheek was balmy, but Chelsea grew stiff with anticipation as she watched Smee row into the blue-black water. Even at this late date, so much could go wrong. When a British sailor had come to Beatrice with the fragment of a letter from her son and the portrait of a young boy he proclaimed to be her heir, she'd immediately sent an investigator to find her family. The man had been able to determine that Richard Albert and his wife had died and that her grandson had been living on the island where her son had made his home.

Upon hearing that news, Biddy had immediately hired a pair of men to rescue poor Richard. Calling upon the good graces of the captain of *The Seeker*—who was an old family friend—she had implored the gentleman to fetch Richard. But months had passed since then. Long, endless months.

In all that time, they'd received only one message. A few weeks ago, a crew member from a swifter vessel had delivered a brief missive:

> *Prepare payment. Richard, Lord Sutherland, found. Evidently raised a heathen and a savage. Make necessary arrangements.*

Several times, Chelsea had wondered what "necessary arrangements" they were supposed to have made, but the strange content of the note was of no consequence now. Richard Sutherland had finally arrived in England. Although Richard Albert and his wife, Julie, had presumably died since no trace of them could be found, the boy had been freed from the horror of his parents' exile. With education and nurturing, he would soon become the refined gentleman he'd been born to be. Chelsea would see to that herself. It was something she'd become very good at doing.

For some time, she'd been one of the most sought-after women in all London. Not because of her supposed breeding but because of her reputation as a governess. She had cared for the youngsters of earls and dukes, foreign dignitaries, and royalty. After a brief sojourn as companion to the Princess Victoria, she'd been able to select her positions from a plethora of offers, even though she'd grown to abhor her work.

Chelsea's clear blue eyes surveyed her surroundings with an innate restlessness developed by years of begrudged privacy. She'd grown to hate the word *governess* and all it entailed. She hated the pranks, the long hours, the snobbishness. But most of all, she hated the men who'd thought she'd been free for the taking. Titled "gentlemen" who'd believed that because she educated the children of the manor, she must have something to teach the master as well. She'd become so skilled at rebuffing their inappropriate attentions that not one of them had ever guessed how close they'd come to the truth.

Chelsea would have left them all—the children, the sour-faced mothers, the lecherous fathers—if not for the fact that she had no other means to support herself. Her father had died just weeks after Chelsea celebrated her thirteenth birthday, leaving her destitute. Only one man had been drawn to her beauty and spirit and stepped forward to help her. Nigel, Lord Sutherland, the seventh Earl of Lindon.

Completely naive, shy, and astounded that such a great man would deign to serve as guardian to the impoverished daughter of an Irish ferryman, Chelsea had allowed him to sweep her away from her home . . .

Into the very depths of hell.

It had taken her three years to escape. Three years of imprisonment behind the sugared bars of pretty clothes, the finest of private tutors, and a pink marble manor. Only when she'd begun to realize that Nigel was grooming her for the position of his mistress and not for a place in society had Chelsea found the courage to leave.

Within days of fleeing her guardian, she'd found herself embroiled in an untenable situation. Penniless, she'd searched for some means of support, only to discover that even with her extraordinary education, there was a dearth of employment opportunities. The only positions she'd found available to women were those of dressmaker, prostitute, or governess. Since Chelsea had shown no skill with the first two choices, through Beatrice Sutherland's help she'd accepted the third. But she'd never forgotten the man responsible for her plight.

The wind lashed the smooth contours of her profile, but she remained immovable, the fiery heat of her determination burning even brighter. She knew her actions over the next few weeks would threaten her very existence. If things went awry, she would never find employment in England again. Nigel Sutherland would see to that. She had changed her name and her identity since that morning she'd run away from Lindon Manor, a home hidden deep in the Earl of Lindon's Scottish estate. But Chelsea knew he was quite aware of where she'd gone and what she'd done. He dogged her every step like an ominous cloud. Her current position in the community remained secure only because of the things she knew about him, the intimate, awful details. He had chosen not to challenge her—yet.

But the thought of possible repercussions did not dissuade her. She would see to it that Nigel paid for his indiscretions. He had hurt so many people, ruined so many lives. She wanted him to admit his sins to all the world. Then, if she went hungry for the rest of her days, her triumph would amply feed her.

Mr. Smee approached *The Seeker*. She could see by the faint trail of phosphorescent bubbles left in the wake of his skiff that he'd pulled abreast and had taken hold of the cargo ladder draped over the ship's side.

Soon. Soon.

Any minute now, Lady Sutherland would have her grandson. Her heir. Nigel Sutherland—the usurping cousin who had taken the titles—would have to crawl back beneath the rock from whence he'd come. He would be defeated without ever knowing how close he had come to destroying Richard Sutherland IV.

Her hand slipped into the pocket of her gown, closing over the miniature portrait that had been brought to Biddy. Richard Albert could by no means be considered a master artist, but the likeness of the painting should be near enough for her to recognize a dark-haired, hazel-eyed youth. There was no telling when the painting had been done, but she estimated young Richard would be somewhere between the ages of five and fifteen.

Chelsea peered into the ebony stillness around her to ensure that no one had noted the unusual activity on the deserted stretch of beach. Perhaps she'd grown overly suspicious in the past few years, but she couldn't ignore a chance that something had gone amiss—a shadow out of place, a flutter of movement. Nigel Sutherland could not be completely unaware of their activities. She had heard that the same seaman who had come to Biddy for a reward had gone to him as well. Chelsea could only hope that Nigel was not yet cognizant of how close they had come to retrieving the heir.

In order to keep Nigel from discovering that Richard was being brought to Britain, she and Beatrice Sutherland— Biddy, as her friends called her—had taken a great many precautions. Lady Sutherland had hired a coach and had gone to London as a diversion. Chelsea had come with Biddy's servants, Smee and Greyson, to Scotland. There, they had opened Bellemoore Cottage and prepared for Richard's arrival before riding on to Firth on Forth to retrieve the boy.

A threat of danger still remained, despite their careful arrangements. A single mistake could alert Nigel Sutherland to Biddy's grandson's arrival. If that happened, Chelsea had no doubts Nigel would do all he could to prevent Richard from inheriting—even going so far as to kill him. Nigel had gone to great lengths to guarantee that Lady Sutherland's lineage would forfeit the title so that Nigel could inherit and pass the estates on to his own son. He would not allow the interference of another Sutherland male.

Far away, Chelsea heard the slap of oars. She watched the swell of waves and prayed she could spirit Richard away before anyone realized he'd been there. They must be on the first leg of their journey to Bellemoore and reach the inn at Dungetty tonight.

The rowing noises grew steadily louder as the little vessel bucked its way through the surf, then hurtled to shore. As the hull scraped across the sand, there was no more time to think or to worry.

Chelsea rushed forward to help secure the boat, then stood beyond the hungry lap of water as a pair of shapes disengaged from the bulk of the skiff and stepped onto the ground.

Immediately, she recognized the two men Beatrice Sutherland had hired to retrieve her grandson. Chelsea felt, rather than saw, their slick perusal and greedy smiles. She could not deny the warning rash of gooseflesh that raced over her arms as they approached.

Motioning for Smee to remain with the boy, she approached the investigating duo. According to their agreement, no real names had been exchanged, no records kept. Chelsea had never seen their faces in daylight, but their effect on her was so instantaneous, she was sure that she could have picked them out of a score of similarly clad escorts.

"Gentlemen." Knowing she must keep in control of the situation, Chelsea was the first to speak. "I trust you've brought the boy?"

The taller man, who went by the name of Smythe, stopped mere inches away. Of the two, he had always presided over the business transactions. His dark eyes, long, equine face, and receding hairline should have exuded an aura of trust; but after each encounter with him, Chelsea had the incredible urge to wash her hands.

He insolently dragged the cloth cap from his head. Chelsea had the feeling that the action had not been performed so much out of courtesy as because the jut of his visor had blocked a silver beam of moonlight from falling across the curves of her bosom.

"Yes, m'dear. 'E's in the skiff."

"We 'ad to put 'im there ourselves, we did," added his companion, a man known only as Jones. In Chelsea's opinion, he was a nasty, ill-featured ruffian—the sort proper women avoided by crossing to the opposite side of the street.

Noting her scrutiny, Jones stretched his lips into a suggestive grin that revealed cracked and blackened teeth. "When 'e 'eard we was bringing 'im to England, 'e put up a royal fuss. We 'ad to offer 'im a bit of . . . persuasion."

"What did you do?" Chelsea drawled in her most forbidding tone.

Jones chortled in delight. "Now, missy. Don't be gettin' your pretty ribbons in a bunch. We was only followin' what you tol' us t' do."

"You were instructed to bring him home, but not at the expense of his well-being."

"Nothin's been done that won't wear off in a day or two."

"The bloke's right on that account, missy," Smythe inserted smoothly after throwing Jones a look rife with warning. "We were told t' fetch Richard Sutherland at whatever cost, and we 'ave. Therefore, I believe there's a matter of coin due."

With a great deal of effort, Chelsea managed to conceal her own distrust. She didn't like these men. She'd pleaded with Biddy to find another source of help. But Biddy had insisted that there was no one else. Only Chelsea had seemed concerned that Smythe and Jones would abduct some poor fool from the docks and try to pass him off as the long-lost Sutherland heir.

"How do I know you've delivered Richard Sutherland and not an unwitting islander?" she asked. Chelsea's gaze darted toward the boat long enough to ascertain that there was indeed a shape hidden by a canvas tarpaulin. But she had no guarantees of his identity.

Smythe sighed. "I knew you'd be doubtin' our fine work an' would insist upon a token o' proof." He tucked his thumb into the watchpocket of his vest. "This was taken from his very person whilst on the island where we found 'im."

He removed a heavy gold signet ring that Chelsea recognized long before the man dropped it into her palm. For thirty years, the family piece had been lost to the Sutherlands; Lady Sutherland had described the intricate design to perfection.

"Where did you find this?"

"Took it off 'is pinkie, we did," the nasty little man blurted.

The tiny hairs at the back of her neck prickled in warning. Somehow, she sensed that their methods of attaining the ring had not been as innocent as these men would have her believe. "I see. Then our business is concluded, gentlemen. I trust no word of your activities will be passed on? To *anyone.*"

Smythe smiled, a feral upward slash of lips that brought a creeping sensation to Chelsea's skin. "As long as you got the rest o' the jewels, we've never 'eard o' Richard Sutherland." He bowed imperceptibly. "Or o' you, Miss Wickersham."

They knew her real name; she'd never given it.

The two men must have sensed her shock because they snickered. Then Jones pinned her with an expression bordering on a leer.

Not wishing to detain them a second longer, Chelsea withdrew the pouch she'd kept in the pocket of her skirt. "I believe you'll find everything in order."

"What 'bout the trans-por-tation you promised?"

"Two horses await you beyond the point."

After inspecting the contents of the bag, Smythe settled his cap over his head again and touched the brim. "It was a pleasure doin' business wi' the likes o' you . . . Miss Wickersham. Give our regards to 'er ladyship when she comes to collect 'er kiddie."

He grinned and walked into the night, but his assistant lingered, spying Chelsea's red-gold hair and the fitted bodice of her woolen gown revealed beneath the slit of her cape. Chuckling to himself, he scurried after his partner. The scrabbling sound of their footsteps faded into nothingness as they rounded the bend. With them, they took the last of Lady Sutherland's personal jewels and her only spare team.

To the soles of her shoes, Chelsea was profoundly relieved to see them go now that their errand was finished.

"Is there a problem, Miss Chelsea?"

Smee came to her so quietly, she hadn't heard his approach. Reminded once again of the boy they'd spent so much time and effort to bring home, Chelsea hurried toward the skiff. "Everything is right as rain, Mr. Smee." She was proud of the way her command emerged strong and clear, belying the nervousness that churned within her. "Come. We've got to get Richard into the coach at once."

"Yes, mum."

They waded into the surf, paying little heed to the hungry waves that caught at their clothing. By pushing at the rear of the boat, they anchored the craft more firmly upon the beach, then moved toward the sprawled figure obscured by the cloth.

"Did he appear ill to you, Smee?"

"I don't know, mum, they kept him wrapped up. It took a half-dozen men to help him inside."

"But he's only a child."

"No, mum."

"What?"

"He was a big 'un, he was. 'Bout as tall as Greyson, I'd say."

Chelsea's heart tripped on an irregular beat. "But surely . . ." Her words melted away, and her fingers closed around the canvas. Moving slowly for fear of frightening her new charge, she drew the covering away, inch by inch.

Dark, sea-kissed hair.

Tanned skin.

Rugged features.

Beard-roughened jaw.

"Oh my," she whispered to herself. A heady disbelief churned in her as she continued to pull the material free.

Muscular shoulders.

Broad chest.

Narrow waist.

Lean hips.

"Oh *my!*" she murmured again.

Richard, Lord Sutherland, was most definitely *not* the child she and Biddy had been expecting. He was completely grown. That fact was made abundantly clear by the sculpted symmetry of his torso, the concave flatness of his stomach, and the well-endowed masculine bulge shielded by a brief loincloth.

"He's not a little tyke, is he, mum?" Smee said, stating the obvious.

Although Chelsea knew she shouldn't give in to the temptation, she stared with a blatant intensity at the figure sprawled on the planked flooring. A curious tingling began to lick at her nerve endings.

No. Richard Sutherland was not a boy—in any sense of the word.

He was a *man*.

A very primitive, savage man.

Chapter
3

A moan spilled into the early-morning hush of the still-sleeping inn. The sound—so completely out of character in the first hours of dawn—wriggled into the dark skein of Chelsea's dreams and tugged her inexorably toward consciousness.

She resisted the intrusion upon her rest. She hadn't had a full night's slumber in weeks, months. After she'd finally claimed the elusive state of oblivion, something called her back. Something disturbing.

Chelsea stirred upon the bed, automatically groping for the rumpled covers beneath her chest. The last wisps of sleep skittered away, and she blinked against the murky predawn gloom cloaking the cramped bedchamber.

Dungetty. The inn at Dungetty.

The delayed recognition of her surroundings caused the evening's events to come hurtling to the fore: the half-naked savage in the bottom of the skiff, the struggle to carry him to the carriage, the long ride with his damp head cradled in her lap.

Peering at the watch pinned to her bodice, Chelsea groaned in dismay when she noted she'd fallen fully clothed onto the counterpane and had slept but a quarter-hour. Not even enough time had elapsed to dry the still-sodden hems of her traveling costume.

Rubbing her eyes, she tried to settle into the arms of Morpheus, but her body ached and her thoughts whirled. She was disoriented after spending hours galloping through the night intent upon a single goal: covering as many miles as possible before the first kiss of the sun.

Struggling into a sitting position, Chelsea propped a pillow behind her, realizing rest was not going to be so easily obtained. She shivered against the damp that had soaked through the layers of clothing she wore, but she couldn't summon the strength to rise, strip off her gown, and change into her night rail.

Sighing, she plucked at the pins that anchored the swirl of braids to her neck, then unraveled the plaits until the waves spilled over her shoulders in a rippling curtain. Because of the utmost need for secrecy, she and Smee had ridden pell-mell to the Hog's Head Inn at Dungetty, where they could shield themselves during the daylight hours. The drugs Richard had been given by Smythe and Jones had taken their toll. Throughout the journey, he'd been so still, so sick. She'd been supremely grateful when the Hog's Head Inn came into view and she could see her charge placed in a proper bed. She regretted that they couldn't stay any longer than nightfall. But once under cover of darkness, they must continue on their way to Bellemoore.

A cry split the darkness. Rough, deep, masculine.

Richard! Flinging the bedclothes aside, she bolted from the room.

A pink stain of sunlight crept down the narrow hallway, revealing the shabby runner and the cracking paint on the walls. Doors on either side of the passageway squeaked open, and censorious eyes followed her travel-stained figure as she hurried toward the chamber bordering her own.

Chelsea paid little attention to the curious guests who followed her progress. Her only thought was on the man she'd sworn to protect.

Drat it all, she shouldn't have left him alone! She'd been so worried about propriety that she hadn't taken into account how ill he was. She'd left him in an unfamiliar place, an unfamiliar bed. Careless. Very, very careless.

She burst into his quarters and ran to the bed. Richard lay sprawled on his back, the covers tangled about his hips and dripping onto the floor. His skin was dappled with sweat and chalky in color. Arching his head into the pillows, he cried out as if tormented by his dreams, the sound like that of a wounded lion, pitiful and tortured.

"Richard? Richard!" She sank down on the feather tick and reached out to him, but at the contact he reared free.

"Miss Chelsea!" Smee burst into the chamber, followed by the innkeeper and his wife. "What is it, mum? What's frightened him so?"

Seeing that they were drawing a collection of gawking, half-dressed tavern inhabitants, Chelsea stared pointedly at the door. Smee, heeding her tacit request, quickly shut it, allowing the proprietor and his portly spouse to stay.

Once they were closed in the privacy of the small cubicle, she turned her attention to the bare-chested man. "Richard?" Speaking comfortingly to him, she edged nearer. The gray tinge to his skin had intensified over the last few minutes; his breath came ragged and swift. "Shhh . . . Richard . . . shhh."

The lulling melody of her voice seemed to calm him somewhat, but when she touched him, he rolled from the bed and retreated to the corner of the room, where he propped his spine against the wall. He faced them all like a cornered animal, teeth bared. His eyes were open but glazed, as if he focused on some sort of demon manufactured by his mind.

"What in the world has come over him, mum?" Smee asked, his mouth agape. "He was fine a minute ago. I peeked in on him before retiring."

The innkeeper's wife *harrumphed* and folded her arms tightly beneath her ponderous breasts. "He's naught but a loony. Give him another dose of laudanum, and he'll be right as rain."

Chelsea, who had been inching toward her charge, felt a chill creep over her, then a slow anger. Straightening, she swiveled to face her, slowly, haughtily, staring at the woman as if she'd heard incorrectly. "I beg your pardon?"

"Laudanum. Give him a bit of laudanum. I put a healthy dose in his tea little more'n an hour ago, and he slept like a baby."

"You gave him *opium?*" Chelsea asked, her tone forbidding. "Without my permission?"

The woman faltered, her mouth opening and shutting like a fish, when she realized her news had not been favorably met. "It's the best thing for his kind, I tell you."

"His *kind* . . ."

"You know. Tetched. Mad."

Chelsea's spine became ramrod straight, and she glared at the woman down the slender bridge of her nose. "This man is not crazy. He's been drugged. *Drugged!* To top it all off, you've just given him a healthy dose of opium!"

The woman's arms dropped. Her throat worked. "I never—"

"Get out."

"But I—"

"Out!"

The innkeeper, seeing that his wife was about to dig an even bigger hole and he was about to lose a shiny coin for the use of the room, tugged her into the hall. "Come along, Bess."

"But—"

"Come along!"

The pair departed, leaving a bleak, throbbing emptiness. A fulminating fury burned in Chelsea's breast long after she heard the slap of footfalls disappearing down the corridor. Damn them. She'd needed Richard fit and alert. That woman had delayed their plans another day, maybe two or three. There was no telling how long it would take for her charge to regain his wits.

"Richard?"

He braced his palms flat against the wall. Before she could reach him, he slid down on his haunches. When she tried to touch him, he growled and caught her in a crushing grip. For the first time, she noted the brackish bruises that marred his

27

wrists and ankles—marks caused, no doubt, by the sort of iron manacles used to restrain dangerous prisoners on ships.

"Shh, shh."

He didn't release her. The longer he held her, the more a horrible realization rooted in her brain. Judging by his need to protect himself through force, he'd been beaten during the journey. Beaten, penned up, and abused. His mind was too hazed to realize he had been liberated from his prison. He thought she meant to hurt him—and for some reason, that thought disturbed her unbearably.

"Is he ill?" Smee whispered, concerned.

"No, Mr. Smee." Chelsea had seen this reaction before. The shaking, the perspiration, the unhealthy pallor. "He's seeing things that aren't really there."

Smee, obviously lost by her cryptic reply, tiptoed forward. "Can you help him?"

"Yes. I can help him."

Leaning closer, she ignored the salt-sticky encumbrance of her hems. For the first time she could remember, appearances held a minor priority. Since he still held her hands in a punishing vise, she rested her forehead against his, willing him to hear her, understand her as she said, "Richard? I won't hurt you. Richard, look at me. You're not on *The Seeker* anymore. You're nearly home."

He didn't acknowledge her. If he noted the content of her statements at all, he gave no sign. She wriggled free from his imprisoning clasp, touching his hair and stroking the tousled waves as if he were a boy—or a frightened beast.

"Richard . . ." His labored respiration rasped against Chelsea's heart, plucking at the cords of her compassion in a way no child had ever been able to do. Minutes ticked past. Long, tension-fraught seconds. Then he looked up, his eyes a brilliant gold and green and brown. So piercing was their intensity that Chelsea could nearly believe he was cognizant of his surroundings. Then he smiled, a silly, drunken grin that spoke of little boys and naughty thoughts.

"Mr. Smee, can you help me get him into his bed?"

"Yes, mum."

But when Smee tried to approach, Richard snarled at

him—sounding so much like a wounded bear snapping at a dog that Smee jumped.

Chelsea stifled a grin at Smee's abashed expression. "Never mind. If you'll just fetch me some water, a face cloth, and my silver-handled brush."

"Yes, mum."

Smee disappeared, leaving Chelsea alone with her heathen.

"Come along, Master Richard. Back to bed."

He didn't stir. The smile he'd worn faded, replaced by a much more potent expression. He visually roamed her features as if disbelieving what he saw, and he reached out to catch her head between his palms.

Chelsea instinctively reared backward, but he held her firmly, almost cruelly, his grip digging into her skull. He grunted, squinted. Then his clasp gentled, soothed.

Chelsea began to push him away but soon halted. At the contact with his bare skin, her pulse began a slow, sluggish beat. A heat seeped into her limbs, an icy chill.

No.

A slow, delicious languor stole through her senses. A wanton, soul-wrenching physical response to his nearness. But she refused to accept the phenomenon. She couldn't allow this to happen. She wouldn't. She was his governess.

"Come to bed, Master Richard." Old regrets, long-lost urges knocked at the closed door of her memory, but she kept them snugly contained. She wouldn't be caught in a man's spell. Never again. Never.

He petted the waves of her hair, her cheek.

"Please, Richard," she whispered, more desperately this time. "Come to bed."

He bent close. His lips parted.

He was too near, too close, too dangerous. Yanking free, she rushed to the opposite side of the room, but once she'd put a safe distance between them, she refused to cower. Instead, she assumed all the hauteur, all the pride that she could muster.

Richard didn't immediately follow, but he blinked at Chelsea in confusion. He struggled upright and peered at her from the slit of half-closed lashes. The laudanum had caused his pupils to grow large and black; he seemed to study her with the hunger of a jungle cat. His chest gleamed in the weak light of morning probing through the grimy windows. Never had his loincloth seemed so brief, so ineffective. Chelsea knew without a doubt that she had unwittingly intrigued him. Aroused him.

More unnerved than she would care to admit, Chelsea stared him down much as she would a recalcitrant bully. But her silent warning had no apparent effect. Instead, this man seemed to drain her of her stoic professionalism, leaving her flushed. Unsettled.

"No."

She didn't realize she'd spoken the word aloud until it pounced into the heavy stillness.

As if drawn by that single bark of sound, Richard wavered, then shuffled forward.

She didn't speak again, but she didn't retreat. Not even when he stood so close that she could feel the heat of his body, smell the musk of his skin. Silken threads bound her, preventing her from moving, but she refused to give in to the pleasure being offered. She stood as coldly as a block of ice. She would not be ensnared by this man's drugged overtures. She would be strong. Resolute. Unapproachable.

His head dipped.

Hers tilted away.

He edged closer.

She stiffened.

Then, to her infinite dismay, his nose slid across her jaw. A rash of sensation began in her cheek and raced down her body to settle low in her stomach.

Instinctively, she pressed her palms against his ribcage, silently ordering a retreat, but he refused to budge. "No, Master Richard," she commanded again as he explored her spine from her waist to the small of her back, then splayed his hand wide to pull her inexorably closer. *"No."*

She fought to remain rigid and unaffected. But the feverish quality of his skin burned through the layers of her clothing. His fingers walked down the length of her thigh as far as he could reach, curling, bunching, seeking. Her lashes flickered closed momentarily as the hem of her traveling skirt responded to his quest, the heavy fabric shuddering, lifting, skimming over the flounces of her petticoat, and leaving a wake of need-awakened flesh.

"No," she whispered again.

The single denial was ineffectual when uttered in such a mixture of longing, uncertainty, and dread. A part of her brain recoiled in horror at her flagrant breach of propriety. But another part of her soul, one kept hidden and secret, struggled for rebirth.

It had been so long, so very, very long since she'd allowed herself to yearn for the strength of a man's embrace. His kiss. The rush of heat and light. The thrum of feminine power settling into her veins.

Fantasy battled with reality. Old emotions and customs fought to escape the chains she'd bound them in years ago. She couldn't explain how, but a string of inconsequential overtures made by a drugged man had resurrected the ghost of the girl she'd once been. One who had run barefoot over the moors. One who had devoured life and its adventures. One who had never been afraid to feel.

Before she knew what he meant to do, Richard bent to touch his mouth to her own. Soft as a dove's wing, the caress was little more than an innocent meeting of lips, but Chelsea wrenched free as if scalded. Standing out of his reach, she dragged huge gulps of air into her lungs, aghast at what had just happened. Not the kiss itself, but her own inability to stop it before it occurred. Deep down, she had wanted it to happen. She had wanted to know what it would be like.

And she'd liked it.

Immediately upon the heels of that thought, Chelsea hardened her heart, denying that she'd experienced anything but a momentary twinge of lust. Lust, as she'd discovered long ago, was a transitory emotion that soon faded into heartache.

She bent to pull back the covers. "Bed, please."

He didn't move. He seemed to dare her to come and fetch him.

"Master Richard, I will not tolerate any more of these shenanigans. You must sleep. Now."

How easily the role of governess settled over her shoulders, cloaking her in its familiar warmth. Regardless of the wanton tumble of her hair and the rumpled condition of her traveling suit, the role she played dropped into place.

A part of her mourned the fleeting taste of excitement she'd enjoyed, but she ignored that impulse. She was a grown woman. A respected member of the community. She couldn't possibly long for those days when, as a young girl, she'd been wild and uncontained, filled with passion and whimsy. The years had changed her from the unfettered imp who'd swum naked in Paddy's pond . . . indiscriminately kissed the hostlers at Lindon Manor . . .

Posed nude for the man she'd adored.

"Bed, Master Richard." Her voice was unaccountably brittle. "Come to bed. You'll feel better if you do."

He swayed on his feet, reached for her, stumbled, and all but fell onto the mattress.

Before he could continue his seduction, Chelsea dragged the linens over his chest and tucked him in with practiced efficiency. But when she would have left him, he caught her.

His eyes were eloquent. Betraying his confusion, his incoherence, his vulnerability.

"No, Master Richard. I have my own room. It wouldn't be proper." *Proper.* There had been a time when that word had held no sway in relationship to her behavior. Now it bound her in links of iron.

Richard didn't relent. He seemed to beg her to be kind. Even as large as he was, as wild, as masculine, he seemed overtly vulnerable. She couldn't refuse.

He tugged.

She obeyed.

Sinking onto the side of the featherbed, she rested against the splintered frame. He sighed and rooted at the pillow with his head, grunted unhappily. He seemed so sad, so confused. But the expression soon faded beneath a heated spark.

Shifting closer, he reached to explore her face with his

fingertips, much like a blind man would. He strayed to chart her neck, her shoulder, the tiny jet buttons beading the closure of her bodice. Each exhalation of air he made seeped through the cloth at her waist, warm, moist, undeniably arousing. A sigh melted from his lips. A masculine groan of thwarted ambition. Irritation. And then . . .

He slept.

When Smee burst into the room sometime later, Chelsea quieted him with a gesture. But long after the portly man had left, she couldn't deny that she longed to trace Richard's profile, his hair, seek out the hills and valleys of his torso, and explore his body in much the same way as he'd explored her face.

She resisted the forbidden temptation. Just as she had so many times that day. She sat for hours, until her back grew stiff and her hands clenched together in a tight knot.

If only her mind were so easy to control.

Chapter

4

*L*indon Manor huddled in the onslaught of a summer storm. Its pink marble walls shimmered with slick runnels of water dammed here and there with the plastering of petals and leaves wind-tossed from the garden.

Inside, rain spattered against the window panes as if seeking entrance, hissing in a strange, unintelligible language. To Nigel, Lord Sutherland, seventh Earl of Lindon, the sound seemed to taunt him, tease him, urge him on. Desire warred with caution, tenderness with an inexplicable rage.

Lord Sutherland automatically tamped down the roiling emotions. Control. Over the years, he had learned the importance of control. Self-discipline had become his mantra, obscuring beneath the stoic mask he wore that he was constantly weighing and judging, sentencing and meting out punishment. No one was free from his censor, not his family, his business associates, his employees. To maintain this appearance of calm implacability, he had become a creature of daily habit. He hid his true thoughts and urges beneath a thin veneer of civility.

But there were days when the facade grew wearisome. Days when the pressures of life escalated and the threat of his own mortality knocked at the gate of his consciousness. At such times, he found himself fighting for his usual mien, ultimately recognizing his greatest fear. Death. Not because of what he'd done but because of what he hadn't done. Nigel wanted more. *More.* Of late, his greed had become all-consuming.

Nigel's pulse thudded in a deliberate, sluggish beat as he waited outside the doorway that led from his own private chambers into his wife's bedroom. The minutes ticked by, doled out in a miserly fashion by the old repeater clock situated on the mantel, until finally he heard the lulling cadence of Estella's even inhalations. Soft, shallow, sweet. At long last, she had fallen asleep.

The hinges made no noise, but that did not surprise him. Each morning, long before his wife awoke, Nigel dipped the tip of a feather into a bottle of oil he kept hidden in the false bottom of his dresser drawer. Then he eased inside, the fluid silence of the well-tended hardware keeping his ritualistic visits private.

Stepping farther into the room, he lingered in the shadows, savoring the secret stolen moments. Thirty years ago, Nigel had made Estella his bride. She had not been an easy prize. Many men had sought her hand—including his arch rival, Richard Albert Sutherland III. But Nigel had wooed her with the calculated devotion of an avid swain. He had showered her with flattery and plied her with gifts. Later, when she had agreed to become his own, he'd known that Estella had married him for one reason. That uncommon, unheard-of commodity: love.

Silly, vain, foolish creature.

Walking silently forward, Nigel stood at the foot of the bed, his figure impressive, hard, lean—even at two-and-fifty years. If Estella were to awaken, his rugged form would be a darker patch in a sea of blackness, framed between the heavy velvet bed curtains. But her sleep continued undisturbed.

Lightning flickered briefly, illuminating the delicate shape swathed in the linen sheets and down comforters. How like an angel she was. Perfect in every way. Her skin was as pale as fresh cream, her hair as delicate as spun silk.

She was his most valued possession. Other men had openly confessed their envy of Nigel's good fortune in obtaining such a woman. She came from a sterling family— solid aristocracy. Her dowry had been ample, her devotion unwavering. For thirty years, this female had cared for him. She had seen that his house was a home. She had kept herself beautiful, doting upon his whims of fashion. She had nursed him through ague and calmed his fits of rage. She had teased him and pampered him and hung upon his every word.

So why had it never been enough?

The air became cloying, thick, trapping in his throat until Nigel thought he would choke. A rage swelled deep in his soul, burning him like a hot tide of bile. Damn it all, she *loved* him, she *adored* him. Every breath she took was for his benefit. Every decision she made was for his comfort—and it wasn't as if he were completely immune. His own feelings for her were all-consuming. He would kill a man for staring too long at her. He would destroy anyone who might harm her. She was his, bound to his side by emotional shackles that even he couldn't begin to explain. He would never allow her to leave him. He would never satisfy the cravings he had to possess her body again and again.

But it wasn't enough.

It had never been enough.

Slowly, just as he always did, Nigel turned away from the bed. Not touching her. Not disturbing her. Closing the door behind him, he disappeared into his own room. Looping the heavy folds of his dressing gown over his arm, he clasped a branch of candles from his bedside table and eased into the hall. Pulling aside the heavy grandfather clock, he slipped into the secret passageway built a hundred years ago by the designer of Lindon Manor, another Sutherland heir.

He found his way with ease. He could have traversed the path blindfolded, but the candles provided a much-needed pool of amber light as he entered his study through the door behind the bookcase and crossed to the far side of the room.

Setting the candelabra on a nearby table, he delved into his pocket and withdrew a key which he inserted into the hidden panels over the mantel. The sharp relief of his shadow danced, shivered, then stretched up the dark walls. Leisurely, he reached over his head and opened the mahogany doors.

Just as his possessiveness for Estella would never wane, he knew he would never tire of this familiar sight. As long as the stars hovered in the heavens, he would feel the same keen pang of hunger each time he performed this familiar ceremony. It had become his religion, his shrine. His obsession.

A subtle dancing heat settled low in his loins as he surrendered to the moment. With a thirst akin to that of a desert wanderer, he absorbed the stroke of candle glow as it slipped between the crack of space he'd created and caressed the ever-widening sliver of canvas being exposed to view. Although he had seen the painting a thousand times and had studied it for countless hours, he would never overcome the rush of adrenalin, the surge of power, the shudder of anticipation.

She was so beautiful. Everything his wife was not. Strong, willful, hot-blooded. Instead of delicate blond waves combed away from a wide forehead, her tresses were wild and uncontrolled, gleaming with the wanton shade of sunset. Instead of skin the color and texture of milk, a smattering of freckles dappled the smooth contours of her shoulders. Where Estella was shy and reserved, roses and sunshine, this woman was passion and fury, fire and ice. Where Estella had always approached him with open adoration, this woman had countered his advances with barely concealed distrust. She had foiled him at every turn. She had managed to escape and remained free through the tacit threat of all the knowledge she'd gathered. His standing in society could be completely ruined if the peerage were to discover all she knew.

Even so . . . he still wanted to own her. Heart and soul, mind and body.

There was no noise behind him, but Nigel stiffened,

37

immediately sensing a presence. The hairs at the back of his neck prickled until a familiar dark voice asked, "Brooding?"

He swiveled to find Reginald Wilde, his personal secretary, lounging against the wall. He had entered the room so stealthily that even the click of the lock had not interrupted Nigel's meditation.

Nigel didn't immediately speak. He waited, counting the beats of silence that would emphasize his superiority, then said, "Your people. What do they say?"

Reginald grinned knowingly. He purposefully took time to wipe the rain from his face, the mud from his hands. Always challenging. Not in a rebellious manner, but more in the way of an indulgent spouse who failed to be impressed with such posturing.

"Beatrice Sutherland is staying with friends near Hyde Park," he said at last. *"The Seeker* was in a London port last fall but left again as soon as it took on supplies. The captain, as you well know, received the ship due to a condition mentioned in the previous earl's will. It is thought that his loyalties to the Dowager Lady Sutherland are still quite strong. Before leaving on his voyage, he was seen with a young, respectable woman. A Miss C. Wickersham." He paused for effect. "Chelsea Wickersham resigned from her post with the Barrinshrops a few months ago. No one has seen her since."

"Damn it! How could this have happened? We sent our own men to investigate the rumors. They told us the Sutherland brat was dead. *Dead."*

Reggie rubbed the side of his nose and stared at Nigel pityingly.

"What?" he demanded impatiently.

"If you will remember, they reported a fire which *supposedly* resulted in his death as well as the deaths of the natives who cared for him. There is a difference. Since they had no positive description of Richard Sutherland, they could not prove such a claim. They merely had a body. One burned beyond recognition."

Nigel pounded his fist against the desk. "I want you to hire someone to find her!"

An impatient scowl creased Reggie's features. His clothes were wet, his boots filthy from his cross-country ride. Stepping to the breakfront, he poured a healthy draft of brandy into a snifter. "Don't you mean *him?* If Richard Sutherland IV has eluded his hunters, perhaps he should warrant our first consideration."

"If he exists, he'll be with Chelsea."

"How can you be so sure?"

Nigel's attention returned to the portrait, displaying the intensity of a man possessed. "I'm sure." His expression grew hard. Bitter. "They all mean to ruin me—Biddy, that impostor, Chelsea—and she'll be more than happy to show them the way."

"What can the little governess do?" Reginald shrugged in disinterest and sipped at the brandy in his glass. "Even if Dowager Lady Sutherland has managed the impossible and has found another Sutherland heir, nothing will come of it. The little brat was raised in a remote corner of the world— no doubt without any kind of formal education. In order to replace you, Beatrice must *prove* his lineage and his ability to perform the duties of a titled gentleman. That Wickersham woman might have time to teach him to speak and dance and converse with the ladies, but she'll give him nothing more, nothing of consequence that will demonstrate his noble blood."

"Don't be so sure. Chelsea was always a very good teacher. She has . . . ways to make a man respond." Sutherland's voice grew thick as he studied the painting once again. "There was something about her . . ."

Wilde glared in disgust at the canvas. "You seem to have an unhealthy attachment to that thing."

Lord Sutherland tried to look at it as Wilde must see it, dissecting each line, each brush stroke. The portrait had been expertly drafted, so expertly, in fact, that at times Nigel honestly thought he could reach out and touch warm, willing flesh.

But Reginald must consider it little more than the clever representation of a woman *en deshabille* upon a bed of tangled linens. She was turned away from her unseen audience. Barely a shred of profile could be discerned, underscoring her vulnerability. Rich, luxurious hair the color of glowing embers tumbled down her naked back, while the covers she clutched to her breast dipped low about her spine, exposing the swell of her hips and the perfect shape of her buttocks.

She'd been so beautiful then.

She was beautiful now.

"I want to know where she went after leaving the Barrinshrops. Find her," Lord Sutherland ordered again. "She knows things that could endanger my standing in society," he muttered, at once drawn and repelled by the woman's visage and the turmoil of emotions it inspired.

Wilde snorted in derision and took another healthy swallow of the liquid swirling in the bottom of his glass. "What can she possibly say or do to harm you? To expose you, she must first expose herself." He offered his employer a crooked smile. "It appears to me that she has already exposed quite enough in that painting. Certainly more than she would ever want on public display."

Sutherland's hands knotted into tight fists. A brittle cast sharpened his countenance, revealing a streak of cruelty he was accustomed to concealing beneath a reserved expression.

"Find her." Rising, he strode forward to stab his finger against his secretary's chest. "Then bring . . . her . . . to . . . *me!*"

Chapter
5

*T*he ticking of a distant clock deafened him, rebounding in his skull with a strength to wake the dead.

Half-roused, half-drugged, Sullivan knew that something had changed. His head ached with the effort, but he was able to determine that the splintered wood of the cargo hold had given way to an angel's cloud. Mercifully, the rocking and swaying he'd endured for weeks had stilled. Sullivan could almost believe he'd been cast ashore on solid ground.

No, it couldn't be. He'd been locked in a cramped and barred cell. His captors had treated him like an animal, feeding him only once a day. Sullivan had known his food had been altered somehow when he'd grown disoriented each time he partook of his single meal, but his body had craved the nourishment enough to damn the consequences.

But things had changed.

Wading through a morass of confusion, Sullivan tried to concentrate. Vaguely, he remembered seeing Rupert and Richard.

My lover's eyes are nothing like the sun . . .

He remembered donning the costume of a savage.

If lips be red . . .

He remembered the two Englishmen who had ambushed him on the road. The struggle. The pain.

Then her lips . . .

He remembered being penned like a wild dog. The sailor's sneers. The lack of light.

My lover . . .

Drawing upon the last scraps of coherence he could lay claim to, Sullivan forced his lashes to lift. As he gradually focused on his surroundings, he couldn't believe what he saw.

He lay within the confines of a four-poster bed. A rain-spattered window set high and thick in the wall revealed a dim patch of daylight while a small table beside him held a branch of squat candles to augment the limited supply of illumination. While in the corner . . .

A ghost? A vision? Vaguely, he wondered if he were witnessing a tantalizing hallucination. A weak smile tugged at the edges of his mouth. If so, he longed never to wake.

In the mellow pool of firelight, he saw a woman standing with her back toward him. She wore nothing more than a modest cotton chemise and a flounced petticoat. Even with his addled senses, Sullivan surmised that she must have been caught in the grumbling of the storm. The flickering glow from the hearth gilded the sheen of moisture clinging to the naked flesh of her arms and shoulders. Occasionally, the *drip-plop* of water nudged the quiet as beads of moisture fell from the water-stained hems of her skirt to pool about the delicate shape of her feet. To his cloudy senses, she appeared both illusion and reality. Saint and temptress.

My lover's eyes . . .

He fought to understand her words, then determined she wasn't speaking to him at all but sang under her breath.

Are nothing like the sun . . .

Her arms lifted in a single graceful motion. Skin as pure and taut as a ripe peach was caressed by the mellow glow of the coals in the grate. One by one, she began to pluck the pins from her hair, rich, waving, golden tresses.

Sullivan's eyelids drifted shut, their weight becoming too heavy to maintain. When he opened them again, the woman had not vanished as he had feared. She stood before him, the damp locks spilling about her hips like a thick mantle—too curly to appear fashionable, too sensuous to be considered proper.

My lover's eyes . . .

In utter fascination, he watched as she reached for a silver hairbrush and stroked the tangles free. Static crackled in the room, tugging at a ribbon of tension that threaded his veins. His lips curved in masculine appreciation. Rather than taming the wild mane, she inadvertently made it curlier. To Sullivan's utter delight, the waves rippled down her back in a mass of naturally formed ringlets. The kind that would twine around a man's fingers and spill over his skin like liquid silk.

The seconds slogged past, marked by the grating tick of the clock. The woman seemed unaware of his scrutiny. She continued her ministrations, oblivious to his intense regard.

At any other time, the steady rhythm of her brushing might have soothed him, but his expectancy prevented him from relaxing. He prayed she would turn. He wanted—*needed*—to see her face. Anticipation settled in his gut like a slow-burning fire.

He attempted to speak, but no sound emerged. Trying once more, he swiped his tongue over dry, cracked lips and groaned.

The woman whirled. The brush clattered to the floor. Wide blue eyes the color of a crystal stream clashed with his.

She was older than he'd expected. Nearing a score-and-five if he guessed correctly. Delicately chiseled features comprised her face—wide brow, slender nose, finely pointed chin. Nothing about her would have stopped a man in midstride. She wasn't classically pretty. Not in the sense that women of the times were supposed to be—fashionable porcelain dolls with the constitutions of orchids.

No, there was a resiliency to her. A strength. If a man were to catalog her features one by one, he would be disappointed. But when taken all together, she was striking, exotic, aristocratic.

She scrutinized him long and hard, the swift rise and fall

of her breasts betraying her agitation. For a moment, he was sure he saw something else settle over her expression. A hint of languor, a taste of stark sensuality. A wistfulness.

Then, to his utter disappointment, the woman recovered her poise and grasped a woolen cape from where it had been flung over the chair behind her. In a moment, she'd covered herself from neck to toe. The temptress vanished, and in her place stood a woman of determination and strict formality. The room dipped slightly. Spun.

"My lord," he heard her say from a long distance.

My lord?

Richard . . .

Chelsea gripped the edges of her mantle tightly against her, but she could see that Richard Sutherland had fallen into another drugged sleep.

A trembling began deep in her bones, but she fought the reaction, refusing to give it leave. He was just a man like any other. She had been ogled by far more intimidating sorts than this. There was no reason to become jittery and warm simply because he'd studied her so thoroughly from beneath heavy eyelids.

A knock came at the door, and she bent to retrieve her hairbrush from the ground before crossing the room. "Who's there?" she called softly.

"Smee, mum. I brought you a cup of broth and a bit of lamb from below."

Chelsea quickly twisted the key and opened the door. Smee's balding pate shimmered with a fine sheen of sweat, and his chubby features radiated with a flush of exertion. Waddling inside, he placed the tray on the dresser, still trying to catch his breath from his climb up the staircase. He spied Richard Sutherland and shook his head. "Poor man, poor man," he huffed, then offered Chelsea a gap-toothed smile and crossed his arms over his ample middle. "Are you sure I can't talk you into letting me stay with him, mum? I'd be more than happy to help."

"Thank you, no, Smee. You need your rest. After yesterday's debacle at the Hog's Head Inn, I think I should watch over him personally. We've come a long way to reach Albee tonight, and we've still a good distance to cover tomorrow to reach Smedlyton."

"Very good, mum." He marched into the corridor. "I'll be ready with the coach at dusk, Miss Chelsea. The rain slowed us down a bit, but I think we can make up the time we've lost this evening. If so, we should reach Bellemoore in a day or two."

"Thank you, Smee."

Once he'd disappeared, Chelsea twisted the lock. She doubted the flimsy hardware could discourage anyone determined to enter, but at least it offered a measure of privacy from drunken patrons who might stumble up the staircase in search of their beds.

Her attention was drawn back to the man in the fourposter. Visually exploring the peaks and valleys hidden by the coarse linen, she noted the lean lengths of his legs, the narrow box of his hips, the corrugated shape of his torso. Her mouth grew dry. She'd expected to be responsible for the needs of a boy. A boy!

But Richard Sutherland was no boy—not by any stretch of the imagination. His masculine frame crowded the narrow bedstead, and his feet pushed against the covers as if seeking extra space. He was fully grown. Mature.

Wild.

Her pulse began an erratic rhythm. If she'd known he would have shaken off the effects of the laudanum, she wouldn't have dreamed of changing her clothes. It had been a mistake she wouldn't likely forget again. When she'd turned from her ablutions to find him looking at her, she'd caught a glimpse of the heathen buried in him. His thorough scrutiny had seemed to strip the clothes from her body, leaving her naked and vulnerable. Not just physically, but emotionally as well. Judging by the flare of interest she'd witnessed, she knew that he had been intrigued, not dissuaded, by what he'd seen.

Chelsea was aware of the risks involved in this unlikely

mutual attraction better than anyone. To pursue such an amorous folly could be dangerous—*would* be dangerous. Especially to a woman like her.

So why couldn't she relegate him to the long list of reprobates and rakes who had failed to capture her attention in the past? Why couldn't she seem to erect the formal, professional barriers that had always served her so well?

Although she hated to admit it, this man unlocked a hidden vault deep in her soul. She was flooded with quick snatches of fantasy that had no place in her well-ordered life. She couldn't seem to stop the odd reaction. It was as if she were being pulled backward in time.

Closing her eyes, she tried to ignore the young woman she'd buried so long ago. Papa had despaired of ever teaching her to be a lady. During her childhood, she'd been so wild and filled with a greediness for life that he'd chastised her regularly. When he died, leaving her alone to fend for herself, Nigel Sutherland had taken his place as her provider, having been drawn to her by that very passion, that reckless *joie de vivre.*

Lord Sutherland hadn't stifled her natural drives—in fact, he had encouraged them. Beneath his tutelage, she'd become a passionate woman. He'd seen to it that she had every opportunity, money, education. It wasn't until later that Chelsea realized such gifts would exact a terrible price.

She approached the four-poster as a prisoner might approach the block. But she couldn't resist. She was drawn to Richard Sutherland as firmly as if pulled to his side by a magic string.

Reckless images came faster, stronger. Bare flesh golden and sun-kissed. Long, waving hair tossed by the wind. And hands. Square, strong, masculine hands.

His hands.

Her hands.

Twining.

Caressing.

How could he do this to her? She didn't want to feel anything for this man. She wanted to remain cool and aloof.

Chelsea's bare feet made no sound on the floorboards

when she halted next to the bed. So intent was her study of Richard Sutherland that the cape dropped unheeded from her shoulders and pooled around her ankles.

Before this night, she'd never considered herself cheated. She'd never believed herself less fortunate because of her lack of male companionship.

Now she felt empty.

Hungry.

Her palms grew moist. The need to touch him swelled inside her breast.

He lay quietly beneath a single sheet. The opium had snared him in its tenacious embrace. She doubted that he would be able to distinguish his dreams from reality once he regained his wits. He wouldn't remember this day or what he'd seen. He would never know if she reached out to touch him.

She shouldn't.

But she wanted to. Her pulse thrummed with the overwhelming desire.

Touch him.

Just this once.

Though each gesture seemed to be weighted, Chelsea moved closer, much like a toddler examining a torte she'd been forbidden to taste. Only when she sat beside him, her petticoat lapping against the bed frame and spilling around her icy feet, did she stop.

Her lungs fought the crushing weight of guilt and delight. Her pulse knocked against her throat. Her fingers trembled as they stretched out, hesitantly at first, then with more determination when she realized he showed no signs of consciousness. She had this one opportunity to indulge herself. A single chance.

Chelsea filled her mind with details. Her knuckles skimmed the hair fanning about his shoulders. The brown-black tresses gave way beneath her exploration, then sprang back into place, tickling her palms. The strands were fine-textured. Fascinating. She had never known that a man's hair could be soft and inviting.

She knew she should stop there, but now that her restraint

had been broken, she couldn't back away. Not yet. Following the feathered hairline, she trailed a path to his cheek, noting the smooth skin below his lashes, then the raspy texture of his jaw. The stubble of his beard abraded her with a delicious friction. A flurry of sparks raced through her body.

Chelsea savored the storm of reaction she inspired. He felt good. Warm. Oh, so male. She wanted to surrender to the strength of his body, the faint musky scent of his skin. She wanted this moment to stretch into eternity until—

His lashes flickered open, and Chelsea issued a gasp of sound.

Golden, green. His eyes pulled at her, drawing her into a vortex of physical awareness. So intense was their power that when he caught her elbows, bringing her closer, she couldn't resist.

The heat of his body seeped into the dampness of her clothing, warming her, scalding her. Broad hands, callused and strong, cupped her shoulders, molded the gentle flesh. His hold was far from gentle but could never be considered cruel. It contained an urgency, a need, as he dragged her toward him.

Their lips met, parted, met again. Then, as if a match had been touched to a pyre of dried grasses, the hesitancy exploded in a burst of flame. His mouth opened, hers responded. His tongue swept into the honeyed sweetness, hers parried, clashed, challenged.

Passion surged through her body. Never had a man's caress consumed her so quickly. Never had her reason been swamped so completely. The fantasies she had begrudgingly entertained became reality as she plunged her fingers into his hair and submitted to his seduction.

A loud crash of cutlery from the main hall below caused Chelsea to jerk free. Her lashes sprang open, and propriety rushed over her in icy tides as she noted the heavy-lidded gaze of the man she had embraced so freely. She shouldn't be doing this! It was wrong. So very, very wrong!

Shocked by the depth of her response, Chelsea wrenched away and retreated to the opposite side of the room.

The man in the bed struggled to prop himself on his elbow

and extended his arm to her. But she soon realized it wasn't merely passion that had caused his pupils to dilate and his limbs to tremble. He wavered, fighting the encroaching tentacles of unconsciousness.

The lingering effects of the opium proved too powerful, and he succumbed, falling back. One last time, he attempted to focus on her face, then he grunted in supreme irritation. Slept.

Even drugged and unconscious, his lax body called to her like a siren's song. Desperately, Chelsea delved within herself for the poise and control she'd created over the years. She sought to dredge her soul for the stern, dictatorial governess who'd lingered there only minutes before.

The emotions came as soon as she called, but somehow they did not feel as comfortable as they once had. This man made her want things she couldn't have.

No, Richard Sutherland was not the little boy she had expected. He was a man. An overwhelming, compelling, irresistible man. In many ways, his maturity would make her task easier. She could reason with an adult. She could focus on deportment instead of behavior. But Chelsea rued the fact that she had been torn from the safe misconceptions of a childish Sutherland heir.

A loss filled her chest with the weight of a thousand stones. Because—for the first time in ever so long—Chelsea Wickersham wanted a male to wake and see her, not as a servant or an employee, but as a woman.

But that could never be. Not with this man. Richard Sutherland might intrigue her, he might excite her, but he was out of her reach. She couldn't have him. Not now. Not ever.

Not without destroying them both.

Chapter

6

Waves crashed against the bow of the *Regal Hind*, spewing over the railing to cascade onto the slippery deck. A single figure stood in the early-morning gloom, the sharp angles of his face clearly highlighted against a backdrop of swelling iron-gray waves and a sky the color of lead. He leaned against the supports that cradled the carved prow fashioned in the shape of a golden-haired mermaid. But he spared no attention for the scantily clad creature. His eyes were turned toward the horizon, where he had been told that "anytime, now, anytime" the faun-colored dunes of Calais would appear.

Another surge of seawater crashed against the swift vessel, and the fizz and burble of thwarted intent filled the man's ears. But not so much that he missed the uneven gait of another passenger who approached him from behind.

"Come below, Gregory."

"Where's Richard?"

"He's fine. Sleeping peacefully. He seems stronger. I think the sea air has done him a world of good."

Gregory nodded to show he'd heard, but he continued to search for the elusive coastline.

"All will be well, you'll see."

"Will it?" Gregory turned to his brother. "How could you let him do such a foolhardy thing?"

"He meant to make inquiries, nothing more. How were we to know those men would abduct him?"

"You should have anticipated such an action. Father warned us that Nigel Sutherland was not to be trusted. His men have been tracking us for years. What were you thinking, man?"

"We still have no proof they were Sutherland's men." Rupert cautiously broached the subject they had avoided for far too long. "What do you intend to do once we reach London? We have no idea where Sully's been taken or how to find him. We would have better luck finding a rabbit in a forest."

"Then we'll search for the hawk first and wait for the rabbit to come to him."

Sullivan Cane smothered a yawn and pushed back the frayed brocade *portieres* framing his bedroom window. Grimacing, he looked out at the profusion of flowers beyond. For days, he'd been locked in this room with nothing to do but stare out the window at the same blasted flowers.

Sullivan was not amused.

His predicament was his own fault. How naive he had been to think he could merely talk to the English bloodhounds, convince them of his "savagery," then twist their nefarious purposes to his own means. He'd not been twenty minutes in their company before they'd crashed a club over his head, trussed him up like a goose, and bundled him onto a ship for Britain. From that day on, Sullivan had been beaten, drugged, and taunted. Trapped in a charade of his own making, he'd been branded a heathen and treated as such.

His situation had not improved. If the truth were known, the last clouding traces of drugs had lifted some time ago, but he had yet to inform anyone. After his . . . adventure at sea, he'd decided that he needed to prepare himself with as much information as possible before revealing his true state of mind. While on Isla Santiago, he'd underestimated his foe, a fact that had led to his being taken away by force. He would not allow the same thing to happen again.

In the last forty-eight hours, he'd been able to gather a number of interesting facts. He knew he'd been brought to the British Isles—most likely Scotland, judging by the view from his window—but there were still too many pieces of the puzzle that needed to be settled into place. Vaguely, he remembered a room with a four-poster bed and a carriage ride in the darkness. Rain. Since he had faded in and out of consciousness, Sullivan had no idea how many of these images could be traced to actual events. His only true memories dated to his arrival at this house. This bedchamber.

Nevertheless, he now resided at a place called Bellemoore—a grand appellation for a stone cottage set in a tiny piece of land which had been gardened to the point of obscuring the black earth beneath. Except for a split-rock path descending to the main road, the dwelling seemed lost in a sea of flowers—flowers he had overheard had been planted by Lady Beatrice Sutherland. His grandmother.

Sullivan's hands dropped from the draperies, and his fingers clenched. It wasn't the view that caused such tension. It was his predicament.

The game had twisted so suddenly. He'd simply meant to confront the bloodhounds seeking Richard, throw them off-guard with his heathenish appearance, and drain them of information.

But things had gone wrong from the very start, and he'd awakened to find himself in a strange land. Thanks to the interference of his grandmother—not Nigel Sutherland, which had probably accounted for his not being killed outright.

Sullivan doubted his grandmother would prove to be a foe, but she had unwittingly thrown him into a dangerous situation nonetheless. If Nigel Sutherland were to learn of his existence—which he most certainly would—Sullivan's life wouldn't be worth a pinch of dust.

Time was his only ally. His meeting with Nigel was inevitable. From what Sullivan had been able to gather, the dowager had traded the last of her dowry jewels to bring him home and now expected him to be her heir, to challenge Nigel Sutherland and right three decades of wrongs.

Sullivan was more than happy to avenge his father's good name. He wouldn't waste the opportunity to confront the man. But Sully could never remain in this country or become a titled lord and heir—and neither could Richard. Too many things had happened for time to be erased. The Sutherland clan had a life elsewhere. They had no need of lands and family that weren't their own.

At this late date, Sullivan realized he should have taken more precautions. But then again, he hadn't expected to be kidnapped and brought north like a common criminal. He hadn't expected to be secreted away to a secluded cottage in the wilds of Britain. And he *certainly* hadn't expected the presence of a personal governess.

Miss Wickersham.

Though she had yet to speak to him since he pretended to sleep whenever she entered the room, he had heard the two servants consulting her opinion on everything from the evening meal to what hour to close the shutters.

Miss Wickersham . . . Sullivan mused again, turning from the window. He could have sworn that he'd met her before arriving at this place. For some reason, he couldn't banish the tantalizing image of Miss Wickersham's bare shoulders from his mind. Yet he had no grounds for such a vision. Since arriving at Bellemoore, he'd seen her dressed in an assortment of severe day gowns and conservative skirts and bodices. She'd never worn anything that could be construed as comfortable, let alone inviting.

And yet . . .

Once again, Sullivan was teased by a niggling memory. Damned if he knew whether it was something that he had actually experienced or if it had been a dream, but somewhere, *somewhere,* he was sure he'd seen a woman like her before.

But . . . *not* like her. Not exactly.

His lips pursed in concentration and disgust at his inability to place the facts half buried beneath a haze of drug-induced recollections. Even now, he could picture a female with long, flowing hair and eyes the color of a clear fresh-water stream. He remembered music—soft, lilting strains that trickled over his senses with a gentle rhythm. And he was sure, quite sure, that the woman had touched him. So vividly did he recall the tracing of feminine fingertips, he didn't think he could have imagined such a thing. But since the rest of the memories invariably disintegrated into the stuff of fantasies, he couldn't be sure. Perhaps he had seen Miss Wickersham upon entering this house and had invented such an unlikely set of circumstances. After all, her hair was reddish in color, her eyes blue.

Nonsense. He couldn't imagine the woman unbending enough to untie her shoes, let alone disrobe in front of an unknown man. She was rigid, proper, and above reproach. Passionless.

Wasn't she?

Shaking his head to rid himself of such ideas, Sullivan stretched and yawned. His situation could be worse. He had not been poorly treated upon arriving at Bellemoore. Consigned to the care of Miss Wickersham, he'd been fed like a king, washed and shaved by her servants, and put to bed amidst a wealth of woolen blankets and down pillows. But he had yet to receive any clothes.

Unfortunately, the house had a tendency to grow a little cool. Even now, gooseflesh sprinkled Sullivan's naked skin. Except for his bedding, there was nothing in the room he could use to cover himself. Nothing but the threadbare robe his "hosts" had thrown over the footboard. Sullivan had tried it on—once—then discarded it when the shoulders had proven too narrow and the garment had refused to stay closed.

He didn't know if the lack of appropriate apparel was an effort to keep him prisoner, or if no such supplies existed. But he had to admit he was beginning to feel the confines of the room closing in upon him. And though he had no idea what Miss Wickersham intended to do with him, he would like to be dressed when she did it.

His mouth widened in a quick grin. Save one activity, of course. If Miss Wickersham were to loosen her rigid stays enough to resemble the woman of his imaginings rather than a red-haired fire poker, he'd be more than happy to spend the afternoon in bed. As long as they didn't use *his* bed.

His smile faded as he surveyed the room. He could see that preparations had been made for Richard, Lord Sutherland, long before his actual arrival. It was quite obvious his grandmother and her servants had not been expecting a man of Sullivan's age. They had apparently been anticipating the arrival of a boy. The bed was a small trundle affair, and the shelves were laden with toys. Sullivan could only wonder who had told them to prepare in such a manner. He wondered why he had not been moved, and could only suppose that the nursery was the only room in the house with a lock on the door.

The soft creak of the stairs warned him that someone was coming to his room, and he dived under the covers. The old house groaned and complained like a cranky old crone—a fact that had dissuaded Sullivan from picking the latch and making any midnight investigations until he could learn to avoid such traps.

Turning, he sprawled facedown across the pillows and curled his legs a bit so that he would fit upon the mattress. He had learned enough in the last two days to doubt that Miss Wickersham or the two aged servants could be numbered among his enemies. Sullivan sympathized with their plight, but he refused to allow his original purpose to be swayed. His strategy might have been altered by a change in locations and players, but the objective still remained clear. Sullivan had to prove to these people that he was an unfit heir. He had to force them to send him home. He had to see to it that they would never want to contact him in the future. Otherwise, his family would never be free from the responsibilities of the Sutherland name.

A key grated in its hole from the opposite side. The latch to the door snicked softly in the early-morning quiet, and he knew within seconds who had brought him his breakfast tray. Miss Wickersham's perfume was most distinct. It held the sweet scents of spring—lilacs and roses—with the subtle underlying spice of jasmine.

When she stepped inside, he peered at her from beneath the merest slit of his lashes. Miss Wickersham had dressed like a governess. Her hair had been tamed and drawn away from her face into a heavy coil she'd fastened against the nape of her neck. She wore a severe gray day gown, and its fitted bodice and full skirt effectively proclaimed that this woman took her duties seriously. Even the metal shanked buttons marched down her chest in rigid perfection, stopping at the point where she'd wrapped a snowy apron around her skirts. Each item of clothing had been starched and ironed so intently that the fabric crackled in protest when she moved.

Sullivan saw the way she glanced in his direction, then moved to place his morning tray on the tiny table and chair ensemble that had been assembled in the corner. He opened his eyes a little more to follow her movements as she set out the fresh bread and bitter marmalade upon delicate bone china pieces.

"We are not amused by your pranks, Master Richard."

Sullivan started when she spoke. *How in bloody hell had she known he wasn't the heathen he pretended to be?*

To his surprise, she didn't turn to confront him. She began to pour milk and tea into a child-sized cup.

"We are fully aware that you are awake," she chided. Sullivan relaxed. She hadn't divined his masquerade. Not yet, anyhow.

Miss Wickersham turned and caught him staring at her. Frowning in his direction, she folded her arms and shook her head in disapproval.

"It is most impolite to deceive people. We shall await your apology."

We?

Sullivan cast his gaze about the room in a purely automatic gesture. Evidently, England had endowed its monarchs and governesses with the use of the royal pronoun.

Miss Wickersham fixed him with such stern disapproval,

Sullivan fought the urge to squirm like the young boy she considered him to be. Finally, by the slightest softening of her expression, she relented. "Very well. We shall anticipate your apology when you have gained a better grasp of the king's English. Until then, we shall simply have to teach you more of the graces and manners expected of an English earl." Her brows arched. "After all, we don't want people to believe you are a savage. Do we?"

But that was exactly what he intended. A grin teased the corners of Sullivan's mouth, but he tamped it down. Suddenly, he saw the path to his goal as if it lay before him like a shimmering strand of gold. What better way to prove himself unfit to become the next earl of Lindon than to convince this woman? His governess. His staid, stern, conservative, British governess. She'd probably never been outside her own charmed circle of childish charges. Why, he'd wager she'd never even been kissed—not properly, at any rate.

As if she'd sensed a portion of his thoughts—or caught a hint of his inner amusement—she grew grim. She made a *tsking* noise and frowned at him in supreme disappointment.

"Master Richard. One of your first lessons is that a proper gentleman should not keep a lady waiting." She motioned for him to join her. "Come and eat your meal while it's hot. Otherwise, you'll disappoint Greyson, who has prepared it especially for you."

Sullivan waited only a moment. Long enough to study her and anticipate the way she would soon blanche in shock and maidenly surprise. Then he rose to a sitting position and swept the covers aside, exposing every inch of his naked body.

To his supreme disappointment, Miss Wickersham didn't gasp, didn't pale, didn't flinch. Indeed, she appeared almost disinterested as she appraised him from head to toe, then back again.

"Quickly now, or the food will grow cold," she urged a second time, signaling that he should move forward.

Sullivan felt a sting of disappointment. He'd expected

more of a reaction—he'd expected *some* reaction. But Miss Wickersham observed him as if his bare backside was of no more consequence than that of a family pet.

"Richard!" Her voice became more pointed. Evidently deciding he had not understood her at all, she grasped a warm piece of bread from his plate and held it enticingly in his direction, swinging it back and forth like a tempting delicacy. "Greyson has fixed you fresh sweetbread, tea, and raspberries with cream," she coaxed in a voice so melodious, so inviting, that Sullivan could scarcely credit it came from such a formal woman.

"Come along," she encouraged, beckoning to him. "Come and eat."

Deciding his empty stomach was paying far more attention to the aromas of food than Miss Wickersham was paying to his unclad body, he stood and sauntered across the room. In one last effort to shock her, he walked with a purposeful gait. One that he hoped proclaimed: *I am man at his most primeval, and you are but a fragile woman.*

But if Miss Wickersham had entertained a lustful thought in her entire life, she wasn't doing so now.

"Sit, please."

Giving in to the game—for the moment, at least—he turned his attention to the glorious sight of food spread upon the table before him. Since he'd been feigning unconsciousness, he'd eaten nothing but the scones and milk left three times a day on his bedside table. The meal spread before him seemed like manna from heaven.

He reached for the thick chunks of bread arranged on a plate but recoiled when Miss Wickersham slapped his wrist.

"Please be *seated*, Master Richard." To emphasize her point, she stepped behind him and pulled out the minuscule chair.

He jerked in reflex when the fabric of her skirts tickled the backs of his legs. Knowing there was a limit to the extent he was willing to embarrass himself in order to prove he was a savage, Sullivan sank awkwardly into the little seat and grabbed one of the linen napkins, quickly settling it over his lap.

"Very *good,* Master Richard."

Miss Wickersham beamed at him as if he'd laid claim to the crown jewels. Then she had the audacity, the unmitigated cheek, to reach out and pat him on the head.

She grasped her skirts and rustled from the room, and Sullivan watched her with narrowed eyes.

One day, Miss Wickersham was going to pay for that pat. In spades. Before he left, Sullivan intended to crack her calm governess-to-the-queen-of-Sheba exterior. Because surely, *surely,* a real woman lay somewhere beneath all that ice.

He intended to expose her.

Chelsea closed the door behind her until the latch slipped into place with a reserved click. Twisting the key in place, she demurely laced her fingers together and held them against her waist. She walked from the bedroom, down the staircase to the vestibule, and toward the front entrance.

"Miss Chelsea? Was there something you needed, mum?"

She waved to the roly-poly figure of Smee, who had wrapped himself in the former housekeeper's frilly apron and now sat hunched over the kitchen table, where he ruthlessly polished the last place setting of silver.

"Thank you, no, Mr. Smee." Offering him a serene smile, she stepped into the morning sunshine and closed the door behind her.

At first she moved slowly, deliberately. But as the trembling of her limbs increased and she felt the heat of a blush rising to her cheeks, she quickened her pace until she ran the last few steps to the pump hidden in the farthest corner of the garden.

Sweet Mary and all the saints, she hadn't thought she was going to make it out of the nursery without coming completely unhinged!

Chelsea had known that Richard Sutherland would have to awaken sometime soon. She had taken every possible precaution she could think of to arm herself emotionally.

But nothing could have prepared her for the way he had flung the covers aside and stood before her as brazenly as a

Whitecastle doxy. Even though she'd known he'd worn no clothing beneath the sheets, she had provided him with a robe for his use—one she'd borrowed from Greyson. Why, the man could have even used a sheet, if he'd had a mind. But no. He had paraded before her like . . . like . . .

Like some wild thing stalking his prey.

That thought brought another burst of heat, and she grasped the pump handle. Frantically, she worked the mechanism until a gush of water tumbled free. Then she splashed the flowing stream onto her face, paying little heed to the moisture that dribbled down the flushed column of her throat.

She straightened, realizing that the cool water had offered little or no real relief. The heat that lingered radiated from within. Huffing in frustration, she hurried up the winding path that led from the garden onto the moors. Though her lungs gasped for air once she'd reached the top of the rise and her skin held an unladylike sheen of perspiration, she didn't care.

Something had happened to her since meeting Richard Sutherland. Something she found terribly disturbing. For years, she had fought so hard to appear the ideal lady. She had patterned her speech most carefully, she had dressed to perfection, she had mastered each nuance of courtesy and gentility.

But lately, none of that mattered.

She found herself resisting the most outlandish temptations. She wanted to run barefoot through the grass at dawn. She wanted to unlace her corset and take a good deep breath.

By heaven, she wanted to *want* Richard Sutherland.

No!

Turning, she studied the cottage below her. The profusion of jewel-like colors of the garden should have caught her eye, but she stared at the window leading into the nursery instead.

No.

Her hands curled tightly into her skirt.

No.

Bit by bit, the thumping of her heart returned to normal. The heat faded from her body.

She had a responsibility to Biddy and to herself. Richard Sutherland must be taught. In just a few weeks' time, he would be taken from his hiding place in Scotland, back to England. There he would attend a weekend with the prominent duke of Burkshire. During that time, a formal petition would be made and legal claims set in motion.

In order for such claims to prove successful, Richard would have to comport himself with utmost dignity. Such a fuss had been made by the *ton* from the moment Richard Albert Sutherland III and his wife, Julie, had jumped ship. Now that the rumors of a Sutherland heir could be proven true, there must be no stains against his name from the first. He must exude the aura of a perfect English aristocrat. He must be ingrained with the proper modes of ceremony and behavior.

Most importantly, he must never, *ever*, be found guilty of consorting with his own governess. That road led to destruction. For them both.

The restless breeze teased the hair drawn tightly away from her brow until tiny curling tendrils began to escape and drift around her face. The grass at her feet sighed, the leaves chattered in hushed tones like matrons gossiping behind their fans. The very air seemed to be filled with secrets. Her secrets.

Life had a strange way of turning back upon itself—like a winding highland road. Chelsea had been so sure she had control of her destiny and every facet of her everyday schedule. Then, within the space of a few days, events had mushroomed out of control, and she found herself groping minute by minute to stay in charge. First, with Richard's arrival, then with her unsettling feelings for him. And last of all, her proximity to Lindon Manor.

Turning, she moved toward the copse of trees on the far side of the ridge. She could have found her way blindfolded. Yet, little more than ten years ago, she had sworn she would never return.

Chelsea traveled along a familiar, nearly invisible path

and edged through two huge boulders jutting out of the spur of land. There, spread below her like a fairy-tale palace, lay Lindon Manor.

She leaned her back against the rock, feeling the heat of the day seep through the weave of her gown. But she was still chilled. Funny, she hadn't expected to experience any type of reaction. Not now, after so much time had passed. If she had anticipated any emotions at all, they would have been those of anger or revulsion, not the pervading sense of loss that crept deep into her soul.

Far below, she could see the tiny specks of color caused by Lord Sutherland's guests as they lounged about the formal gardens, laughing, walking, playing cards and lawn tennis. If she closed her eyes, she thought she could hear their laughter, the faint strains of music.

It wasn't difficult for her to imagine the sights and sounds and smells. Since his ascension to the peerage, Lord Sutherland spent the peak summer months in Scotland at Lindon Manor in order to oversee the estate's mining and agricultural concerns. Legally assigned as his ward, Chelsea had endured three such summers with Lord Sutherland. Lindon Manor had been her home. She had witnessed the gamut of his emotions: his elegant charm, his subtle posturing, his brooding, his anger.

But work and harvest hadn't been the only things on Nigel's agenda. Each June, he came with his wife and his son, Cecil, intent upon hosting a month-long fete. The first day of the month heralded the arrival of the crème de la crème of London's *haute ton,* who swarmed like locusts to the country. Many people claimed that to be invited to Lindon Manor for the season was the equivalent of being asked to vacation with royalty. Lord Sutherland shamelessly showered his guests with fine food, imported wines, musicales, galas, and hunting expeditions.

Chelsea had been part of that world. Although Estella, Nigel's wife, had ignored her and Cecil had looked down on her, she had basked in the opulence and extravagance offered to her by a wealthy, powerful, handsome man, not knowing how Nigel had meant to lead her into a false sense of security. He had hoped to blind her with his excesses as surely as he had hoped to buy the approval of the British aristocracy. He had intended to woo her into his way of life as surely as he'd meant to woo her into his bed. Every overture had been brazenly performed in front of his wife and heir beneath the guise of simple Christian charity.

Later, Chelsea was to pray for summer to arrive. Not because of the onset of such lavish entertainments, but simply because then she could hide herself in the crush of people. Witnesses. Nigel would have to leave her alone for a time.

A gust of wind caused the tree branches to rattle together like old bones, and Chelsea shivered in the muggy heat, knowing she lived on borrowed time. Nigel had always known where to find her. However, she had managed to evade him by slipping away from the Barrinshrops under the cover of darkness. Nigel would have heard of her escape by now. He would be searching for her soon. He wouldn't be happy. Chelsea recognized the innate danger of living so close. She knew that if he ever caught a wisp of an idea that Richard Sutherland lay ensconced in the walls of Bellemoore Cottage, their situation would prove dangerous.

But Chelsea was not a fool. Lord Sutherland had been following each move she'd made for years. When she had agreed to meet Richard's ship, she'd known her sudden disappearance would infuriate Nigel. She had been forced to find a hideout. Somewhere he could never find her or her charge. Her only hope was that he wouldn't think to look here. In the one place she'd vowed never to return to in her lifetime.

Chelsea chafed her palms together, stilling the nervousness that settled in her stomach like a coiled snake. Below, a stray stream of sunlight broke free from the cloud cover and struck the pink marble of the manor house, making it glitter. The building rested like a delicate carnation in an emerald field. So beautiful, so serene.

So deceiving.

Closing her mind to the years she'd lived in those very walls, Chelsea straightened, denying any emotion but sheer

The walk through the moors served to remind Chelsea of her true purpose for being at Bellemoore Cottage and the formal relationship she should be establishing with her charge. By the time she had reached the flagstone steps leading into the house, she had herself well under control. This . . . infatuation with Richard Sutherland was but a brief aberration. A moment of poor judgment. When she became more accustomed to him and his heathenish ways, the unnatural temptation he exuded would vanish into the dark recesses of her soul from whence it had come.

Issuing a sharp nod to herself as if to echo her own concurrence with such a conclusion, she once again prepared herself to enter the lion's den.

Built nearly fifty years before, Bellemoore was a replica of a cottage Lady Beatrice Sutherland's husband had seen in France. The rooms were butted next to each other like a row of children's blocks, joined together by a series of doorways. On the lower level lay a large studio, the center foyer with its winding staircase to the upper levels, then the dining hall, and finally the kitchen and scullery. Above lay the nursery and four private bedrooms.

At one time, Bellemoore had basked in the glory of the

Sutherland empire. It had been the prize secluded in the wilds of the border country of Scotland, lying only a few miles from the main house. The cottage had been built on the site of one of the original edifices of the Lindon estates, and after Lindon Manor had been erected to serve as a summer home, Bellemoore had become more of a private retreat.

Currently, it was the only piece of property Dowager Lady Sutherland had left. After her husband's death had stripped her of her monies and influence, the cottage had been awarded to her by Nigel Sutherland as a token means of support.

The reason Nigel had been so generous was painfully clear. The house came with no real land to speak of. None that could be farmed or grazed for profit. The cottage stood well within riding distance of the manor so that Nigel could keep his eye on Biddy's activities yet far enough away so that she couldn't interfere with his.

Other than the building itself, Nigel had offered no concessions. Bellemoore's upkeep had drained the dowager of what little wealth she had managed to bring with her. Over time, the jewel of the Sutherland estates had begun to dim—except for the garden, which grew more beautiful each year. The house itself was in an obvious state of decline.

But Richard Sutherland could change all that. As a new earl, he could reendow her with all she'd lost. Although Biddy was gambling that her heathenish grandson would be a better lord than Nigel Sutherland, at least Biddy could have the satisfaction of seeing the title passed on to her own blood. If Richard proved to have some measure of heart for his grandmother, he *could* see to restoring Bellemoore and the rest of the Sutherland estates. He *could* see that Biddy had some means of support other than the moldering cottage during her last few years.

Chelsea endured a niggling pang of concern. Biddy had used the last of her own personal wealth to bring Richard here. Most of the silver and furniture had been sold long ago. Nothing of any real value remained. Nothing but Richard Sutherland IV. The true heir.

Crossing into the dining hall, Chelsea realized that her task had taken on a new significance. If Richard Sutherland had been a child as they had expected, they would have appointed a solicitor as the boy's legal protector. The fight to regain his titles would have been no less bitter, but Richard could have been kept fairly free from the actual battle in deference to his tender age.

Things were more complicated now. Since Richard was an adult, he would have to prove to be a true gentleman. A Sutherland.

Which brought Chelsea full circle to the original problem. Richard Sutherland must be transformed into a titled lord as soon as possible. He couldn't do that if he persisted in frolicking about in a state of undress!

"Smee."

The man interrupted his task, hanging upon each syllable she uttered with the eagerness of a lapdog. With his black eyes, chubby features, and the shock of curly sand-colored hair surrounding his balding pate, he closely resembled Lady Sutherland's cocker spaniel, Dudley. Originally serving at Lindon Manor as the hostler, he had followed Biddy into her "exile" with more devotion than had been shown to her by her own family.

"Yes, mum."

"Will you see if Greyson is available? I would like to confer with you both, if I may."

Grinning in delight, Smee hurried into the kitchen, his stout legs churning and the ruffles of his apron fluttering like a conclave of moths. He soon returned with the dour-faced butler in tow.

That Greyson had been born and bred to his position, Chelsea had no doubt. He towered above Smee by a good measure, his figure gaunt, his features permanently grim. Even though Chelsea had known Lady Sutherland for years—and had thus known Greyson for some time—he never seemed to age. He seemed old. Had always seemed old. Would continue to seem old. His pale skin and even paler blue eyes caused one to doubt that he left the house during daylight. The shock of parchment white hair which grew from his head was so thin that he persisted in combing the strands from one ear to the other in an effort to conceal the fact that he was just as bald as Smee.

"You called, Miss Wickersham?" he asked, inclining his head in a courtly manner.

"What do we have in the way of money?"

Smee and Greyson exchanged glances. But while Smee stepped from foot to foot like a schoolboy caught with his hand in the larder, Greyson merely answered her with stoic blandness. "Nothing, Miss Wickersham."

"Nothing at all?" she repeated, although she knew Greyson had no reason to lie. He and Smee had probably not seen wages in the better part of a year. Like Chelsea, they donated their time out of love and respect to an old woman.

"No, miss."

"Have we anything left to sell?"

Once again, Greyson and Smee locked eyes, but, as usual, it was Greyson who spoke. "No, miss. Nothing of any real import."

"Drat," she muttered. "We simply have to find something for Richard to wear until we can obtain some sort of appropriate garb."

Greyson moved toward the sideboard and slid open the drawer. "There's always this, miss."

He lifted the burnt-orange-colored scrap of cloth that Richard had been wearing when they'd retrieved him from *The Seeker.* The wisp of fabric could barely pass as an undergarment.

Since Greyson and Smee had bathed Richard and attended to his personal needs upon their arrival at Bellemoore, Chelsea hadn't seen the garment since their arrival. The simple raiment brought back a host of images from her first encounter with Richard Sutherland—when she'd pulled aside the canvas to find a heathen beneath. Even now, thinking about the way that scrap of material had covered his . . . well, the image had become emblazoned upon her mind.

When asked, Chelsea had told Greyson to throw away the inappropriate covering. Now it seemed her only alternative to Richard Sutherland's utter nakedness.

"Very well, Greyson, give it here."

He walked toward her with all the dignity of a well-trained majordomo and gave her the inappropriate covering which he had cleaned and pressed in the interim. Chelsea doubted such ministrations were necessary, considering the size of the colored strip. She nevertheless took the vesture, holding it between two fingers as if it would explode in her face.

As a governess, Chelsea's primary duties had always been to teach, but there had been times when her responsibilities had sometimes bordered those of a nanny. In the past, she had condescended to help with all manner of intimate rituals. She had bathed children—girls and boys—and had helped them dress and undress. But never, in all her years, had she been forced to condone the use of such underthings.

"Smee, with your permission, I'd like to augment this with a pair of your trousers and a shirt. I am afraid Greyson's clothing has proved to be far too narrow."

"Yes, miss. It would be my pleasure."

As she marched from the room, holding the loincloth away from her body like a dead rat, Smee sighed in regret. "Master Richard needs proper clothes," he remarked.

"I quite agree," Greyson ponderously intoned.

"What we've got to offer won't do—especially once Miss Wickersham takes him into town."

"Indeed."

"We must find a way to help her," Smee continued, clucking softly. "She appeared so worried. We have to get her some coin—and we haven't a moment to lose."

"I concur wholeheartedly." Greyson took a slow breath, held it in his lungs so that his chest puffed out as if he were an admiral in full dress uniform. "I've been pondering that same dilemma all morning, and I might have the solution."

"Oh?"

Greyson considered the now empty threshold. "We'll need a pair of horses."

"We can use the carriage mounts."

"You'll have to dye their stockings. The animals must not be recognized."

"There's some stove blacking in the stables."

Greyson's narrow lips pursed in thought. "I think I can find some appropriate costume, but you'll need to locate toggery of your own. Something dark and flowing."

"I've got that cape Lady Sutherland gave me Christmas past."

Greyson finally turned to study him with a measuring glance. "And a mask."

Smee grinned. The excitement fairly bubbled inside him until he could barely stand still.

A mask!

How delightful.

Sullivan had just reached for the last piece of bread when the door creaked open and Miss Wickersham appeared.

Afraid she might take the food as some sort of belated punishment, and unsure of when his next meal might come, Sullivan heaped a huge spoonful of marmalade into the center and stuffed the whole thing into his mouth.

To his utter consternation, Miss Wickersham merely sighed as if her patience were extremely pressed upon and walked toward him.

With each step, he felt a wave of some emotion that seemed very much like guilt. Had she meant to dine with him? Was he supposed to have saved her something? From what he'd gathered, Miss Wickersham and her employer were suffering beneath slightly impoverished circumstances. Had he consumed the only meal left in the house?

But Miss Wickersham didn't seem inclined to chide. She approached the table with a determined gait and placed a small pile of clothing opposite his dishes.

"We would be very pleased if you would change into these things, Master Richard."

Not willing to show her that he had a perfect understanding of her words, he offered her what he hoped was a blank look.

Her mouth pursed ever so slightly, then she *hurrumphed* and muttered, "Though you probably haven't a clue of what I'm saying, I refuse to lower myself to grunting and gesturing and speaking to you as if you were a deaf aunt instead of a poorly educated barbarian."

Richard felt a spark of amusement but kept his features carefully masked.

"Master Richard, we shall return in ten minutes, and we expect you to be dressed." She pointed to the stack of garments, then to Sullivan, and repeated, "Clothe yourself." Turning on her heel, she disappeared again.

Sullivan sat back as comfortably as he could in the tiny chair and eyed the nursery clock. Just as the little yellow bird finished a rousing rendition of cuckoos, the knob turned, and Miss Wickersham entered.

She spied the amount of bare skin still available to her eye and heaved a frustrated sigh. "So we're going to have to teach you the proper modes of dress as well, are we?"

The very idea proved interesting.

She went toward him and scooped the borrowed items from the table. "Stand, please."

When he remained where he was, she bent to take the napkin from his lap and hesitated in mid-motion.

"Of all the stubborn, ill-managed children it has been my pleasure to teach, you've got to take the prize."

She appraised him for a moment with a determined blue gaze. One so clear and steady that Sullivan could nearly believe she had the ability to see straight through him.

"Give me your hand, Master Richard."

She held out her own, palm up. He was confronted with incredibly slender fingers. The skin was smooth and lady-like, but he could see by its character that Miss Wickersham was not a stranger to hard work.

"Your *hand.*"

Realizing he must not press his "savageness" too far,

71

Sullivan obeyed. Just as he'd imagined, her flesh was delicate and soft. But the bones and muscles beneath were tensile and strong.

She indicated that he should rise and led him toward a privacy screen which had been placed in the corner to disguise the porcelain chamber pot.

Pushing the clothing into his arms, she said, "A proper gentleman does not disrobe in front of anyone other than his manservant. Not even in the presence of his wife. Consider this for future reference, Master Richard."

She shooed him behind the elaborate wooden shield, but even though his governess was hidden from view, Sullivan could feel her presence on the other side. He could almost see her waiting impatiently, her arms folded, her toe tapping a restless tattoo against the polished floorboards.

Sullivan quickly investigated the things he'd been given. To his utter disappointment, he realized his governess had offered him an oversized rough linen workshirt, a huge pair of broadcloth trousers, and the scrap of fabric he'd worn as a loincloth when he'd first arranged a meeting with Lady Sutherland's bloodhounds.

Briefly annoyed that he had none of his own clothing, Sully sighed. What he wouldn't give for a decent pair of breeches and a solid pair of boots in this cursedly cold country. But his captors had taken his disguise at face value and had never bothered to see if he owned a wardrobe more extensive than a single scrap of linen.

Sullivan considered his governess, then swiftly covered himself with the loincloth. After slipping his arms into the billowing shirt, he stepped from behind the screen.

Miss Wickersham looked up from the spot she'd been glaring into the floor. For the first time since his arrival, Sullivan believed he might have caught her off-guard. He thought he detected the briefest glimmer of shock.

But then she frowned, marching from the room like a general in search of her troops.

"Greyson! Greyson, come teach this heathen how to clothe himself properly!" he heard her call as she stamped down the staircase.

Chuckling softly to himself, Sullivan leaned against the bedpost and waited.

Where was that man?

Chelsea came to a halt in the doorway of the scullery. Both Greyson and Smee had disappeared for the time being. Just when she needed them most.

Tamping down a groan of frustration, Chelsea reluctantly returned to the foyer.

If she had been given any real idea of what it would be like to care for Richard Sutherland, she would have refused to participate. She would have offered her apologies and been quit of the whole affair. No woman alive—no proper woman—should have been asked to involve herself in such a scandalous muddle of affairs.

No *proper* woman, a voice echoed deep in her head.

Chelsea hesitated in midstride and drew to a reluctant halt. Could she even lay claim to such a title now? No *proper* woman would have touched Richard Sutherland while he was unconscious. No *proper* woman would have gazed upon him while he was unclothed.

Most notably, no *proper* woman would have allowed herself the burst of undeniable pleasure she'd experienced when he'd emerged wearing nothing more than a loincloth and a loose, flowing shirt.

True character will out.

Chelsea's eyes squeezed shut for a moment as the words resounded in her head. Hadn't that always been Papa's favorite phrase?

Evidently, he'd been right. Though Chelsea might appear the conservative, genteel woman to those who met her, deep in her own heart she knew the truth. That Chelsea Wickersham was but a name she'd plucked from thin air. That her lineage had no more breeding to it than if she were the daughter of an impoverished Irish ferryman.

Oh, Papa, why didn't you live longer? Why didn't you see what would happen once you died?

Pushing away the flood of brackish images that invariably

descended at the memories of her father, Chelsea moved determinedly toward the stairs.

She had developed a reputation for herself. A place. She had abandoned her previous identity as if it had never existed, and she refused to feel any guilt for making such a clean break from her past. Once she'd made a gentleman of Richard Sutherland, she would move on again. To another employer. Another nursery. She couldn't deny that the idea was far from inviting. But what other choice did she have? A woman alone had to find a means of employment. Even if it meant working with the likes of Richard Sutherland.

Chelsea flung open the door with the deft flick of her wrist. Richard Sutherland leaned indolently against the bed. His hair had been washed and combed, but Greyson had not yet had the opportunity to cut it, so it hung in dark, thick waves to a point just beyond his shoulders.

The black-brown waves might underscore his primitive state, but it was the way Smee's shirt hung about the lean sculptured mass of his body that caused a tingle of desire to dance in her veins. If possible, the scant covering of the loincloth and the rumpled drape of the linen shirt seemed more dangerous than when he'd stood before her completely naked.

She opened her mouth to speak, hesitated, then stated, "Greyson is unable to serve as your manservant for the time being, so I suppose I shall have to take his place since Smee has disappeared and your grandmother is still in London."

She eased toward him, wondering how to accomplish the task of dressing her charge without losing every last shred of her own personal dignity. Finally, steeling herself for the worst, she decided to look upon the next few moments as a challenge. She would regard him as a wayward child. A mischievous boy.

"Master Richard, I think you should button your shirt first of all."

He blinked uncomprehendingly.

"Have you no grasp of the language at all?"

He offered no sign of having understood.

"Very well." She began the task of fastening the garment.

His skin was warm. Firm. Intoxicating. Midway down his chest, she stopped. "Finish, please."

To her complete shock, he reached out to begin unfastening the buttons of her own bodice.

"Master Richard!" She slapped his hands and backed away as if she'd been burned, praying that her cheeks were not beginning to reflect a rosy hue.

He adopted such a crestfallen expression, she realized he must have misunderstood. "Your buttons." She pointed to his chest. "Tend to *your* buttons."

Though he seemed subdued, he complied. Only after he was completely covered by the huge shirt—from neck to midthigh—did she feel any measure of relief.

"Finish with your trousers," she instructed, backing away. But before she could move too far, he grasped her arm.

An immediate charge radiated from that point of contact, like a match touched to gunpowder. Chelsea's mind willed her to retreat, but her feet remained welded to the floor. She could only stare at the broad masculine fingers wrapped around her elbow. A sparse dusting of dark hair beckoned to her. His wrists were strong and well formed.

"Ye—" She cleared her throat when the word emerged as a squeak, then repeated, "Yes?"

He offered her a long, soulful glance. One that caused his ice-green eyes to gleam with bits of brown. She felt quite sure that he had sensed her disquiet. Then he solemnly reached out to refasten her dress. A wanton wildfire spread through her chest to drizzle deliciously through the rest of her body.

Once he'd finished, he didn't withdraw. Hesitantly, he touched her chin, her mouth. Not in an overly familiar way, but in the manner of an artist who searched a statue for texture and form. Just when she feared the last of her grand avowals of control would tumble to her feet in a pile of dust, he stopped.

Chelsea barely managed a husky "Thank you for fixing my buttons, Master Richard." *Touch me. Touch me again.*

Shaking her head to clear it of such thoughts, she armed

herself against this man's appeal and moved to retrieve the trousers from where Richard had left them behind the privacy screen. Sitting on the edge of the bed, she held the breeches out and motioned for Richard to put them on.

His head tilted in confusion.

"You must finish dressing, Master Richard." It was the only way she could maintain her sanity.

When he didn't respond, she tapped his calf and urged him to comply. The strong muscles rippled as he stepped into the leg. Dark, wiry hairs tickled her skin. She shifted with untold reluctance.

"Again, please," she murmured, barely able to speak without having the command emerge in a kittenish purr. She hated herself for displaying such weaknesses—she who had always been so iron-willed. But from the moment Richard Sutherland had entered her life, years of training and dedication had seemed to drain free like sand from an hourglass.

Richard climbed into his breeches, and she automatically complimented him on his obedience. "Very good. Soon, we'll have you more than adequately prepared for the afternoon." Standing, she drew the pants up to his waist. All the while, she thanked heaven that Smee's trousers were so wide that they could be held at a relatively safe distance away from Richard's body. She didn't know what she would do if her knuckles were to skim against his flanks.

"Button, please."

When he didn't do as he'd been told, Chelsea knew that she could not, would not, fasten the placket. Luckily, he seemed to interpret her command, because he obeyed after an interminable pause. Heaving a silent sigh of relief, she took a piece of twine and circled it around his lean waist, then folded the top band twice to hold the makeshift alterations in place.

Finished, she regarded her charge with a critical eye. If possible, he seemed even less the titled gentleman and more the savage. If the women of society were to see him this way, they would either swoon at his feet in delight or run screaming into the night. And the men . . . well, there was no telling what a man would do. Probably challenge him to a duel simply on principle.

She hoped Richard would never be seen by anyone outside of Bellemoore in such a state. Clad in the too-large shirt and too-short pants, he had the appearance of a bizarre rendition of Robinson Crusoe. By the time she had him trained in his duties, she hoped he would seem more like a mysterious gentleman of means.

Tugging at her apron strings, Chelsea crossed to the armoire in the corner. Removing a larger, dove-gray Mother Hubbard pinafore, she exchanged the smaller wrap for the all-encompassing shield. While her back was presented to Richard, she repaired the tatters of her professionalism. By the time she had knotted the bow at the base of her spine, Chelsea Wickersham, governess, had returned.

"We are pleased with your progress this morning, Master Richard," she announced, offering him a huge smile as she walked to the door. "Come along. It's time for our lessons."

Gesturing for him to follow, she marched into the hall.

Sullivan hiked his pants more securely around his waist and trailed behind her with a secret smile. Somehow, he sensed that he'd rattled Miss Wickersham. She might not show it in any particularly betraying expression or action, but he could tell.

For this time—*this time*—she hadn't dared to pat him on the top of his head.

Chapter

8

The clatter of carriages and the cacophony of foot traffic cloaked the sound of Gregory Cane's boot heels striking the cobbled walk. Dodging into a narrow alley, he escaped the bustle of the London side street and climbed the rickety steps leading up the side of a timber structure named the Wayfarer's Inn. It was a quiet little establishment run by two women who had once served as Episcopal missionaries in the Indies. They doted upon strangers who needed a place to sleep—for an hour, a day, or a year.

Gregory entered by the upper landing, assuming a stealth that came second nature to him now. His green eyes glittered. His blunt features were etched in determination and remained slightly bitter. No one saw him enter the chamber at the end of the hall. Just as no one had seen him leave.

Rupert looked up immediately, betraying the fact that he had not been reading the book resting in his lap. "Any news?"

Gregory glanced at the figure sleeping in the nearby bed and kept his tone low in deference to the recovering invalid. "No one could tell me anything about Sully or a mysterious

Sutherland heir. But I've located Nigel. He's staying at Lindon Manor for the summer."

Lindon. The name lingered on his tongue, bittersweet, and inexplicably enticing.

"When do we leave?"

"Tonight."

"What will we do once we arrive?"

Gregory's expression revealed a brief flash of anticipation, regret, and fury before becoming set and determined —and therefore much more menacing.

"We return the good Lord Sutherland's attentions in kind—but first we must dress for the occasion."

Hundreds of candles rained light upon the opulent ballroom of Lindon Manor. The crush of people in the overheated dancing hall caused the tapers to don misty halos. The room seemed to be cloaked in an ethereal cloud. Broad windows had been thrown open to catch the slightest hint of a breeze, but the musky odor of an impending storm offered little relief. Except for the tortured dance of the delicate lace curtains, the heat had drained the room of its vibrant energy, shifting the focus of the evening's activities from dance and recreation to slander.

Nigel, Lord Sutherland, seventh Earl of Lindon, damned the interminable evening. Feigning an interest in the conversations being bandied about, he laughed heartily at the joke he'd been told by the Baron de Guy. Slapping the man on the back, he congratulated the florid-faced Frenchman for his sterling wit while inwardly he prayed that the pompous ass would move on to a fresher audience.

The baron began yet another tale, and Lord Sutherland clenched his jaw in irritation. Short of offering this influential man his back, Nigel was pinned as effectively to his place as a bug to a board. His only outlet for the restlessness he suffered was to roam the room with his eyes.

The gala was about to decrescendo from its frenetic high. Already, he could feel the submerged drive of the evening beginning to ebb. Soon, the attendees would grow as restless as he, and the latent entertainment being offered would not be as attractive as an evening in bed—either one's own, a lover's, or a stranger's.

Sutherland surveyed the chattering clumps of people milling about the grand gilt-and-laquered ballroom in a jaundiced manner. In all honesty, he doubted if any of his guests had come with their minds set on much more than "seeing and being seen." They had downed ungodly amounts of champagne and imported delicacies from the buffet while distracting one another with bits of gossip, verbally placing themselves on a pedestal while dragging a friend or acquaintance through the mire. But Nigel didn't care. His own objectives for the gathering had been just as selfish.

His position as Earl of Lindon had not been easily obtained. For all intents and purposes, he had inherited the title when Richard Sutherland III had been exiled for treason and no other Sutherland males could be found.

Nigel's lips twitched with remembered satisfaction. He would never forget the sweet revenge he'd experienced when Richard Albert and his wife had been taken bodily onto the convict ship. He would never forget the tang of triumph when he'd watched the elder Albert Sutherland wither away from the daily drops of poison Nigel put in his tea.

He'd been little more than twenty years of age, but he'd still managed to obtain his goals. He'd become lord of the manor, the seventh Earl of Lindon. Unfortunately, he'd been unable to completely escape the whispers of innuendo that had accompanied his quick advance in station.

Thirty years should be long enough to prove oneself, he thought, especially when no solid evidence of his complicity had ever been uncovered. But the peerage was slow to forget such a titillating bout of conjecture. No one cared that Sutherland shipping had boomed over the last decade. No one bothered to congratulate him on the tripling of his fortune. No one wanted to peer beyond the intriguing scandal.

So every year, beginning the first week of June, Lord Sutherland hosted a three-week celebration: hunting, picnics, dinners, and sport. He invited his guests to the renowned Sutherland summer retreat in Scotland and launched the festivities by throwing a party. The biggest, most expensive, most exclusive party of the season. If some of the *ton* felt he was trying to buy their approval through a display of excess . . . they were right.

Lord Sutherland felt an imperceptible tap against his sleeve, an action that would have gone unnoticed in the push and bump of the celebration if he had not seen the figure who had approached him with a quiet sense of urgency.

Reginald Wilde was—as always—impeccably dressed. An elegant black cutaway clung to his sinewy figure, revealing the compact frame of a man accustomed to regular exercise and moderate diet. His wheat-blond hair had been combed away from a high forehead; his brown eyes constantly searched the assemblage.

"Excuse me, Lord Sutherland." The words were nearly lost in the crush of voices and the *oom-pah-pah's* of the brass band in the corner of the room. A band, of all things, Lord Sutherland thought absently as he checked to see if the Baron de Guy had noted Wilde's appearance. When Nigel's wife, Estella, had informed him that she had hired a brass quintet—as was popular in those damned soirees the colonies hosted—he'd nearly succumbed to a fit of rage. But she'd been right again. His guests had been entranced by the sounds emanating from the shiny horns and had scrambled to find room on the dance floor among the crush of people already there. The strains of a waltz by Chopin took on an entirely new personality when interpreted by the deep-throated lilt of the shiny instruments.

"Lord Sutherland?"

Nigel shifted, tucking his thumbs into the watchpocket of his vest. Clamping a fragrant cheroot between his teeth, he squinted at the man veiled through the screen of smoke. "What is it, Wilde?" When Wilde didn't immediately speak, Lord Sutherland responded to his silent cue by saying, "Baron, have you met my secretary? Reginald Wilde."

The Frenchman held out his hand for a firm handshake. Before he quite knew what had happened, Wilde had flattered him, bolstered his ego, and deftly introduced him to a plump matron a few feet away. Once the new pair had begun to converse, Reginald's gaze briefly clashed with Lord Sutherland's. Casually, he strolled to a small pocket of space wedged between the huge guillotine window and a potted palm.

Calmly, lazily, Lord Sutherland ambled toward him, still patiently puffing on his cigar. But he became more watchful and intent.

Even after Sutherland joined him, Wilde stood just behind his employer, close enough to impart his information but far enough away to appear as if he weren't speaking to him at all.

"You should have been a spy, Reginald. Damned if you don't have a flair for such things."

"Perhaps." Wilde addressed his cravat rather than his employer, his voice so low it seemed to melt into the thick air. "I think you should come to the library at your earliest convenience."

Nigel smiled and nodded to a trio of ladies on their way onto the portico. Once the females had ducked beneath the heavy sash of the man-sized window and disappeared outside, he heard Wilde punctuate his odd remark with a single word. "Immediately."

Lord Sutherland's gray-flecked brows rose in surprise at such an odd request. Wilde knew there was nothing more important on his lordship's schedule than entertaining the dicey combination of dignitaries, aristocrats, and adversaries who cluttered his home. Yet, the man had still extended his odd request.

"Really?" Lord Sutherland drawled in an imperious tone, one that was at the same time bored and laced with curiosity. "What business is so pressing that it can't wait until morning?"

Wilde hesitated, clearly torn about speaking aloud in so public a place. Finally, he admitted, "If you remember, several months ago we were approached by a strange duo who claimed to have been hired to find Beatrice Sutherland's long-lost grandson. They wanted to play one end against the other and receive a salary from Biddy as well as from you. You chased them away, saying the information they brought was a scam." He paused for effect. "Well, they have returned from their voyage. They claim their mission was successful."

Lord Sutherland looked at Wilde then, really looked at him. An iron-hard sparkle lay embedded in his assistant's dark brown eyes. Taut lines of tension bracketed his handsome mouth.

"Come with me." Nigel Sutherland didn't even wait to see if the younger man followed. Determinedly, he began to weave through the crush of petticoats and pantlegs, ivory fans and walking sticks.

Once outside the ballroom, he nodded now and again to couples chatting lazily in the vaulted corridors. His pace remained slow enough to avoid attention but purposeful enough to waylay interruptions.

Soon he reached the darker portions of the east wing, where fewer candles had been lit in the hopes of keeping the guests away from this part of the estate. Without pause, Sutherland threw open the door to the study. The strains of the waltz followed him like phantom threads, spilling into the room and making the mausoleum quality of the library even more pronounced.

Cold marble and polished wood glistened in the scant crimson light cast by the coals left glowing in the fireplace. Gargoyles sneered from the ornately carved mantelpiece. Grotesque African masks leered from the walls. Nigel had decorated the room himself with the care and precision of a calculating surgeon. Each item had been purchased and arranged with the intent of intimidating his business associates and discouraging the staff from entering the room to dust.

A pair of candles sputtered from the wall sconces on either side of the window. The tapers barely provided enough of a glow to illuminate the two men sprawled upon the horsehair settee.

Lord Sutherland crossed to the huge mahogany desk. He

stood tall and stiff, effortlessly conveying a sense of arrogance and disapproval, an aura that clung to him as surely as the muted scents of cigar smoke and wine.

"Gentlemen." The greeting was imperious, haughty, cold.

If the two men noted the less than cordial greeting, they did not let on. They remained seated, ignoring courtesy that stated they should rise at the entrance of the seventh Earl of Lindon.

Reginald wisely shut the door, slowly, silently, without even a whisper of wood brushing carpet to draw the attention of a passing guest.

Lord Sutherland pinned a baleful gaze upon the duo on the sofa. "I told you never to return," he growled. "I will not be drawn into your charades. Not then, not now."

"But we've got a bit o' news, guv'ner." The crowing taunt came from the smaller man. A nasty, ill-featured bloke with the face of a gutter rat.

His companion placed a calming hand on the little one's arm. "Jonesy, don't be so quick t' fly off the beam with his lordship." The placating smile he offered Sutherland was oily in its obvious effort to please. "We knew you'd be wantin' t' speak t' us right away. We would've come sooner, but we only just arrived in town."

Refusing to rise to their bait, Lord Sutherland circled the desk and sank into the tufted chair. He pulled a sheaf of paper toward him as if any news these men might impart was of no import. But the sudden heaviness of his chest made it difficult to concentrate. His thoughts grew as muddled as London fog.

For years, he'd lived with rumors that Richard Albert III had survived. Each month, he'd brushed a dozen such tales off as a hoax. But when an elderly sailor had brought proof of an heir, Nigel had hired his own team to investigate. Those men had returned with news of a horrible fire and a death. They had been sure it was Richard Sutherland. Quite sure. Somewhat sure.

Thinking his position secure, he'd been amazed when Biddy had continued with her search. When the rumors of sightings began again, Nigel had sent the same men anew to confirm the child's death. He had never seen the pair after that. Nor had they corresponded with him in more than a year. Certain that his own team had eliminated the problem, he had ignored the offer made by Smythe and Jones when they had tried to gain two rewards for one job.

Had he made a huge tactical error? Could Beatrice Sutherland have found something? Someone? Or had she become so desperate she was willing to gamble the last of her possessions to chase a dream?

Bosh! It couldn't be true. Nigel's position was secure, his crimes well covered.

Except for one stray thread. Chelsea Wickersham.

The thought caused a bead of sweat to form between his shoulderblades. Chelsea. The same woman who had escaped his clutches a decade before. The same woman who had disappeared from the Barrinshrops' in London. The same woman who had reportedly gone to fetch the elusive Sutherland heir.

Refusing to appear worried in front of this overly solicitous pair of bandits, Nigel offered carelessly, "Come back tomorrow if you think it's necessary. As for tonight, I have no time for such games."

"I don't think you want us t' be doin' that, guv—"

Once again, Jones was restrained by his companion. "We woulda come to you first, mind you, but you dinna believe us when we came before, so's we took our time." He grew sly. "You'll want t' listen good to us this turnabout. We got news, we do. News 'bout a Sutherland heir. We know where t' find 'im."

Nigel couldn't help a slight start of reaction, but he masked the reflexive action by leaning back in his chair and peering at the men over the tips of his steepled fingers. "Of course you do. I'm also quite sure there's a price connected to such information. Information which will prove ultimately worthless."

"*She* was willin' t' believe us."

Sutherland waved away that piece of trivia with a negligent hand, then hid it behind the lip of the desk when the faint sheen of the candles caught the way he trembled. "Beatrice Sutherland is an old woman, willing to grasp at any lost straw—"

"Not the old one. The young miss. The pretty one."

Nigel sensed the way even Wilde's interest was piqued by that tidbit of information. Their eyes met, clung, and bounced away, just as they had in the ballroom. All in the space of a heartbeat.

"Some parlor maid, I suppose." Sutherland dismissed it, lifting a silver letter opener from the desk and tracing the elaborate etchings. A nervous tension began to swell in him, but he tamped it down, focusing his energies on the blade he held, absorbing the tensile strength of the metal, the cool kiss of the razor-sharp edge.

The feral man leaned forward, the poor lighting making his nose seem sharper, like that of a fox. A cunning, quick-witted fox. "No, sir. The governess. The one old Lady Sutherland plucked away from Lord Barrinshrop's kiddies."

Panic flowered in Nigel's belly. He stilled.

"Calls 'erself Wickersham. Chelsea Wickersham. But I 'ear that's not 'ow she was christened." Knowing he had the full attention of the Earl of Lindon, the wily man stood and scooped his hat from the settee. When Jones didn't immediately follow, Smythe grasped the little man's elbow and yanked him up. "But if you're too busy t' speak t' the likes o' us, we'll just be on our way."

"Stop!"

The moment he spoke, Lord Sutherland realized that the single word had revealed too much, hanging naked and quivering in the cryptlike tension. Gathering his control, Nigel tossed the letter opener onto the desk and stood. "Sit down."

Rather than appearing cowed by the implacable command, Smythe chortled. "I don't have t' take orders from the likes o' you."

"Sit."

The word fairly seethed, but Smythe still didn't back

away. "Only if you intend t' make it worth my while . . . yer lordship. I got debts t' pay. Especially," he taunted, "after such a long and fruitful trip. One I'd be willin' t' tell you 'bout if—"

Without warning, a woman invaded the study.

"Nigel? Whatever are you doing? Our guests are wondering . . . where . . ."

The sudden silence of the room was a tangible thing, alive and crouching in the corners. The beautiful lady who entered must have sensed it somehow, because her head jerked slightly as if she were a faun sniffing the night air. Soft gray eyes, pearlescent like the wings of a pigeon, roved the room. "Dear?"

"Not now, Estella."

"Is something wrong?" Always the proper hostess, Estella offered a serene smile in the direction of her unfamiliar guests.

Nigel pushed his shoulders back and rolled his chin to ease the constraint of his collar. Offering a glare of warning to the men who had dared to confront him, he tugged down the hem to his vest and crossed to his wife's side. "Nothing's wrong, my sweet."

Unable to help himself, he touched the sweep of blond hair that framed his Estella's heart-shaped face. The woman he'd married was still, at forty-eight years of age, so tiny, so petite, that his own stature seemed to make her shrink even more. But rather than intensifying the tension that throbbed in the stillness of the library, by her very smallness she diminished it. There was nothing more intimidating than a fragile woman.

"Just man-talk, my dumpling. Why don't you return to our guests? I'll join you shortly."

"Could I bring some refreshments?"

"No, dearest." He added pointedly, "Our meeting will be short."

"If you're sure I can't be of some service," she offered, referring to the two strangers.

"Quite sure, my pet. Go and see to our other guests.

They'll be retiring to their rooms anon and will wish to thank their adorable hostess for this evening's entertainment."

She offered Nigel a fleeting, teasing smile, one that held an echo of the coquette she'd been in her youth. The attitude dimmed when she studied Smythe and Jones. Nevertheless, she obeyed her husband's whims. "Very well, then. Good evening to you, gentlemen."

"Now see 'ere—wait just a minute! I don't suppose you've got another bunk or two. Willie 'n me are old friends of his lordship. An' if it wouldn't be a hardship on y', mum, we'd like t' accept his invitation t' stay."

Estella consulted her husband, and he offered a curt nod.

"I'll see to it, then. I feel certain the footmen can be moved from the room next to the kitchen if you don't mind the simple accommodations."

"That would be fine, just fine, I assure you."

Jones grinned.

"I'll send someone once the room is ready. Good evening, gentlemen."

"Yer ladyship."

"Mum."

Her departure down the corridor was much more reluctant than her arrival, as if, unsettled, she wished to linger to test her own disquiet. But soon, she disappeared, her indigo gown melting into the gloom, until only the faint trail of her perfume remained.

Sutherland waited until the last lamp at the end of the hall caught the golden highlights of her hair and limned the exquisite formation of her profile. Then he closed the door and turned the key.

The answering silence coiled around him like the dusky spirals of smoke rising from the pair of tapers. Pungent, silken, alive. Deep within the house, the gala continued. Laughter rose and fell like a sparkling wave. He heard the rumble of men's voices, the women's teasing replies, and the exuberant thump and rumble of a gavotte. Combined, the noises should have stoked him with success. The party continued to be a triumph, an overwhelmingly entertaining affair. Nigel, Lord Sutherland, had always delighted in impressing his neighbors and confounding his business rivals.

But lingering beneath the tinkling melody of the party lay a heavier tone. A twisted chord of unease which played in a pulsing, vibrating minor key, thrumming unheard by anyone but him. It weighed against his soul and wrapped around his heart. Unfamiliar emotions roiled within him, struggling for supremacy: denial, disgust, disappointment. Fear. The rivulet of sweat he'd felt earlier plunged down his back to pool at the base of his spine. Turning, he leveled a fulminating gaze upon his unwanted visitors.

"I want you to say what you have to say, then be out of this house by morning."

"Not so fast, guv'ner. We're a bit tired after our trip. I don't think I could remember all the details. 'Ow 'bout you, Willie?"

Jones guffawed. "M' mind's a blank."

Lord Sutherland visibly controlled his urge to throttle them both. "Perhaps, after a good night's sleep, you will remember."

"Maybe we will, an' maybe we won't."

A soft tap heralded the footman who'd come to fetch the new arrivals.

"Sleep well, gentlemen," Lord Sutherland muttered harshly as the door was opened and they followed the liveried servant into the hall.

"'Ere's hopin' you can do the same, yer lordship. It might be the last good night ye'll be havin' in a long, long time."

Reginald eased the door shut and turned to his employer. "Well?"

Nigel returned to his desk and lifted the letter opener, stroking, testing the sharpness of the blade with one blunt-tipped finger.

"See to it that our . . . guests are given a bottle or two of wine with my compliments. Not enough to level them, just enough to inebriate them and make them more talkative." His jaw took a harsh edge. "Then bring them to me in two hours' time. I'll await you near the entrance to the abandoned mine shaft below Willoby's Point."

Chapter
9

*T*he screams awakened her.

Chelsea jerked from a complete sleep, sitting up in bed, her heart pounding, her mouth dry. She flung the covers away and ran into the hall. After throwing open the door to the nursery, she came to a shuddering halt mere inches inside the threshold.

He slept. Not like a boy. Not with the covers bunched beneath his cheek or his knees drawn close to his chest. No, he lay sprawled on his stomach, one arm flung above his head, the other draped over the side of the bed. His hands were curled, relaxed. The linens puddled low over his hips, baring one tight buttock and part of a hair-roughened thigh. Chelsea stood trembling, shocked not only by her reaction to his sleeping form but by the overwhelming relief she felt upon finding him safe and his rest undisturbed. So telling, so revealing, that her first thoughts had been of him. Sure that he had endured some horrible dream or had suffered from an accident, she'd rushed to his side without even bothering to retrieve a robe.

She'd found him safe, and although she wondered who had made such macabre screams, she was loath to leave.

He was so beautiful. If she had possessed some artistic

abilities, she would have painted him that way, with the moonlight gilding his bare skin, his hair spilling over the pillows. Or perhaps she would have sculpted him from smooth marble. Every peak and valley, each dip and swell, would have known the sweep of her touch.

But this man was flesh and blood, no painting, no sculpture. Moreover, she was a woman grown, not some adolescent unskilled in the beguilement of the flesh.

So why, with each succeeding day, was it becoming harder to remember such things?

Knowing that if she didn't leave now, she might not find the strength to do so at all, she backed from the room, waiting for the snick of the latch to inform her that the door held true.

"Miss Chelsea?"

Chelsea gasped and whirled. Smee, upon seeing her agitation, hurried forward, the flame of his candle dancing and skipping at his haste, nearly extinguishing itself in the pool of melted wax near the wick.

"Is anything amiss?" Greyson asked from where he stood near the back staircase.

Smee hovered like an eager parent, waiting for the slightest sign of renewed fear, as if he thought she would display poor judgment and faint without the benefit of someone to catch her. Stiffening her spine, Chelsea summoned her best governess's mien lest these men divine even a portion of her previous wicked thoughts.

"No, Greyson, I'm fine."

"We thought we heard a scream," Smee murmured, offering her a worried look.

"I heard it, too." Her eyes skipped from the tall, somber butler to his cherubic companion.

"Master Richard?" Greyson intoned.

"I checked on him when I heard the cries. He's still sleeping."

Greyson offered a thoughtful "Mmm," then added, "Perhaps Smee and I should inspect the grounds."

Chelsea searched the mullion windows set in the thick wall at the end of the corridor. For the first time, the sparkling glass and the delicate lace curtains made her feel incredibly vulnerable. She felt as if anyone could be watching them. Gusts of wind caused the panes to rattle slightly. Distant streaks of lightning warned of an impending storm. "Wait until morning, Mr. Greyson, Mr. Smee. I'm sure it was nothing. Nothing at all."

"Very well, miss."

"Goodnight, then." Lifting the trailing hems of her gown, she disappeared into her bedchamber, leaving the two men alone.

"What do you suppose made the sounds?" Smee breathed.

"Don't you mean *who?*"

"A man?"

"Nigel, Lord Sutherland, resides not far away. In my opinion, that in itself bodes little good. No doubt, the sounds were a result of one of his more . . . private forms of entertainment." Greyson shifted, shaking away his gloomy expression. He motioned for Smee to follow him into the nursery. "You're sure he drank the tea?"

"Every last drop."

"Fine. The sleeping draft should have done the trick." The two men crept into the master's room with the stealth of a pair of criminals. "Did you bring the measuring tape?"

"Yes."

"Give here."

Smee slapped the tailor's twill into Greyson's hand, then took out a small notebook and a stub of a pencil. "Whenever you're ready."

Greyson cautiously approached the sleeping form.

"I feel quite guilty, you know, drugging him like this so soon after he's gathered his wits," Smee whispered.

"It's only for the night."

"I know that, Greyson, but . . ."

Greyson peered at him from beneath bushy brows. "We must do whatever is best for Richard, the dowager, and our own Miss Chelsea."

"Yes, Greyson."

Greyson lifted the sleeping man's wrist, then let go. It

dropped limply, whacking against the bed frame in a manner that made both servants wince. But the savage didn't stir. Immediately, Greyson began to take the supine figure's measurements, calling them out like a costumer's assistant while Smee copied them down.

Then the two men covered the Sutherland heir with the bed linens and withdrew. While they tiptoed down the corridor, the butler inquired, "Have you finished blacking the horses?"

"Yes, Greyson."

"And pressed the costumes?"

"Yes, Greyson."

"Fine." His square jaw became implacably firm. "Come Saturday, we'll ride."

The huge house echoed with an eerie, post-celebratory silence. If Nigel, Lord Sutherland, were to close his eyes, he could almost hear the faint murmur of voices, the ebb and fall of laughter, and the silver-toned glissandos of the long-forgotten band.

The party had been a huge success, his wife was delighted, his guests impressed. But Nigel didn't think of that now. He couldn't escape the hollowness that threatened to consume him, the restless tension.

Taking another huge gulp of the brandy, he drank straight from the bottle, not even flinching when the liquid splashed onto his shirtfront. Wiping his lips, he glared at the portrait over his desk and tried to tamp down the burning fury that mixed with the liquor in his stomach.

"You should be in bed."

The voice melted from the shadows. Turning, Sutherland confronted the slender frame of his secretary. For once, Reginald Wilde was not impeccably groomed. He had abandoned his jacket. His shirt had come untucked from his breeches on one side, his cuffs were unbuttoned and hanging loose around his wrists, and gilded chest hair winked from the strip of skin exposed between the open edges of linen. The legs of his fawn-colored riding breeches were mud-spattered.

"Our guests?" Nigel asked, not moving from where he slouched on the settee.

"They . . . departed. I arranged for them to be sent to a far better place soon after you left the mines," Reginald carelessly answered. Striding across the room, he opened the windows and flung the shutters outward, allowing the muggy breeze and the faint trails of washed lightning to spill into the stuffy room.

Quiet reigned for only a few seconds before Nigel slapped the sofa and shouted, "Damn her! Damn her all to bloody hell! *She* is responsible for this mess. Biddy never would have done such a thing on her own."

"You have to admire her spirit."

"No. I damn well . . . do . . . *not!*" But as his words reverberated around him, Nigel confronted the sliver of profile from the painted portrait. His lie hung in the rain-laden air. Little more than a decade ago, he had been drawn to Chelsea Wickersham because of that very thing. Her spirit.

He sprang from his seat and stalked toward the portrait. Grasping the letter opener from the blotter, Nigel circled the desk and lifted the blade to trace the painted curve of her shoulder, the delicate indentation of her spine. The action was a telling threatening caress, vividly conveying that he had once explored those same dips and hollows with his own hands.

"Damn it! Find . . . *her!*" Whirling, he stabbed the blade, tip first, into the exquisite wood of his desk, then stormed from the room and slammed the door.

The embedded weapon swayed from side to side. To the man who remained, it represented a symbolic sort of metronome, measuring what little time remained before Nigel Sutherland would have to confront his past, his rival . . .

His obsession.

At that moment, Reginald decided that he would wait until morning to impart his news: that just before the bodies of their uninvited guests had been tossed into the mines, one of them had summoned enough strength to mutter a single word.

Bellemoore.

Chelsea spent the next two weeks with her charge, trying to find some core of civilization in his makeup. Instead of breaking through to the well-behaved man she felt sure lingered underneath, she found that he was even more uncouth than she had ever dreamed possible.

On their first outing together, she sent Smee and Greyson to serve as guards on the hill and took Richard on a walk through the gardens. Within minutes, he had evaded her completely. She'd found him hours later, perched asleep on the bow of a tree.

After that, she kept him locked in the nursery and tried to read to him. He countered her measures by prowling the room like a caged beast until she thought she would scream.

Nearly a fortnight passed, and Chelsea grew determined to forge ahead in some small way, so she gave Richard full rein of the house, hoping he would explore and begin to come to terms with his new life. Rather than taking advantage of his freedom, he dogged her every step while Chelsea tended to the front rose patch. Needing to give herself a little room to breathe, she had provided him with a pair of shears to help. Minutes later, two of Biddy's favorite bushes were unrecognizable save for the shorn blooms and branches scattered on the path.

In the following few days, she found that any attempts at formal lessons were of no use. She simply tried to fill his time. But, like a mischievous toddler, he seemed bent upon clinging to her one minute and driving her insane with worry the next.

Stewing the whole night about what to do, Chelsea decided that perhaps she was taking this assignment from the wrong tack. Richard Sutherland needed to know that he wasn't a barbarian but a gentleman. For that, he must look like one.

What Chelsea hated to admit was that her actions would

benefit her own cause as well. Perhaps by taming his appearance, she could tame her thoughts. She didn't know why he continued to fascinate her. Was it because he was in essence a savage? Because he reminded her of urges better left forgotten?

Or because he was forbidden to her?

"Greyson? Smee?" Stepping into the empty kitchen, Chelsea frowned. She had counted on having the two men help her with her task, but since Saturday tended to be a day of last-minute chores, they seemed to be off on their own private errands, leaving her completely alone in the house with her charge.

Alone.

Reluctantly, she climbed the back steps and opened the nursery door. Richard lay sprawled on the bed, his back propped against a mound of pillows. His long legs crowded the narrow bedstead. She was thankful he wore his borrowed clothing, but the buttons of his shirt had not been fastened, leaving a too-healthy strip of bronzed flesh to her view. The picture book he held was clearly upside down, but he didn't bother to right it.

"Master Richard?"

He lazily turned his head to acknowledge he'd heard her but made no effort to rise. Leisurely, he surveyed every inch of her body, making her overtly aware that she had chosen her most staid, unflattering gown and all-encompassing apron.

"Come with me, please."

He didn't stir.

Blast. Chelsea did not want to go in. When they shared the same space, the very air seemed to crackle. Her skin became sensitive, her commands scattered.

"Master Richard, come here."

Still he didn't move.

Drat it all! If he were any other man, she— The thought came to a screeching halt. If he were any other man, she wouldn't be so conscious of his bare skin, the copper color of his nipples, the dip of his navel.

Disgusted by her own traitorous tendencies, she marched toward the bed. She tugged at his sleeve until he rose with feline grace.

"Come . . . with . . . me," she ordered again. Releasing him, she left the nursery with the sure steps of a military attaché, offering a sigh of relief when she heard him follow.

Not giving him time to change his mind, she led him to the kitchen and gestured for him to take his place on the bench next to the huge oak table. "Sit, please, Master Richard."

When he didn't respond, she stifled the urge to huff in impatience. Really, this language barrier was proving to be quite annoying. It wasn't that Chelsea didn't sympathize with his plight or have the persistence necessary to break through their problems in communication. There just wasn't time to be playing these kinds of games.

Panic laced her veins like a black mist. The list of skills Richard needed to master was enormous. The stakes involved were dear—not only to Biddy but to Chelsea as well. If they failed in their endeavors to restore Richard's inheritance, she didn't even want to contemplate the consequences.

The dank foreboding threatened to undermine her usual efficiency, but Chelsea stiffened her resolve. She would succeed. She would teach this heathen what he needed to know if it was the last thing she did. Starting today, she intended to attack her campaign head-on.

Of all their goals, his language skills held prior sway. The rest of their plans would fall neatly into place once she and her pupil shared a common tongue. By all the laws of probability, Richard should be nearly as British as she. His parents—providing they had survived during a portion of his childhood—should have taught him at least a portion of their native tongue.

But Chelsea had no idea if that had happened. Richard's background was vague. Obviously, the portrait they'd been given had been painted many years before. Looking back, she supposed she should have thought of such a possibility.

It had always struck Chelsea as odd that Richard Albert and Julie Sutherland had not had a child for twenty years.

Nevertheless, the date Lord and Lady Sutherland had died and left him alone was a mystery. She could only hope that sometime during the last two decades, his parents had taken an active part in his upbringing. If so, it would only be a matter of jarring loose old memories.

But right now there was the matter of his grooming.

Taking his wrist, she pulled him after her, much as she would a recalcitrant little boy. Ignoring the way the bones beneath her grip reminded her that her pupil was far from immature, she forced him to sit down. "Stay." Much like Biddy's spaniel, he obeyed.

Sullivan watched as his governess busied herself as if the task she performed was of the utmost importance. Working quickly, she gathered a tea towel from the pantry, a metal basin, and a pair of scissors. Setting them on the table, she withdrew her own metal comb from the pocket of her pinafore and arranged all of the items on the polished oak as if they were soldiers being prepared for war. Using the hem of her apron to protect her hands, she lifted the tea kettle from the rear of the brick and iron stove and filled the basin.

"Today we shall begin working on your appearance, Master Richard," she informed him after dispensing with the kettle. "Though I'm sure your . . . er . . . current fashion sense is suitable for the wilds of your previous home, most Englishmen have a much more . . . conservative view on such things as mode of dress and hairstyle."

Sullivan's eyes narrowed, and in another quick glance he surveyed the comb and scissors. She meant to cut his hair.

The thought filled him with annoyance, then a burst of frustration at having her force her mores upon him without so much as a show of concern. The fact that he supposedly couldn't understand English registered only a moment. What caught and held his attention was that she intended to shear him like some blasted, pasty-faced fop, when in fact he needed every last shred of savagery at his disposal to keep his enemies off-guard.

Chelsea looked up from her preparations to find that her charge's eyes suddenly glowed with an inner light. One that made him appear a little dangerous. Summoning most of the inner mettle she could muster, she tried to study him dispassionately, imagining what his broad shoulders would look like when better defined by a tailored jacket and vest. His calves, bare beneath Smee's breeches, would be more appropriately garbed in well-fitted trousers. With his hair cut and trimmed more closely to his face, he would indeed appear very much like the titled gentleman. If only she could find a way to douse the gleam that had kindled in his eyes.

"First, we must protect your borrowed clothing. Smee was kind enough to loan you his shirt and trousers, so you'll need to take care of them properly." Continuing her running monologue, she settled the towel over his shoulders. "After being so gracious, Smee would be most distressed to discover one of his shirts ruined, don't you think?"

He didn't answer. Not that she'd thought he would. He watched every move she made, like a hawk trailing a mouse.

"There are many changes that will need to be made over the next few days, Master Richard. Somehow, we'll have to find a proper wardrobe so that you can accustom yourself to the current styles. In a day or two, we will work on deportment and etiquette. In my experience, even a gentleman without means can convince people otherwise if he can adopt the proper balance of reserve, discretion, and arrogance." Wryly, she added, "Judging by some of our past encounters, I fail to see a problem in developing your arrogance."

Arms akimbo, she continued, "Today, we will deal with a few of the simpler things. We will take you into the garden again for a walk and describe some of the flora, then show you the path up to the moors. But first there is the matter of your hair."

Reluctantly, she fiddled with the lock that habitually spilled over his forehead. Soft. Silky. She hated to cut the waves. The sensual way the tresses hung to the middle of his shoulderblades had become the source of fantasies, and she had so few left to cling to, she hated to destroy what harmless imaginings remained. But some things had to be done just because they had to be done. Richard Sutherland couldn't appear in front of the *ton* looking like a shipwreck survivor.

The shears awaited her command, reminding her of the minutes that ticked past. Chelsea grasped the comb in one hand and the scissors in the other. She was procrastinating. All because of some foolish nonsense that should have been banished long ago.

"Master Richard, I—"

She had no more than said his name before he caught sight of the cutting implement.

"Don't be afraid. This won't hurt."

But when she grasped a large chunk of his hair, he began to struggle.

"Master Richard, please!"

The blades yawned, and she fought Richard's hold, determined to cut the locks to prove to him that he wouldn't be harmed. But when he saw the amount of hair she intended to trim, he roared and sprang to his feet.

There was no time to adjust to his instinctive flight. Chest clashed with chest, hip with hip. Chelsea gulped for breath when the force of the impact knocked the air from her lungs. She felt him push her out of the way and lunge to the side.

Dropping the scissors, Chelsea caught one elbow, clinging to him like a burr to a bucking steed.

"Master Richard! Stop this nonsense at once!"

Growling, he tried to disentangle himself. Fearing that she had frightened him, she wrapped both arms around his waist. "Master Richard! Please. We won't harm you. We promise. Please!"

He stopped, his sudden inactivity jarring her. The realization of the way she held him, her palms cupped intimately around his ribs, crept into her consciousness like a thief. A war of indecision consumed her. One part of her brain demanded that she wrench free, but a corner of her heart whispered that she should stay.

Before she could gather the wherewithal to react, he dragged her tightly against him. At the intimate meshing of their thighs, an instantaneous heat struck her like a bolt of lightning.

His expression had grown dark. But she knew it wasn't anger that she saw. Whatever fury he might have felt had been driven away by a more primitive, carnal emotion. One that—no matter how thick her veneer of civilization might appear—Chelsea knew she matched, measure for measure.

He parted his legs to draw her closer. His gaze zeroed in on hers as if testing her reaction, then scanned the contours of her face, her breasts, before returning to settle upon the moist curve of her lower lip.

Suddenly, Chelsea realized that there were things in this world that were universal. Language barriers and cultural differences held little power against the elemental urges of a man and a woman. It had a lexicon all its own. An unspoken set of rules. An elaborate choreography of gestures and signals.

Richard's head eased down, tipping slightly to one side. His lashes closed partway, his mouth hovered above Chelsea's.

"No." She tried to pry their bodies apart, but her actions only managed to bring them even closer together. To her horror, she could feel the first faint stirrings of his arousal. "Let me go," she demanded. "Immediately."

He didn't release her. His fingers spread wide as if seeking some way to delve beneath the yardage of her gown.

"No!" Using all her strength, Chelsea tore free from his embrace, staring at him in combined horror and self-recrimination.

"You mustn't do that. You mustn't!"

But her reprimand was husky and needy.

He paid little attention. She recognized his intent as he ambled toward her. Other men had looked at her that way. Just before they had tried to "pat a little arse," as she'd heard one baronet phrase it.

"No," she repeated more sternly. Her mouth grew dry,

her pulse thumped. Not from fear, not from distress, but, quite honestly, from anticipation. But she couldn't let this happen. Not now. Not ever.

He drew close, pinning her arms to her sides, just above her elbow, and she fought against the rush of eagerness that spilled through her body.

"No, Master Richard."

His head dipped, his mouth parted, and he bent to kiss her.

Chelsea reacted instinctively, drawing upon years of experience. Her hand arced into the air, her palm cracking across the hollow of his cheek.

The resulting silence in the room was deafening. Richard snapped to attention, touching the reddening spot.

Chelsea thought he would appear contrite, perhaps abashed, even alarmed. He merely straightened, his mouth settling into a thin line. Then he walked from the room, shutting the door behind him.

Never had she felt so small, so mean. She had struck a man for reacting honestly with her. While she, who supposedly knew better, had stifled her own wishes to reciprocate and had played the hypocrite.

But she'd done what she knew to be best for all concerned. Hadn't she?

Her heart didn't think so. It still pounded madly in her chest. Her arms had unconsciously folded to keep from reaching out.

She'd been right in her actions, she silently reaffirmed. She knew she had. There was too much at stake for her to believe otherwise. She had come to Bellemoore as an employee. The task she'd been asked to perform was critical. Richard Sutherland was being given a fresh start. He would build a new life and a brilliant future. She would have no part in that world. She must never forget that. She must never forget that once her work was finished, she would leave.

Sighing, she rubbed at the tension gathering at the nape of her neck. Her outburst had left her with emotional barriers to repair and a relationship to reestablish. Afraid she had hurt Richard Sutherland or scared him, or both, Chelsea went outside in search of her charge.

Within minutes, it became quite apparent that he had disappeared.

Damn, damn, *damn!* Sullivan stormed down the garden path and into the screen of foliage beyond, cursing the cool Scottish climate, the bite of pebbles beneath his feet, but, most of all, that snip of a British governess who had slapped him—*slapped* him—because he'd dared to kiss her.

He would admit to himself that matters had gotten a little out of hand. He would admit that perhaps he had pressed liberties that were not entirely honorable. But by heaven, she hadn't been completely innocent in the affair, either. For the last few weeks, she had treated him with the same attention given to a five-year-old. She had bullied, babied, and prodded him until it was all he could do to keep from snapping at her to give him a moment's peace. When she'd looked at him that way in the kitchen, all soft-eyed and soulful, he hadn't been able to control his thoughts. When she had begun to touch him, he hadn't been able to control his actions. But, by damn, he *hadn't* forced her. She'd been more than a willing participant. In fact, she'd clung to him as if she'd never wanted to leave. She'd returned each caress in full measure. She'd . . .

Sullivan swore again, damning the fickleness of women, the impossible nature of his predicament, the sting of his cheek.

But most of all, he damned the way his body responded even now to the thought of kissing her again.

Greyson and Smee huddled low in the screen of trees and watched the road into town. The air fairly crackled with glee. Smee hugged himself in excitement, while Greyson's features were flushed with an unaccountable pleasure.

Far in the distance, the slow, muffled clop and squeak of a pony cart sifted into the dappled quiet of the afternoon.

Greyson drew upright, assuming a military posture. "Ready, Smee?"

"Ready, Greyson."

"Have you everything I asked you to bring?" The butler's pale eyes adopted a determined glint.

"I think so, yes."

"Rope?"

"Yes."

"Spyglass?"

"Yes."

"Saber?"

"Yes."

"Bonbons?"

"Yes!"

"Good." Greyson inhaled through his nose, held it, puffed out his chest, then released the air through his mouth. "You have the outline of events?"

Smee tapped his bald pate. "Memorized."

Greyson noted his companion's dark floppy hat, silk scarf, and flowing black cape. "Might I compliment you on your costume? You look quite the part. Quite the part, indeed."

Smee grinned. "Why, thank you, Greyson. I do so like the mustache you've painted on. I believe it's the finishing touch."

Feeling unaccountably expansive, Greyson inquired, "Really? You don't think it's too much? After all, it's only a bit of blacking."

"Oh no! Not at all. Smartly done, I'd say. The frock coat and trousers . . ."

"You like them?" Greyson sucked in his stomach and preened beneath the dated evening togs. "Clothes make the man."

"I've found that to be quite, quite true."

"Crime is no excuse for sloppiness."

"My thoughts exactly."

"Shall we take our positions?"

"After you."

"No, my friend. After you."

"You're too kind."

"Not at all. Glad to do it."

The two men separated, Smee lurking behind a boulder that careened sideways into the road, Greyson hiding in a thick stand of trees.

Only a few minutes elapsed before the rattling sound of the approaching conveyance intensified. Smee lifted the spyglass and squinted at the diminutive pony cart, then waved to Greyson. "Lady Appleby and her sister Lady Greene."

"You're sure?"

"Quite sure."

"Are they alone?"

"As far as I can see. They must be returning from the garden party at the manor, just as we'd hoped."

The clattering was quite near now. Throwing Greyson the other end of the rope, Smee secured the binding to a tree on one side of the road while Greyson did the same on the other.

"On the count of three, Smee."

"Right-o, old boy."

"One . . . two . . . three!"

Huffing and puffing, Smee clambered on top of the huge rock. When the cart rounded the bend, he stood upright, pounded his breast, and bellowed fearfully.

The sleepy pony, startled by the noise, reared, then balked at the rope strung a mere foot before its nose. The women in the carriage squealed and gasped, trying to maintain control of the suddenly lively animal.

Smee attempted to jump from the rock, found it too high, retraced his steps down the back, then approached the frightened gentlewomen, brandishing his pistol. "Aargh! What ho, what ho!" he shouted in his best brigand imitation. "Yer money, yer jewels! Or I'll have yer virtue, I will."

The women screamed, their withered faces paling beneath the huge brims of their bonnets. Fragile, glove-encased hands clutched at the shawls slung over their shoulders.

Before the women could dissolve into swoons, there was a

rustle of leaves, and a figure dressed in a woolen jacket with shiny patches at the elbows broke free from the trees. He struggled to draw a saber from the scabbard at his side, swore, then whipped the blade free. "Do as he says, lassies, and you won't be hurt."

Smee waved the pistol back and forth in emphasis.

Greyson approached their victims. "Please, my dears. If you would be so kind."

Rebecca Appleby and Marvella Greene—both well into their seventies if they were a day—cowered, then quickly yanked at their jewels, tugged their reticules from around their wrists, and held out the lacy bags. The tassels at the bottom shook with the women's obvious trembling.

"Take them, take them! J-just p-please don't hurt us!"

Greyson motioned for Smee to take the proffered items. "You ladies have displayed a genuine depth of human charity." His lips tilted in a devilish smile. "We do appreciate your kindnesses. Truly, we do." Taking Rebecca Appleby's hand, he leaned close and then tugged her toward him, bussing her on the lips. Before she could react, he pulled a tiny tissue-wrapped package from his coat pocket and tossed it onto the lap of Marvella Greene.

Within seconds, the women's hiccuping gasps of panic subsided into coos of astonishment.

"Until we meet again," Greyson drawled, winking from behind the eyeholes burned into his best black silk handkerchief. "Farewell, my lovelies." His arm swept wide as he bent in a stiff, courtly bow. Then he and Smee quickly unhitched the rope from the tree, struggled onto the backs of their mounts, and half-trotted, half-galloped into the obscuring underbrush.

Leaving the two aged women blushing and staring after them both in delighted astonishment.

Chapter

10

The indomitable Chelsea Wickersham was weakening. She had tried to be the person she'd been hired to be, but after each encounter with Richard Sutherland, the years of propriety and reserve were being stripped away, leaving the aching heart beneath.

She didn't want to be this way. She didn't want to feel this much—not just passion but honest regard. She thought about Richard at the oddest moments of the day. When she did, the persona she'd created seemed to sift away, like so much dust, leaving her staring at a woman she thought she had abandoned long ago.

Chelsea had always prided herself on being strong. On not needing the arms of a man to make her feel whole. Now she discovered that she was no better, no worse, than all of the daughters of Eve who had longed throughout the ages to find someone who would adore them. She didn't want this to happen. But she couldn't seem to make the emotions go away.

Chelsea had a great deal of time to ponder this unexpected twist to her personality during her search for Richard Sutherland. He had vanished as if he'd never been, and with each succeeding hour she'd grown more upset.

When she considered the fact that Nigel stayed so near, her worry had quickly escalated into panic. She was about to ride pell-mell into town in search of Greyson or Smee—or chance calling to her charge aloud—when, much later, she finally located him down by Deidre Pond.

By that time, she was frantic, picturing Richard Sutherland IV stumbling closer and closer to the one man he should avoid. When she topped the rise and pushed aside the branch obscuring the water from the view of the path, she thought at first she must have been mistaken in thinking she'd heard a splash. But as she drew nearer, she saw the sleek head swimming away from her toward the rocky outcropping on the opposite side.

She hid her trembling hands in her skirts, but she refused to admit to herself how relieved she was to find him. Not just because he was Biddy's grandson and her pupil, but because she had been worried about him. *Him.*

But as she saw him gliding effortlessly through the water, she wondered why she had ever felt any qualms about his safety. This was no adolescent who couldn't fend for himself. In fact, judging by his temper and reflexes, she pitied anyone who might dare to cross him. She was quite certain that Richard Sutherland could be ruthless when provoked. Which only served to make her feel even more guilty for striking him. He had never been anything but kind to her. For that, she had slapped him as if he were some masher about to take her virtue.

Had she hoped to provoke his anger? If he had forced the embrace, then she could have felt justified in striking him. Then she wouldn't have had to confront the guilt of responding so wholeheartedly.

Somehow sensing her scrutiny, he rolled in the water, floating half-submerged on his back. His arms rose to the surface, skimming back and forth in front of him. Silky ripples ebbed from his shoulders outward in ever-widening circles, the effect nearly hypnotizing her so that she couldn't bring herself to look away.

She didn't know what to say to him. An apology, a demand for more appropriate behavior, a teasing remark would all be wasted. The man couldn't speak. He didn't seem to understand a word she said. If not for the way he watched her so intently, she would have wondered if he heard her at all.

At a loss for what to do next, she regarded him quietly. He remained where he was, effortlessly treading water. His dark hair had been slicked away from his face and shone in the sunlight. His expression was stern and unreadable, but there was a difference in the way he looked at her. More than ever before, he masked his emotions, watching her with eyes that had once been so expressive and now were cloaked with their own brand of secrets.

In that instant, Chelsea realized that she had done him even more of a disservice than she had originally admitted. This was no boy. She had known that from the beginning. But she had continued to treat him as if he were a child. She hadn't bothered to take into account that he had been abducted and horribly mistreated during his return voyage. He had awakened to a world completely foreign to him. He had no grasp of the language and no one to trust but strangers. Inadvertently, in trying to help him, they had led him into danger.

So how did they go on from here? She was already struggling to resist this man. How could she reassure him that she wouldn't willingly harm him when the imprint of her blow probably still stung his cheek?

"Master Richard?" she called.

Sullivan didn't stray from his spot in the center of the pond. He eyed the woman who approached with a hint of distrust, wondering what sort of punishment would be meted out by his governess for his improprieties.

But, to his surprise, she didn't seem inclined to chide. Rather, she seemed slightly chagrined. Her eyes had grown dark, troubled. Her skin had pinkened as if she were embarrassed.

The silence grew longer, and Chelsea opened her mouth again but didn't know how to continue. Even if he had been able to understand her words, she couldn't have explained. She couldn't possibly tell him that she dreaded each moment she spent in his presence. Not because she disliked him or her position as his governess, but because he aroused feelings in her better left forgotten.

"Richard?" She edged closer. Her gaze dropped to the pile of clothing that had been abandoned on the shore, then zeroed in on him again with the strength of a desperate homing pigeon.

There wasn't a single doubt in her mind that he was naked. Completely and utterly naked.

A nervous flutter swept into her stomach. But she didn't care. She was about to walk a tightrope, and she prayed that in balancing the slender thread she didn't pull them both down.

Extending her hand, she uttered the only words she could think of. "Come home with me, Richard." She had meant to make the words a command; they were an invitation.

Something flared in his visage. Perhaps it was the dulcet tone of her voice or the way she dropped all pretense and merely looked at him the way a woman looked at a man. Either way, he continued to tread water for some time, then slowly, sinuously swam toward her.

He sliced gracefully through the water. The crystal liquid rolled over the golden skin in a manner that was completely innocent yet undeniably intoxicating.

Several yards from the shore, he stopped and allowed his feet to sink to the bottom. When he stood, water rushed down his torso in brilliant diamond drops. His arms hung curved at his sides, dripping water from his fingertips and the heels of his palms. Gooseflesh riddled his tanned skin, reminding Chelsea that the pond never reached a comfortable bathing temperature. He would be lucky if he didn't catch his death after such a stunt.

"Come home where it's warm, Richard. A storm is brewing, and you'll become chilled." Her shoes scuffed against the rocky shore. "Please."

Sullivan stood still for some time, wondering what had happened to change the woman before him. She had watched each move he'd made with an intensity that bordered on hunger. Rather than backing away from her emotions and relegating him to his role as child to her role as tutor, she remained what she was, a woman who was very aware that he was a man.

"Please come out of the water, Richard."

He obeyed.

Chelsea watched in abject fascination as he emerged. The murky sunlight and dappled shadows beneath the trees caressed each line and indentation of his chest. The swirling sluice of ripples dropped below his hips, his thighs, his knees, until finally he stood before her, quite bare, quite brazen, and quite beautiful.

She didn't flinch at his nakedness, and that seemed to spark a flame of admiration. Several minutes inched past as he took his measure of her, but she refused to back down. She even allowed herself a leisurely survey of his body, and though she trembled at what she saw, she refused to appear the meek, frightened virgin.

Evidently amused by the silent test of wills, Richard reached to touch her cheek, then halted midway, a curious frown appearing between his brows. Tipping his head in consideration, he traced the wind-tousled ringlets that had escaped the confines of her coif.

Chelsea stood stock still, her pulse scrabbling at her throat. Surely he couldn't remember how she had caressed him so wantonly during their journey to Bellemoore. Surely he couldn't remember the way they'd kissed. Until now, she had seen no recognition, and she'd thought herself safe. But she feared that even through his drugged haze, some shred of a memory remained like a seed waiting to sprout.

He seemed to consider some monumental puzzle. Then he grinned. A slow, secret grin that sent tingles down her spine. She didn't trust that smile. It made her think of exposed secrets and hidden delights. He had remembered something. She could only pray it wasn't much.

"I think we'd better return to the house."

When she tried to retreat, he caught her behind the neck. His flesh was icy and damp, smelling of clear water and male musk.

He scoured the length of her body as if he'd never really

noticed her before. Then, without warning, he released her, scooped his clothing from the ground, and brushed by her to return to the house, leaving Chelsea with the task of following the taut curves of his buttocks the entire way.

"Mast—" She broke off and began again. "Richard?"

He twisted to shoot a questioning glance over his shoulder.

"I think you should dress first. It would be best." When he didn't move, she pointed to the clothing he held. "Dress, please."

Richard blinked uncomprehendingly, then grinned in evident amusement, and he dropped the items to the ground. He took his shirt. Chelsea watched, unabashed, as he drew the linen garment over his shoulders, thereby obscuring the lean line of his back and the narrow square of his hips. But when he began to don the scrap of red-orange cloth, she averted her head.

Her first clue that he had finished was when a set of wet fingers twined between her own. He had approached her so silently, she hadn't been aware of his arrival. He had dressed in his shirt and loincloth, but the breeches were tucked under his free arm.

"Your trousers," she prompted, pointing to the bundle.

He shook his head and tugged. Although it wasn't proper for a woman in her position to allow a half-dressed, semi-educated savage to take her hand and lead her down the garden path . . . .

Chelsea didn't demur.

Nigel was not at home when the stranger approached Lindon Manor. Reginald was the first to see him. The summer air had grown hot and heavy so late in the afternoon, and most of the guests had retired to their rooms to rest. Except for one couple listlessly exploring the grounds and an eighty-five-year-old matron snoring from the rocker placed under a tree, Reginald had the estate virtually to himself.

Not normally in the habit of searching the road for travelers, Reginald had come to the front steps to smoke one of his rare cheroots. Upon looking up, he had paused. The man in the saddle was tall, lean, impeccably groomed. He was big-framed—not flabby—but of the sort whose bones were solid, his flesh pure muscle. His hair curled carelessly about his face and touched the collar of his frock coat in a manner that proclaimed: *I don't give a damn.* His face reflected that sentiment—cleanly cut, bluntly shaped—its expression bordering on arrogant disdain.

When the stranger brought his animal to a trot, then a slow walk, Reggie ground his cheroot beneath his heel, automatically noting the fine breed of the stallion and its owner's excellent command of the beast.

The man swung to the pea-gravel path and tossed the reins to a waiting footman with the careless abandon of a person accustomed to being waited upon. He appeared unaware of Reggie as he scrutinized the neoclassical facade of Lindon Manor.

"I would like to speak to the Earl of Lindon."

The words were issued without warning and contained a barely noticeable chill.

"In what capacity?"

"Business."

"Your name?"

"Cane. Gregory Cane."

Nigel Sutherland ambled forward, keeping to the trees that surrounded the garden at Bellemoore. Legend said that dead men told no tales. But those who were about to die told volumes.

Reginald had told him that Smythe and Jones had confessed that Richard Sutherland was abiding at Bellemoore. After cooling his heels for more than a week because of unexpected business, Nigel had finally managed to come see for himself. Minutes ago, he'd approached the cottage to find the windows flung wide to catch the surly breezes. Odd, since, according to his sources, Beatrice Sutherland was still in London and no one was supposed to be in residence.

It was at that precise moment he'd seen Chelsea Wickersham.

When she'd stormed out of the kitchen and hurried up the path leading into the moors, he'd been momentarily stunned by the changes he'd seen in her. So much so, he hadn't been able to summon the presence of mind to follow her. He'd been riveted by the first sight of her hair, her face, her form, that he'd witnessed in over ten years.

Chelsea Wickersham had grown even more beautiful in a decade. Where the painted features of the portrait he owned still held a hint of things to come, the woman he'd seen had met those implied promises. Her manner was controlled and determined, her posture proud and feminine. Her face . . . he had guessed she would become this exquisitely beautiful. That was why he'd spirited her away from her homeland so early in life. He'd known that if he waited for her to mature, some other man would snap her up.

Nigel flinched, experiencing the tight burn of need. Time had not dimmed his desire to possess this female. She was on the verge of destroying him, and he found that it wasn't Richard Sutherland who entered his thoughts, or their ultimate confrontation, or Chelsea's machinations.

It was this woman. His hunger for her had not been blunted. His obsession had not waned. He would have her. He would see her kneeling at his feet, begging for his forgiveness, his mercy, his touch.

Then he would own her. Once and for all.

Mounting his horse, Nigel pointed the animal toward home, not even bothering to wait for a glimpse of the elusive Sutherland heir. There were plenty of opportunities ahead for all that. Right now, he wished to indulge himself in a bit of sport. It was time Chelsea Wickersham was given a taste of her own medicine. When she'd run away from him, enlisting Beatrice Sutherland's help, she had made him wait in an agony of suspense, wondering if she dared to expose him and his crimes to all of society. He knew she'd suspected his efforts to accuse Richard Albert Sutherland of treason and to arrange his father's death over the succeeding months. He knew she could ruin his future by going to the authorities. But she hadn't done that. She'd bided her time, tacitly threatening him with the powerful knowledge she

Chapter
11

Sullivan leaned back in his seat and eyed his governess down the long length of the dining-room table. On the opposite end, nearly twenty feet away, Chelsea Wickersham finished her supper.

It *was* her. He hadn't been dreaming.

Sullivan lifted his spoon and tapped it idly against the damask cloth, staring at his companion with ever-growing glee. The visionary temptress who had lingered on the fringes of his consciousness ever since he had awakened at Bellemoore had not been a figment of his imagination. She was his governess. Miss Chelsea Wickersham.

He wanted to crow in triumph at the very idea. Who would have thought someone so alluring could be his own Miss Wickersham, governess extraordinaire? He was quite sure that if she knew he'd divined her secret, she would be mortified. After all, he'd seen her adorned in little more than her undergarments and the wild tumble of her hair. He didn't think that particular state of attire appeared in the *Handbook of English Educational Etiquette*.

Since he had uncovered the knowledge of her indiscretion, Sullivan didn't know exactly how he planned to use it. Perhaps in the future, he could employ the information to demonstrate his own unsuitability as a peer of the realm. After all, why would they want to trust a man who would seduce his very own governess?

In the meantime, the secret colored their relationship in a subtle, inexplicable way. It made him see her in a totally new light. Not as his teacher, but as a woman.

Chelsea lowered an earthenware mug and blotted her lips with a napkin. Looking up, she found him watching her over the branch of candles.

Neither of them moved. The air around them grew rich and warm.

Earlier that evening, she had come to fetch him from the nursery, surprising Sullivan by treating him more as a guest than a pupil. She had ushered him down to this room and had shown him to the far end of the table, where an elaborate place setting of crystal, china, and silver had been laid. After quietly naming each of the pieces, she had retreated to her own seat, where a cruder set of pottery dishes awaited.

They had dined upon simple fare—leek soup to begin with, an entree of boiled potatoes, lamb, baby peas, and thick crusty bread, and finally a sliver of custard pie. Sullivan had purposely used all of the wrong forks and even his fingers, but Chelsea had not seemed inclined to chide. They had continued the meal without interruption. A portly man—whom Sullivan surmised had been the mysterious Smee who had donated the clothing Sullivan wore—served each course with the flair of a master chef serving a gourmet feast.

Through it all, Sullivan studied his teacher. The gilded halo of light diffused from the center of the table caressed her cheeks and brought out the fiery highlights in her hair, but she remained unaware of the picture she made. She was poised, quiet, and dignified. A lethal paradox when that excruciatingly proper demeanor was compared to the woman of passion he'd seen in his arms earlier that day.

In honor of the meal, she had abandoned her apron; but she still wore a discreet gray gown beneath. Her only adornment was a simple onyx brooch fastened at her throat.

Not even a shred of lace or braid softened the line of her bodice. Her hair had been combed back from her face and fastened at the nape of her neck with innumerable unobtrusive hairpins.

If his mind was correct in insisting that she had stood before him in her underthings, how many of the other hazy memories were true, and how many were the product of the drugs he'd been given? He remembered only bits and pieces. The stroke of light on feminine skin, music, a kiss . . . and a fleeting caress. A delicate touch like butterflies winging their way down his chest.

"Are you finished?"

With some difficulty, Sullivan brought his mind back to the present.

"I hope you enjoyed your supper. It's good to see you eating your fill. Don't be afraid to ask for more if you're hungry."

She couldn't know what interpretation he applied to her last remark as the intimacy of the room filtered into the corners and warmed the air they breathed. The French windows had been opened to catch a breeze. The soughing of the garden foliage and the grate of the crickets provided a lulling serenade that invited thoughts of bedtime and quiet nights.

But Sullivan was far from sleepy.

Chelsea reached for her mug, toyed with the handle, then abandoned it again without drinking. "Come with me, Richard. I think there's something you should see."

She didn't wait to ascertain whether or not Sullivan had understood her request, but took the candelabra from the table and disappeared. He was too intrigued to press his charade. Rising, he followed her through the rooms which were arranged gunshot fashion—butted back to back with no hall—into the foyer, then to another set of double doors.

"I've learned a great deal about your family in the last few years. Biddy has a wealth of stories to tell and delights in finding a new audience. I sometimes think I belong to them as much as you do. This was your grandfather's studio," she explained, her voiced hushed, nearly reverent. "He fancied himself a bit of a painter, although he never tried to sell any of his work. It was merely a means of relaxing from the pressures of his businesses. Perhaps that is why your father took up painting during his exile. He must have learned some of the rudiments from Albert."

Turning the brass knob, she ushered him inside a huge area that smelled of lemon oil and roses. The candles shed a weak, buttery wash around them, but the rest of the studio basked in sooty darkness.

"This was once a lovely spot filled with settees and velvet carpets, but most of the furnishings have been sold. Luckily, we were able to keep a desk and chair. I placed those in the center of the room since this is where we will have your lessons." She repeated, "Les-sons."

He didn't speak, but he absorbed the earnest cast of her face and the warmth of her skin on his own. He wondered if she were aware of the way her thumb swept back and forth against his wrist in a manner that was more in keeping with a lover than a teacher.

"Come." Twining her fingers between his, much as he had earlier that afternoon, she led him to the side wall. "I want you to meet your family. Perhaps by seeing them, you will see something that might jar you into remembering who you truly are."

She stopped in front of a long line of portraits, and Sullivan immediately understood her intent.

"Originally, your grandfather's paintings were hung here, and these were housed in the portrait gallery at Lindon Hall, one of the family estates in London. But when your grandmother was forced out of her home, she managed to secrete these away. Nigel, your cousin and the man who inherited the title, planned to sell them. Imagine. Selling your own people."

Chelsea's voice trailed away on a note of sadness, the emotion so tangible that Sullivan wondered what could have caused her to feel so deeply for a dozen painted strangers.

Lifting the candles, she drew him closer. She spoke in a confidential tone, one used with foreigners, knowing they understood only a fragment of what was said, yet expressing everything that came to mind nonetheless. Sullivan sensed that because she didn't think he comprehended most of her remarks, she was more inclined to be honest in the information she gave him.

"This is Roland Sutherland, one of the first portraits to be commissioned. He was a great naval hero during the rein of Queen Elizabeth, and it is from him that you received your title. Next to him is his wife, Lucille."

Sullivan eyed the couple with a scant amount of interest, noting the starched ruffs and elaborate clothing. The oiled patina of the portrait clouded the features of the couple who stood beside a marble pillar. The yellowed effect served only to make them seem even more indistinct and forbidding.

Chelsea led him toward the next picture. "Lubeck Christopher Sutherland. He lived during the latter part of the seventeenth century. He is credited with building the main wing of Lindon Manor and siring fourteen children—only three of whom survived their infancy. His wife, Nan, is the subject of the next painting."

Lubeck stared from the canvas, a devilish grin slashing over his features. But Nan, poor Nan. Even though the artist had not been incredibly skilled in proportion and perspective, Sullivan could also see a weary pain.

"This is Corbet Sutherland, black sheep of the family. Late in the previous century, he journeyed to the colonies and fought against England during their rebellion. Biddy— your grandmother—told me once that when the family discovered his activities, the painting was nearly burned along with the rest of his belongings. Luckily, it was salvaged by his elder sister, Marjoram. If you peer at it closely"—she bent and squinted at the lower corner—"you can see the scorch marks."

Sullivan had already noted the marks. He didn't really need to bend to see them, but by doing so he could smell the clean freshness of Chelsea's hair. The faint scent that clung to the tresses revealed that she must rinse it in lilac water after scrubbing it clean with some other perfumed soap.

Sensing his close proximity, Chelsea straightened and continued down the line. "This is Annabeline Stark, your . . . great-great-grandmother, I believe."

Sullivan noted the stern, sour-faced woman who had left beauty behind at birth.

"This is your namesake, Richard Albert Sutherland, fourth Earl of Lindon."

Prepared to notice it politely and move on, Sullivan was struck by a strange sense of recognition. There was something about the handsome man who posed on the back of a gray stallion that was familiar. Perhaps the arrogant tilt to his chin. Hadn't Sullivan seen it on Rupert often enough?

No. His father.

Emotions stirred within him like a phoenix shifting amid the ashes. Half-buried memories flashed like quicksilver, then were gone before they could be grasped.

"There is no true portrait of his wife, Lucrece. She posed for a painting soon after their marriage, but since she became *enceinte* shortly thereafter, she refused to continue sitting for the artist until the child was born. Several hours after delivering a fine, healthy son, she died. Richard Albert Sutherland was so distraught that he ordered the painting to be completed anyway.

"In the original sketches, she was holding the family dog. After her death, the artist revised the composition."

A sober-faced child sat in the arms of his mother, seeming to cling to her as if bidding her to stay. Ethereal hands held him still. Sullivan's hold unconsciously tightened around Chelsea's as she continued in a near whisper.

"It is said that the artist painted her face a half-dozen times, using the line and pencil drawings done months before. The earl was never pleased with the representation. He said she had grown more beautiful while carrying his son. So the artist finally left her features completely in shadow—unpainted. I'm told that the earl hung the portrait in his own private chambers, and that for him he saw Lucrece's face undimmed by time."

Chelsea's voice had grown husky in telling the story, and

Sullivan became quiet and introspective, wondering at the empathy she displayed for a stretch of canvas covered with daubs of colored oil.

"Richard?" She spoke slowly, as if she needed to impart the meaning of each word. "Richard, that baby is your grandfather."

The pang of surprise shouldn't have occurred. He should have anticipated what Chelsea would reveal. But the sight of that chubby, wistful boy had seemed unreal to him until that instant. The two-dimensional faces took on new meaning. They stretched from being impersonal representations of people long dead to . . .

Family.

Chelsea led him to the next frame. Sullivan felt as if he'd been punched in the stomach. He lifted a hand that shook, ever so slightly. His father's face. It wasn't exactly as he remembered it. A little younger, rounder, more innocent. But the brown-black hair and slender features were so familiar. He saw them echoed in a slightly diluted fashion in the mirror each morning.

He touched the canvas, nearly expecting to encounter flesh and blood. This was the face that had haunted Sullivan's dreams and filled him with untold regret. This was the reason a burning fury filled his heart day after day. Judging by his father's deathbed confessions, Richard Albert had been crushed by his enemies, his name dragged through the gutter. He'd been exiled from his homeland, then left to rot on some godforsaken island. From the moment Sullivan had heard the half-whispered tales, he had vowed to avenge Richard Albert's honor.

"Richard? You recognize him, don't you? He looks quite a bit like you, the same mouth and jaw. Your grandfather was quite striking."

Sullivan shot her a quick glance. *Grandfather?* This wasn't his grandfather, this was his . . .

"This is your father."

The next portrait was so exact, so lifelike, that Sullivan was thunderstruck. He understood the discrepancies he'd noted in the representation of the first figure. It wasn't age that had caused the subtle differences, but an entire generation. The image was younger than Sullivan remembered his father being, yes, but it was accurate down to the very last detail.

"Your mother."

Before he could assimilate the avalanche of emotions that threatened to bury him, Chelsea held the candle higher.

"You have her eyes."

Sullivan had never seen his mother. Much like Lucrece, she had died in childbirth after bearing her husband a son. Sullivan Arthur Cane.

Cane. How ironic that the name Sullivan had honored from birth, the name he had fought to uphold, had been one his father had adopted, not owned. A title Richard Albert had used to protect his family from discovery, while all along his father had been a Sutherland. A *Sutherland.*

A vise seemed to squeeze around his throat. The air he drew into his lungs scraped like sand against the obstruction. Rupert had told him their mother was beautiful, but Sullivan's childish imaginings had never come close.

She was so young in the picture—little more than sixteen, he'd wager. Soft brown hair had been drawn away from her forehead and cascaded down her back in a riot of ringlets. A sheer scarf had been wound, *à la française,* around her tight bodice, and billowing skirts spilled to the ground. But it was the laughter that lingered in her ice-green eyes and the saucy tilt of her lips that held him captive. No wonder his father had never really recovered after her death.

Chelsea lowered the candle again, throwing the painted face into obscurity. But she didn't move away. Instead, a sadness stole into her expression.

"You come from a long line of distinguished people, Richard Sutherland. You should feel very proud of your heritage. Each succeeding generation has built upon the legacy and made it better. But when your father was slandered and sent away, the title was passed to a cousin. It nearly killed your grandmother. She never gave up hope that her son would be found. When that sailor came with a snatch of your father's letter and your portrait, she didn't know if she had the strength to hope, but she intensified her search."

Her grip tightened, becoming nearly painful. "I can't destroy that. I can't allow anything to harm your campaign to regain all that belongs to you." She turned to him with barely submerged despair. "But I'm not very strong. Not as strong as I used to think." Her words dropped to a whisper. "Help me to be strong."

Sullivan remained motionless, knowing that she thought her confession had been utterly private and that he hadn't understood. But, heaven help him, he had.

Briefly, Sullivan wondered what would become of them all if he were to join league with Chelsea Wickersham, her servants, and Dowager Lady Sutherland. In order to do so, he would have to admit his Sutherland lineage and take a stand to defend it instead of leaving Chelsea and her allies to fend for themselves. It would mean ultimately exposing the Sutherland brothers. It would mean embroiling himself in a thirty-year-old deceit. He might sympathize with the dowager. He might even pity her. But she was nothing to him but a name. He owed her no loyalty that might endanger his brothers. They didn't belong here. They had no desire to take upon themselves the same titles that had ultimately killed their parents.

On the other hand, in denying such a task, Sully would risk losing this woman. He didn't know why such a thought made him panic. It wasn't as if he'd known her for any great period of time. But he would be a liar if he professed to be unaffected by her presence. She touched him in myriad ways. The paradox of her personality only heightened her effect on him. He wanted her. He wanted to know everything about her. But he feared disappointing her.

Cupping her jaw, he tried to avoid seeing the earnest entreaty reflected in her face. He tried to ignore the vulnerability and think only of himself and his brothers. But in the space of a single evening, she had slammed a door of selfishness in his soul and forced him to look outside his own small immediate circle of concerns.

He thought of Richard. He'd sworn to protect him—*would* protect him, with his very life if necessary. Surely there was some plan that could help them both.

An acrid defeat tainted his tongue. No, the only way to come to Chelsea's aid was to expose Richard's identity. That was something he could not do.

I can't help you, please don't ask me.

He wanted to say the words aloud, but he couldn't. Not because he shouldn't reveal that he spoke English, but because he knew the sounds would never push free of the obstruction lodged in his throat.

He touched her jaw, resisting the intoxicating reaction he experienced when she melted into him, her lashes closing in delight.

A curious wonder flared. A spark of need ignited. He wanted more than that simple exploration of her cheek. He yearned to hold her, kiss her, absorb her into his very being.

Her eyelids flickered open, and she must have seen a portion of his thoughts, because she clutched his wrist to push him away, then paused, then clung.

He didn't understand all that he saw in her face: hunger, pain, fear. But he understood the wanting. The hunger that overflowed and spilled into every facet of her being. Her posture lost its rigidity, her lips parted in invitation, her grip became a caress.

Sullivan savored the moments as they beaded together like rain on a spider's web. He absorbed the texture of her skin against his, fine to coarse, smooth to rough. He reveled in the scent of her hair, the slight gasping puffs of breath she made against his chest.

She didn't release him, but rather followed each step with a counter of her own. Like some intricate ballet, they drew together, shifted, touched, retreated, until Sullivan thought their movements more closely approximated dancing than evasion.

He indulged himself in each of her reactions. He brought

her close enough so that the fabric of her gown whispered against his legs. She smiled, a delicate flush tinging her cheeks as he parted his legs and tugged her against him. Briefly, hip nudged against hip, then she side-stepped.

When she would have freed herself from his grasp, he held tight. But soon he realized that she didn't wish to escape him. She moved to the desk and set the heavy candelabra on the far corner. Then, turning, she toyed with the buttons of his shirt.

"I don't want to want you," she whispered. The words held both pleasure and pain, regret and joy. "Until now, my life has been all I thought it could be. You spoiled all that. You made me long for more. You made me yearn for things I can never have. But not without endangering us both."

Sullivan frowned, wondering how she could possibly believe that what blossomed between them could be wrong. He had lived long enough in this world to experience the allure of women, the lust, the friendship, the rejection. But he had never felt the potent combination of desire and possessiveness, passion and confusion that he felt now.

Chelsea closed the gap, standing so near that the folds of her skirts flattened between them and the shank buttons at her breast rubbed at his chest. Lifting on tiptoe, she smoothed away the creases of tension.

"Shh, shh. Don't worry about me. I know I'm flirting with disaster. I know I should storm from this room and never return. I should leave you to your life, your family, and your future. But tonight I'm lonely and just a little sad." She explored his chin. "I know I'll come to regret this evening more than I've rued anything I've ever done. But I've lived with regret before. I've learned to survive it." She approached for a kiss. "I just don't want to be alone. Not tonight."

The pressure of her lips against his was questioning at first. When he parted his mouth in reassurance, she kissed him with the fervor of a woman denied. Tongue clashed with tongue, warm, wet, and willing.

Greedily, she fought to absorb his very being into her

own. The buckle of her gown dug into his flesh, she grasped at his shirt, taking great handfuls of linen, then continuing to seek for satisfaction.

Lifting her high in his arms, Sullivan returned each caress with one in kind. Never had a woman been so responsive, so alive, and yet so utterly fragile. Her desperation touched an aching chord, making him wish he could wrap her in lamb's wool and protect her, even as he wished to initiate her to his flagrant need.

When he began to tremble, not from carrying her but from the overwhelming need to deepen these delicious sensations, he set her on the desk. Lifting her skirts high about her knees, he stepped between her thighs, damning the flounces and frilly underthings that bunched between them, preventing him from finding the bare skin he craved. Seeking solace, he cupped her buttocks, then mapped the delicate line of her spine and caressed her shoulder blades.

She was so beautiful, so astonishing. How could he have ever doubted that she was the fiery temptress who lingered on the fringes of his consciousness?

She broke away, trailing kisses down his throat. Grappling with the fastenings on his shirt, she tore them free, then continued to press tormenting caresses down his chest. Finally, dragging the fabric from the waist of his trousers, she wrenched the garment off his shoulders, imprisoning him in the sleeves.

Gasping, she watched him, wildly, daring him, inviting him to follow her lead. Then she bent forward to circle one nipple with her tongue before following the line that dissected his torso, down, down, ever down . . .

Tearing free, Sullivan stopped her mere inches from his navel. His heart pounded, his flesh seemed on fire. His mouth closed over her own, hungrily, passionately, no holds barred. The desk beneath her creaked as he tried to press forward. A pen fell to the floor, the inkwell, then, jarring free from its foundations, the candles.

At the clatter of brass to stone, he felt her pause. Her hands curled into his back. Her face buried in the hollow of his neck.

He could feel the intensity of the embrace they'd shared melt into the darkness. Below them, one candle fought to survive amid a puddle of dark ink. It sputtered and choked, throwing a spasmodic light.

Chelsea did not grow rigid and unfeeling. Sullivan had to give her credit for that. But when he tried to comfort her, she did not renew their embrace. A sadness had settled over her, an overwhelming regret.

"I can't." She clutched at his shoulders, once, twice, then released him. Easing from his arms, she slipped from the desk and peered around her as if she had forgotten where she'd been. At long last, she saw the portraits.

Walking forward, she touched the unpainted face of Lucrece Sutherland. He heard the ragged tempo of her breathing, and knew it was not just the result of their mutual desire. The weary set of her shoulders and the droop of her head spoke of a silent, overwhelming pain.

She took a step back, another, then retreated toward the doorway. "I'll leave you with your kind." Her skirts whispered of her shame and her untold longing. He thought she would disappear without another word, but at the doorway she turned.

Her hair had come loose from its pins and tumbled down her back, warm, alive, beautiful. The placket of her bodice hung open, exposing smooth, creamy skin and a hint of tatted lace at the yoke of her chemise. Ink and wax spattered the hem of her gown, but she didn't appear to notice—or if she did, she didn't care.

He took a step as if to follow her, but she shook her head, a small smile lifting her lips. But it was not a gesture of happiness, more a gesture of farewell.

"Good night. Lord Sutherland."

Sullivan stood for some time, waiting, hoping she would return. She never did. So he scooped his shirt from the floor and went in search of a rag to clean the dark stains of ink that bespoke the intensity of their clinch, all the while feeling the gazes of his ancestors looking on.

* * *

Chelsea was unaccountably weary as she climbed the staircase and made her way down the corridor to the last door at the end of the hall.

Why had life taken such ironic twists? How could fate offer her hope with one hand, then snatch it away with the other? For years, she had been denied friendship, companionship, and love because of her past association with Nigel. She had battled to deny urges ingrained in women since the beginning of time. She had lived her solitary life—quite comfortably—with only a few regrets. Just when she was about to reverse the tables and fight to prove her worth, she was shown in a single fickle turn of fortune's wheel how little one sweet moment of revenge meant compared to a lifetime of loneliness.

Letting herself into her room, Chelsea closed the door with more care than the action deserved and leaned her forehead against the jamb. She was beginning to believe that her burgeoning feelings for Richard Sutherland were not going to be transitory. Until now, she could pass them off as an aberration or poor judgment. But she feared that the yearnings she experienced could no longer be classified so simply. Lately, she depended far too much on seeing his smile and spending every minute of the day in his company. It didn't seem to matter that he couldn't converse with her. It didn't seem to matter that he dressed like a savage and had the manners of a heathen. He made her feel good. He made her feel needed.

He made her feel whole.

You can't have him, she told herself for the thousandth time. But the threat behind the phrase was beginning to lose its sting. The issues had not changed, nor had the circumstances. She couldn't escape the fact that he was titled while she was not. He was her pupil while she was his teacher.

But matters of position and tradition paled against her overriding concern. Chelsea Wickersham was not who she appeared to be. She might find a way to flaunt convention and encourage a relationship with her student, but she would never be able to outrun her past or the very real demons that pursued her. Every hour of peace she obtained was borrowed from a lifetime of regret. To draw him into her world would destroy him.

She couldn't do that. As much as her body throbbed for satisfaction, as much as she longed for the succor of his presence, Chelsea had experienced the agony of being denied a future. She couldn't force the same emotional and physical exile upon anyone else. Least of all a man who filled her with passion and tenderness, desire and love.

Regret knocked at her heart. Turning, she tugged at the buttons of her bodice and slipped the garment from her shoulders, dropping the boned article on her bed.

Sweet, gentle Smee had already turned down her covers and fluffed her pillows. The sight caused a reluctant smile to flicker at the edges of her lips. He and Greyson never ceased to watch out for her. Like a pair of aged fairy godfathers, they saw to her welfare in a thousand different ways.

After flinging open the windows to allow the murky breezes to flood the room, she crossed to the armoire and withdrew her carpet bag. Biddy would understand why she would abandon their plans in midcourse and run away. Chelsea only prayed that the old woman could find someone else to help her. Although Chelsea knew her actions could delay Richard's return to society—perhaps even endanger them—at least this way both of them would be given a small measure of peace. These forbidden feelings would be stopped before they became overwhelming.

Chelsea stepped into the bathing room where Greyson had spread perfumed towels over the floor and had left a kettle of water on the fire. Stripping off the rest of her clothing, Chelsea quickly washed in the shallow footbath, then drew a batiste wrapper over her naked body. She would leave on the morrow. After she had found a way to notify Beatrice of the change in plans.

She was braiding her hair as she returned to the bedroom. Sighing softly to herself, she began to extinguish the candles, one by one by one. A solitary light remained by the bed. Shaking the thick plait over her shoulder, she bent to blow the flame out, then froze.

On the pillow lay a single white rose.

Fear and horror raced through her so quickly, she thought she would shatter. Her chest became encased in ice. Straightening, she whirled to confront the empty room.

Running to the windows, she slammed them closed and bolted the latches, knowing all the while that her precautionary measures had come much too late. *He* had been here.

Panting, she frantically searched the darkness, wishing she hadn't extinguished the other lights so hastily. She tried to tell herself that the bloom had been an offering from Smee or Greyson. But her pillow had been bare before she had begun bathing.

Richard had brought it, her mind feebly argued. But there were no white roses on the Bellemoore estates. Biddy was passionate about pink, pink roses, pink hollyhocks, pink petunias. If another color was used, it was a splash of vibrant color—never white.

White.

Purity. Grace. Fidelity.

White.

Ice. Waste. Sterility.

Shivering now, she ran across the room to retrieve the flower, taking it to the bathing room, where she threw it into the coals beneath the kettle. The fragile petals shriveled, writhed, then turned to ash.

She was trapped. Trapped. If she were to leave Bellemoore, Richard would be harmed, she knew he would. She was the only thing that stood between him and his enemies. No one but Chelsea would ever know how she had stumbled upon the knowledge of secret crimes, thereby becoming a pawn. A knowledge for which she had no tangible proof to bring to the authorities.

Sinking to the floor, Chelsea fought back the tears and the panic. She had known Nigel Sutherland would hear she had been in league with Beatrice and helped the true heir to return. She had known she would not escape his fury.

But she had hoped he wouldn't find her nearly so soon.

Chapter
12

Reginald sighed and continued to wait for his employer to awaken. The rustlings of their guests strolling toward the staircase in search of breakfast had so far failed to rouse the man.

Impatiently, Reggie tapped his foot against the rug but wisely did not consider waking his employer. Lord Sutherland had still not returned by the time his guests had begun to retire. Reginald, who had spent the night talking with the intriguing Mr. Gregory Cane, had grown more and more annoyed as the night progressed. He knew where his employer was. With that woman. Once again, Nigel was neglecting duty, business, and his own impression upon his visitors, for that . . . that . . . girl.

Reggie had watched as Mr. Cane surveyed each room, each dignitary, with a keen, hard gaze. He'd seen him grow more tense, his expression more masked with every tick of the clock, and he'd blamed Nigel for it all.

Mr. Cane had refused to be drawn into talking about his business with Nigel, so to keep him from tiring of the wait, Reginald had drawn him into a sporting game of backgammon. To his chagrin, he'd lost thirty pounds to the man in little less than an hour. But at the very least, he'd convinced the stranger to return within the week to meet with Nigel Sutherland.

Reggie shifted in the wingback chair situated in the corner of the master bedchamber and studied Nigel's sleeping form. Judging by Mr. Cane's willingness to bet large sums of money on such a game of strategy, Reginald had surmised that he either was very wealthy or felt he had nothing to lose.

Nigel shifted, grunted, and opened his eyes, blinking owlishly at the meager light offered by the cloudy day.

"Well?" Reginald demanded without preamble. "Did you take care of our little problem?"

Nigel scowled at him in annoyance, and Reggie swore. "You didn't, did you? You went up to that house, found them there together, and didn't do *anything!*"

"Shut up, Reggie." Nigel swept aside the covers and padded naked to the armoire to retrieve his robe.

"Did you even see him? Did you even bother to go that far? To identify the man who intends to destroy you?" He could tell by Nigel's expression that he hadn't. Reggie glared at him in disgust. "She has possessed you like a demon for years, but you couldn't even gather enough control over yourself to eliminate Richard Sutherland. Instead of thinking with your head, you thought with your—"

"Enough! Do *not* forget your place, Reginald."

Reggie lapsed into a grudging silence, waiting until Nigel was nearly dressed. "What do you intend to do?"

"I've set matters in motion, Reginald. Leave the worrying to me."

Reginald's eyes creased in thought. "That's it, isn't it? You want her back. You've always wanted her back. And you're going to use Richard Sutherland to do it."

Nigel merely offered him an enigmatic smile.

"I hope you've thought this through."

"Believe me. I've taken care of every last detail."

As Nigel slipped into his jacket and headed for the door, Reggie felt a brief flashing desire that, just once, things wouldn't go exactly as Nigel planned. But then, as he stood to follow, Reginald knew it was a wasted thought. Even the

Fates themselves wouldn't dare to challenge this man when he'd decided upon a plan of action.

"Good morning, my boy."

Sullivan rolled to his back on the narrow bed, abandoning his contemplation of the view outside his window. Frowning, he watched as Smee entered the room and shut the door with a bump of his shoulder.

Sullivan had purposely stayed abed, hoping that his governess would come early to rouse him. After what they'd shared the night before, he knew their first few minutes together might be awkward, even uncomfortable. But he had been sure he would be able to sway Chelsea toward another quick embrace. What he hadn't counted on, however, was having her ignore him.

Rising, he lunged toward Smee with the intent of demanding that the little man tell him where Chelsea was hiding. But Sullivan had momentarily forgotten that he had spent the last few days playing the savage.

When Smee saw his advance, he gasped, throwing his hands into the air in reflex. The tray fell. Cutlery jangled. Biscuits and tea flew wide as the portly man flattened himself against the wall, his eyes bugging. "Don't hurt me, please, please, don't hurt me, please," he whispered.

His desperate litany took Sullivan completely by surprise, and he stopped in midstride. The poor man looked as if Sullivan were about to pole-ax him.

At the first sign of an aborted attack, Smee offered him a shaky smile in return. "Good boy, good boy." Then he eyed the litter of the breakfast tray with open dismay. "Oh-dear-oh-dear-oh-dear."

Sullivan crouched, intending to help pick up the mess, but Smee misconstrued his movements, thinking he meant to eat the soiled fare. "No, no. No, I'll get you some fresh," he said, stopping him. Quickly gathering the scattered breakfast things, he scurried from the room, saying, "I'll be right back with another tray, I will. Don't you fret."

As soon as he'd disappeared down the creaky staircase,

Sullivan stood. The charade he'd played up to now was beginning to wear on him. There were things he needed to do and information he needed to gather. He was tired of grunting and groveling and playing the fool. He'd done all he could with his current identity. It was time to move on.

But first he had to find his governess.

Once in the hall, he began opening doors. The two chambers next to his own were vacant, the huge pieces of furniture shrouded in linen, dismantled beds propped against the walls. Dust motes danced in the weak sunbeams that managed to wriggle through the slats of the shutters. The murky light only seemed to underscore the abandoned air that lingered in the unoccupied chambers. The house should be filled with people. And the nursery should be filled with children. Sutherland heirs.

That Sullivan would think of such an idea shocked him a little. He was growing far too possessive of things that didn't belong to him. This cottage, these rooms. Chelsea.

Opening the last door, Sullivan finally found evidence of an inhabitant. His governess.

Stepping inside, he knew immediately that his hypothesis was correct. The air smelled faintly of lilacs. The bodice she'd worn the night before had been folded over the foot of the tester bed. And a carpet bag . . .

Sullivan frowned. A carpet bag? A slow-dawning suspicion crept over him. Grasping the tote, his lips tightened in anger when he saw that it was already half full.

He threw the bag to the floor. He'd never thought his governess a coward, but now he wasn't so sure. There could be only one reason for her abrupt departure. She was running away. From him. From the feelings they'd shared.

This time, Sullivan felt no guilt at their behavior, only outrage. She'd been an equal participant in the previous evening's activities. She had responded with passion and fervor. And now, it seemed she was about to run from those emotions. To deny that they were unique. Special.

Storming from the room, he jogged down the back staircase into the kitchen. Smee looked up from the tray he was preparing and beamed. "Oh! You've come down to eat with us."

Sullivan acknowledged him absently, then hurried past him into the garden.

Empty. The kitchen, the stables, the rose path. All empty.

"My lord."

It took a second for Sullivan to realize the low summons was being directed to him. When he met the dour face of the butler, the man asked, "Are you looking for Miss Wickersham? Your governess?"

Richard cocked his head.

"She is in the studio."

When Sullivan didn't respond, the gentleman shifted the vase of cut flowers he held and motioned for Sullivan to follow. "This way, please."

Sullivan trailed meekly behind him, not so much because he was expected to but because he was actually astounded. He hadn't bothered to look for Chelsea there because he had been quite certain that Miss Wickersham would not hide from him by returning to the location of their last encounter.

Greyson opened the front door to the house, then those leading to the studio. "In here, my lord," he whispered.

She was sound asleep.

Sullivan came to an abrupt stop halfway through the threshold, seeing the woman bent over the desk, her head cradled in her arms. She looked so serene, so vulnerable, so young. Yet her dreams were not untroubled. A frown creased her brow, and her fingers twitched restlessly.

"Would you like your breakfast in here?" Greyson inquired.

Sullivan didn't answer. Taking a fuchsia peony from the arrangement of blooms, he padded forward, slowly, silently, so that he wouldn't wake her.

It amazed him how she grew more beautiful to him each day. Not that her features had changed or her manner of dress. No, it was because he had begun to anticipate her smile, her laughter, even the sparkle of anger that sometimes appeared in her eyes.

Creeping forward, he wondered what it would be like to see her this way, asleep, her head resting on his own pillow. His chest.

A pang of desire struck him at the thought. Not just a physical pang, but an emotional one as well.

Yes, the game had grown wearying. He didn't know when the rules and objectives had changed, but he needed more—much more—than a pat on the head. He needed to converse with this woman, to uncover every facet of her personality and maddening turn of her intellect. He wanted her views on politics and poetry and art. He wanted to argue and banter and tease.

Most of all, he wanted her to see him as something other than a barbarian.

From the far side of the room, he heard the faint click of the door latch being set into place. Standing slightly behind and to her side, he reached to touch the petals of the flower he held to the dainty curve of her ear.

Chelsea Wickersham jerked awake, startled so completely from her dreams that they scattered before she could properly recollect them. She was left with little more than an unsettled sensation of longing for something but being unable to have it.

Cupping her forehead in her palm, she squeezed her eyes shut again and propped her elbow on the desk. After finding the white rose on her pillow, she'd been unable to sleep in her own room. Chased by fears and memories that refused to die, she'd returned to the studio to clean up the mess that had been made and to work. But upon finding the floor mopped and the candelabra restored to its proper place, her concentration had flagged.

Ignoring the stubby candles which had testified that she'd been there only hours before, she'd forced herself to compose a formal letter to Beatrice Sutherland, informing her of all that had occurred in the last few weeks. Once she'd finished, Chelsea had noted that there were a great many omissions she'd unconsciously made. Such as her growing *tendre* for this man. The way he infuriated and invigorated her. The way she looked forward to each second in his presence.

Then, just when she was debating how to tell Biddy about the rose, she'd fallen asleep.

A faint prickling at the back of her neck caused Chelsea to stiffen. Opening her eyes, she blinked against the rush of cloud-fuzzed sunlight spilling through the huge French windows that lined one wall. When the velvety touch of a peony petal kissed her cheek, she started, whirling in her seat.

To her infinite consternation, she found the object of her thoughts looking down at her, holding the end of the stem. He didn't smile right away—that was something she had noticed from the very beginning. Used to students who tried to manipulate her favor through childish grins and playful antics, she was still disconcerted by the intent stare of this man. His eyes, those incredible eyes, were the true test of his emotions, able to change chameleonlike from icy green to a bemusing hazel. But this morning, they seemed at once opaque and fathomless, not giving him away.

"Good morning, Master Richard." She automatically used the title that would remind him of their proper relationship, then damned the way her greeting emerged in a husky, sleep-tinged voice.

Something within his expression darkened, grew more piercing. Then he lowered himself onto his haunches so that his gaze was level with her own.

Chelsea steeled herself against the way her mind immediately recorded each detail. At times like these, she despaired of ever teaching Richard Sutherland the proper modes of dress. Once again, her charge wore nothing more than that bright orange scrap of fabric over his loins and Smee's huge shirt.

"Master Richard, a gentleman should always remember to properly clothe himself before emerging from his bedchamber. Especially if he plans to entertain the company of a lady." The firm instruction was blunted by the whisper of yearning embedded in her tone. She prayed he hadn't heard it or that, if he had, he hadn't heeded the hidden message.

As usual, he didn't speak, didn't react. Not even so much as the flicker of an eyelid revealed that he'd understood even a scrap of her instructions, let alone the heartache underneath. He waited, his body seemingly relaxed, but still giving the impression of being coiled for action.

Her eyes dropped.

She couldn't help the action. She knew it was wrong. As a woman of gentility, she should certainly show more self-control. But by confronting her when the wispy cobwebs of sleep still clung to her brain, he had battered down a few of the defenses she had erected so hastily in the predawn hours. She couldn't remain impervious to the man who knelt beside her chair.

His legs were bare, the skin still retaining the golden cast of a tropical sun. His thighs were lean, the wrapping swell of each muscle clearly defined. The loincloth he wore was so brief it was nearly nonexistent, cupping his sex yet leaving his hips and buttocks nearly naked. His chest and abdomen were smooth, without the tufts of curly hair Chelsea had imagined covered all men's chests.

Yanking her thoughts and her eyes back to a more appropriate line of focus, Chelsea cleared her throat. "Today we shall begin your lessons in . . ."

Her train of thought abandoned her entirely. Once again, Richard had lifted the peony to her cheek, trailing it down her jaw, touching the curve of her lips.

He smiled. A slow, potent smile that bashed at the ramparts of her professionalism.

"Flow-er."

Unconsciously, her jaw dropped and her mouth parted. He'd spoken! In English. His first English word!

"Richard?"

His grin widened, becoming devilish and mischievous. A naughty boy smile that tugged at her heartstrings, and deeper.

"Flower." This time the word was uttered lowly, a tiger's purr.

A sinuous tension gathered low in her belly. She tried to

ignore it. She tried to tell herself that she would not give in to it. She refused to allow him to affect her this way. She couldn't afford to settle into the role of a woman trapped in a sensual spell. She had to remain detached. Aloof. Now more than ever.

Fear gripped her, but before she could acknowledge the sensation, the flower teased her again, the dewy petal clinging to the moist flesh near her teeth. Richard followed the progress of that petal with such avid fascination that Chelsea felt as if he'd touched her. Not with the flower, but with his finger. Or his lips.

She tried to turn away; in all honesty, she really tried. But she could no more abandon this tension-fraught encounter than she could fly to the moon.

Character will out, the cautioning voice of reason taunted her, warned her. But the intoxicating thump of her heart and the tingling of her senses overpowered her conscience.

"We really must do something about your hair." The remark should have been a simple statement of fact, but it was an excuse. A flimsy reason for her to stretch out.

The tresses clung like liquid midnight, twining around her fingers with the silken heat of a sultry summer evening. Long, wavy, they feathered over her skin with the familiarity of a lover's caress, mocking her with all of the might-have-beens.

She had never known another male with such long hair. Though a similar style had been in vogue during her mother's time, Chelsea had never considered that a man could remain . . . well, a *man* if his locks were as long as his mate's.

Now she knew differently. There was nothing effeminate about Richard Sutherland. He was entirely masculine. And completely and utterly pagan.

As if he'd divined her thoughts, she watched his eyes darken and zero in upon the fullness of her lips. He meant to kiss her. And heaven help her, she wanted him to crush her in a savage embrace, she wanted—

No! Not again.

Her chair screeched across the parquet floor as she surged to her feet. But before she could take more than a step, he was in front of her, blocking her path.

Chelsea was not a tiny woman by any means. Of average height and stature, she rarely felt intimidated. But something about the breadth of this man's shoulders and the sharp delineation of each muscle in his stomach caused her to feel overtly feminine. Delicate.

But not powerless. No, the way he looked at her made her understand how Eve must have felt just before she tempted Adam with the apple. Richard Sutherland might not particularly like her at times. He might find her bossy, overbearing, and annoying. He might chafe at her instructions and balk at her commands. But he was very much aware that she was a woman. He was intrigued by her prim manner of dress and rigid manners. And after he had managed to shatter her flimsy image of control the day before, she knew it wouldn't take much to lead him into destroying that facade altogether.

His grin became rueful, and his eyes gleamed. When he gestured for her to take the peony from his hand, she delved for the goals and values she had always harbored. But her objectives were blunted by a too potent rush of desire. As she reached for the fragile stem, she couldn't prevent the way she purposely brushed against him.

Assuming a stoic facade, she went past him on her way to the kitchen. Distance. It was time she put some distance between them.

"Come and eat your breakfast, Master Richard. Then we shall go to the moors for our lessons. We have work to do if we're to extend your vocabulary to the fauna as well as the flora."

But as she led him out of the room, she knew it was only a matter of time before Richard Sutherland touched her again. She could see his intent in his eyes.

She could only pray that this time she wouldn't melt toward him like wax in the afternoon's sun.

* * *

Greyson marched past the empty stalls, his portly companion in tow like a battered skiff behind a stately barge.

"Come along, Smee."

"Yes, Greyson."

As soon as Master Richard and Miss Wickersham had taken their places at the dining-room table to break their fast, the two men had tiptoed from the kitchen into the honeyed sunlight and scurried into the stable house. There, beyond the hostler's bench, hidden behind a pile of rugs, a barrel, and a trunk, lay a dented strongbox.

Since Greyson was in charge of finances, Smee waited impatiently, shifting from foot to foot, as the dour man added the money they'd received from their latest escapade and counted the pile of coins.

In the past week, the Avengers—as Smee and Greyson liked to call themselves—had organized a half-dozen daring daytime heists on the village road. Their fame was beginning to grow, especially among the female population. Carriages filled with women had taken to trolling the byways in search of the mysterious men they called the Kissing Bandits. The townsmen were furious, of course, and vowed to bring the thieves to justice. They had gone so far as to put the criminal's descriptions in the *Addlebury Post* and offer a reward for their capture.

Smee couldn't be more pleased. In the past, such adventures had always been beyond his placid life-style. Finally, he was being allowed to indulge himself in a bit of whimsy.

"Well? How much have we amassed, Greyson?"

"We've enough for a set of everyday togs, but not enough for evening wear."

"So what do we do?"

Greyson quickly counted out a handful of coins. "Keep Miss Wickersham busy this afternoon. I'll take these to Mr. Gulch, the tailor in Addlebury. Surely he has something on hand he could alter for Master Richard as soon as possible. In the meantime, I'll instruct him to fashion a full set of clothes—day, evening, and riding—based on Master Richard's measurements, then leave this as a down payment."

"What about the balance of the amount? We'll be needing more coin, don't you think?"

"It will take Gulch a week or so to finish the order. In the meantime, the Avengers will ride again." His chest puffed in importance. "Perhaps we'll even raid the guests at Lindon Manor. Such a feat would prove poetically just, don't you think?"

"Oooh," Smee cooed, rubbing his hands together.

How delightful!

Chapter
13

*T*hroughout breakfast, Sullivan carefully bided his time, waiting and watching for the first crack in Chelsea's veneer. He hadn't forgotten the fiery vixen who'd slapped him, or the teacher who'd led him into the studio to see the portraits. But for now, Miss Chelsea Wickersham, governess, had returned.

Sullivan was far from daunted. There was something about all that starch and steel that made him want to unpeel the layers of her personality like the skin of an onion until he discovered the true woman hidden beneath. He planned to do just that. Soon.

He knew that she would be especially vulnerable to such a sensual campaign. Her stoic facade was paper-thin. Sullivan sensed a cauldron of conflicting emotions. Passion and ice. Anger and compassion. Above all—hunger. Her eyes followed him like a hummingbird, darting from place to place, never allowing her gaze to linger, but making him quite conscious of her interest nonetheless.

After their meal, Chelsea insisted that he dress. Sullivan obliged only after as much pointing and cryptic instructions as he felt she would indulge. Then, once Smee had returned to the kitchen from some mysterious errand, Chelsea immediately returned to business. "Smee, if you'd be so kind as to bring the rug and this small basket into the garden. Today we will continue our lessons outside. Come along, Master Richard."

Controlling the automatic grin of amusement her address inspired, Sullivan followed Miss Wickersham as she darted out of the kitchen door and marched down the path.

Sullivan tagged along as quickly as he could, wincing at the pea gravel that dug into his bare feet. Regrettably, neither Smee nor Greyson had been able to loan him a proper set of shoes. He could only wonder when Chelsea planned to remedy that fact. He had heard her speaking to the servants about finding him a more suitable wardrobe, but each morning he woke to find the same shirt and trousers, carefully laundered but growing steadily more worn with each passing use.

"Master Richard, today we shall begin your lessons in earnest."

She glanced over her shoulder to ensure he trailed her. Behind them both, Smee trotted along like a faithful lapdog, panting for breath at the end of the yard where a patch of grass had been grown in the middle of a love knot hidden behind a privet hedge.

"We will be quite comfortable here, Mr. Smee."

"Yes, mum." Smee dropped the wicker basket and quickly arranged a woolen carriage rug upon the ground. "Will you be needing anything else, Miss Chelsea?"

"No, thank you, Mr. Smee. Please, don't let us keep you from your duties. Master Richard and I have a great deal of work to do." A shadow passed over her features, and Sullivan thought he caught a genuine hint of fear. As Smee trundled toward the house, she added, "We've so little time, Master Richard. I had originally hoped to force a confrontation between you and Nigel before the summer solstice, but now . . ." She nervously pleated the folds of her skirt, adding, "I'm quite sure Nigel Sutherland knows you're here. You must be very careful where you go and what you do. Never leave the house unless you are in my company." Her voice became strangely husky. "He will not harm you if you are with me. Lord Sutherland will not endanger his bargaining power in such a manner."

Sullivan wondered why she would make such an odd remark, especially if he was supposedly unable to understand her. But before he could garner more clues, she changed the tack of her conversation.

"He'll be expecting you to make your claim. Our major obstacle to your education is, of course, your grasp of the king's lexicon. But after your stunning breakthrough this morning, we have faith in your abilities to rally to the occasion. After all, your father was British, as was your mother. Surely, you must have heard your parents speak to you. We just need to jar that portion of your memory free."

She spoke of her educational objectives quite freely, but a sheen of perspiration dotted her lip. The nervous plucking at her skirt increased. She kept sneaking peeks at the hillside as if she expected Nigel to appear at any time.

Seeking to allay her unease, Sullivan sank onto the blanket and stretched out on his back, assuming a picture of perfect comfort. The action caused his shirt to pull free from his baggy pants. The concave hollow of his stomach attracted her attention before she yanked it away again.

"Now, Master Richard . . ." She knelt upon the blanket as well, choosing the corner farthest from his own and smoothing her skirts about her legs until the folds obscured even a hint of the shape of her limbs beneath. Though her position was more relaxed than before, her spine remained rigid and her posture stiff. "Today we shall begin with some of the basics. Perhaps by being out here in nature, we can prod your memory in regard to your language capabilities. Since the garden helped you to remember your first word, I am hoping more time here will stimulate the rest of what we require."

Sullivan was feeling stimulated, all right, but not by the exotic flowers. More by the crackling tension that settled between them, the moist sheen of her lips, the full curves of her breasts.

Delving into the basket, she removed a shiny red apple. "Ap-ple. Apple."

Sullivan opened one eye. Two.

"Repeat after me. Apple." She held the fruit a little closer. "Ap-ple."

Not bothering to respond, Sullivan took it from her and bit the ripe red flesh.

He heard her unconscious huff of surprise. But rather than pursuing an obviously dead subject, she fished into the depths of her basket again.

"Carrot." She waved a stubby baby carrot in front of him. "Car-rot."

Sullivan took a few more bites of the apple and offered her a blank uncomprehending look. She was so beautiful. Sunlight gilded the fire of her hair.

"Repeat, please. Carrot."

Tossing the apple a few feet away, Sullivan caught the carrot and crunched on the crisp tip.

This time, Chelsea's frustrated sigh was more obvious. "You seem to be under the misconception that this is a picnic instead of a lesson." Three fruits and two vegetables later, Sullivan was beginning to be quite full, while Chelsea was obviously maintaining a tenuous rein on her patience.

Her blue eyes snapped in a way that Sullivan found entrancing. A slight blush flooded her velvety complexion. He decided that the time had come to escalate the stakes of the game.

"You're not trying, Master Richard." She poked a finger in the direction of his chest in emphasis.

Sullivan frowned in confusion, then mimicked her action and tapped his sternum. "Richard."

Her expression of stunned delight was entrancing. "Yes. Yes! You are Richard. Richard Sutherland."

"Richard." Rolling into a sitting position, he closed the distance between them by half. He pointed to her. "Richard."

"No. Miss Wickersham. Wick-er-sham."

"Chel . . . Chel . . ."

Reluctantly, she supplied, "Chelsea."

Sullivan could tell how much she hated the informality of

having him address her by her given name, but she wasn't willing to endanger such inroads into his progress.

"Richard—" She gestured to his left breast, her palm flat "Chelsea—" She reversed the position, grazing the buttons studding her own chest.

Sullivan caught her hand and pressed it against his own skin. "Richard." When she tried to snatch free, he held her captive against the bare skin exposed at the opening of his shirt.

He heard her slight inhalation, felt the way she twitched against him. Before she could draw away, he laid his opposite palm against her ribs. He thought she jumped slightly in reflex. "Chelsea."

Sullivan altered his posture so that he faced her more directly, one of his knees bent, the other crooked to provide him balance. She tried to retreat, but he refused to release her wrist.

Some of the iron seeped out of her posture. Her lashes flickered closed, the velvety fringe pooling against her cheeks before lifting again.

He wondered if she knew how much she told him, all without words. He read the longing and need. Fear?

Sullivan sought to eradicate that last emotion. He might want her breathless, he might want her grappling for control. But he didn't want her to be afraid.

He took her hand with both of his now, kneading the sensitive hollow. She resisted him at first, soft unintelligible sounds of denial and distress whispering from her throat. But she didn't back away. Spellbound, she seemed intent upon absorbing each sensation. The more he charted the sensitive skin, the more her spine eased.

"Chelsea . . ." he murmured, half in invitation, half in amusement.

She wriggled slightly in a final effort to release herself. He held fast, and bit by bit she surrendered. Her lips unconsciously parted, and she swayed toward him.

Sullivan had hoped that meant their lesson was at an end, but even though her customary posture might have slipped, she valiantly clung to her role of educator. "Hand," she supplied. "You are holding my *hand.*"

He wasn't diverted. He soon realized that Miss Wickersham might sometimes play the innocent or the prude, but there were things she could teach him, things that they would experience together. If only he could find the key to unlock her natural reticence.

"Hand," he repeated dutifully, dipping to brazenly kiss the hollow of her palm, touch it with the tip of his tongue. Her lips parted in the faintest wisp of a gasp. Sensing his "governess" would return at the slightest provocation, he continued his sensual reconnaissance.

"Wrist," she supplied when he tarried there.

"Wrist?"

"Yes. Wrist."

He continued his foray with his lips, following the path of a vein to the sensitive hollow above.

"Elbow," the word was slightly unsteady.

"El-bow?"

"Elbow."

Using his index finger, he explored the fullness of her sleeve. The friction of fabric was no less delicious.

When he encountered the sensitive area of her inner arm, a huskiness emerged in Chelsea's voice. "Arm."

"Arm." He bent closer, his thigh pressing into the fullness of her skirts until he discovered the answering shape of her leg. His hand spread wide, cupping the rounded ball of her shoulder.

"Shoul . . . der," she supplied, the word barely audible.

"Shoulder."

He shifted again, tucking her neck into the notch formed between his thumb and his outstretched fingers. Smiling, he tested the delicate strength he found there.

Sullivan noted the ragged rise and fall of her chest, the blush in her cheeks. She enjoyed his caress, she craved it. He knew she did. He could only wonder how long she would continue to stall the natural course of events. Soon, a mere taste of passion would not be enough, an embrace would lead to hardship, a kiss to inexplicable longing.

Her pulse knocked unsteadily, eloquently testifying that what had begun as a simple English lesson had developed into something far more erotic, far more dangerous. She must have sensed a portion of his thoughts, because her head shook slightly from side to side.

Sullivan smiled, a smile heavy with promise. He idly toyed with the ridge of her high collar, teasing the sensitive skin, playing with the button, ruffling the lace. Tarrying there, he pressed his hand to the hollow of her throat. Then, without warning, he allowed it to plunge down the line of her sternum from neck to navel.

She arched her back, a greedy sound escaping from her lips. Leaning forward, he kissed her chin, her jaw, her ear, then opened his mouth to suckle the side of her neck.

"No! You mustn't." Chelsea jumped to her feet, but he quickly followed, hauling her tightly against him. Her spine pressed into his chest, her buttocks into his thighs.

She trembled, and it surprised him. She'd always sported a will of iron. The idea that he could affect her so completely intrigued and aroused him.

She wanted him. She wanted *him*.

"No, Richard." She grappled with his hold, trying to pull free.

"Chelsea."

"No!"

She tried to release herself, but he touched the taut bead of her nipple, and she shuddered against him and grew still. Her head fell to the side like a bud too heavy for its stalk, exposing the sensitive skin of her neck.

He had only meant to calm her, reassure her, but at that blatant invitation, he couldn't resist. His head bent, and his lips touched her skin, once, twice, then returned like a starved man. His tongue traced the velvety column of flesh above her gown, and he experienced a bolt of white-hot heat.

He couldn't remember a woman tasting so sweet. He couldn't ever recall wishing to drown in a scent so elusive yet so tantalizing—the innocence of lilacs and the exotic undercurrents of jasmine.

His tongue continued its moist path, reaching the hollow behind her ear. Then, unable to stop himself, he took the lobe between his teeth and tugged.

Her reaction was instantaneous. She reached behind her and gripped his hair while her lashes squeezed shut as if to savor the sensations more fully.

One of Sullivan's hands splayed wide over her ribs, while the other climbed higher, tracing the whalebone strips of her corset beneath her gown until he reached the firm mound of her breast above. But even though he ached to cup the swell, he tormented them both by dragging just his thumbnail across the tight, aching nub of her nipple.

She moaned, low in her throat. A sound so uninhibited, so sensual, that he was stunned. She arched her back, pressing her hips against his arousal. "Rich-ard," she gasped.

Sweet bloody hell, she was so alive in his embrace. So natural. To think that all this was hidden beneath her staid governess' uniform. The thought alone caused his heart to thunder so hard he was sure it could be heard half a county away. Why would she want to leave him? Why would she pack her things if she meant to stay?

She twisted against him, not to escape but to draw closer. Pressing chest to chest, thigh to thigh, she kissed his chin, his neck, his chest. Kittenish sounds of distress poured from her throat.

Then, in a choreographed movement of mutual desire, her head lifted, his dipped. Despite the aching hunger that consumed them, the rage of passion that drove them, they both paused, a mere hair's breadth away. Eyes locked in anticipation. They stilled. Until slowly they closed the distance. Mouth blended to mouth, heart to heart.

The embrace held the gentle heat of spring and the fervent promise of summer. What had begun so simply was suddenly not so simple. His head slanted, bringing their lips more tightly together. Mouths parted, tongues met, retreated, then finally dueled.

In an instant, their mutual desire swept away all thought of caution. Sullivan moaned as Chelsea fought to get closer. Need stumbled, then roared. Passion glowed, then exploded. He wanted her, heart, soul, and body. His body strained toward her, caution scattered to the wind.

There was only one possible conclusion to their actions. Gently disengaging himself from her embrace, Sullivan made her look at him. He saw what he had hoped to find. A consummation of fire and passion. Ecstasy and delight.

But what disturbed him were the shadows he found there as well. Guilt. Shame. Fear.

Fear.

Gently, he began to woo her again. Smiling in reassurance, he kissed her lightly, quickly. He couldn't resist her. He couldn't deny her. Pressing his lips to that sensitive arc, he drew her down onto the ground, pressing her into the softness of the rug.

When he would have removed the pins from her hair, she stayed him, one last vestige of propriety hanging poised by a silver thread. Her gaze grew dark. Tormented.

"Shh, shh," he whispered.

Her head shook slightly from side to side. A tear fell down her temple.

"I meant to be strong," she whispered. "I meant to help you. I meant to protect you. I would have run away if I could, but now I'm powerless to go."

Sullivan sensed the anguish behind the words and an overwhelming defeat. But his own body pulsed in relief to hear she wouldn't escape him. His heart pounded against his ribs. He wanted to take her in his arms and love her until they both grew senseless. But suddenly he couldn't finish what they had begun. He couldn't take her this way, defeated and unsure of herself.

When did I grow so noble? he thought self-deprecatingly. Mere days ago, he would have ravished her here, on the grass, with little thought of possible witnesses or future consequences.

So what had caused him to develop such an interfering conscience? Had it happened the day she'd brought him his breakfast tray and refused to blanche at his nakedness? The day she'd tried to cut his hair? Or when she had introduced him to the long-lost Sutherland heirs?

He smoothed away the teardrop that had melted into an almost indistinguishable silver track. He kissed her once, twice, and breathed deeply of her scent. Then he rolled onto his back and drew her into the hollow of his shoulder, holding her, soothing her, as the maelstrom of fading passion and confusion seeped from her body, leaving her drained and quiet in his arms.

Never would she know how much he ached for her then. Never would she know the inner hell he suffered as Sullivan was brought face to face with his own brand of dilemmas.

He desired this woman. Not just physically but emotionally as well. He wanted her to rely on him. He wanted to strengthen that elusive bond that grew steadily between them each day. He wanted her as his lover and his friend.

But how could he possibly resolve the obstacles that lay between them? He was sworn to help his brother but wanted to help this woman. To aid one would be to endanger the other. If by some miracle of heaven he could find a way to resolve that particular problem and help them both, how could he make her love *him*, not the title? It was still too risky for him to abandon his masquerade of adopting Richard's identity. Was it fair to offer her the enticement of position, wealth, when all he possessed was a tiny parcel of land half a world away? How could he live with himself if she accepted him, thinking he was Richard Sutherland, seventh Earl of Lindon, and he was forced to take such luxuries away?

Thunder rolled overhead, seeming to echo his own confusion. Clouds spread thready wreaths over the brilliant sun, bringing a chill to the air and the heavy muskiness of impending rain.

When she would have withdrawn, Sullivan held her still. Just a few more minutes. He needed a little more time to dream of the impossible becoming suddenly possible.

The thunder rattled again, closer this time, lingering, drawing nearer, until Sullivan realized that this time it wasn't thunder he heard but the clatter of a carriage approaching the cottage below.

The woman in his arms stiffened, hearing it, too. Twisting

free, she scrambled to her feet, lifted her hems, and hurried to peer past the hedge.

Sullivan was awarded with the flash of petticoats and the sight of trim ankles clad in ivory silk stockings with an elaborate clocking design embroidered over her ankle. For some reason, the sight of such frivolously feminine undergarments hidden beneath her severe gown caused a bolt of reaction to course through him. Someday, someday soon, he would love her. When he did, she would be wearing those stockings. And nothing else.

Propping his elbow beneath him, he rested his chin on his fist. But when she didn't immediately return, he experienced a shiver of foreboding. The heaviness of the air gathered around him, settling like a lead weight deep in his chest.

Long before she faced him again, he saw the way she cloaked herself in an emotional armor, piece by piece. By the time she faced him again, her stance was brittle.

Despite her obvious effort of outward calm, she hadn't guarded her soul. He read the traces of a tortured hunger. Then the shadows encroached. She stood, still silent. He became witness to a flash of haunting pain, so eloquently expressed that it tugged a response from his soul. Not lust but empathy. Compassion.

One of her arms wound around her waist and the other crossed diagonally over her chest so that her fingers curled around the base of her neck. It was a defensive stance. A vulnerable one. But the determined tilt of her chin and the fire that flared briefly in her expression negated her own posture.

"It seems we have guests, Master Richard. Your grandmother, Dowager Lady Beatrice Sutherland, has arrived."

Chapter
14

After making her announcement, Chelsea waited for Sullivan's reaction, but he didn't move. Not because he wasn't supposed to understand her, but because he didn't know what to say or how to act. This woman on whom Chelsea placed so much importance was nothing to him. A face without a name.

"Come, Richard. Beatrice will be anxious to see you."

Anxious to see him? After she had endangered his family? After she had paid bloodhounds to bring Richard home?

His father had been sent away from this place in shame. He had died cursing the geography, the people, and his enemies. He'd thought himself abandoned by his family. So far, Sullivan had not been persuaded to the contrary. He saw no reason to stay. Moreover, he saw no reason to drag Richard the length of the globe to return him to a climate that would probably kill him.

"Richard?" She crooked her finger, then turned and began the trek back to the house.

Sullivan fell into step behind her but followed much more reluctantly. He was annoyed and angered by the intrusion of this old woman. Not just because his body still thrummed and he wanted to lie upon the grass with Chelsea

Wickersham, but because he did not want to meet Beatrice Sutherland.

It was this woman who had forced Sullivan to adopt an elaborate masquerade in order to protect those he loved. If not for her persistent attempts to find Richard, he and his family could have lived their entire existence quite happily on Sutherland's Roost. But no, she had been intent upon immersing them in the mire of deceit and intrigue, without a thought that they might not wish to become involved.

How could she be so thoughtless, so insensitive, so completely wrong? She might call herself his grandmother, but she was nothing more to him than a foreigner.

By the time he and Chelsea rounded the hedge and began to return, the carriage had rolled to a stop. Before the driver could alight to help, the door was thrown open, and a tiny gray-haired woman emerged. Limping quite noticeably, she stumbled up the walk as fast as her feet could carry her, then ran into the house. A small dog clambered down and yapped about her heels, making her journey even more awkward. Sullivan was offered no more than a glimpse of the tiny birdlike woman before she disappeared, her yapping spaniel in tow. Despite the distance, he could hear her calling, "Richard? Richard!"

Sullivan ignored the note of panic and longing that tinged her words. She was an interfering, meddling old crone who didn't deserve another thought.

Within seconds, she appeared again, directed by Smee, who pointed to the two figures in the distance. She stopped and squinted in confusion, asked something of Smee, who pointed more emphatically at the couple before disappearing inside the cottage.

Sullivan stopped at the bottom of the path, unwilling to go any farther. He didn't want to meet her. He didn't want her to know anything about him. He wished she would climb into her carriage and leave. He wished she would turn away from his savageness in disgust. He wished . . . he wished . . .

Why did she have to look their way so longingly? Why did she have to demonstrate such confusion and hope?

Chelsea took his elbow and, short of balking against her like a stubborn mule, he was forced to follow.

Each step he took seemed to make the elderly woman shrink inside herself even more. Huge, watery blue eyes watched his approach, her gaze moving up and down his frame as if she couldn't believe the evidence of her own senses.

She was so old. So small, so fragile, so vulnerable. But there was nothing weak about the joyful anticipation that spread over her face as she turned to Chelsea.

"Where is he?" she whispered, then more strongly, "Where is he?" Limping forward, she smiled in delight. "Where is my boy?"

Other than another quick glance, she didn't bother to study Sullivan again, and he grew tense and angry. He wasn't some stablehand to be ignored so easily. This woman had no right to make him feel inadequate and low. No right!

She came to a halt directly in front of him, and Sullivan appraised her with arrogant disdain. So this was the woman who had caused so much upheaval and pain? This was the old dowager who had overturned heaven and earth to find them when they had fought to remain hidden?

"Biddy," Chelsea began gently. "This is your grandson, Richard Albert Sutherland IV."

The old woman's skin pulled tightly over her cheekbones, fading to an unnatural pallor. Her stare flicked to Sullivan, then to Chelsea, then back again in confusion. "But . . ."

"I wrote you a letter last night, explaining—"

"I couldn't wait any longer. I had to come. I know we agreed that I should stay in London until you sent word, but . . . He's not a boy. He's grown."

"Yes."

Her eyes clouded. "The information we were given was wrong. The portrait was much older than we believed."

"Yes."

She shuffled forward, and for the first time Sutherland noted that she carried a small bundle. It had been wrapped in brown paper and tied with a velvet ribbon. She smoothed the package in embarrassment and quiet regret. "I'm afraid

I'm caught unprepared for such . . . I thought you might enjoy something of your father's, but . . . you're grown."

Sullivan looked suspiciously at the parcel. Something of his father's? What could she possibly have of his that she would think Sullivan would want? His father had already passed on his legacy. A legacy of pride and honor.

Biddy hesitated, then gave him the package anyway. "Perhaps you will find it amusing."

Sullivan reluctantly took the present but did not reply. When the silence stretched taut and interminable, Chelsea inserted, "He doesn't speak much English, I'm afraid."

"No English?" The woman appeared dumbstruck.

"However, we're getting along famously as of this morning." A fullblown pause followed that statement, as if Chelsea were remembering just how "famously" they'd been getting on. She added, "Wait and see, he'll be chattering to you like an old friend within a few days."

They waited in expectant silence, but Sullivan refused to speak.

Beatrice's face became starkly vulnerable. Her chin quivered. "He's so thin."

"He's strong and healthy, Biddy."

"He's pale."

"Nonsense, he's got a nice golden glow from the sun."

"He's weak."

"He has the constitution of an ox, I assure you."

Biddy's chin crumpled, huge tears appearing. Sullivan tried to push away the pang of reaction he felt as he saw her struggle to blink them away before they were noticed.

She took a step forward. Two. "Richard?" she whispered, reaching out to touch his face. "How like my Albert you look. Come. Won't you give your grandmother a kiss hello?"

She reached out as if to draw him down to her, and he jerked back, stunned by how much raw emotion this woman displayed. He was no one to her. He was a barbarian. An unknown quantity.

He didn't want her to touch him. He didn't want her to get to know him, to learn to like him, to decide to love him as her own. He didn't want to admit that there was anything between them but hard feelings. He didn't want to come to terms with the naked love and adoration he saw.

That was the way things had to be.

When she tried to restrain him, he twisted free, stormed to the cottage, and disappeared inside.

"Richard. Richard!"

He heard Chelsea call to him, but he didn't stop. He slammed the door resolutely behind him, refusing to acknowledge the dart of guilt he felt for such an action.

Chelsea had never been so angry and ashamed of another human being in her entire life. She had dealt with cruelty before. She had been raised at the knee of a dour, petty man. She had evaded the clasps of lechers and sycophants and fools. But never, ever, had she seen such deliberate hatefulness toward a helpless woman.

It took her some time to settle Biddy in her room upstairs, to reassure her that Richard was merely confused and overwhelmed. The whole time a fury burned in her chest. How could she have thought this man gentle and noble? How could she have misconstrued his apathy for tenderness?

Riding on a storm of inner castigation for believing this man could be something good when he was not, she marched down the corridor and threw open the nursery door.

"That was cruel, Master Richard. Completely and utterly cruel!" She planted her hands on her hips. "That woman has pinned her whole life upon the hope of seeing you. She has sacrificed everything she owned and everything she held dear. You turned away from her as if she were nothing but a chambermaid. How dare you? How *dare* you be so ungrateful."

He stood with his back to her, his head bent. Incensed that he hadn't even acknowledged her presence, she stamped toward him, forcing him to turn.

The anger drained away as she found a still, silent confusion radiating from his features. He held the small, stubby shape of a stuffed dog. Blunt masculine fingers stroked the rabbit's fur that covered the toy. There were bald spots where a child had already rubbed the pelt away.

"Oh, Richard." Chelsea squeezed his wrist. Part of the shame she felt became her own. "This hasn't been easy for you, has it? You must be extremely confused about all that's happened. After this morning's success, I expected you to understand the import of meeting your grandmother. But to you, she's just another strange face."

Sighing, she continued more gently. "I wish there were some manner of communication we could share. But there's no easy way to explain how you came to be here and how imperative it is for you to stay. Some things can't be put into words." She thought for a moment, then continued. "Biddy, your grandmother, is a special woman. She is kind and loving and devoted. She would never see another person in pain, but if she found herself in trouble, she wouldn't say a word. For years, she's fretted and agonized and worried about your father and mother. After she learned of their deaths and your existence, she began to worry about you." She gently asked, "Why don't you meet with her?"

She tried to draw him toward the door, but he refused to budge.

"Please don't punish her this way. She's lived through so much unhappiness. She deserves a little joy."

But the man she spoke to remained immovable. Knowing he didn't understand and guessing that at the moment he needed some time alone to gather his own thoughts and impressions, she backed away.

At the door, she turned. He stood exactly where she'd left him, his expression grim. "Rest, Master Richard. We'll come and fetch you in time for supper."

The door closed behind her with the care and gentleness of a new mother leaving her babe to nap. Quiet settled over the nursery. A nursery that should have been filled with children—a dozen grandchildren for the old woman who had expected a little boy.

Sullivan's eyes lifted from the dog to the dark panels of the door. Everything had changed. He didn't know when exactly. Sometime between the realization that his governess was not all she appeared to be and his grandmother's arrival.

Grandmother. A stranger, yet not a stranger. Blood of his blood.

Squeezing his eyes closed, Sullivan massaged the ache at his temples. This latest development complicated things tenfold. He'd meant to protect his family through whatever means he found necessary. But Sullivan found himself yearning for other things. He wanted to avenge his father's betrayal. He wanted to hurt those who had hurt him. He even toyed with the idea of finding a way to help a lonely old woman who thought he should recognize her and kiss her cheek.

And tangled somewhere in the middle of it all was Chelsea Wickersham.

As much as he might wish to return to those few idyllic hours in the garden, things weren't so simple anymore. Without really knowing how, he found himself yoked with responsibilities and commitments that he had never even imagined existed.

So what was he going to do?

The first silver beams of moonlight trickled from behind the tattered *portieres* and cast whiskers of stardust over the carpet. The tiny yellow bird in the nursery clock finished a round of sleepy cuckoos, and midnight crept into the house like a velvet tide.

The sigh of the nursery door being opened was so slow, so silent, that the sound melted easily into the shadows. For several long minutes, a stoop-shouldered woman stood motionless in the threshold. One gnarled hand gripped the molding, not with a white-knuckled tension but softly, gently, merely providing support to limbs weakened with age and rheumatism.

Clutching the worn dressing gown more tightly against her throat, she shifted, as if to turn away and leave as quietly as she had come. But she had taken only one step when she stopped and glanced over her shoulder, staring with such love, such reverence, at the figure upon the bed that her eyes sparkled and her chin trembled.

Leaning upon the walking stick she was too vain to use by day, Biddy crept into the room. When her presence didn't seem to disturb the man who slept, she grew bolder still, until she stood so close to the bed that the lace of her robe rasped against the linen bedcovers.

The ticking of the clock served as the only measure to the passing of time as she greedily absorbed the sight of her grandson's frame. Then, holding the gilded head of the walking stick more firmly, she bent forward. Fingers that were withered and crippled tenderly pushed a strand of hair from his forehead.

He didn't stir. The pattern of his breathing didn't alter. The delicate skin stretched thinly over her joints was so soft, her caress could have been that of a moth or some fairy queen.

She gripped the covers bundled about his waist, drawing them up around his chest and tucking them beneath the featherbed. Then, on a note of whimsy, she reached for the stuffed dog which had tumbled from the nearby rocker to the floor.

After petting its balding fur, she slid the toy beneath the blankets, "Take care of my grandson, MacDuff," she whispered. "See that the beasties of the night don't visit his dreams—for he is special to me. More precious than gold."

With one last pat, she turned and shuffled from the room, closing the door behind her. She had come and gone so silently that except for the faint scent of carnations that lingered in the air, she could have been a dream.

Sullivan's head rolled against the pillow and his eyes opened, focusing upon the mahogany portal. Though he steeled himself against the sensation, he felt a tug of guilt, pity, in addition to something more.

Somehow, in all the planning and plotting and scheming, he and his brothers hadn't really considered Beatrice Sutherland. She had been some nebulous idea, not a person. She had been an outsider, not . . .

Not an old woman desperately clutching at wisps of hope. She had so many dreams for the future and such fond memories of the past.

But Richard must be protected at all costs. What else could Sullivan do?

He stroked the fur of the toy, feeling the spots that had been worn away years ago by another small child. Another Sutherland heir.

His father.

What could he do?

Frustrated, Sullivan whipped the covers back and strode to the window, parting the curtains and glaring out into the blackness. Deep within the house, he heard a whisper of skirts, the soft fall of leather shoes. The frustration he felt over the predicament with his grandmother eased into another, entirely tormenting emotion.

Chelsea.

It amazed him how quickly he'd come to recognize the sound of her tread. He thought he even caught the tantalizing scent of lilacs and jasmine that clung to her skin, her hair. She must have been keeping the old girl company and was about to retire for the night.

He savored the awareness, the burst of anticipation he felt as she moved toward his room. Paused. Then passed.

Damn. She hadn't come in. She was still avoiding him, as surely as night followed day.

Since confronting him earlier, she had barely spent a minute's time in his company. She hadn't spoken to him all evening, hadn't seen him at all except in passing. He'd spent dinner with his grandmother, alone, while Chelsea had chosen to eat with Greyson and Smee.

He'd seen through her ploy with little trouble at all. She hadn't been thinking solely of the old woman. He knew that by the way she refused to look at him squarely, or avoided so much as a brushing of hands. She'd eaten with the servants, then disappeared after dinner, as if to silently remind him of her position as a mere employee in this household.

But her intent had backfired. She removed herself from

his presence, so he began to search for her. She refused to touch him, so he wanted to campaign a seduction. She underscored her position as his governess, so he yearned to find the real woman beneath.

He knew she was struggling against her innate reserve, her sense of duty, and her private vows of respectability. The angst she felt was clear. But he also knew her defenses were crumbling beneath the strength of her need. He'd seen evidence in the unguarded glances she'd given him as she'd accompanied his grandmother and him out of the dining hall and back to the nursery. Once he'd passed through the threshold into his chamber, she'd reached to close the door. He'd seen the blatant desire.

Sullivan willed her to return yet damned his own obsession. Bloody hell. How, in so short a space of time, could he progress from being infuriated to intrigued to bewitched by such a woman? He couldn't seem to push her from his mind. Despite all of the emotional upheaval he'd suffered, his attention wasn't on his family or his father's honor or his stranger-grandmother. It was on a woman. A slim, mysterious woman with hair the color of spun sunlight and eyes as deep as a cool crystal spring. A woman with secrets in her gaze and fire in her soul. A woman of innocence one minute and experience the next.

Pursued by urges he couldn't ignore, Sullivan donned his shirt and trousers and prowled the close confines of his room. The rest of the house wallowed in somnolent silence, but he couldn't bear to go back to bed. Not yet. He felt as restless as a caged animal. Sleep wasn't something he even wanted to think about.

Over the next hour, Sullivan tried to settle the chaotic jumble of his nerves with reading and pacing, but nothing seemed to help. Nothing at all. So he thought about Chelsea—and suffered the consequences.

Midnight bled into one o'clock, then two. Then, to his infinite surprise, hinges squeaked far down the corridor. Sullivan waited, his heart pounding, knowing who it would be by the steady, stealthy creak of the floorboards. Chelsea.

He waited, barely breathing as she walked toward him. But when there was no pausing in her stride as she continued to the staircase, Sullivan fully intended to follow her.

Moving as soundlessly as he could, he tiptoed down to the lower level, stopping on the final tread. The narrow windows to the side of the front door had been left open, allowing the redolent scent of flowers to waft into the foyer, but he didn't think she'd stepped outside.

His eyes roamed the foyer, falling upon the entry to the studio. When Biddy, Chelsea, and he had left the room earlier, the doors had been closed behind them. They now stood ajar.

Sullivan saw a brief flare of light against the far wall. The honeyed flicker eased into a steady glow, and he knew that she had lighted one of the candles on the desk.

Sullivan stepped from the staircase. An urgency surged in him, a nameless drive. For hours he had agonized over Richard, his grandmother, his own decisions, and Chelsea —this tormentingly complex woman. But he didn't want to think anymore. He wanted to *feel*. He wanted to drown himself in sensation rather than in thought. He wanted to experience all Chelsea had to offer and more. He needed her kindness, her sweetness, but he also craved her fire with an intensity that threatened to consume him completely.

The yearnings that had simmered in his belly all day intensified. From this moment forward, there would be no slaps, no servants, and no arriving coaches to interrupt them. Moving decisively, he clasped the doorknob and entered, prepared to force Chelsea to admit she needed him, whether he had to reach his goal through seduction or trickery.

But he wasn't prepared for the sight of his governess.

She was clad in nothing but her night rail. An embroidered shawl had been slung loosely over her shoulders, and her hair spilled wildly down her back. The candle on the desk painted the strands with a tender brilliance. The wavering flame shed a halo of light that pierced the fine weave of her garment, throwing her body into shadow.

Reaction rushed through Sullivan when she whirled to

find him watching her. Her body, sharply revealed, was lithe and slim, her breasts high and firm, her waist narrow, her hips gently contoured.

She didn't move, didn't speak. But in the space of a heartbeat, she changed, and Sullivan saw a near-stranger.

Gone completely was the reserved, didactic educator. In her place was a soft, yielding woman, passionately longing for him.

No words were spoken. No words were needed. A shivering, violent need pulsed in the room, unbidden but there nevertheless. Sullivan tasted her hunger as strongly as his own. An almost tangible force, it hung over them, electrifying the air.

"Richard?" she murmured, the call more of a caress than an audible query.

Sullivan barely noted the cool parquet floor beneath his feet as he walked forward. He saw the way she clutched the folds of her shawl, bunching the delicate fabric against her neck. But she didn't back away. Of that he was glad. For hours, he had been tormented by their afternoon together. He wanted to experience each sight and smell and texture anew.

Driven by the need to prove to himself that he wasn't imagining this woman and her unproclaimed feelings for him, he was far from gentle. Tipping her head, he bent and crushed her lips beneath his own.

Desire burst upon him instantaneously. Abandoning all thought of wooing her into participating in his embrace, he opened his mouth and silently demanded that she do the same.

To his overwhelming surprise, there was no hesitation on her part. Her lips parted. Her body swayed. When his tongue slid into the moist haven, hers challenged, parried, advanced.

Moaning deep in his throat, he parted his legs. He scooped her hips forward and up until they rubbed intimately against his, then more forcefully, grinding, pressing, seeking satisfaction and torment, agony and bliss.

The shawl dropped to the ground. She clung to him,

writhing beneath his touch, seemingly trying to crawl inside him. So furious, so passionate, was her response, that she stunned him into hesitating.

At once, she became the aggressor. She yanked at the fabric of his shirt, tugging it from his waistband and tearing at the placket so that buttons snapped from their foundations and scattered across the floor. Running her fingertips down the bare expanse of his chest, she pressed her thumb into his navel, withdrew, then repeated the action.

Gasping, he reared back. She watched him with avid interest, like a spider watched a fly caught in her silken trap. Her eyes assumed the luster of the clearest of aquamarines. Her lips were moist; her chest heaved.

Sullivan peered at her in astonishment. How could she seem an innocent one moment and a woman of experience the next? How could she act the virgin and the courtesan? At times, he thought a simple embrace would cause her to swoon. Then, in a heartbeat, she became a seductress.

Sensing his confusion, she drew his head down and kissed him again. Slowly, sweetly, like a maiden testing sensual waters. The contrast to their previous embrace had his head spinning, his heart thumping uncontrollably. Then, before he could completely adjust, she tipped her head to bite his ear, his chin. She returned to tease the dip of his navel, taunt him, torment him, circling the silken indentation with her nail.

Sullivan was incapable of logic. He only knew that he had to bring her closer. Tucking his hands beneath her arms, he lifted her high against him so that her hips pressed against his stomach. To his infinite delight and pleasure, she wrapped her legs around his waist and looped her arms around his shoulders. He supported her, bending forward to take her mouth, and she returned his kiss, measure for measure.

Never before had a woman affected him so completely. Her sweetness filled his senses, ruining him for any other female. What had begun as an intriguing flirtation mere days ago now bloomed into something more. He had to have her. Arching beneath him. Tonight.

He angled her head back and broke away from the delicious torment of her lips. He struggled to fill his starving lungs with air, while at the same time he beaded kisses down her neck to the demure neckline of her gown. Frustrated by the barrier of cloth, his teeth tugged at the lacy edging, his tongue dipped below the delicate border. Still unsatisfied, longing to see what lay beneath, he struggled to support her with one hand while the other reached for her buttons.

She allowed him to unfasten a few of the pearlescent discs. Before he could do much more, she was bending forward to press moist kisses over his neck and across his shoulder.

"No," he whispered.

"Yes."

No longer patient, Sullivan took the batiste at her shoulder and jerked it down over her arm. The sharp rend of tearing cloth punctuated his haste. The awkward angle of their twined position allowed little more than the baring of her shoulder and most of one full breast.

Although the nipple was coyly shielded by a wisp of fabric, Sullivan felt a reverence steal over him. She was so beautiful. So passionate. So honest.

Seeing his expression, she rubbed his cheek, nuzzled the hollow at the base of his neck. The tip of her tongue darted out to lave that spot. Then one foot dropped. The second.

He clung to her for several seconds, keeping her suspended in his embrace and forcing her hips to press intimately against his arousal. A soft sound, half groan, half sigh, melted from her throat, and she pushed away until she firmly touched the ground.

One finger strayed to explore the washboard-like indentations of his stomach. She seemed to be wrestling with some inner dilemma, but within a moment she smiled.

"Come with me."

169

Chapter
15

Sullivan was struck to the core. He knew when a woman's invitation involved something more than sipping tea in the drawing room. Yet, he had never seen any other female look at him with such blatant desire.

She led him from the studio up the stairs. Without the benefit of a candle, they were left in warm, murky shadows. Moonlight streamed through the curtains at the end of the hall, throwing lacy patterns on the floor and clouding their fevered expressions.

Climbing each step was an exercise in torture. He saw clearly the sway of her breasts and the lulling swing of her hips. Her hair streamed down her back in a mass of tiny ringlets which beckoned for his touch. Her lips begged for his kiss. If not for the presence of his grandmother and two servants, Sullivan would have considered ravishing her on the staircase—taking her like the savage she thought he was.

Chelsea paused by the door to the nursery. To his infinite astonishment, she twisted the doorknob and led him inside. He wondered if she were going to refuse him again. But as soon as he joined her, she closed the door and leaned back, offering him a tempting smile as she twisted the key she had removed from the other side.

"Biddy's room adjoins my own, so I think we'll spend the night here if you don't mind. Besides . . . this is still the only room in the house with a lock."

He didn't respond.

She didn't appear to have expected him to.

Straightening, she toyed with one of the buttons of her night rail, watched his reaction, then slipped the disc free in blatant invitation. Another creamy inch of flesh was exposed to his view, this time allowing a glimpse of the shadowed valley between her breasts.

Sullivan's patience for wooing and teasing vanished, but when he stepped forward to haul her into his arms, she stopped him. Her head shook from side to side. "Shh. Not yet. Not yet. We have all night." Her lips curved, her smile was filled with latent promise. "If I'm to do this, if I'm to suffer the consequences that will surely follow, I mean to make this a night worth remembering."

Her words summoned a pang of conscience in Sullivan. He was not naive enough to think that there would be no repercussions for their actions. Even if no one were to discover what had happened, bonds would be formed, emotionally and physically. But too many ties already joined them, Sullivan realized. What was occurring was very real. To his infinite astonishment, he found himself wishing to ensure they became permanent.

Niggling doubts rose, churned, but they were quickly doused when she circled him, studying him as if he were a slave upon the block. Her fingers trailed his stomach, marking her path, feathered over his back, then returned to rest upon his waist as she faced him again.

Seeing her this way, with her eyes dark, her hair flowing, he knew he would never forget this night, whatever the future might bring. He would see to it that the pleasure was worth the pain.

"For once you are far too respectably attired, Master Richard," she murmured. "Allow me to play the gentleman's gentleman for the evening."

Stepping behind him once again, Chelsea slid the garment

free. When the shirt finally dropped to the ground, she spread her hands wide, testing the resilient flesh.

He was so firm, so warm. So male.

This was what she'd imagined doing from the moment she had drawn back the coverings in the skiff to discover that Richard Sutherland, heir to the Lindon estates, was more heathen than gentleman. Now that her fantasies had become reality, she didn't quite know what to do. She supposed she should think of the future. She supposed she shouldn't allow things to continue. But she found she couldn't stop the fire that burned within her—*wouldn't* stop it. It had been so long since she'd allowed herself to feel valued. It had been so long since she'd felt beautiful and alive. It had been so long since she'd felt cherished.

As she faced him once again, Chelsea had no doubts that Richard desired her. His restraint was tenuous. When he would have reached out, she eluded him. "Not yet, Master Richard." The fact that he couldn't understand a word she said didn't dissuade her from speaking aloud. In fact, his lack of understanding added a boldness, a dangerous flavor, to the evening. She could say anything, speak of her most secret wishes, and he would never know.

Crossing to the fireplace, she withdrew a piece of kindling from a tin mug on the hearth, touched the sliver of wood to the burning coals until it ignited. Glancing at him over her shoulder, she noted the way he stood still, watching her with an overwhelming intensity.

Moving about the room, she lit three candles. One on the hearth, one on the dresser, and the last on the bedside table. Then she blew out the tiny flame, prolonging the simple action so that he absorbed the pursing of her lips, the slow exhalation. Licking her fingers, she watched the flare of reaction he displayed as she pinched the last burning ember into oblivion. Then, without a thought to tidiness, she dropped it onto the floor, reveling in the burst of freedom she experienced at that uncharacteristic act of carelessness.

"Do you want me, Richard? Do you need me?" She expected no answer. She needed none. She caressed his stomach as she passed, then continued on to the bed. "I don't think I've ever thought of this room in relationship to a tryst, but I think—with a little imagination—we can manage."

She took the silk duvet from the bed and dragged it over the velvet carpet in front of the hearth. The counterpane fell to the ground in a billowing, glistening, down-filled cushion. Richard eyed her questioningly.

"I'm rather fond of Mozart, you know. *The Abduction from the Seraglio* is one of my favorites." She pushed a wayward strand of hair away from her forehead, slowly, sensually, aware that he watched the sway of her breasts, the inner curve of her arm. "As part of your education, we really must go to the opera in London. Then you could see why I'm so intrigued. Imagine. An opera about a harem."

Taking the pillows from the bedstead, she scattered them over the coverlet upon the rug until the area in front of the hearth resembled a sultan's lair. Next, she draped the sheet at one end, a blanket over the other, artistically arranging the linen and wool with the care of a master painter. "In case we get chilled," she explained, pausing in her preparations. "Though I don't think there's much likelihood of that, do you?"

She didn't know what had intrigued him, the lulling sound of her voice or her careful preparations, but his eyes burned, glowed, searing into her flesh.

"Do you know what happens when you look at me that way?" she whispered. "I don't feel very much like a governess." Standing, she spied the stuffed dog which had tumbled to the floor. Retrieving it, she approached Richard once again. "But then, you don't remind me much of a child."

She stopped, a mere fraction of an inch away. So close she could feel the heat of his body being absorbed into her own. "Before you came, Biddy told me about MacDuff. She said once that he kept the beasties of the night away from your father."

She touched one furry ear to Richard's chest, feathering it back and forth over the flat copper nipple bare to her view until it beaded into a hard nub. "You won't be needing MacDuff tonight, Richard. Tonight I'll see to the beasties.

Tonight and tomorrow and the night after that." Her chest grew suddenly tight, heavy. "In return, promise me you'll keep the beasties from my door. If only for a little while. Please."

He didn't speak, but his hand clamped around her wrist. He threw the dog aside. Chelsea knew that she had pushed him about as far as his control would allow. But she didn't care. She exulted in the fact.

"Richard," she managed to whisper mere seconds before his lips slammed over her own and he took her mouth, ravaged it, savored it, gentled it.

A storm of emotion rumbled through her. She responded to him just as greedily, then just as tenderly. For each caress he bestowed, she offered one of her own. For each kiss, she added another, until they were both clinging, straining, struggling to grow closer.

He pushed her away. He stared at her as if he didn't know what to think, what to feel. Chelsea knew it was because she responded too eagerly, too passionately. A woman was supposed to be reticent, to acquiesce to a man's desires, not respond in full measure.

"I surprise you, don't I?" Her tone was ragged. "You don't know what to think about me, what kind of person I am. Don't think. Don't sort my parts, my attributes, and my foibles and stuff the findings into a little cubbyhole. I'm me." She rubbed the dip of his navel. She didn't know why that part of his anatomy seemed to fascinate her so. Perhaps because it was surrounded by taut masculine flesh. Perhaps because it was forever bare to her view in the heathenish costume he continued to wear. Perhaps because it was unseemly for a woman like her to want to touch it. Or the woman she pretended to be.

"I'm me," she said again. "Maybe for a little while tonight . . . I'll be a part of you."

He gripped the fabric of her night rail. Then he was moving, lifting, drawing circles around, over the dainty curve of her shoulder.

The convulsive movement caused the cloth to lift, shift, tease. Shuddering, she leaned into him for support as the batiste whispered over the sensitive tips of her nipples, teasing, taunting, caressing. Never had she thought that an action so simple in intent could have such earth-shattering results. The fire she had purposely banked suddenly raged. Her breathing quickened, her pulse slammed through her veins.

His fingers laced through her hair, bringing her up for his kiss. Then there was no time for words. Mouth clashed with mouth. The silence of the room was split with the sharp tear of cloth as Richard rent the garment from neck to waist.

Chelsea gasped, surrendering to the torrent of sensation. When he released her to tug at the fastenings of his trousers, finally releasing the string that held them to his waist and pushing the garment free of his hips, she did not demure.

Glancing down, she noted that he was aroused, ready, barely contained by the scrap of cloth that covered him. While she watched, he released the knot of his loincloth, that tempting, tormenting, tantalizing garment, freeing him to her gaze. Large. Powerful. Completely male.

Then he was crushing her to him. Chest to chest, hip to hip. She had barely the time to gasp at the intimate contact before he took her lips with his own. He lifted her, holding her close, so tightly that their pulses beat as one, feeding from the frenzy of their need.

Breaking their kiss, he knelt upon the nest of blankets she had formed on the floor. He laid her down with a gentleness that was at odds with their haste. But when she touched the sensitive rope of muscles at his flanks, the fierceness flared out of control. Taking her lips, he rested his upper body over hers. He cupped her breast, kneaded it, molded it.

A hot bolt of pleasure sank deep into her belly. She hadn't thought a man's lovemaking could ever make her feel so charged, so overwrought. She didn't think she could take another minute of this unbearable pleasure.

Still, he continued. His thumb dipped into her navel, much as she was wont to do to him. She gasped at the sharp burst of sensation.

He continued his search, measuring the span of her hips, the sensitive hollow, the prominent bones. She grappled with a fistful of his dark, silky hair as it spilled over his shoulders, silently bidding him to stop. But Richard didn't abandon his intimate foray. He merely smiled against her throat, kissed her there, painting the spot with his tongue, while his blunt, nimble fingers delved lower, seeking, testing, finding.

Unable to hold still, she clutched his hips, sinking her nails into the flesh and bucking against him.

He smiled, The smile of the victor. The invader. The savage. In a single motion that made her overtly aware of his overpowering masculinity, he shifted, rolling onto his back and drawing her over his stomach so that her legs cradled his hips.

She arched her torso at the intimate friction. Male to female. Hard to soft. Tensile to pliant. Then she bent, her back rounding, her hair spilling about them in a tangled curtain.

Never had she thought that anything could feel so sweet. A heavy wave of pleasure-pain thrummed through her veins. Pressing her mouth to his, she kissed him with all the pent-up passion she'd denied for so long.

He rolled over, bringing her with him. Looking into the intensity of his eyes, eyes as green as a roiling river, she knew the last thread of his control had snapped. The savage would have his way.

Sensation crowded upon sensation, hot and fast and strong. Richard propped himself on his elbows as she held him tightly around the waist. His fingers slid low to test her, finding her more than willing, more than ready. Gasping against the gentle caress, she reached down to urge him on.

She had no more than brushed the sensitive ridge of his manhood before Richard moaned and tore her away. Twining their hands together, he crushed her lips with his own and slowly thrust into her, a little at first, then all the way.

The reflexive cry that tore from her throat at the rending of her maiden's barrier was swallowed by his mouth. But when he would have drawn away, she clung to him, wrapping her legs around his waist. She felt him inside her, large and heated. Strong.

Opening her eyes, she met his look of concern. Smiling, she murmured, "Continue, heathen. I defy you to finish what you've begun."

Acknowledging her mock-challenge to prove he could pleasure her now, mere moments after rending her asunder, he began to rock, slowly at first, then faster and faster. Harder. Until both of them were straining, yearning for some faraway goal.

Just when Chelsea didn't think she could bear any more, it began. A violent implosion of sensation, a rippling shudder of pleasure. Dear heaven, she'd heard stories, but she'd never thought, never *dreamed,* that they could actually be true—and yet so false, so inadequately expressed.

This was what saints had sinned for. This was what martyrs had died for. This was why women throughout the ages had been willing to throw caution and propriety to the wind. Not just an animal act, not just a blending of bodies, but a searing meld of heart, mind, and soul.

She savored the trembling release. The last few aftershocks. Sighing, she forced her eyes to open. She saw his face. Taut, expectant, triumphant.

"Chelsea," he whispered against her cheek. He kissed her jaw, her neck. Then, to her infinite surprise, he began again, moving slowly, drawing back, hesitating, easing forward.

She swallowed in surprise. She hadn't thought, hadn't known that a man could continue so, without taking his own pleasure. Especially after the way she'd brought him to the edge of insanity.

Ignoring the heavy ache of her body, denying the twinge of pain, she allowed him to lead her again.

This time, there was a languor to their intimate dance. A savoring. This time, Chelsea was aware not so much of her own body as of his. She wanted to give him joy. She wanted to give him satisfaction. She absorbed each texture, each whispered sigh, each silken caress. She studied his movements and copied them, exploring, kissing, tasting, giving.

Soon their pace increased, intensified. Richard's features adopted a grimace of sweet agony.

"Give in to me," she urged into his ear. "Surrender."

He growled against her neck. No longer gentle, he moved more boldly, more quickly.

Chelsea hadn't thought it possible, but her body quickened, the taut string of passion grew tighter, tighter. Straining with him now, she gripped his buttocks, urging him to linger, withdraw, return.

Sensations began crowding in upon her in a heated frenzy. She grasped at the pillows, the blankets, anything that might provide some sort of stronghold. She moaned his name, mouth open.

One last time, he plunged into her. Her body responded by convulsing again and again and again. Sweetly. Tormentingly.

He tensed. He clasped her hips, holding her tightly, firmly. Then he shuddered, taking his own release and forcing the hot tide of his seed into her body.

"Chelsea, dear sweet bloody hell, Chelsea. I can't get enough of you. I can't get enough!"

Chapter
16

Damn you," she hissed. *"Damn you!"*

The stunned mixture of guilt, exhaustion, and wariness she found on his features gave witness to the befuddled accusation of her brain. The accent she'd heard might be odd to her ears, but there was no denying the fluency of the phrase. He had spoken to her in the heat of passion. In English. *English!*

Filled with a sudden rage, she pushed him away, pummeling his shoulders with her fists. Scrambling to the far side of the blankets, she stabbed him with open accusation.

A weary curse slipped from his lips. One arm lifted to cover his eyes, and he took a deep, jerky breath. Time hung brittly about them. The annoying grate of the cuckoo clock in the corner only seemed to underscore the sudden silence.

Chelsea didn't know how long they remained that way, trapped in some indefinable morass of emotion. She only knew that enough minutes spilled into the silence to steady her pulse and cool her ardor.

Realizing she sat bare before him, naked, vulnerable, Chelsea took the sheet from the floor and wrapped it tightly around her body. "You've understood me all this time, haven't you?"

He raked his hands through his hair and rolled to a sitting position. "Chelsea—"

"Haven't you?" she demanded more forcefully.

"Yes."

"For the entire time? Or did you have a day or two when you honestly couldn't remember English, or . . . or the drugs kept you from speaking."

"The entire time."

A slow chill seeped into her expression. "Damn you. *Damn* you! Were you so lacking in entertainment that you needed me to play the fool?"

She pushed to her feet, and he lunged to stop her. "No!"

"How could you have done such a thing? Are you completely devoid of honor and compassion? Or were you just amused by the entire situation? By your grandmother's plight?"

"I didn't know her. I didn't know *you.* Bloody hell! I was forcibly taken from my home and imprisoned aboard ship. For weeks I was kept in a cramped cell below deck and drugged like an animal. How would you react?"

"With honesty."

"Oh, really," he drawled. "Are you quite sure that word is in your vocabulary?"

She jerked as if she'd been slapped. Unspoken between them were the feelings that she had tried to deny, tried to push away, but which she'd displayed most eloquently and most brazenly only minutes before.

"At least I never deliberately hurt you." She scooped to retrieve the remnants of her night rail, then tried to dodge past him, but he caught her and forced her to turn.

"What do you mean by that?"

"You never planned to help Biddy, did you? Even today, after you finally met her, you were willing to walk away. She was just another old woman in dire financial straits, but no one who should require your aid."

Sullivan didn't speak. He couldn't. Not when the truth jammed in his gullet like a stone.

"I can't *believe* I fell for your tricks. I can't *believe* I could have been so gullible." Striking out, she hit him with the side of her fist, then again and again. When he tried to pin her arms to her sides, she wrenched free and retreated to the opposite side of the room.

"Damn, damn, damn you!" She kept repeating the same phrase, so angry she couldn't find a more punishing imprecation. Grasping a book from the table, she threw it at him, then another, and another. He dodged her missiles, but she came up empty of weapons. He prowled toward her.

"Stop it. Just stop it!"

When he would have held her, she slapped him away. "Don't you dare touch me. Ever," she hissed. Drawing the sheet around her like a queen's robes, she marched toward the door.

But she couldn't leave him. Despite the anger, despite the embarrassment, despite the abused pride, her most overwhelming emotion was disappointment. Her head rested against the smooth mahogany in abject defeat. "Why couldn't you trust me?" she whispered, so softly the query was nearly swallowed whole by the darkness.

He didn't answer her right away.

She finally peered at him over her shoulder. "Why?"

He sighed, raking his fingers through his hair. "Sit down, and I'll—"

"No."

"This would be much easier if you would—"

"No."

He threw his hands into the air as if to say "Fine." Pulling a towel from the warming rack next to the fireplace, he wrapped it around his hips with utmost care before speaking. "Thirty years ago, my parents were sent away from England in shame. My father was accused of treason, my mother of coercion. No one fought to prove their innocence, no one believed their pleas."

"Biddy believed. So did your grandfather."

"They abandoned us."

"They spent their whole lives trying to find you. After your parents' ship went down, they sent *The Seeker* to the area where your parents jumped ship at least a half-dozen times. They were desperate to locate you."

"But we didn't want to be found! My parents *died* because of this place." He made a sweeping gesture of the room and the garden beyond. "They died for a title and a collection of moldering estates that meant nothing in the grand scheme of things. They died cursing their enemies, their homeland, and their family."

"But Biddy loves you."

"She doesn't know me. She doesn't know anything about me."

"She wants to."

"Does she? Or does she just want another cookie-cutter Englishman in tight breeches who spends more time on the knot of his cravat than on his own character?"

Chelsea didn't respond. She didn't know what to say because she didn't know if Biddy could ever resign herself to the fact that this man, this savage, would never conform to the image she'd carried in her heart.

"So you're going to refuse to help her."

"I have a home of my own."

"But what kind of home? A thatched hovel, a primitive island?"

"I want you all to leave me alone once I go."

"Why? So that you can pretend that none of this happened, that we don't exist, your grandmother doesn't exist?"

"I have a life there."

"You could have one here as well. A good one. A fulfilling one."

"As the Earl of Lindon."

"Yes. Yes!"

"What if I don't want that?"

She held the sheet to her chest. "Help her, please help her," she begged, dodging his question.

"Why? Why are you so bent on this?"

"I care for her."

"She must have paid you dearly for such loyalty."

"Yes." She could barely force the words free. "Yes, she paid dearly. Not with money, but with compassion, empathy, charity. I can never forget the love she gave me."

"She's an old woman."

"She's your grandmother!"

"That fact might inspire you, but it does not bring an answering fervor to my mind."

"Then what about me?" she asked woodenly. "Would you do it for me?"

"Why?"

She couldn't answer. Not after all that had occurred between them.

"What do you gain from all this if I succeed?"

She fought the crushing pressure that seemed to close over her chest. "Peace."

"From what?"

"Myself. I have old debts to settle. One, a debt of kindness."

"To Biddy?"

"Yes."

"Why?"

Her knees quaked, and the color drained from her face. "Because years ago, she walked into hell and drew me out." When he would have pressed for more information, she opened the door and crossed the threshold. There she paused. Without turning, she said, "Dreams are fragile things, Richard. Once destroyed, they aren't easily replaced."

"What about the other debts? Are they for past kindnesses as well?"

She paused, wondering how much she should say and how much she would reveal. Finally, she offered, "Past cruelties."

Chelsea, moving with the brittle care of a survivor of some overwhelming tragedy, closed the door behind her. Sullivan was left in the echoing void, alone, wondering how one simple mistake in judgment could have dominoed into such a sorry state of affairs. What worried him most was not that he had bungled things but that he'd hurt her. That alone caused him more pain than he would have ever thought imaginable.

Dreams are fragile things, Richard. Once destroyed, they aren't easily replaced.

Her statement had rung with such stark pain. Sullivan cringed. Somehow, he knew that she wasn't speaking of Biddy but of herself.

He couldn't imagine what dreams she must have had that could have created such a bleak despair once they'd been lost.

Sullivan woke midmorning, having fallen into a restless slumber mere hours before.

The house remained silent and still. Lying in bed, he stared up at the cracked ceiling and waited. But no one ventured upstairs, let alone came to the nursery. Soon he realized no one would come at all.

Far below, he could hear the good-natured banter of Smee and Greyson. He heard the grate and slide of Dowager Lady Sutherland's cane against the gravel as she walked the length of the garden.

He didn't know if Chelsea had informed them all of his masquerade, or if the ensuing peace was a measure of respect for an old woman who should avoid any upsets to her nerves. Either way, he found he didn't want to wait any longer. The burden of playing the savage had become unbearable. It was time he showed his true colors.

But first, first, he had to see Chelsea.

Drawing on Smee's oversized trousers and the linen work shirt, he padded silently down the hall. Before descending the staircase, he stopped, considering, then entered his governess's room.

He didn't know what he had expected to find. He thought there should be some change, some proof of what they had shared. He felt different—older, more finely tuned to the little sounds, the shadings of light and shadow, the unsettling quality of the stillness of the cottage.

In Chelsea's chamber, however, there was no evidence to confirm or deny what had occurred the previous night. No betraying peek of the sheet she'd covered herself with, no torn nightgown. In fact, the private arena was nearly sterile in its neatness. The bed had been made to military perfection. The armoire door was closed, the toiletry articles on her dresser rigidly arranged. The carpet bag which had once born witness to her efforts to escape him had been folded and neatly placed beneath the dresser.

The ordered regimentation disturbed him. Now more than ever, he knew this wasn't the life-style Chelsea Wickersham was meant to endure. She was a woman of passion. She had so much to give a man, so much to offer. Yet she had entombed herself in a sterile, solitary existence. *Why?*

The complexity of her personality never ceased to amaze him. How had she ever managed to hide the sensuality of her nature behind the prim and proper facade of a British governess? How could she remain a virgin for so long when she was so instinctively well versed in the art of bringing a man to his knees?

The mystery tormented him. He wondered what had driven her into shielding her true self. He wondered what hopes she'd once had. What dreams she'd once lost.

Withdrawing, he closed the door silently behind him, determined that one day soon he would find the answers to all of those questions. And more.

Smee and Greyson hovered near the front landing and watched Richard disappear down the back stairs.

"Do you suppose they've had a tiff?" Smee whispered.

"What they've had or haven't had is none of our affair," Greyson answered stiffly, striding down the hall to enter Lady Sutherland's room and begin tidying the bed—a chore that a few years ago would have been beneath his dignity but now he bore like a badge of honor.

Smee quickly followed and fluffed the pillows. "Miss Chelsea left in a hurry this morning. You don't suppose she's gone to the village, do you?"

"No. I don't."

At Greyson's odd response, Smee blinked in surprise.

The older man fiddled with the edge of the coverlet, then added confidentially, "I followed her—just to assure myself of her safety, mind you," he hastened to add.

"Where did she go?"

"Onto the moors. She's been staring down at Lindon Manor all morning."

Smee's eyes rounded to the size of saucers. "Poor thing. Poor thing!"

Greyson's head dipped in emphatic concurrence.

"But we must help her!"

"No one can help her but Master Richard."

Smee's lips folded together at their quandary. "Then we must help *him* to help *her.*"

"Exactly."

"What should we do?"

"First we should see about his clothes." Greyson flicked the last edge of the counterpane into place. "Hurry, Smee. Go into town immediately and fetch the togs being made."

"What if they aren't finished yet?"

"Take anything Mr. Gulch has completed. Quickly! While you're out, I'll prepare the guest room for Master Richard. I don't see any sense in keeping him in the nursery any longer. Miss Chelsea hasn't locked his door in well over a week."

Smee dipped his head in acknowledgment, hiked his pants more securely about his rotund middle, and toddled from the room, rushing down the stairs and out to the stables. Like Sir Galahad of old, he mounted his trusty steed and galloped into town, ready to brave hell itself in order to defend his lady.

Sullivan's search for his governess proved futile. He found the kitchen empty, as well as the garden. The servants, Smee and Greyson, had disappeared for a time, leaving him no clue to where Chelsea could be found. Returning to the house, he wandered from room to room until reaching the studio.

Weak sunlight spilled from the narrow windows, painting the tiles with splashes of buttery yellow. A wind gusted from the west, proclaiming that the intermittent sunshine was but a passing fancy and another storm would be blowing in come eveningtide.

The weather seemed an echo to his senses, full of hope one

minute, somber disquiet the next. Sullivan couldn't help feeling that things were changing, rushing out of control before he had the time to recognize their passing. Where he had once been so clear-cut and decisive, he now found himself doubting his actions, his objectives, his goals. A hunger burgeoned within him. But he didn't know what he needed, what he wanted. He only knew that something was missing. Something that would fill the hollowness that lingered deep in his heart where a burning anger had been mere days before.

His hand closed over the doorknob, and he stepped into the studio.

He would remember this room for the rest of his days. When he thought of it, he would recall the musky scents of roses and petunias, the bright splashes of color from the portraits arranged on the walls. Most of all, he would remember his grandmother. The frail, elderly woman looked up, her eyes suddenly sparking with an unspeakable joy.

"Well," she sighed, her lips pursing into a quick smile. "So you've awakened at last."

He didn't answer. He couldn't bring himself to admit that he had committed a lie of omission. He had played the savage and taken her for a fool.

Far from abashed by his silence, his grandmother gestured for him to approach. "Come in, Richard. Come in. I won't bite, I promise. Sit with me if you'd like."

He walked toward her with some reluctance, seeing that Greyson or Smee had unearthed a rocker for her comfort. She sat in a far corner, the dog on the floor beside her, a pile of worsted in her lap.

His bare feet made no sound, and Sullivan was immediately conscious of his unconventional appearance. Why this woman did not run screaming, he'd never know. His hair was loose and flowing, his shirt unbuttoned. The ill-fitting pants revealed a healthy measure of his calves.

"Bring a chair up, and help me with this mess," she grumbled, plucking at the yarn.

Sullivan was still unsure whether Chelsea had revealed his deception or not, but he ultimately decided that either way, there was no sense in continuing with the charade, so he placed the chair nearby.

"Hold this, please." She wound the worsted over his wrists, then proceeded to roll it into a tidy ball. "It was naughty of you to pretend you didn't speak the king's English."

"Chelsea told you." After remaining silent for so long, his voice sounded rusty and gravel-toned even to his own ears.

"No. Actually, she didn't."

"Then how—"

"No son of mine would allow his boy to be raised without education. I realized that last night. Still, I must applaud you on your ingenuity. You must have learned quite a bit about us that way."

Sullivan refused to reply, and she chuckled. A delighted sound that was more like that of a young girl than an elderly lady. Then, sighing to herself in pleasure, she continued rolling her yarn. Her gnarled fingers struggled to perform the simple task, but she didn't complain.

Silence bathed them in twisted motes of summer. The dog snored softly and occasionally paddling its legs in the air as if chasing hedgehogs in its dreams.

"You'll be leaving us, I suppose," Biddy said after some time.

"Why would you believe such a thing?"

"You have the appearance of a tiger who's been kept in his cage too long," she confided. "It was selfish of me to think that it would be enough."

"It?"

"The title. England." After a beat, she added, "Me." Around and around the yarn went. "Forgive an old busybody for her selfish fantasies." She studied him then, without blame, without recrimination. "You wish to go home."

He couldn't lie. Not while she watched him so intently. "Yes."

Her head dipped in a nod.

"I belong there," he insisted, wondering why the words did not comfort him as they should.

"I can see that." When he shifted uncomfortably in his chair, damning the gape of his shirt and the baggy pants, she hastened to reassure him. "I don't mean your . . . *avant-garde* attire or that delightfully long, flowing hairstyle—just as my husband wore it at one time, it is." She shook her head. "No, it's more of a bearing. An attitude."

He lifted a brow in silent query.

"When I look at you, I see strength. Pride. Plus a healthy measure of arrogance." Her voice grew husky. "For years, I have lived with the horror of your father's fate—and yours, when that sailor told me of your existence. I worried you would be emotionally beaten, your spirit broken. But now I see that wasn't the case. I hope that my son—your father—enjoyed much the same fruits of success. That his bearing remained as impressive as yours?" Her words lilted to a hopeful question.

Sullivan envisioned the broken, slump-shouldered man of his childhood. "Yes."

Biddy considered her wool for the longest time. "I'll see to the arrangements of sending you back to Isla Santiago. I won't trouble you now that I know you're happy." She pressed her lips together, her fingers stumbling. "If you would be so kind as to send me a note now or then. Just so I know how you're doing."

He nodded, and she added the last bit of yarn onto the ball. "There now. Thank you for your help."

Sullivan stood, sensing Beatrice wished to be alone with her memories. He was about to step into the foyer when she called, "Richard?"

"Yes?"

"How did he die?"

Sullivan studied her for some time, seeing the age-riddled features, the pain, the kindness, the love.

"In his sleep," he lied huskily.

"Did he . . . did he say anything . . . before?"

A tense quiet beaded the air. "He whispered your name," Sullivan said, unable to tell this kind old woman the truth.

That her son, Richard Albert Sutherland III, had not died blessing those he loved . . .

But cursing his enemies.

Gregory Cane tapped the flanks of his mount, easing it more firmly into the shadows of the trees surrounding Lindon Manor. This was not the first time he had returned to watch the house. He tried to tell himself that he was merely waiting for some sign of his brother. But it was difficult believing such a lie.

Day after day, hour after hour, he'd studied those pink marble walls, the grand columns, the graceful arcs and pillars and windows. He should have grown immune to the sight. But his stomach continued to knot, his hands to clench. It was for *this* his parents had been killed. His wife. Lydia.

An unseen hand clamped around his throat, and he fought to swallow, but the action only seemed to force the tightness deep into his chest. When Nigel Sutherland emerged and mounted the horse waiting at the block, Gregory's eyes grew bleak and stormy.

You will pay, old man, he promised himself and whatever spirits might be near enough to hear his whispered curse.

A hot, muggy wind gusted over the bleak promontory, tugging at Chelsea's skirts, seeming to beckon her closer and closer to the jagged outcropping and the bird's-eye view of Lindon Manor. The keening sigh of the breeze had an almost human quality. Sighing, gasping, pleading. Whispered voices seemed to echo in her ears, beckoning her to abandon her tenuous facade of control and surrender to the forces of the past.

She resisted the invisible entreaty, enduring it stoically, much as she had endured the interminable stretch of years spent in a job she had always hated in order to escape a monster she had grown to fear.

Nigel Sutherland.

No man should have the power to change a life so quickly.

No man should have the power to take an innocent young girl, mold her for his own pleasure, then teach her the true meaning of horror.

Their relationship had begun innocently enough—at least, it had seemed so to Chelsea at the time. If she were to close her eyes, she could see everything that had happened the first day she'd met the seventh Earl of Lindon. Each second had become emblazoned upon her memory, engraved so clearly she would never forget. She saw the barren ocher-covered grass, the ebony earth, the jagged tumble of boulders. Far in the distance, she could hear the lash of the surf and, nearer, the drone of the vicar. She'd shed no tears as they'd laid her father in the cold, unforgiven ground, but she'd ached. Ached for the man he might have been, the life they might have had.

Paddy O'Rourke had been a cruel taskmaster. Hard as flint and crusty as an old seaman, he'd had little time for a gawky young girl filled with more energy than her growing body could contain. From the first, he'd thought she'd been possessed of the devil—or, worse yet, had inherited her dearly departed mother's tendencies to dream.

In many ways, his death had been a release for Chelsea, ceasing once and for all the cruel lash of his tongue and his harsh code of behavior. However, she couldn't help thinking she was to blame for his passing somehow because she'd wanted to be free to follow her own will. She'd envisioned a thousand times what she would do once she left Paddy O'Rourke and Ireland behind.

But in all of her fantasies, she had never imagined that her father would die. She wasn't ready to be on her own. She was only a girl of thirteen. Terrified of what the future would bring, she'd shivered against the cruel bite of the sea breeze and swallowed back her alarm. What would she do? She had no family. No friends. Her home and all its furnishings would be sold to pay Paddy's debts, and she would be left without a farthing—she had no family to rely on. No real friends who could help her.

Staring into that hole, she'd felt a pang of frustration, then a wave of anger. Furious at the hand life had dealt her and the injustices of fate, she'd lifted her head, glaring at the sparse gathering of acquaintances, then looking up, up, up.

There he'd been, on the top of the hill. Mounted on an ink-black steed, Nigel, Lord Sutherland, had cut an impressive figure against the cobalt-blue sky. He'd sat so still, but somehow she'd sensed that he had been watching her for some time, noting the flash of emotions crossing her face. The anger, the frustration, the yearnings. She'd seen him before in town. In fact, she'd thought he might have followed her a time or two. So much so, she was sure that he knew where she lived.

She'd been so young, so innocent, so stupid. Returning from the graveside services, she'd opened the door to her father's cottage, a house that would soon be sold beneath her, and she'd wanted more.

"I took you away from all that, Gelsey."

The voice melted not from the past but from a point just behind her. Real. Chilling. Chelsea froze, sure that she had imagined the words, the subtle, silken tone, the proper Oxfordian accent.

No. No. No.

A shadow washed over her body, and she sensed his presence like the weight of doom settling over her wool-clad figure.

"My sweet, sweet child, why do you seem so surprised? I could always read you. I knew every thought that crossed your mind, every dream before you dared to dream it."

A warm, masculine hand curved over her shoulder, and Chelsea fought the immediate wave of revulsion that tumbled through her veins. Prickles of ice needled her skin, and the years melted away as if they'd never been. All the education, polish, and poise withered into cold ashes that fell to her feet, leaving her a naive, trembling adolescent girl afraid of what the future might bring.

She remembered how she'd foolishly allowed him to take her home from the funeral. She'd listened as he told her about the business that had brought him to Ireland. Impressed by his title and his responsibilities, she'd offered him a cup of tea and asked him to sit and stay for a while.

After that, she was never able to escape him completely.

"Gelsey, Gelsey," he crooned, the words little more than a whisper.

"Lord Sutherland." The acknowledgment was a bare whisper of sound, but he heard her, she knew he did. She could feel him edging closer, could feel the greedy sweep of his gaze.

He made a *tsking* sound and tightened his hold, not cruelly, not yet, but allowing no refusal to his command. "Come now. There's no need for formalities. Not between *us.*" Exerting a subtle pressure, he forced her to turn, forced her to acknowledge the one face she had hoped to avoid seeing in a London crowd or a seaside retreat.

He was still handsome. Tall, lean, incredibly fit. Well into his fifties, his hair had grown grayer, and lines creased his face. But those qualities only seemed to enhance his latent sensuality. Chelsea had seen females cross the street just to brush elbows with him as he passed. She had witnessed staid, proper gentlewomen fawn upon him at social gatherings. Ladies of the highest moral caliber had been known to proposition him. Yet Chelsea knew that in the past thirty years, there had been only two women who had ever truly tempted him. His wife, Estella . . . and a thirteen-year-old-girl.

His keen eyes slipped from the top of her head to the smooth sweep of her hair, her mouth, her chin. Then his scrutiny dropped with a slow, unnerving thoroughness. By the time he reached the tips of her shoes, Chelsea felt as if he had stripped her bare, leaving her naked and shivering, while behind her a young idealistic artist sought to capture the moment on canvas.

"I still have the painting," Nigel murmured.

Chelsea didn't comment upon how easily he'd read her mind. It was a phenomenon that had occurred too many times for her to be startled by it now.

"How did you know where to find me?"

"I'll always find you. Just as I'll always care."

His broad shape crowded her, cutting off her supply of air. "My sweet little Gelsey." He wrapped one arm around her waist and dipped his head to nuzzle her ear. "Why have you stayed away for so very long?"

Chelsea gripped his waist to push him away, then found she couldn't. Trapped in a vortex of time, she struggled to thrust back the shadow of a shivering, intimidated young girl. Her lashes squeezed closed, and she was swamped with the smells she had fought so hard to forget, cigar smoke and Tammany cologne.

Just as it had so long ago, his overwhelming personality sucked her back into a whirlpool of indecision and pain. In a flashing series of time-fuzzed pictures, she saw the first day she'd stepped from Lord Sutherland's conveyance onto the carriage block of Lindon Manor. She saw the bedchamber with its white damask counterpanes and cherub-painted ceilings. She saw the ballroom where the dance master had showed her how to waltz. The back lawn where the fencing master had taught her to fight.

The master bedroom, where a courtesan had instructed her in the art of seducing a man.

A scalding tear seeped from her lashes and bled down her cheek. "No," she groaned. Then more strongly, "No!" Wrenching free, she strode past Nigel, then whirled to confront him. "I won't let you do this to me again. I won't!"

Far from being upset, Nigel merely smiled at her reaction, as if he'd anticipated each syllable she'd uttered.

"You disgust me, do you understand that?" she continued. "I was only thirteen years old!"

"Age has little bearing on what occurs between a man and a woman."

"I wasn't a *woman*. I was only a child."

"I respected that fact, if you'll remember."

She snorted in disgust.

"I gave you a home."

"You made it a prison."

"I supplied you with rich foods and beautiful clothes."

"You tried to buy my affection."

He advanced. "I hired the finest of instructors, who showed you how to speak like a lady and think like a scholar."

Her chin lifted to a proud angle. Her eyes shimmered with unshed tears. "And act like a whore."

His lips lifted in a slow, self-satisfied smile. "Come now, my dear. Of all the things I'd expected to happen over the past few years, I never thought you would become a prude."

Memories she'd shoved deeply into her mind strained to be free. "You had no right."

"I had every right. I saved you from a life of poverty and despair. If I hadn't come along, you would have sold your body on the streets."

"I suppose you think it was better for me to have bartered it with *you?*"

"You never wanted for anything. You had only to think of something and it appeared. I treated you like a princess. I gave you all I had to give—including my affection. But I never tasted the fruits of my labors," he reminded her, stalking closer. "If you will remember, I went to great trouble and expense to have you trained. I saw to it that you were quite well versed in the arts of seduction, that you knew how to please a man and take pleasure yourself. Then you disappeared."

Chelsea had the sudden urge to strike him, to wipe the complacency from his face and mete out a measure of the pain he'd inflicted so long ago.

"I never wanted that kind of life. You lied to me when you said you wanted only to be my guardian, my friend."

He shrugged. "You would not have come with me otherwise." When she continued to step away from him, he stopped. "But you will come back to me, my dear. Of your own free will. Soon."

"Never."

"Ahhh, you think not." His voice became silky, dangerous. "Then consider this." Pursing his lips, he thought for a moment and said, "I am quite aware of the man you've attempted to hide in Biddy's little cottage and exactly what you intend to do with him."

A brittle expectancy settled over Chelsea. She hadn't expected Richard's arrival to remain a secret. The night she'd found the rose, she'd known his whereabouts had already been compromised. But she had thought—hoped—that Nigel would not dare to touch him. Not when Chelsea knew so much about him, not when she could reveal so many of his secrets. At present, she wasn't so sure. Nigel's eyes held a fierce sheen of determination, one she had seen before and come to avoid.

He noted the dawning comprehension registered on her face. "Yes, my dear, I know all about your endeavors to bring the true Sutherland heir back to England. I know how you have pampered him, coddled him, and bullied him into submitting to your plans. But I'm sure you must understand my position when I state that I will not allow you to continue with such an escapade. I will not let you disturb my well-ordered life with that impostor."

He sniffed and peered up at the wisps of clouds as if in thought, but Chelsea knew he was merely relishing his power over her. She shivered at the velvety shards of malice embedded in his tone.

"I sense that you and the mysterious Sutherland heir have developed a . . . *tendre,* if you'll pardon my turn of the phrase." His voice dropped, becoming harsh. "You really should be more careful to draw the draperies when you . . . entertain your students in Biddy's studio."

Chelsea experienced a stab of unease, a shudder of fright, wondering if he knew the extent of their embraces, if he had peered into the nursery windows as well. But Nigel continued before she could manage to think clearly.

"Get rid of him, Gelsey," Nigel warned. "Get rid of him now. Send him back to his horrid little island, and hide him as far away from me as you possibly can." His threats became chilling, deadly. "For if you don't, I shall have to take matters into my own hands. Just as I did with that ill-fated artist so long ago."

After issuing that final parting remark, Nigel leaned down to kiss her, softly, gently, briefly, as if to whet his appetite for things to come. Then, after touching her cheek, he crossed to his mount, swinging into the saddle. Throwing her a mock salute, he tapped the animal's flanks and cantered away, leaving a shattering silence.

Chelsea stared at the spot where he'd been and tried to dam the rising terror. She wiped the taste of him from her lips in disgust. Her chin crumpled. What was she going to do? Dear sweet heaven, what was she going to do?

Whirling, she hurried across the moors, not really seeing where she went, not really caring. Nigel's threats lingered in the air like the acrid scent of lime and decay. Alarm tainted her tongue. She had no doubts that he would see each horrible promise through. Nigel had always been fanatically possessive. He wouldn't take kindly to the thought of another man reaping the rewards of his careful tutelage. Just as he hadn't taken kindly to the discovery that Chelsea had once, regrettably, allowed herself to care for another man.

Jaime. Jaime. The name alone brought a swirling vision of that ill-fated artist to the fore. Tall, thin, eccentric. How he'd flattered and teased her. From the moment he'd breezed into Lindon Manor, her life had never been the same. She'd been enthralled by his devilish smile and quick wit.

Nigel had commissioned Jaime MacDonough to paint her portrait one fall. It was to have been a present, proof of rite of passage into womanhood upon her sixteenth birthday. Lord Sutherland had interviewed a dozen men, finally selecting a Scottish gentleman whose talent he considered bordered upon genius at recreating on canvas what was found in life. Returning to London to take care of sudden business, he had eagerly awaited the outcome of his newest venture. But what Lord Sutherland hadn't bargained on was that in the intervening weeks, she and Jaime would become friends.

From the first, Jaime had intrigued her. He'd taught her to smile again, to laugh. After three years of being told what to do and how to do it, Jaime was the first person who asked her what *she* wanted from life.

The answer had been so simple back then. She'd wanted to be loved.

Jaime had loved her. For three weeks, they'd been inseparable. Nigel had left her with a host of chaperones, but under the guise of making preliminary sketches, Jaime had followed her through the routine of her days. They'd talked and laughed, eventually kissed and embraced.

Chelsea had been reluctant to let him touch her at first. She hadn't wanted to see his ardor die when he discovered how comprehensive her education had been. But from the very beginning, Jaime had swept away her misgivings, assuring her that he found her unusual talents to be delightful. He'd even painted her that way, upon the bed, draped only in a sheet. It was to have been a private gift. Another more respectable portrait was to have been made for Nigel.

She shouldn't have agreed to pose in such a compromising position. Chelsea had known from the very beginning that it was foolish to agree to such a dangerous plan. Slipping secretly into his room each night, she'd known that one careless mistake could reveal her betrayal.

She'd been so young. She'd wanted to do something for Jaime—something no one else had ever done. She'd wanted to arouse him and entice him. She'd hoped to shake Jaime's last foothold of gentlemanly reserve so that he would worship her not just with his heart and soul . . . but with his body as well.

She'd known Nigel would be furious if he ever discovered the extent of their burgeoning relationship. Still, she hadn't demurred from posing so intimately in front of the man she'd adored. She'd been so sure that his love would conquer all. When the right time presented itself, she and Jaime would run away together—hadn't they said that very thing to themselves often enough? No one could shatter their hopes and dreams.

Chelsea shivered, hugging her arms even tighter to her torso. No one but Nigel.

Years later, she still couldn't block the phantom screams from her memory. The unearthly animalistic cries of the one man who had dared to accept her heart and had paid dearly.

The cries had awakened her from the dead of night.

Chilled to the bone, she'd swept aside the covers and run down the pink marble halls. She'd barely felt the cold stone against her bare feet as she flung open the door to find a horror like none she could ever have imagined.

Nigel stood facing the newly finished painting. A knife glinted in one hand, something dripping from its tip. Dripping.

At her soft cry, he'd turned, his face harshly illuminated by the pale moonlight streaming through the windows. "So nice of you to join us, my sweet," he murmured. "It seems the painting is finished."

He walked toward her, his movements slow and calculated, like a cat creeping up on a sparrow. "Judging by the . . . unusual pose, I can see that the two of you have been hard at work. Although it's not exactly what I asked for, I'm pleased with the results. Quite pleased."

He cupped her cheek, and she recoiled from a sticky wetness that clung to his skin. The faint, sickly odor of blood assaulted her nostrils, and she started, her back pressing against the jamb in her haste to escape, searching the obsidian and gray shadows for the artist in question.

She finally found his figure lying unconscious amidst a tangle of crimson-streaked sheets. Vaguely, she absorbed the hulking shapes of Nigel's men lurking near the bedstead, saw the way they hovered like death's angels, their expressions grim.

"Shh, shh," Nigel soothed when she gulped in horror and ground her fist against her mouth to press back the rising nausea. "Don't fret. Hush. I've taken care of things once and for all."

She managed to choke out, "You killed him."

Nigel regarded her in much the same way a parent might have if forced to explain a difficult fact to a disobedient child. "Nonsense. I haven't killed him. I merely took the proper precautions necessary to protect you from his advances."

Blood. So much blood.

"What—"

"Gelded, my dear. He won't be bothering you again."

Ten years later, Chelsea still couldn't forget the overwhelming guilt, the self-recrimination. That night, she'd realized how well and truly caught she was in Nigel Sutherland's web. By keeping Jaime alive, he'd trapped her so securely there could be no escape. She couldn't abandon Jaime. Not like this. She kept telling herself that once he was well again, they would find a way to leave. Together. Somehow.

That day had never come. Three weeks later, in a fit of delirium, Jaime MacDonough committed suicide. His only crime had been to love her. For that, Chelsea had consigned him to death as surely as if she had held the pistol to his head and pulled the trigger.

Chelsea's chest ached unbearably, a stinging pricked at the back of her eyes, but she refused to give in to it, refused to cry for a man who had been dead for over a decade. A man who had teased her. A man who had cherished her. A man who had taught her that fear had no place in a woman's heart when she rested safely in a man's arms.

Safe.

How long had it been since she'd experienced such an emotion?

Cherished.

How long had it been?

Last night.

Chelsea hesitated on the edge of the promontory, gazing down upon the rolling hills of the Lindon estates. Beneath the gloom of the approaching storm clouds sat the elegant pink marble manor house. So beautiful, so innocent, so fairy-tale perfect. Who would have guessed that in its walls were trapped such untold secrets and violent emotions?

An icy foreboding settled into her bones. Not because Nigel Sutherland rested so near. Or because the house reminded her of all she'd tried so hard to forget.

No, the feeling that doused her in panic was a result of realizing that once again, she'd tasted those same emotions she'd once shared with Jaime: safety, love, and more. So much more. Never had she craved a man's company so completely. Never had she experienced such a passion, an all-consuming adoration—one that made her adolescent infatuation with Jaime MacDonough pale in comparison. One that seemed suspiciously like love.

Richard.

When had she begun to care for him so much? When had each breath she'd taken centered upon his well-being?

Her heart began to thud in her breast, jarring against the restraint of her ribs. A terror for this man's safety rushed through her muscles like a numbing drug. She was caught in a snare with no way to escape.

Nigel Sutherland already wanted the man dead. If he ever were to discover the leanings of Chelsea's heart, he would stop at nothing to arrange such a state. Once and for all.

Jaime MacDonough's cries seemed to howl in the wind. The picture of his body, broken and bloody, swam into her mind.

Crying out, Chelsea rushed away from the promontory, nausea churning in her stomach. Once again, Nigel had taught her an invaluable lesson. But this time, this time, she would have to find a way to thwart his efforts. She would remove Richard Sutherland from his grasp.

Now. Tonight.

Even if she had to trade her soul with the devil to do it.

Chapter
17

Sullivan Cane stepped into the nursery to discover a package had been left on his bed. Thinking it was yet another gift from his grandmother, he unwrapped the simple brown paper. What he found inside, however, caused him to sigh in pleasure.

Clothes.

He tore the rest of the paper away like a stripling lad opening his presents Christmas Day. He soon discovered a jacket, three lawn shirts, two pairs of breeches, a vest, stockings, dressing gown, and undergarments. All crafted of the finest wools and cottons, all obviously well tailored and artfully made.

By the foot of his bed, he found another box. Upon lifting the lid, he uncovered a pair of riding boots, a soft pair of kid dress shoes, and a fur-lined set of slippers.

Sullivan handled them greedily, not knowing until that instant how much he had missed having a proper wardrobe. A loincloth and oversized shirt might be appropriate for the island surf; but here in Scotland, the brief attire did not suit the climate. Not to mention that the garb of a savage tended to make a man forget his own code of values—as if by shedding the outer veneer of civilization, one let a bit of the heathen creep into one's soul.

Sullivan realized such had been the case with him. He had hardened his heart and concerned himself with only the needs of his immediate family. It was time to extend those lines. His sojourn in the English Isles might be short, but ties had been formed. Ties that linked him as strongly to these people as those that bound him to his brothers.

The familiar *tap-slide, tap-slide* of his grandmother making her way down the hall caught his attention. Taking one of the shirts, Sullivan stepped to the doorway and leaned his shoulder against the jamb.

"The clothes are beautiful, thank you."

"Clothes?"

"Yes, the things you left on my bed."

She limped closer to peer around him. "Ooh, such lovely things. Who brought them?"

"You mean you didn't—"

"No."

"Then who?"

She shrugged. "Perhaps Chelsea found an extra penny or two in the household budget."

If there was one thing Sullivan had learned while playing the barbarian, it was that there was no excess money in this particular household. Even the food placed on the table came from the garden first, and through a trade of items and services second. The articles on his bed were of too fine a quality to have been exchanged for Smee's expertise as a blacksmith or for a pint of Greyson's aspic.

Ignoring the bell pull, Sullivan marched to the head of the staircase. "Smee! Greyson!"

In a half-dozen ticks of the clock, two heads peered around the landing.

"You called, sir," Greyson droned, not so much as a raised eyebrow betraying the fact that he had never heard the master of the house speak before.

"Come up here, please. Both of you."

Greyson and Smee exchanged glances but complied nonetheless. The butler was the first to take the stairs, moving slowly, calmly, and with infinite dignity. Behind him, the portly hostler darted from one side of the treads to the other as if wishing to pass his companion but daunted by the results should he succeed.

"This way."

Sullivan led them into the nursery and gestured to the clothing that spilled over the worn counterpane of his bed. "Explain, please."

The clock ticked in a rusty, wheezing manner.

After some time had passed, Greyson responded dryly, "I believe they are clothes, sir."

"I know that, Greyson. I would like you to be a little more specific, however."

"Woolen frock coat, silk vest, three shirts, one each of cambric, lawn, and—"

"The specifics I require are not about the garments themselves, Greyson, but how they came to be here."

"Oh. I see."

He darted a guilty look at Smee. Smee pursed his lips and scuffed at the rug with the toe of his shoe.

"I couldn't say, sir," Greyson finally said.

"Couldn't or shouldn't?"

"A . . . little of both, sir."

Sullivan studied the duo, sensing that there was more than the mystery of the new garments abubble here. Turning to the older woman, he bent to kiss her cheek lightly. "Grandmama, I do believe you seem a bit tired. Don't let me keep you from your nap."

Beatrice Sutherland touched the spot where he'd bussed her. So delighted was she by the unexpected caress and the title of *Grandmama,* she didn't refuse but limped into the hall and disappeared into her room.

"If there's nothing further you require, Master Richard . . ."

Before Greyson or his companion could take another step, Sullivan closed the door, shutting them all in the nursery.

"There are many things I still require," Sullivan interrupted smoothly, a determined expression hardening his jaw. "The first of such is a few answers."

"I don't know what you mean, sir."

"I think you do. If my suspicions are correct, I also think that you know a good deal more about Nigel Sutherland and his endeavors than you have heretofore been willing to admit."

Rupert eyed his brother across the room and tamped down the worry that had been dogging him for some time. Gregory had returned from his reconnaissance several days earlier, and Rupert hadn't needed the "sight" to know he'd been to Lindon Manor. Since then, he'd grown even more gloomy and morose than he'd been before—and that was a remarkable description of his present black mood, since he hadn't been fit company in more than a year.

Rupert sympathized with him, he really did. Nigel Sutherland had been responsible for Lydia's death. He had sent the bloodhounds who had tracked the Sutherland brothers to the coast of Brazil. The trackers, thinking they had finally cornered Richard Sutherland IV and the natives who cared for him, had torched the hut where Gregory and Lydia and two of the family servants had been hiding. The dried grasses and palm fronds thatching the roof had ignited with stunning speed, collapsing before all of its occupants had escaped into the darkness. Rupert could still hear the screaming . . . the screaming . . .

Gregory had never been the same since. His brief sojourn at Lindon Manor had only served to intensify his grief. Rupert had tried every trick he knew to bank the bleak light that doused what little joy remained in Greg's eyes, all to no avail.

"Gregory?" His brother, who was staring out the window, didn't even blink. "Gregory!"

Gregory, muscular, overwhelming, brooding Gregory, finally glanced his way.

"I've got to go out for a bit. You'll see to Richard, won't you? After his walk, I persuaded him to rest for an hour."

A simple nod was the only answer he received. Knowing he must do something soon, Rupert decided the time had come to find Sullivan. Nigel Sutherland had to be stopped before Gregory's spirit became his latest victim. He only prayed he could find Sully without drawing attention to the fact that Nigel thought he had only one heir to contend with.

When, in fact, there were four.

Chelsea ran back to Bellemoore as if the hounds of hell snapped at her heels. She sprinted as fast as she could go, holding her skirts above her knees and scrabbling down the uneven path. She was driven by the sights and sounds of past horrors as well as visions of future repercussions.

"Smee! Greyson!" Bursting into the house, she rushed from empty room to empty room, searching for signs of Richard. But the echoing halls were her only answers.

Dodging back out of doors, she hurried down to the stables, where she found Smee, dressed in his apron, throwing grain to a pair of chickens—the only animals other than the horses that still existed on the grounds of the cottage.

"Smee, where's Master Richard?"

His features wrinkled in obvious dismay. "Well, I—"

"Where?" she asked, seeing a flush steal into his cheeks.

"He left."

"Left? Where did he go?"

"I don't know, miss." Smee wiped his hands on the front of his apron. "We tried to stop him, we did—Greyson and I. But he wouldn't be stopped."

"What—"

"We managed to provide him with some proper clothes. He appeared most grateful—even had Greyson help him with one of the cravats. But when he couldn't find you anywhere about, miss, he took one of the mounts from the stables. Before we knew what he meant to do, he was galloping down the lane like the banshees were after him. Greyson followed him, he did."

"Which way?"

Smee pointed toward the direction of Lindon Manor. "That way," he admitted hollowly.

A sick swirl of fear roiled in her chest. Surely he hadn't gone to confront Nigel. *No. Please, no.*

She ran down the path, scouring the horizon. But she saw no sign of a lean, heathenish form. Except for the churned trail of the earth, she would not have known that he had been there at all.

Richard Sutherland sat easily upon his gelding, unconsciously adopting the posture of a man who had ridden all his life and had been trained by an expert horseman.

Greyson awarded the younger man his grudging approval. Although he didn't condone Master Sutherland's unorthodox methods of introduction to the family, he couldn't fault him, either. To bide his time and gather information, all the time playing the savage, why, it was something . . . something the Avengers would have done.

"This is as close as I dare let you ride, sir," Greyson advised, bringing his own animal to a halt. They were shielded in a heavy thicket of trees. Only a few hundred yards away lay Lindon Manor.

Greyson never ceased to feel a sharp twinge of regret each time he traversed this road. He had served with the Sutherland family for years—nigh on to fifty, if the truth were known. He remembered the good times, when laughter and love had echoed from this house.

"Sutherland lives here, then."

"Only during the summer months, sir. There was a time, a few years back, when he frequented the manor house more regularly," Greyson hesitantly admitted. "But that has not been the case in more than a decade."

"Why is that?"

Sullivan saw the way the butler chose his words carefully, then responded. "He had a ward, sir. A young lady. He visited her off and on throughout the year to check on the progress of her . . . tutors." The old man's words resounded with hidden meaning, but Sullivan sensed he would refuse to explain himself further.

Sullivan experienced a twinge of unease, having known Greyson to be so protective of only two people: Biddy and

Chelsea. But he pushed his disquiet away, determined to keep to the matter at hand. "How many people reside there now?"

"Normally, just the staff—the assorted footmen, housemaids, and estate servants. Nigel Sutherland, his wife, Estella, his son, Cecil, rarely visit anymore. However, each June, Lord Sutherland entertains. This year, he brought only his wife, secretary, and personal servants."

"How many guests are in attendance, Greyson?"

"Upwards of a dozen. The present Earl of Lindon prides himself on being very discriminating."

"They all stay at the manor?"

"Yes, sir."

"For how long?"

"Another few days. A masquerade will be held tomorrow evening in honor of the summer solstice."

"A masquerade . . ."

"Yes, sir."

Sullivan felt a stir of an idea, a spurt of satisfaction. "Tell, me Greyson. Are there other servants who still reside at Lindon Manor who worked with you thirty years ago?"

"Yes, sir."

"How many?"

"Quite a few, sir."

"Are they loyal to Beatrice?"

"Yes, indeed, sir."

A smile tipped his lips. "Good, good. See if you can't round them up for me, Greyson. I'll need to see them as soon as possible. Tonight, if feasible. But later. Midnight. I don't want their positions put in jeopardy."

"Very good, sir."

Sullivan's grin widened even more. "Tell me, Greyson. How came you to be so knowledgeable on these matters, hmm?"

For once, he thought he saw a flash of discomfiture flit across the butler's face. "Why, I'm sure it's common knowledge, sir."

"I wonder," Sullivan drawled mischievously. "Of course,

when one is an Avenger, one is also privy to all sorts of information, isn't one?"

He chuckled aloud when the butler's jaw dropped open, literally dropped, and he gaped at Sullivan like a fish out of water. "You see," Sullivan murmured, leaning close, "not only can I speak, but I can read as well. There seems to be a good deal of newsprint stacked on the breakfront. Old issues of the *Addlebury Post*. A common thread of subjects seems to be folded to appear on top. A pair of dastardly brigands tormenting the female population of the countryside. The two men, one tall and thin, the other short and round, bear a remarkable resemblance to you and Smee."

Finally regaining his voice, Greyson sat poker-straight in the saddle, assuming an air of wounded dignity. "I don't know what you mean."

"Never fear, Greyson, your secret is safe with me." Sullivan dropped the teasing facade, adding, "We may have need of your talents sometime soon. Meanwhile, I think it's time I paid a call to Lindon Manor."

"Oh, but you can't! Nigel, Lord Suth—"

"Never fear, Greyson. It's not the master of the house I intend to visit. But the mistress."

Greyson stared at him, long and hard, evidently testing his will. His jaw remained stiff, square. But then, to Sullivan's infinite amazement, a flicker of some warmer, gleeful emotion appeared in the old man.

"You mean to help her, don't you, sir?"

Sullivan didn't know which "her" he spoke of and thought it better to remain silent.

Greyson didn't seem to need any more confirmation of his thoughts. He merely looped the reins around his palms and stated firmly, "I'll wait for you here, sir. The shade beneath these trees is quite refreshing. I shall be quite comfortable provided you do not remain too long."

"Aye, aye, Greyson."

As Sullivan rode to Lindon Manor, he realized Greyson had extended his protectiveness to include one more person besides Biddy and Chelsea. In all honesty, he couldn't account for the warmth that settled around his heart like a sea of melted butter.

Nigel Sutherland brought his horse to a stop next to the steps leading up to Lindon Manor. A hostler scurried forth to take the reins as Lord Sutherland came forward, nodding companionably to the people milling about the veranda and the front lawns.

As always, Estella had seen to it that his guests were entertained. Originally, a croquet tournament had been planned for the afternoon. Because of the inclement weather, his wife had organized an impromptu musicale. Even now, the strains of the pianoforte could be heard spilling through the halls, accompanied by the warblings of a tenor imported all the way from Rome for the occasion.

Nigel grinned at a particularly high note. Pity that Mac-Donough fellow had shot himself. Otherwise they wouldn't have had to inquire on the continent for a man able to hit a high C.

Chuckling, Nigel flicked a spot of dust from his jacket and joined Lord and Lady Selby near the back of the room. He had only just offered his hellos when his secretary appeared.

"Lord Sutherland."

"Yes, Wilde." Damned if Reginald wasn't slinking about again.

"There are some papers to be signed. I put them in your office."

"Not now, Wilde, I've got things—"

"I really feel you should take care of them. Immediately." With an almost imperceptible shake of his head, Wilde cautioned Nigel against protesting once more.

"Very well. If you'll excuse me," he offered to his guests.

He followed Wilde to the opposite wing of the house, closing the door behind them. "What's so blasted important it couldn't wait until later? I told you those reports—"

"It's not the reports, sir." Wilde stepped to the window and motioned for Lord Sutherland to follow.

"Damned cloak-and-dagger theatrics," Nigel muttered. "What in bloody hell . . ."

Then he saw her. Estella. She sat in the cool shadows of the arbor. Despite the gusting wind and hazy day, she had braved the miserable weather and now sat alone—

No. Not alone.

"Who is it?" His eyes clung to the lean masculine frame and powerful physique. Estella's petite stature only served to emphasize his height, the width of his chest, the slender hips and powerful legs. Such an impressive figure would have seemed quite at home in blacksmith leathers or farmer homespun, but his form was sheathed to perfection in the well-tailored habit of a gentleman. Shiny black boots coated muscular calves. A set of faun-colored riding breeches clung to powerful thighs. His shirt had been fashioned of the finest lawn, the cravat tied in a simple yet elegant three-corner knot and his shoulders covered in a dun-colored jacket.

"I don't believe he's one of your guests."

Nigel had always been a jealous man, a possessive man. Even though Estella and the stranger were separated by a good three feet, he felt a pang of fury. Spinning on his heel, he marched back into the hall, intent upon confronting his wife before the brigand could get away.

"Hello, Estella."

Estella Sutherland started at the low, whiskey-toned voice. She had come to the garden for privacy. She'd always hated entertaining on such an extravagant level. She detested the noise, the pressures, the constant upheaval. But Nigel insisted they cling to tradition, even when she begged him to allow them to have one summer free from such lavish ceremonies. Just one summer.

Now yet another guest had interrupted her solitude. Since her infrequent minutes alone were the only pleasures allowed Estella these days, she was highly irritated. But she was also a hostess, a genteel Englishwoman, Nigel's wife. Subduing her automatic frown, she summoned a hollow smile and turned.

The words she'd been about to say were trapped in her throat, unuttered. A choked cry escaped. That face. That form. The book she held in nerveless fingers slid from her lap onto the ground. The years rushed away, and she was immature, greedy, and so very, very foolish.

"Richard Albert?" she said, knowing even as she used the name that it couldn't be. Richard Albert was dead. Had died years ago. If he had survived through some miracle of heaven, he wouldn't be so young, so vital. So changed.

Clearing her throat, she snapped her head away, damning the flood of heat washing into her cheeks. With a single utterance, she'd betrayed herself. After nearly thirty years of guarding her secret, she had unwittingly revealed all.

"You look the same as he described you."

"I don't know what you mean."

"I only heard a few scattered stories about you—just before he died."

His last word wrenched her attention back again. "Died? When did he . . ."

"Three years ago."

"Then he survived. When the ship went down, he survived."

"Yes."

"And . . . Julie?"

"They lived together for nearly a decade before she passed away during childbirth."

Estella's already pale skin blanched even further. "I see."

"No. I don't think you do."

Her shoulders stiffened as if anticipating a blow.

"He never blamed you, Estella."

"I don't know what you're—"

"He knew everything—your subterfuge, your promises to Nigel, your knowledge of the conspiracy."

Estella burst from her seat and ran to the opposite side of the arbor.

"He also knew about Cecil."

She whirled to regard him with wide eyes. "What do you want from me?"

"Your help."

"My help? My help with what?"

"Justice."

* *

Nigel rushed from the house, but as soon as he stepped outside, he saw that the arbor was empty. His wife stood in the rose garden supervising the clipping of flowers for the evening's centerpieces.

"Estella."

She turned, offering the same dazzling smile she'd given him for thirty years. One that proclaimed that he was her sun and her whole world revolved around him. "Yes, my love."

"Who was that you spoke to in the pergola just now?"

She turned back to her roses with a woman's infinite unconcern. "A business acquaintance of Lord and Lady Wilmonton, I believe. Mr. Sullivan was his name—yes, I believe he said it was Sullivan. Although he did not extend the discourtesy of forcing his company upon our guests, I do think he meant to angle an invitation to our masquerade."

"Oh." Nigel squinted and peered down the lane. "He's staying in Addlebury, I suppose."

"Yes, dear."

"What kind of business did he say he was in?" Nigel asked, remembering that the man's form and the cut of his cloth were worthy of his interest. The stranger's bearing transmitted an aura of power. Power, wealth, and strength. An attractive combination for a man such as Nigel, who was always searching for an ally.

"I believe he said he was in some sort of foreign trade."

"Foreign trade. Hmmm. Perhaps he's an associate of the gentleman Reginald entertained." Nigel tucked his thumbs into his vest pockets. "Send a footman and extend an invitation to the masquerade ball, Estella. After all, we wouldn't want to slight the man unintentionally."

"Yes, dear. If that's what you wish."

Nigel returned to the house, leaving the gusting wind and the squabbling of sparrows fighting over a few stray bread crumbs near the kitchen as Estella's only distraction. Watching the door close behind her husband, Estella took one breath, then another, quicker still, trying to calm the acrid emotions burbling inside her.

She'd tried so hard to forget during the past thirty years.

All the things she'd done. The secrets she'd kept. But her sins had come full circle.

What was she going to do? She took a step, as if seeking an avenue of escape. Then halted, feeling trapped. She had fenced herself into an untenable situation. She had bargained with the devil and lost. Today, she was being offered a chance to redeem herself.

But she didn't think she had the courage to do it.

She had betrayed so many people.

Most of all, herself.

The wind gusted about her, carrying the musky odors of roses and rain. Droplets began to spatter the flagstones about her. The servants darted into the house to finish the centerpieces.

Estella paid no heed. She felt no discomfort. It wasn't until her hands grew moist and sticky that she realized she'd clutched the stems so fiercely, the thorns had pierced her skin and caused her to bleed.

Greyson was waiting in the trees when Sullivan returned. Sullivan couldn't have said why, but he found himself strangely comforted by the sight of the grave-faced butler.

"Have you finished your business, sir?"

"I've made a start."

"Any problems?"

Greyson was so patently nervous, yet trying so hard to disguise the fact, that Sullivan smiled. "If you mean in the form of Nigel Sutherland, I didn't see the man."

"Very *good*, sir."

Sullivan laughed, and the unexpected sound caused Greyson's mouth to twitch.

"Shall we adjourn to Bellemoore, Greyson?"

"Yes, my lord."

The two men trotted down the dappled lane, following the roots of the rolling emerald hills. A sprinkling of rain began, intensifying the smells of summer: grass and dust, storm clouds, and hot earth. Around them, the countryside basked in sleepy silence. The setting should have eased Sullivan's nerves. It had the necessary atmosphere for a holiday retreat.

But rather than feeling an ease of his tensions, Sullivan's muscles coiled as if in readiness for . . . what? Battle? Yes, surely. Self-protection? To some degree. Survival? Most definitely. It was more than that. He discovered that he was no longer so bent upon his own concerns. Yes, he would continue to protect his brothers—but his feelings had become even more concentrated, fierce, extending to others as well. Biddy, Chelsea, even Greyson and Smee. For the first time, he felt he knew the true emotional bonding to be found in the term *family*. Having grown up in a male-dominated world, Sullivan had learned about caring and protectiveness, to be sure. But now, those emotions were sharper, keener, perhaps even more powerful.

"My lord?"

The softly veiled warning came to him in a bare puff of sound.

Immediately on his guard, Sullivan glanced at Greyson first, then followed the man's attention to the top of the hill. A figure on horseback watched them. Juxtaposed against a stand of trees, he was a giant with huge shoulders and powerful legs. Even from a distance, it was evident that he was well armed: a pistol tucked into his waist, a knife sheathed at his side.

Sullivan shouted and prodded his horse into a gallop. Racing up the hill full-steam, he barely noted Greyson's cries of warning. "My lord! My lord, no! We can make a run for Bellemoore!"

Pulling on the reins, Sullivan brought his mount to a skidding halt. He leapt from the saddle, charging at the figure who had done likewise.

From his vantage below, Greyson saw little more than two men, grappling together as if about to come to blows. Urging his gelding up the hill at a bone-jarring trot, he lifted his quirt, prepared to save his master. But it soon became apparent that Richard was far from inconvenienced. Indeed, he seemed joyful as he embraced the man and slapped him on the back.

Becoming aware of the servant's presence, Sullivan released his brother Rupert. As he met the butler's astounded countenance, he realized he probably should have been more subtle. Greyson was no fool. Without an explanation, he would eventually piece things together. Sullivan preferred to explain, but by doing so he would have to take a leap of faith. He would have to trust.

There were few people he'd known to whom he had extended the honor. Fewer still who had deserved it. But after all that had occurred, Sullivan experienced no qualms in what he was about to do.

"Greyson, you must swear that what you have seen today and what you are about to hear will go no farther."

"My lord?"

"Swear."

Greyson appraised the two men, dissimilar in build but sharing the same strong features and piercing integrity.

"Do you swear?"

Brothers. Without being told, Greyson knew what Master Richard would say. A secret glee tickled his insides, but the old man drew himself into a proud, impressive stance.

"Aye, my lord. Upon my honor and my own good name, I swear." When the gentle giant stepped forward for the introduction, Greyson's only thought was: *Won't Biddy be pleased?*

A drizzling storm began late in the afternoon. Alarmed, Chelsea paced the narrow width of the cottage's vestibule. Six steps north, six steps south. The slightest sound sent her rushing to the window in the hope that Richard had returned.

He never did. Greyson came back soon before teatime but offered no explanations of Richard's whereabouts. The light rain deepened into a downpour, eased, then stopped altogether, leaving a brilliant sunset, the smell of fresh-washed foliage, and the restless patter of stray raindrops falling from the rosebushes onto the ground below.

Of them all, only Biddy seemed unconcerned by her grandson's disappearance. She'd offered her a beaming smile. "Don't fret, child. He's a grown man. He can take care of himself."

As Smee and Greyson had escorted the old woman up to bed, Chelsea hadn't been able to summon a retort. Richard was grown, yes, but completely unprepared for the likes of Nigel. She doubted that he had ever encountered such chilling charm, such cloaked cruelty.

Chelsea's only comfort through the entire afternoon came when Biddy had informed her that Richard intended to leave for home as soon as possible. A relief so tangible she could taste it had flooded Chelsea the instant she heard the words. As soon as he returned, she wouldn't waste her time with inanities or demanding where he'd been. She'd simply bundle him into the coach, ride pell-mell for the coast, and put him on the first ship leaving the country. The plan was simple and therefore most likely to succeed.

So where had he gone? If he'd stumbled upon Nigel Sutherland, Chelsea was quite sure she would have heard about it by now. Nigel wouldn't have been able to resist tormenting her with his prize. She could only hope the ensuing silence meant Richard was safe.

But why didn't he return? What was so important to him that he'd spent the entire day away from the cottage? Was he merely surveying the lay of the land? Or had he found more latent entertainments? Was he holed up in some tavern imbibing a pint of grog and the ample charms of a willing woman? The thought sent a pang of jealousy through her heart, so surprising an emotion simply because she had never experienced it before. Not even with Jaime MacDonough.

The clatter of hooves caused her to rush outside. In the last yellow glow of sunset, she saw the shape of a horse and rider on the lane. Her heart pounded, her mouth went dry. She couldn't tell yet if Richard approached the house, or possibly Nigel.

Damning the consequences, she ran outside. The soles of her shoes scrabbled against the pea gravel. The hems of her skirts grew quickly damp, but she didn't give a thought to appearance or propriety.

She had reached the end of the path leading to the stables when the form turned into the drive. She stopped, stunned.

The man who rode toward her was a stranger, yet more familiar to her in many ways than her own reflection. He sat tall in the saddle, his spine straight, gripping the reins with a lax familiarity.

His hair had been combed back from his head and secured against the nape of his neck with a leather thong. Broad shoulders appeared wider still because of the expert tailoring of his jacket. The strength of his jaw was under-scored by his snowy-white cravat. His thighs were covered in a kid-soft fabric that clung to each swell of muscle in an incredibly enticing manner.

Chelsea's heart slowed to a heavy, determined beat. Her skin tingled as if feather-stroked. How she loved this man.

The thought struck her like a thunderbolt, but she couldn't deny it. That was why her fear for him was so overwhelming. Why she found herself willing to do any-thing, *anything,* to see him safe.

He stopped his mount a few yards away. Neither of them moved in the gloaming, a brittle quiet stretching between them. An expectancy. A sweet, silvered longing that spoke most eloquently in its very silence.

Chelsea tried to deny the passion storming through her. She tried to dampen the burst of excitement, the over-whelming relief, the stunned amazement. How could she have ever mistaken this man for a helpless savage? He wore the clothes of a gentleman with such ease, such strength, that had she seen him wearing them before, she never would have believed his ruse.

The memory of the way he'd played her false stung, like the quick prick of a bee. He'd lied to her. He'd led her on. He'd trifled with her emotions and belittled her feelings for him. But like the bee sting, the anger quickly died. Nigel had seen to that. By threatening Richard's safety, he had un-knowingly shuffled Chelsea's emotions into perspective. Her pique melted under a more powerful dose of protectiveness.

Looking at Richard now, it was hard to summon any anger. It was hard to summon anything but the need to close him in her arms to know for sure that he was safe. Her need became a powerful force, causing her to tremble. But she would have to be careful. She could not forget that her prime objective in the next few minutes would be to push him away. As much as she longed to be held, caressed, she could not allow the pleasures of the moment to endanger him for all time. She had the tools necessary in her arsenal to do such a thing: anger, cool disdain, an affected formality. She could only pray she had the strength to use them.

But as she stood there in the darkness, she didn't know what to say, what to do to force him to her will. She couldn't treat a person such as this as if he were a child. But she had been a governess so long, she had forgotten how to approach a man as an equal.

"Good evening, Lord Sutherland."

At her stilted greeting, he prodded his horse into a walk and closed the last few feet. Despite the weak light of the evening, Chelsea absorbed the sharp planes and hollows of his face, the sheen of his hair. His frame was so impressively arrayed that even though Chelsea had seen him in less—far less—there was something about having him clothed, so completely and utterly clothed, that caused a warming deep in her belly. She'd been loved by the heathen. Would it be so very different to be loved by the gentleman? To watch him disrobe, piece by piece?

Richard swung from the saddle and stood beside her. He studied her from head to toe. Yet, unlike Nigel's scrutiny, which had left her weak and unsure of herself, Richard's gaze left a trail of fire.

With each second that passed, she was reminded of how wildly she'd behaved in his arms the night before. She'd held nothing back. She'd kissed him, caressed him, spoken to him . . .

Spoken to him. A ruddy heat flooded her cheeks. She'd said things to this man that she never would have said had she known he could understand her. She'd uttered secret desires and wishes, private thoughts and fantasies.

Her courage fled as quickly as it had come. After what she'd done, said, how could she hope to think she could make him believe she no longer cared? No longer responded?

He must have seen her hesitate, because he caught her elbow, saying, "I think we should talk."

His voice was so low, so knowing, she cringed. She had never bared herself so completely in front of a man. Not just her body, but her heart and her soul.

"I don't have anything to say," she responded. He would never know how much her crisp tone cost her.

"Chelsea, don't. Don't deny what happened between us. Don't demean it. You want to yell at me, so yell. Call me names. Slap me again—whatever makes you feel better. But don't cut me off this way." He grew sober, his voice low and sincere. "I love you."

His words struck her to the core. *Love.* That reciprocal emotion she'd craved for so long. He was offering it to her on a silver platter. Her heart softened, then clenched in pain. He couldn't love her. To do so would spell his doom.

Chelsea watched him in tortured silence. He would never know how much she wanted to rush into his embrace, to feel his arms close around her tight and strong. But quickly upon the heels of such a thought came another, stronger memory of a man quietly bleeding to death from a bullet to the temple.

Jaime. Her ardor was doused by an icy terror. She had to get Richard away from here. She wouldn't see him hurt. She wouldn't see him die.

"No." The word surprised her because she'd spoken it aloud. Trying to release herself from his grasp, she added, "I've nothing to say to you." Her spine grew rigid, her voice cool, as she relied on years of experience to guide her back into a role with which she was no longer comfortable. "What happened was a mistake."

But Richard sensed her intentions immediately. "Damn it, don't shrink into that prim and proper cast-iron mold! We both know how poorly it fits you."

"Don't you dare patronize me!"

"Why not? From the moment we met, you've been patronizing me. You treated me like a little boy or a family pet. But when you let your guard down enough to be a real woman and I responded, you couldn't bear it."

"What I couldn't bear was your deceit!"

"A transgression I have already explained and for which I have apologized. The circumstances of my silence do not negate the passions and emotions involved when we loved each other last night."

Chelsea steeled herself to speak the very words she wanted to leave unuttered. "Love. What we shared wasn't love, it was a mating. An animalistic satisfying of urges."

The lie scalded as it passed. But it was the only thing she could say to kill the light kindling in his gaze and drive him away forever.

Richard dropped her hand as if it had grown red-hot. Without a word, he turned, leading the horse into the stone stable house at the side of the cottage.

Chelsea was left alone in the shadows. So cold. So miserable. The sharp echo of her words rebounded in her head. How consummate a liar she'd become. How petty. How mean. Yet, in order to protect him, she couldn't tell him the truth. She couldn't unravel her past transgressions and her present turmoil. She had to keep her own counsel. Remain quiet.

Just as once, in order to protect himself, he'd been forced to keep his silence.

Chelsea didn't know how long she stood there, how long the soughing wind moaned its mournful tune. She only knew that she had lost something. A precious diamond of hope for the future. All that remained was to garner the will to see things through. She might never defeat Nigel, she might never see justice served. But at least she could thwart his plans to kill the true Sutherland heir.

She bit her lip in hesitation, then followed him into the stables.

The mews were quiet, dark, warm. Richard had removed the horse's tack and had begun to curry the animal with a competent ease. Far from seeming ill suited to the chore, there was something about the calming sweep of his hands and the soft tones of his voice when he spoke to his mount that proclaimed him a man of education, of breeding, of experience.

Chelsea felt a softening, but she steeled herself against it. Horrifying visions kept springing to the fore. Not of Jaime but of Richard. Twisted, bleeding. Dead.

"Biddy said that you wish to return home," she said quickly, needing to get him out of England while she had the power to see him go. "I'll make the proper arrangements for you to leave this evening."

He didn't look up, betraying quite effectively that he'd been more than aware of her presence.

"I won't be returning to Isla Santiago so soon."

Her stomach clenched at his reply, but she managed to maintain her outward facade of calm. He couldn't stay. He had to leave now while she had Nigel conforming to at least a portion of her wishes.

After several minutes of silence, she asked, "When will you go?"

"After I've finished what I came here to do."

"But you were brought here by force! You couldn't possibly have had reasons of your own to—"

"Couldn't I?" His stare took on an unfamiliar glint, shining with an inexplicable hint of ruthlessness. He knew something, sensed something.

"Where have you been today, Richard?"

He patted the horse on the rump, secured it in its stall, then closed the gate. "Visiting family."

Chelsea couldn't even force a puff of sound from her tight throat. Finally, she managed a choked "Where?"

"Lindon Manor."

Chapter

18

*T*he color bled from Chelsea's skin. She grasped the post support to keep from falling. "No." The panicked word was barely audible.

Alarmed by the way she suddenly swayed on her feet, Sullivan reached out to steady her. To his infinite amazement, Chelsea dropped all pretense of cold formality. She hugged him close, clutching his shoulders.

"What did Nigel say? Did he hurt you? Did he tell you—"

"Chelsea!" Sullivan cut into her nervous babbling with a single word. He held her trembling form tightly to his own. "I didn't talk to Nigel. I merely went to his house." What he didn't tell her was that he had talked to Lady Sutherland, thereby sowing a seed he hoped would prove fruitful sometime in the near future.

But Chelsea was far from comforted by his words. "You've got to leave this place. Tonight."

"Why?"

"Don't ask questions, just do what I ask." Tearing free, she backed toward the stable door. An alarming chalky pallor kissed her cheeks.

"Go. Leave. There's nothing for you here. You said that yourself."

"I've changed my mind."

"Stop it! This isn't a child's game of King of the Hill."

"I never thought it was. I'm deadly serious in my intent."

His choice of words drained her face of what little color was left.

Richard snagged her elbow. "What are you so afraid of?"

"You! What he'll do to you." She clapped her hands over her mouth as if regretting that she'd said that much.

At last, he was seeing the woman he loved and not the cold-hearted stranger who had greeted him upon his return.

"What could Nigel ever do to me that would frighten you so?" When she tried to shrug free, he held fast, knowing there was a motive for her odd behavior. He had not imagined her passion, her caring. He would not—could not—believe she didn't return his love. Such an idea was at odds with everything they'd shared. They had set the foundations for a life together. It was up to him to determine why she was denying their destiny.

She tried to dodge away, but he pinned her wrists to the wall on either side of her head.

"Damn it! Tell me." His voice rang with suppressed anger, a violence turned inward at his own impotence to fathom her change in moods.

The fight drained from her stance when she realized he was not about to release her. She finally admitted, "Kill you."

A tenderness flowed into Sullivan's soul. She did care for him. Why else would she fear so deeply for his safety? She was so steeped in her role as his governess, she hadn't realized that he didn't need her protection. That he was more than aware of the dangers present in consorting with the present Earl of Lindon.

"Do you hear me, Richard? He'll kill you."

He wasn't concentrating so much on her words anymore. He was wondering what it would take to bring the blush back into her cheeks. To make her realize that he was a full-grown man, more than capable of taking care of himself and of her.

"I doubt that," he replied lazily, leaning forward to tease the tip of his nose across her cheek, her jaw. She smelled so good. Like a dew-moist garden. "He hasn't got the brains or the nerve."

Chelsea wriggled from his grasp and planted her fist against his chest. "How dare you be so flippant! You're mortal! Mortal! It's time you faced that. Nigel Sutherland will see you killed. He knows a hundred different ways to do it so that no one will ever suspect he's responsible—and none of those methods will be quick or painless. But I won't let you do it. It was because of me and my stupid pride that you became involved. I will not have your blood on my conscience, too."

Sullivan drew back, seeing that she would not be so easily distracted. Shadows lingered deep in her eyes, eyes that were normally so clear and guileless; he could only wonder what secrets had dimmed their clarity.

"You're afraid of him, aren't you?"

She opened her mouth to refute such an idea, paused, then sagged slightly as if in defeat. "Yes. I am afraid of him. I've seen enough of Lord Sutherland's methods to learn I have reason to be afraid. So do you."

"How did you receive such an intimate knowledge of the man?"

She rolled her face away, but he forced her to look at him.

"How do you know him?"

"I've . . . worked with him."

"His son, Cecil, is older than you. Nigel would have no need of your services as a governess. I repeat: How do you know him?"

"It's not important." Her response was filled with such vengeance, such loathing, Sullivan wondered what Nigel had done to merit such a reaction.

"It is to me. I sense something has occurred between you." He added pointedly, "You once mentioned a debt of cruelty. Was Nigel responsible?"

"Yes! Yes, he was!"

"Then help me to defeat him, Chelsea."

At his softly spoken challenge, she wilted even more. "He cannot be defeated. Don't you see? Your only choice is to leave."

"Run?"

"There's no shame in saving your own life."

"I've spent the last few years evading this man. He won't give up so easily."

"He won't follow you. I can arrange that much at least."

Sullivan straightened. Restlessly, he prowled down the length of the cobbled aisle between the stalls before facing her again. "Won't follow me! How can you be so naive? I'm the one person who threatens his current life-style. He won't rest until he sees me dead."

"Once you've left here—"

"Once I've left here, he'll merely send his bloodhounds after me. Again."

"Again?"

"I've been dodging the good earl for years now, living on the run, moving from place to place, job to job."

"But he didn't know about you."

Sullivan issued a short bark of laughter. "Oh, he knew. He even tried to kill me once. Sent a pair of men to do his dirty work—but they won't be coming back here. Not in this life, anyway."

He could tell his succinct retort surprised her, even scared her a little. "I'm tired of hiding, Chelsea. I won't live like that again."

"He won't follow you!" she insisted again, desperately this time. "You have my word."

"How could you possibly guarantee what Lord Sutherland will or will not do?"

She didn't reply, but he could see that she believed her words to be true.

Her militant manner nudged at a shred of information he knew he should remember. Why did the mere mention of Nigel Sutherland make her seem so frightened? What had chased away his indomitable British governess? What had stripped away her innate courage, her overwhelming pride, and left her completely frantic?

"Does Sutherland have some hold over you?"

"No."

"Has he approached you?"

"No!"

"Then why, Chelsea? Why would you dare to speak on his behalf?"

She stubbornly pressed her lips together.

"Why aren't you willing to help me defeat him? Why are you so certain that your way is the only way? Why do you seem so confident one minute and bullied the next?"

"I don't."

"Damn it, Chelsea! You two have obviously talked. Have you bargained with him? Have you traded some sort of information to exact his promise?"

"No!"

He gave her a slight shake. The fragment of memory that had evaded him all evening wriggled into his head. He searched her features with infinite care. "How long have you served as a governess?"

His sudden change of tack confused her.

"What?"

"You're quite experienced. How long have you served as a governess?"

"A little more than ten years."

"Where were you before then?"

She wriggled free and moved away from him, fiddling nervously with the top button of her bodice.

"I was being educated, of course."

"Where?"

She adopted a guardedness of her own. "Where?"

"Where were you educated?"

"In England."

"Then you're not from England originally."

"N-no."

"Where were you taught?"

She stormed to the door, but he stopped her by slamming it shut with his palm. "Do you know that when you're angry, there's a slight deviation to your pronunciation? A lilt. As if the woman you used to be has not been completely hidden."

She blanched.

"Where were you educated, Chelsea? Or should I say by whom?"

She shook her head in denial.

"Tell me, did you once reside with our esteemed Lord Sutherland? Were you his ward? Did you eat the same meals, discuss the same politics, share the same roof?"

"Stop it! Stop!"

"Greyson mentioned today that Nigel once had a ward. Was that you, Chelsea? Did he bring you here to England? Did he set you up in his house? Wine you, dine you, and tutor you? Did he instruct you in the finer points of art, literature, and debate? What else did he teach you, hmm?"

At his words, the color sprang back into Chelsea's cheeks. A defiance shored up her posture. She could see the disgust, the disdain, just as she'd feared. He didn't mind that she knew how to arouse a man. He didn't mind if she acted the wanton. As long as Nigel wasn't the reason. As long as she hadn't been his whore.

"Damn it, Chelsea, what did he do to you?"

"Do you want to strip me bare? Is that how you prove your own worth?" Disappointment tainted her tongue. Dark. Dank. Once again, she'd been tried, judged, and found wanting. She was nothing more than Nigel's plaything. His doxy. Angrily, she began ripping at her buttons. "Fine." She quivered openly now. A sob caught in her throat as she tore the gown from her body. Her shoulders were blurred in twilight. The tight cinching of her corset thrust the mounds of her breasts against the tatting of her chemise.

Sullivan watched in astonishment as she stripped to her shift, removing the corset cover, the petticoats, and the stays. In the shadowy interior, her skin glowed with a pearlescent luster. He could see the shape of her naked body under the delicate silk of her unmentionables. Although she was angry, she possessed the power to arouse him, excite him. She was slim, her bosom firm and rounded, her hips lush and inviting.

Before he could fathom her purpose, she pulled him to the far end of the stables. Her entire demeanor changed, becoming purposeful. He followed in a daze, the tempted trailing the tempter.

Once at the far side of the mews, she stopped, standing directly beneath the high barred window that allowed the warm, musky night air to drift inside. The last sheen of sunset seeped over the ledge and filtered to the floor in trickling dust motes of gold.

When he would have spoken, she dammed his words with her fingertips, then shifted to stroke his jaw, his neck, his chest. There was a lingering reverence to the caress, but at the same time, it was jaded by a blatant, calculated thoroughness. He was at once intrigued and repelled, enticed and put off. This wasn't love that dictated her actions. It was something sharper. Baser.

With each second that passed, each blatant overture, it became quite obvious that she knew just what to do to a man, just how to make him beg. But while she had performed such intimacies through a mutual desire the previous night, now she approached it like a duty.

She unbuttoned his shirt, one inch at a time. Slowly, tantalizingly. As she exposed an ever-widening ribbon of flesh, she bent forward to trail a string of kisses from his throat to his sternum, then down, down, to his navel. She teased the edge of the indentation with her tongue as she breached the barrier of his trousers to trace the sensitive crease of his flanks.

Slowly and deliberately drawing away she spread a tack blanket on the straw behind her, knelt, and reached for the placket of his breeches. She didn't unfasten the buttons but ran her thumbs down the seam, seeking, finding. Her fingers spread wide, wrapping around his pelvic bones, pressing into his skin. She tarried there, dallied, stroked, kneaded. All with the skill of a well-kept courtesan.

Sullivan fought the response he could not contain. He didn't want her like this, her attitude bleak, her efforts practiced. But at the stirrings of his arousal, she lay down on a mound of straw. Her arms rested wide above her head, one knee crooked so that the fabric of her shift draped low over her thighs.

"Have it your way, Richard Sutherland. Men have used me to gain their own goals before. Why should you be any different?"

Chelsea fixed him with the practiced stare of a whore, all glitter and cold emotion.

Her transformation withered Sullivan's instinctive response and killed any ardor he might have felt. This wasn't the woman he'd come to admire, adore, and cherish. This was a stranger. A cold, unfeeling stranger.

He took a step back, wrenching away from her gaze. He didn't speak. He couldn't. Not without exploding in fury. Or was it disappointment? Or hurt?

Sullivan stormed from the stables and slammed the door.

Behind him, Chelsea sank back into the straw, curled into a tight ball, and began to cry. *Damn you, Nigel,* her heart whispered. *Damn you for teaching me how to push him away once and for all.*

Beatrice Sutherland found her grandson much later. He sat upon a simple stone bench that was embedded in the foliage of the garden. When he would have risen upon her arrival, she waved him down and took a seat beside his own sprawled frame.

"The rain leaves such a wealth of scents, doesn't it?"

He didn't answer. He sat brooding in the darkness, his legs spread out in front of him, one elbow resting on the bench's support as he unconsciously traced the lower curve of his lip.

Biddy sighed, realizing there was no sense beating the bush for birds. Best to march right in and catch them herself.

"You've had a quarrel," she stated. To her ultimate satisfaction, he didn't avoid the issue, didn't pretend not to know what she was speaking about.

"Yes."

"You've hurt her, you know."

"Yes."

Biddy fluffed a bit of lace at her sleeve. "Would you like to discuss it with me?"

His visage grew dark and inscrutable. "A gentleman does not tell tales about a lady."

"Ahh." Her lips split in a smile. "I see that my son did educate you, then, on a man's code of conduct."

He dipped his head in concurrence.

"What if I talk and you simply listen?"

He didn't respond, but he didn't refuse.

"I sense that your relationship with your . . . governess has become much more personal."

Not so much as a flicker of an eyelash betrayed his true thoughts, but Biddy knew she'd hit the nail squarely.

"She's not of your station, of course. She was not nobly born. It would be entirely shocking for her to inherit such a title as you will someday possess." When he opened his mouth to retort, she waved him into silence. "Twenty, thirty years ago, such things would have mattered. If you were my son, I would have *forbidden* such an alliance." She tapped her cane on the stones beneath her feet in emphasis. "I would have locked you in your room, cut off your inheritance, publicly shunned you if necessary."

She searched the darkness, her memories. "But I have since learned that such petty differences are not worth the time or the energy. Especially where matters of the heart are concerned."

She patted his knee with obvious affection. How like her husband he looked. How like her son. It was as if the Sutherland blood took control, stamping out near facsimiles from generation to generation.

"You have your mother's eyes," Biddy noted.

"Thank you."

"I did not want your father to marry Julie. Did you know that?"

He nodded.

"Yes, Richard Albert would have told you. His father and I had intended for him to marry her sister, Estella Perry."

"The current Lady Sutherland."

"Yes." She shifted slightly in her seat, seeking comfort on the hard stone bench where none could be found for joints tormented by rheumatism. "I asked Lord and Lady Perry to visit for the summer and to bring their daughters. Estella was so lovely—blond, petite, vivacious—that I felt sure your father would fall under her spell. I never even considered Julie as a match. At sixteen, she was too young, too childlike for such things." She chuckled. "I had not counted on the powers of love. My son caught sight of Julie—little, brown-haired, green-eyed, giggling Julie—and his heart was no longer his to give."

"But you eventually allowed them to marry."

"I didn't really have much choice in the matter. Your father refused to give Estella the time of day. He came into breakfast one morning, proclaiming he'd compromised Julie in the heat of passion and the fog of inebriation and they must be married. Of course, I was quite certain that his protestations were not completely true."

She watched her grandson, noting the subtle nuances of his expression, and decided that he had discovered the real events quite some time ago.

"You were?"

"Richard, I am not a stupid woman. Nor was I ever a sloppy hostess. I am quite aware when one of my guests is skulking through the halls seeking an assignation. I am also quite aware when several bottles of wine mysteriously disappear." She sniffed. "I caught her in the passageway one evening."

"Who?"

"Estella, of course. She had arranged her hair to appear like Julie's riotous locks, worn one of her gowns, a bit of her scent—my son was drunk enough and desperate enough to think it was Julie."

"What did you do?"

"I meant to send the chit packing! But she eloped with cousin Nigel before I could do much of anything. When your father came to me and 'confessed,' I did not disabuse him of the notion that it was Julie he had compromised. Julie was willing to have him by hook or by crook and didn't say a thing to stop the nuptials. I knew they were in love, and time would unmask the truth." She made a *tsking* sound with her tongue. "What a muddle. What a complicated, nasty muddle. If I had known that we were setting such a terrifying series of events into motion, I would have . . ."

"What?"

"I don't know. I've wondered the same thing a thousand times, but I really see no way we could have prevented what happened. Nigel was so young at the time—I didn't think he could prove to be such a foe. I suppose it just goes to show that even baby adders possess a powerful poison."

She touched Richard's cheek. "Be very wary of him, Richard. He can be so charming, so friendly, so civil. Then he'll slide a knife between your ribs without your even being aware of it. More alarmingly, he has cultivated a good many powerful friends."

"Friends who can become even more powerful enemies."

She pursed her lips. "I sense that you know nearly as much as I do about this man."

"My father was away for some time. But his memory never dimmed."

"What of you, Richard? When this is all over, what will you remember of your time here in Britain?"

She saw the way his gaze lifted to the upper windows of the cottage. Chelsea's windows.

She lapped both hands over her walking stick and tamped down her smile of pleasure. "Go to her."

At Richard's grunt of surprise, she chuckled.

"As I stated once before, Richard, I am not a stupid woman. Nor was I ever a sloppy hostess. I am quite aware when one of my guests is skulking through the halls seeking an assignation. I am also quite aware when several bottles of wine mysteriously disappear."

"We never took any wi—"

She chuckled in honest delight at his chagrined expression. "No, not yet. I've placed them on the sideboard in the kitchen for your convenience."

"Grandmama—"

She held up a hand to halt his protests even as she sighed in pleasure, closing her lashes as if savoring what he'd said. "How I love to hear you call me that. You must call me that at least a dozen times a day."

She peered up at the same windows he'd studied earlier. A glow appeared in their depths, deepened, signaling that Chelsea had lighted a pair of candles. Her lithe shadow passed in front of one French panel, then another.

"She was once terrified of the dark, did you know that?"

Richard's gaze bounced from the cottage to Beatrice.

"Yes, it's true. She seems so strong, so secure, so blasted British at times, but it's true."

"She was Nigel's ward. She lived with him."

"Your father could not have known such a thing. So how did you come to such a conclusion?"

"I guessed as much this afternoon."

"I suppose it is only a matter of time before you will begin to demand answers about the rest." His expression grew so black, so stormy, Biddy knew she was right.

"What did he do to her?" He glared at the panes of glass where Biddy could see the shape of Chelsea Wickersham muted by the lace of the curtains. She was lifting her arms, plucking at the pins binding her hair. Then she took her brush and began to groom the riotous strands. From seemingly a million miles away, Biddy heard the soft strains of the tune she sang.

My lover's eyes . . .

"She's forever misquoting that sonnet, you know. How a woman so well educated could make an error with Shakespeare, of all things, I'll never know."

Are nothing like the sun . . .

"What did Nigel do to her, Beatrice?"

If lips be red . . .

"I cannot betray a confidence. But I think you know."

Then her lips . . .

"Will you never tell me the truth?"

"No. She must tell you herself."

My lover's eyes . . .

"Go to her, Richard. She fears for your safety—and she has a right to be afraid. The next few days will be dangerous times for us all. Nigel knows you are here. He will not rest until one of you is destroyed." She gripped his hand. "If I thought sending you back home would stop him, I would beat you into unconsciousness myself and spirit you away this very night. But matters have come full circle in a way we had never anticipated when we first arranged to bring you home. The only avenue left is an open confrontation. The world must see that Nigel Sutherland is not fit for the title of man, let alone that of an earl. I only pray that we are all strong enough to see the challenge through."

She clung to him, testing his strength, his innate goodness, then she smiled. "But tomorrow is soon enough to worry about such things. Tonight, see if you can't steal some happiness."

He stood and took a few steps forward, then stopped. "I sense that you approve of our . . . alliance."

"No. Not entirely. I would have hoped that circumstances were different and you would have wooed her, married her, then bedded her. But I understand that extraordinary situations often dictate extraordinary measures. Right now, I think she needs you, needs you desperately." She lifted a warning finger. "But hear this, Richard Albert Sutherland. I do expect you to make an honest woman of her. She deserves that much, at least."

"Yes, ma'am."

"Yes, what?"

"Yes, Grandmama," he amended, bending to kiss her cheek, then touch her gnarled hand. "Do not stay out here in this damp long."

"No. I'll simply sit for a while and enjoy the cool breeze. The summers seem to grow shorter as the years roll on, and I am much afraid that winter will o'ertake me before I'm ready."

Sullivan discerned the dual interpretation to her words, and they struck him with the force of a blow. He'd just discovered this woman, learned to love her. Pray God, he would have her company for many years to come.

"Once this is over, we'll keep the winter at bay together, Grandmama. You'll come home with me where the sun is always warm, the winds kind. Then you'll never be without family again."

Chapter
19

*N*igel Sutherland's guests were snugly ensconced in the salon, enjoying an evening of games and conversation, when two shapes crept out of the night. They let themselves into the house through the rear servants' entrance and hurried down the dark passageway to a secret door hidden in the wall next to the coat pegs. The clacking of boot heels coming from the kitchen caused them to fumble in their task, but the panel slid shut just as one of the stable hands appeared from the scullery and marched out of doors.

"Whew!" Smee breathed, leaning against the cool wall. His heart pounded fiercely in his chest. The beads of sweat shimmering on his bald pate came into sharp focus as his companion struck a flint and lit a candle. "That was as close as whiskers on a cat."

"Nonsense," Greyson chided, gesturing for his companion to follow.

It had been nearly forty years since Greyson had traversed these secret channels. Richard Albert, Biddy's son, had taught him the tangled network. As an only child, Richard Albert had often enlisted the servants to play in his elaborate games of Dickie Dark—a made-up version of Robin

Hood. Perhaps it was at that point Greyson had unconsciously developed a flair for the life of crime.

"You have the list?"

"Indeed I do." Smee pulled a rumpled piece of paper from his pocket. "First, the cards."

Greyson led them toward what he hoped was the study, backtracked twice, then finally found the door leading to the gloomy room. The hinges made no sound as the men peered into the chamber, conveying quite eloquently to Greyson that he and Smee weren't the only characters who had played Dickie Dark in the last forty years. He'd wager that Nigel Sutherland had done his fair share of skulking since obtaining the house.

The two men went about their business quickly, locating Nigel's gaming table and unearthing his supply of gambling paraphernalia.

"Cards," Greyson snapped out, extending his palm like a practiced surgeon waiting for tools. His eyes glittered purposefully behind his mask.

Smee dug into the carpet bag he held. "What color?" he asked, indicating the design stamped on the backs. To ensure the success of their operation, they had "lifted" every variety possible from a store in Addlebury mere hours ago.

"Green and gilt."

"How many?"

"Two."

"They've been subtly marked?"

"Yes, indeed."

"Very well." Smee slapped the containers into Greyson's hand. Greyson exchanged them for the unopened packets on the table and gave Lord Sutherland's decks to Smee, who tucked them in his valise.

"What is the next item on our list?"

"Invitations."

"Very good."

Greyson and Smee searched the pristine study to no avail and sighed in frustration. Then, as if both were struck by the same bolt of lightning, they whispered, "Reginald!"

Clambering into the secret passageway, they made their way to the office kept for Reginald's use.

Despite the man's fastidious appearance, the narrow cubicle was a mess, filled with empty brandy bottles, overflowing ash trays, and discarded correspondence. An opium pipe lay on the desk and a sickly sweet odor permeated the air, revealing that the hookah had been recently used.

Smee's nose wrinkled in distaste. Greyson stoically ignored such evidence of vice as he rummaged through the desk.

"Aha!" He held up a stack of clean vellum invitations. "Evidently, the good Lord Sutherland's list of attendees was so exclusive, even the printer was unaware of the exact number that would attend."

"Merely adding to our good fortune."

"Quite."

Smee took the invitations, stashed them in his bag, then swiped a length of sealing wax from the desk and added it to his booty for good measure.

"Anything else on the list?"

"Not for this evening's adventures."

"Very well, let us return."

The two men hurried into the passage. Greyson had already sent word to those servants he thought were loyal to their cause about the meeting with Richard Sutherland later that night, but it would not do to be caught in the meantime.

They peeked out into the corridor.

"Clear?"

"Clear."

The Avengers tiptoed out. Greyson was about to step into the balmy night when a gasp erupted behind them, followed by the clash of dishes.

Whirling, they found a portly woman, jaw slack, her mouth opening in preparation for a scream. Smee, without thought, without pause, dashed forward, wrapped his arms around her ample girth, and dipped her backward, planting a long, passionate kiss on her lips.

When he righted the woman, she blinked in surprise and pleasure, touching her mouth as if amazed.

Before she could gather her wits, the two masked men darted into the evening, hopped and grunted and mounted their steeds, then rode into the blackness. Only after they had charged out of sight did Greyson slow their pace and throw his companion a wide smile.

"Why, Smee! I never knew you had it in you."

"It seemed the thing to do."

"I agree wholeheartedly."

"And my form?"

"Flawless."

"Execution?"

"Impeccable."

"Thank you, Greyson."

"No, Smee. Thank *you.*"

Gregory Cane stepped into the salon of Lindon Manor, his steps sure, his posture proud. He searched carefully, judging each face, each form, until he found the tall, distinguished gentleman standing framed in the opening of the huge guillotine window leading into the garden.

Nigel.

For the first time, it was not grief that stabbed. It was anger. A deep, burning, omnipresent anger. At what this man had done, the lies he'd told, the lives he'd destroyed.

Sullivan had been right. Hours earlier, his brother had burst into the inn. Rather than welcoming him, he'd chastised him. Gregory had been irritated at the scolding, then furious, then ashamed. Every word Sullivan had uttered had been true. Gregory had wallowed in self-pity. He had used his sorrow to shield him from the world. He had buried himself with his wife and adopted the role of a coward, shielding himself from the pleasure and pain to be found in his continued existence.

But all that was about to change.

Gregory remembered his mother well enough to know how to make an entrance. He stood poised in the doorway, masked his true thoughts, and waited. Sure enough, within seconds, the heads began to swivel, one, two, then a half-dozen. Women first, then men. A hush lapped over the salon in ever-widening waves until the one man's attention he sought flickered, held.

He knew in an instant that Nigel had surmised he was the mysterious guest who had come once before. He could see it in the way he measured the quality of his clothes, the golden brown color of his hair, the strength of his build. Nigel was careful, Gregory had to give him that. He waited long enough to approach him so that he appeared only slightly interested. But the buried greed in his manner and the purposeful negligence of his attention gave him away.

"Mr. Cane?"

"Yes."

Nigel extended his hand. Cool, dry, like the cast-off skin of a snake.

"My secretary told me you'd come once before." His sweeping gesture indicated the candle-studded room populated with beautiful women and just as beautiful men. "Would you care to join us?"

Gregory kept his features bland. He waited for any sign of recognition—then relaxed when he found none. Evidently, he resembled his mother enough in coloring that Lord Sutherland did not suspect his true heritage. "I've never been fond of such events." An arch of his brow indicated the huddled groups sniping at one another under the guise of sophisticated conversation.

Just as he had hoped, Nigel took the bait. "Then perhaps we can discuss our business elsewhere. Reginald told me you were a man of sporting tendencies. Shall we abandon this group for a game or two?"

"Your assistant wearied me of backgammon, I'm afraid."

"Cards, then?"

"If you wish." Lord Sutherland had snapped at the hook offered. Now Gregory would see it was secure before reeling the Earl of Lindon in for the catch. "Are you a betting man, Lord Sutherland?"

"Provided the stakes are right."

"Meaning—provided the stakes are lucrative."

"It does make the game more interesting, don't you think?"

Gregory smiled. And as his lips moved in an upward slant, he admitted that it had been a long time, a very long time, since he'd done such a thing. But as he followed his adversary into the den, he knew there was an immense satisfaction to be found in challenging an enemy, knowing ahead of time that even though the odds weren't entirely in your favor and an element of danger remained . . .

You *could* win.

Even if you had to cheat to do so.

Sullivan strolled into the kitchen, more at peace with himself than he had been for days. He had finally come to terms with his foe, and plans had been set in motion that would force a confrontation between him and Nigel before the close of the week.

Although his father had never spoken about his true background while Sullivan was a boy, Richard Albert had given his sons more than enough information during his fatal illness. As if sensing his own mortality, he strove to impart as much knowledge of their heritage as possible. He had spoken of names and people and places that Sullivan had never forgotten—and in some cases never forgiven. All that remained for Sullivan to do was to organize that information into a trap that would close over Nigel Sutherland with the swiftness of an executioner's ax. A trap entirely of the present earl's own making.

The gears of their machinations were set. Each step had been arranged with the care of a master mason, stone by stone by stone. One level would drop irretrievably onto another.

Sullivan didn't doubt the arrangements would work. He merely strained at the time remaining before he could act. He wished he could storm to Lindon Manor and take what rightfully belonged to his family. But that would be displaying actions little more honorable than Nigel's own methods to obtain his title. No, Nigel must defeat himself. He must confess his sins and seek recompense.

Sullivan had done all he could until after midnight. Smee and Greyson had helped to set things up; Gregory was currently embroiled in the first phase of their plans. Sullivan needed an army of men to finish his work. Until Greyson summoned his former colleagues to help with the campaign, Sullivan's present task was to wait . . . and to repair the rift with Chelsea.

True, she had hurt him. But after his talk with Biddy—and the tormenting images his own mind had conjured after learning Chelsea *had* been Nigel's ward—he was beginning to understand her motives a little better. Her life had been far from easy. If she had lived with Lord Sutherland, she would have been subjected to a person who knew little about love and caring and a great deal about . . .

Cruelty.

That was the word she had used. She had alluded to her past in a hundred different ways, and Sullivan had ignored the clues. Moreover, he had unintentionally belittled her pain. He had shamed her. He had wounded her.

The thought settled on his chest like a ship's anchor, heavy, damning. That was why, tonight, he must find a way to show her that the past was of no import. He loved her for all she had become, the sensual siren as well as the innocent maid. She was a composite. An amalgam of all she'd learned and experienced. Chelsea was a beautiful woman, a devoted friend, and a challenging educator.

But tonight . . .

Tonight, there were things he intended to teach her.

The umbrous interior of the scullery closed about him with a subtle sense of comfort as Sullivan crossed to the sideboard where two bottles of wine had been left for his use. By his grandmother. His sweet, caring, doting grandmother.

Sullivan's lips tipped in an honest smile. In the space of a few days, his relationship with that woman had changed dramatically. So much so that he was even considering bringing her with him to Sutherland's Roost.

He hoped she would come. He delighted in her quick wit and soothing gentility. And if she would journey home with him to the warmth of the tropics, Chelsea would not lack for feminine companionship during the voyage.

Chelsea.

How would he tell her that he was not all he appeared? How could he tempt her to join him when she discovered that he was not Richard Sutherland? That he had no lands, no titles—

Enough. This evening, he wouldn't torture himself with what the future might bring. Just as he wouldn't torture himself with the past. Chelsea and he had these few precious hours, probably the last they would have before time and circumstance came crashing down over their heads. And he intended to make the most of the opportunity.

After all that had occurred between them, Richard still refused to go.

Chelsea gripped the brush she held and sighed. Less than an hour ago, Beatrice had brought a tray to Chelsea's room and had told her the news. Upon hearing the foreboding tidings, Chelsea had curled into the chair next to the window and pondered the darkness of the garden. As if he'd heard the worried tumble of thought clamoring in her brain, Richard had appeared below.

He'd looked no more happy than she, and she'd suffered a twinge of remorse. What she'd done to him, the way she'd acted . . .

How could she ever face him again? She wanted to run, hide, but the seriousness of her predicament prevented such an action. If she didn't do something soon, Nigel would have his way.

And so she had decided that she would have to take matters into her own account. She would give Richard all she had so carefully guarded, her heart, her devotion, her desires, her passion. Then she would pose her question again: Will you leave? If he agreed, she would escape with him to the ends of the earth if necessary. They would be together for all time.

If he demurred . . .

At least she would have had one more night as his heart-mate. Without regrets.

But first, she had to bridge the gap and wipe away the memory of their previous encounter. She had to find the courage to display her true feelings. Openly. Honestly.

Chelsea drew the brush through the waves and studied the stranger who stood in the mirror before her. Her hair spilled around her in a riot of color, the gilded ringlets emphasizing the flushed quality of her cheeks, the bright sparkle of her eyes. The dark maroon faille of her dressing gown played peek-a-boo with the raw silk night rail beneath. The shift's color was such a delicate peach, the fabric so fine and fragile, that the garment was a mere wisp of color over naked flesh. If she were to drop the robe and stand in front of the flame . . .

A heat flooded her cheeks as she removed a precious vial of scent from her dressing table. Only a scant number of drops remained in the crystal bottle. The perfume had been a gift years ago from an ardent employer. Upon learning of the man's intentions, Chelsea had immediately sought another means of livelihood, but she had found herself incapable of returning the offering. Even then, the scent had struck her as being overtly feminine. And wicked.

Slowly, sensually, she trailed the glass stopper over her breasts, her neck, the insides of her elbows. The cool silk of her gown lapped against her skin with a tantalizing friction as she lifted her hems to touch her knees, the inside of her thighs, her abdomen. Allowing the fabric to fall into place, she replaced the bottle of *parfum français* and surveyed the results of her ministrations.

She was inundated in a fragrant cloud, clothed in the sheerest of fabrics. A wanton color tinged her cheeks. How could he not know that she meant to seduce him? How could he not know that despite all that had occurred, she longed to feel him next to her, over her, in her.

Stepping to the window, she unhooked the heavy brocade *portieres* from their artful swags. Tonight she would allow no one to witness what was about to occur. Below her, the garden was empty, quiet, redolent with summer. If only life itself were as peaceful as nature. What she wouldn't do for a chance to leave the hustle and grind of the everyday world and live in a garden such as this, far from the pressures of earning a living and protecting her precious professional name. Neither activity had ever given her a tenth of the happiness she'd found these last few weeks. With Richard.

"My lover's eyes are nothing like the sun . . ." She sang, the words and tune the only fragments of memories she had of a mother who had once loved her and laughed with her. "If lips be red—"

"The entire sonnet is incredibly unflattering if properly quoted."

Chelsea whirled at the deep voice, discovering that Richard had somehow entered unannounced. He leaned against the closed door. A bottle of wine and two delicate goblets hung suspended from fine-boned fingers.

"As I recall, the piece begins with 'My mistress's eyes are nothing like the sun' and continues on from there, comparing her hair to wires and the skin of her breasts to dun. Hardly an appropriate song for one so young. Or so lovely."

He appraised the color of her hair in the candlelight, her pinkening cheeks, her gossamer gown.

Momentarily daunted by the intensity of his gaze and the task she had set for herself, Chelsea clutched her robe tightly to her breasts.

"Of course, the last couplet of the poem could hold true," Richard continued, padding forward. "'And yet, by heaven, I think my love as rare / As any she belied with false compare.'" When he stood but a hair's breadth away, he murmured, "Good evening, Chelsea."

"My lord."

He *tsked* at her choice of words. "Until you can officially attach such a title to my name, I would prefer you didn't call me that."

"It is a title that is rightfully yours."

"Perhaps." He shrugged and set his burdens upon the dresser. "And perhaps such a title will never be mine." His eyes became dark, searching, mixing with golden shards of brown. "Would you think me less without the name, the titles?"

Chelsea could answer him in a heartbeat. She could honestly insist that she wished the role of heir could never be assigned to him. Then he would be safe. And he could be hers. But dangerous times demanded strict measures in diplomacy. And since her evening's ambition was to seduce him, she must not offend him quite so quickly. Not knowing how best to respond, she merely answered, "I could never care for you less."

Unwittingly, her words took on more meaning than she had ever intended. They hung suspended, achingly honest, undeniably real.

"You *do* care for me, then?"

He seemed so much bigger, so much more dangerous, than he had mere days before. It was not merely the addition of his clothes or the outward facade of civility. No, it was more, so much more. The jut of his jaw, the fierce determination that molded his brow—all bespoke a man of purpose. Never could his visage be construed as vulnerable. There was too much strength, too much overt honor.

How could she possibly appeal to such a man? A complete and overwhelmingly masculine man. She could seduce the pagan she'd come to recognize. She understood the physical needs and drives of such a man. But this gentleman with his neatly tied cravat, snug-fitting breeches, and vest, was difficult to reconcile to her objectives.

Rather than releasing the death grip she claimed on her robe, she held it even tighter.

When she didn't answer him, he stepped closer, so near that she could feel the heat of his body seeping through the faille into her chilled flesh.

"Do you care for me?" he asked again, more forcibly this time.

He was too close, too powerful. Whirling away, she sought

246

some measure of control. *"Care* for you?" she answered in what she thought was a teasing tone. "I don't know you. I know . . . I know a gentle savage. A vulnerable heathen." What she had intended as playful repartee quickly melted into bare fact. Her need for reassurance, her confusion, hung naked between them.

Richard held her shoulders, softly, caressingly. "I am that man, Chelsea."

She abandoned all pretense, responding to him with the fears she harbored in her heart. "No. You're not. The man I thought I knew doesn't exist. You . . . you're . . ."

He slid his arms around her waist, drawing her against his thighs, his hips, his waist. The fabrics she wore could have been air between them, so clearly did she feel each plane of his body, each button, each fold, each ridge.

"I'm what, Chelsea? A gentleman? A titled lord?" His hands swept over her ribs and skirted the swell of one breast before resting on her shoulder. "Is that what has your heart pounding so erratically? That I have become the very man you wanted me to become? My, aren't we the little hypocrite. Wanting a prim and proper Englishman for appearance's sake, but longing for a barbarian between the sheets where it counts."

"Don't be—"

"Honest? Admit it, Chelsea. What disturbs you most about my sudden transformation is that you were never completely certain that it could happen. That I could be everything you longed to teach me to be. You wonder if the savage can ever reappear." He turned her to him and framed her face with his palms. "Can't you see it, Chelsea? Why we're so perfect together? We both know the correct time and place to wear the facade. And the precise moment to drop it."

He saw a flicker of acknowledgment and knew she had admitted the truth to herself.

"So which are you to be tonight?" she challenged. "The primitive or the gentleman?"

His smile was slow and filled with untold promise. "Does it matter?"

She opened her mouth but didn't speak, couldn't think of what she wanted to say, *really* wanted to say.

"I love you, Chelsea."

A soft gasp escaped her lips at his unexpected confession. After what had happened in the mews, she had been sure he would never say such a thing again.

"I love the woman you are, the woman you will become. And I want to make love with you tonight," he continued, stroking her cheekbones with his thumbs. "Will you let me do that? Will you let me stay with you tonight? Not as the savage, but as the gentleman?"

"Biddy—"

"Sends her blessings and her very best wine."

Chelsea closed her lashes, savoring the strength, the safety, to be found in Richard's arms. She absorbed his scent, his form, his manner.

She had grown to love this man so much. She would do anything to protect him. *Anything.* Even if to do so would mean sacrificing her honor in such a way that he could never bear to be near her again.

But she would have this night. And tomorrow. And the next night. She would stretch out as many hours as she could in his company. Then, when the time had come for her to be alone again, she would have the comfort of knowing she had given him all that was in her power to give.

She released Richard, smoothed the crumpled cloth of his shirt, caressed him. She peered at him from beneath the heavy fringe of her lashes. Their glances met, clung, simmered.

"Will you believe in me enough to realize I'm wise enough to take care of myself?"

She didn't answer, merely pressed her lips to the plane of his jaw. The slight stubble abraded her sensitive skin deliciously.

"I'll take care of you, too, Chelsea."

She smiled against him, continuing her foray. "See to it that you do. Care for me, that is."

"I have never felt for any woman what I feel for you."

His words blazed within her, offering her the most

brilliant hope tempered by an agonizing despair. Had she been so scorned by the Fates that she could never lay claim to a lasting love? One that would be hers, through the end of time? Was she always doomed to love, then lose?

But she had this moment. And Chelsea was not so stupid that she did not know when to take greedily whatever the gods were willing to offer her.

"Will you make love with me tonight, Richard?"

His eyes blazed. "If you'll allow it."

"What if I demand it?"

"Then I cannot refuse the earnest appeals of one so beautiful. It would not be—"

"The act of a gentleman? What if I do not wish to spend my time with such a man of means? In my experience, they have little to recommend them. They seem quite cold, quite uncaring, quite self-absorbed."

"Then you have obviously not experienced a *true* gentleman."

Chapter
20

Sullivan kissed Chelsea, softly, tenderly, sweetly. With each response, she silently begged him to continue. But there was no need. It soon became obvious that he did not intend to leave her. He intended to love her.

He touched her hair, her shoulders, bent to press his mouth to her throat, the hollow behind her ear.

"Tell me what you want me to do, Chelsea."

"I . . ."

He smiled against her. "You were not so shy yestereve."

When she ducked her head in shame, he lifted her chin. "There's no need to hide from me, love. There is nothing you cannot say to me, nothing you cannot do, as long as you share the honest regard I feel for you." There was a submerged warning to his words, one that spoke of their time in the mews. Then the glitter was gone, ignited beneath a searing heat.

"Come." He led her to the bed. The covers had been folded away from the headboard, exposing sweetly scented linens.

Upon reaching the bedstead, he stopped her, gently divesting her of her robe. The room was warm, but she trembled beneath his intimate regard, knowing at once that she pleased him.

"You are so lovely," he whispered. "So pure." When she would have shook her head to deny such a thing, he repeated, "Pure."

Bending, he scooped her into his arms and laid her on the billowing goose-down mattress. To her surprise, he did not join her.

"Richard?"

"A proper gentleman does not disrobe in front of anyone other than his manservant. Not even in the presence of his wife." He parroted the advice she had given him so long ago.

He saw the disappointment, the shy intensity, then the gleam of challenge. "Propriety be damned, my lord."

Grinning, he touched his cravat. "Am I to understand that you wish me to breach the most sacred laws of conduct?"

"Yes."

"Then I cannot disappoint a lady."

From his position several yards away, he pulled at the end of his cravat, slowly, tauntingly, so that the artful arrangement disintegrated bit by bit by bit. Then he worked at the front closure of his vest, exposing the fine lawn of his shirt so gradually, Chelsea thought she would faint from the shallow breaths she took. When he shrugged from his vest, she leaned forward in anticipation.

"I have dreamed of being with you thus," he said.

"And I with you, my lord."

He dislodged the fastenings of his cuffs, exposing strong wrists, a smattering of dark hair. Next, he began on the pearl nubs that held his shirt shut. The buttons fell free, exposing a golden streak of masculine flesh. Sleek muscles. Taut skin. Chelsea found it incredible that such a man existed, and that he stood here, exciting her with his subtle strip of clothing.

The shirt gaped open, and he spied the uneaten food on the tray on her bedside table.

"Hungry?"

"Not for food."

Her answer pleased him, and, as her reward, he dropped the shirt. Prowling to the bed, he sat on the side to divest himself of his boots and socks, then twisted to place his hands on either side of her ribcage.

"Perhaps I could tempt you with a morsel or two. A piece of fruit. After all, we cannot have you fainting from lack of proper nourishment."

Taking one of the strawberries from its pool of cream, he held it poised over her chest. A drop of rich liquid fell, moistening a spot above her left breast.

He *tsked*. "I fear I have soiled your gown." He bent and licked away the evidence, dampening her shift, then reached to remove it. "Perhaps it would behoove you to take this off."

When she attempted to speak, he dropped the berry between her lips. Lifting her, he slid the night rail over her hips, her shoulders, then helped her to sit so that he could slide it over her head.

"Better, much better."

When she shuddered in reaction to his sensual growl, he drew the covers to her waist, but no farther, then returned to his strawberries.

"Come, my love. You must eat at least half of this bowl. If you wish, I will finish the rest."

He took another berry and held it above her to allow a pattern of drops to appear on her breasts. Then, offering her the fruit, he once again dipped to lick away the heavy cream.

The act was so erotic, so arousing, that Chelsea gripped his arms, silently begging him to abandon such torment and take her, here and now, but he forestalled such attempts.

"Shh, love, shh. We have all night. An eternity."

What followed was an exercise in torture. Chelsea had never imagined what delights could be experienced in eating a simple bowl of fruit. By the time they had finished their repast, she was writhing beneath him, clutching at his hair, his shoulders.

Clearly as affected as she, Sullivan rose from the bed. He saw her, flushed and panting, ready, and knew they were heart-mates, soul-mates. He would never again be so touched by a woman—not just physically but emotionally and spiritually. Sullivan realized he would do whatever he must to see the haunting distress banned from her eyes.

"Richard?"

The word was barely recognizable, and Sullivan was glad. At this moment, he didn't want to be reminded that she thought him to be someone else.

He stripped off his trousers and stood before her, basking in her greedy gaze, filled with a wondrous power. Then he was above her. Her legs parted easily to accommodate him, and as he probed at her entrance, she accepted him, eagerly, willingly, lovingly.

Their joining was fierce, earth-shattering. While they clung to each other, panting, he knew that he had lied to himself all these years. Home was not an island, home was not a place, home was being safely niched in Chelsea's body, her arms.

Her heart.

"Well?"

A pair of horsemen became two-dimensional shapes set against the deeper ebony of the hillside. If one were to look closely, carefully, one would be able to determine that the two men were not natives of the area but were a pair of travelers who had recently arrived at Addlebury.

"Nigel, Lord Sutherland, was in fine form?"

"Pompous as ever. Nigel was quite sure he could not be beaten. When the opposite proved true, he bet heavily. Again and again and again."

"To what end?"

Gregory grinned. An honest, rake-hell, satisfied smirk. He held out a packet of vellum documents.

"What's this?"

"The deed to Lindon Manor and the surrounding estates in the area—a prize he was reluctant to part with even when he'd been squarely beaten, I might add. I managed to obtain it only upon threatening to expose him as a cheat in front of his guests. That and a promise of a rematch."

"I can't believe he did it. I can't believe the man would be so stupid as to wager his home."

"Nigel reacted just as Sully supposed he would—too arrogant to consider he might lose."

Rupert held the papers up to the light of the moon, squinting at the elaborate writing. He read enough to ensure that they were indeed quite legitimate. "It worked," he breathed. "Sully's blasted plan worked."

"Mmm-hmm." Gregory's green eyes glittered with a devilish mischief. An emotion that hadn't been there in years. Straightening in his saddle, he drawled, "It would seem to me that our good Lord Sutherland is trespassing."

Rupert's own features lightened considerably, becoming no less devilish. "Could be."

"Perhaps we should see about having him evicted."

"My thoughts exactly."

"Should we go about it tonight?"

Rupert chortled. "Nay. I feel quite fatigued."

"So do I."

"But tomorrow . . ."

"The summer solstice. Yes, the longest day of the year should prove a most satisfactory time to break the news. That way, Nigel will have even more time to enjoy a purgatory completely of his own making."

"Damn, damn, *damn!*" Nigel threw the cut crystal goblet into the fireplace. The glass shattered. The amber liquid exploded. A shower of sparks cascaded onto the rug.

"Temper, temper."

Nigel whirled to find Reginald watching him from the doorway. The secretary closed them both into the tomblike silence of the study. "Am I to understand your meeting with Mr. Cane failed to prove profitable?"

Challenging. The younger man was forever *challenging* him. Nigel was growing tired of it all. Reginald was not in control. Nigel was. Nigel was *always* in control.

Nigel growled low in his throat, panic, fury, and frustration roiling in the pit of his stomach, lingering on his tongue like acid.

He and Reginald had shared much through the years. Their bond was unique, and in many ways dangerous. Nigel had shared his blackest secrets with his secretary. They had long since crossed the boundaries of simple employer and employee, yet they weren't quite friends. There was something more to their relationship, much, much more. But not even to his closest associate and the guardian of his soul could Nigel admit the folly of the last few hours. That he had allowed himself to wager Lindon Manor was inconceivable.

But he had done it all the same.

He had been so sure he could best the man. So sure! In retrospect, he realized Cane had toyed with him, played upon him. He had lulled him into a false sense of security, allowing Nigel to win at first—waiting for the stakes to grow high and Nigel to grow cocky. Then the tide had turned, so slowly he hadn't been aware of the IOU's piling up in front of his adversary. A little wine, a few good cigars, a drag or two on the hookah, and *wham!* He'd been caught like a rat in a trap.

"Find him!"

His barked order was issued so unexpectedly, Reggie's brows climbed. "I beg your pardon?"

"Cane. Find him. *Now!*"

"May I ask—"

"No, you may not ask. *I* am your employer. *I* am. I do not need to explain myself; I do not need to ask permission. Your position here is not indispensable. It hinges upon my good will, which at the moment is sorely strained! *Find . . . him!*"

Reggie slowly straightened, unaccountably hurt. When he stormed from the room, Nigel swore, then swore again. Damn it all to hell, it was time that little runt learned his place!

But he couldn't deny that Reggie's reaction unsettled him no little bit.

* * *

Chelsea had turned onto her side, breathing heavily. Her skin was flushed and dewed with perspiration. Her hair tumbled about her in a sea of curls.

Drawing the tresses aside, Sullivan exposed the delightful smattering of freckles across her shoulders. He kissed her there. Then between her shoulder blades. Down the length of her spine.

She took a ragged breath. He felt it against his lips, then felt the gooseflesh rise on her skin. In truth, he didn't have the energy to do much about it. But he smiled to think that even now, when both of them were exhausted and sated, the embers of passion could still flare.

Curling against her spoon-fashion, he rested his head on the pillow above hers, wrapped his arms around her waist, and held her to him. If Nigel had his way, this might be their last night together. But if Sullivan Cane had any say, it would be the beginning of forever.

"Richard?"

"Hmm?" He dipped his head, rubbing the stardusting of freckles with his nose.

"If I were to ask you once more to go away, would you?"

"Nay, my love," he answered. "You could not tear me from your side."

She did not speak, and Sullivan returned to his explorations, missing the stark terror that raced across her features.

But when he turned her for his kiss, she gave it full-measure, then clung to him, silently bidding him to love her yet again. When their bodies fused and his life's seed shot into her, she whispered a silent prayer. That she would have him tonight, the next night, and the next . . .

Knowing full well that Nigel Sutherland would be coming to fetch her. Soon.

Estella preferred the rain. She preferred the musky odor of water-drenched loam, the moist warmth that clung indoors, the quiet patter, the lazy afternoons.

But the rain had stopped earlier that day, finishing too abruptly for her taste, long before things seemed . . . *clean*.

Shaking away that morbid thought, Estella looked into the

mirror over her vanity, coaxing the tangles from her hair with the silver hairbrush that Nigel had given to her for Christmas more than a decade before. The handles of the vanity set had been decorated with an elaborate crest belonging to the Earl of Lindon.

The air crackled as she ran the bristles through the thick golden waves, over and over and over. Nigel had given a second such brush to another woman. No, not a woman. A girl. His ward.

It had been years since she'd thought of her. Gelsey, her name had been. Gelsey O'Rourke. Nigel had introduced Estella to the Irish waif, spouting something about harboring her from the world and displaying good Christian charity. Then he'd ensconced her in Lindon Manor. He'd thought himself so clever. He'd considered Estella so gullible. He'd never suspected that she'd known his intentions were less than honorable.

Estella had known what he planned to do to the child. Yes, she'd known. She'd merely chosen not to confront him. She'd willingly let him shower his attention upon a girl too young to defend herself, because by allowing him to do so, he would not direct his attentions toward Estella.

She met her own reflection in the vanity mirror. She saw a bleak hollowness there. A yawning void.

Mortality was an alarming thing. Just a few years ago, Estella would have shrugged off such memories. She would have comforted herself with the thought that she possessed everything in life she had ever desired.

Everything.

The word had a brassy ring. Especially since, at this point in her life, she realized she had been chasing material possessions. She had thought to salve her conscience with money and power. Trifles. She had bartered her soul for *trifles,* denying that what she wanted most could not be bought. Love.

She had lost that chance at happiness long ago, when first she had begun to spin her webs of deceit. In the succeeding decades, she had paid dearly for her actions. With her pride, her body, even her son. For thirty years, she had played a role. She had become a stranger to herself: biddable, frail. Nigel's prize.

"Dearest?"

The door adjoining her own room opened without a sound, admitting the one man she had grown to hate. In the mere batting of an eyelash, the fire was extinguished, and the sweet, adoring expression she'd developed throughout her marriage was firmly entrenched.

"Yes, my love?"

There was a curious energy cloaking him, a cracking, static nervousness. But when he spoke, it was to say, "You look tired."

"A little. But not so tired that I would bar you from my room." She offered him a gamine smile that echoed the coquette she'd once been. "Our guests have retired?"

He approached her, so tall, so lean, so undeniably attractive, even now. But a brooding intensity cast a pall over his bluntly cut features, frightening her, warning her. She had seen him like this once in their time together. Mere days before the grapevine had reported that Nigel's ward had disappeared, only to surface later under a new name and the auspices of Dowager Lady Sutherland.

"Near as I can tell, they are all abed."

"Then we have what's left of the evening to ourselves," she murmured, her voice a practiced seductive purr. She hoped to waylay some of the anger she saw in his eyes. Cruel eyes. Why had it taken her so long to see that there was no light in their depths? Merely a deep, omnipresent darkness.

His hand wrapped around her neck, stroked her, caressed her. When she did not immediately respond, the fingers tightened, bruising her, before gentling her. "So it would seem."

Knowing she had been subtly chastised, Estella reached to rub his knuckles, following the strong framework of bone and flesh, the tracery of veins. She trailed each inch tenderly, lovingly, clasping him and drawing his palm down to cup her breast. "Then stay with me, my love. Stay with me this eve."

When he bent to press his lips to her throat, Estella

admitted to herself that at least this had not changed between them since their nuptials. She could not fault him his passion or the way he never ceased to pluck a response from her. Her loins quickened, and her breathing became labored, and she admitted that even now, despite his mood, his cruelty, and three decades of wedded hell, Estella could still close her eyes.

Pretending he was the man she wished him to be.

Sullivan rested his chin near the crook of Chelsea Wickersham's shoulder. Their lovemaking to date had been wild and passionate, the stuff of dreams, but try as he might, he could not get her to open up to him emotionally, to believe in him enough to allow him into his mind as well as her heart and her body.

"I don't understand you, Chelsea."

The woman he'd so thoroughly adored mere minutes before lay quietly in his arms. When she did not immediately respond to his words, Sullivan wondered if she had fallen asleep. If not for the tense quality of her posture, he would have believed such a thing possible.

Just as he was about to lapse into silence himself, she said, "Perhaps because I find it more comfortable that way."

He found her statement intriguing but did not turn her to face him. There was a guardedness to her voice that did not encourage prying. Therefore, he was surprised to hear her add, "There are things I've done, secrets I've kept, that I don't want anyone to know about."

"Not even me?"

"Not even you. Especially not you."

She clutched at his arms, strumming a chord of protectiveness that Sullivan had never known he possessed.

"Don't you know there's nothing you could say that could make me love you less?"

This time, she did not answer. Somehow, although she made no sound, no move, Sullivan sensed that she did not believe him. Turning her, he sought to unravel her masked expression.

"It's because of Nigel, isn't it?"

She shifted away, but not before he saw a flash of hurt.

"I'm sorry," he sighed. "I shouldn't have spoken of him. Not now."

"He will always be between us."

"No!" When she would have risen, he held her still. "Can't you see? I don't care that you knew him before. I was the first man to love you. I was the first man you allowed to touch your heart. I don't care what has gone between the two of you. I simply care that you continue to let him rule over your life! Let me take care of him."

"You cannot defeat his kind, I know that now."

"His type doesn't worry me."

She pushed free, dodging from the bed and drawing on her robe. "He should worry you a great deal. Nigel has murdered. He has lied and stolen and cheated."

She rounded the bed. "It was he who framed your father. He bribed a government employee to steal the documents that were later found in Richard Albert's possession. He hired the lawyer to defend him, paying the man well for his incompetence. When he could not arrange their executions, he ushered your parents onto the boat that would send them to their doom, then returned to poison your grandfather. He's done all these things and more. Not openly, not even craftily. But through the sheer pleasure of proving to himself that he could do them.

"Don't you see? You are his worst enemy, his ultimate foe. He won't take you quickly." Her voice dropped to a tortured warning. "He will make a sport of it. He will dangle you over hot coals. He will toy with you, torture you, demean you in every possible way. He will ultimately kill you. Not swiftly, but in the most painful and degrading manner he can devise."

Rather than appearing frightened, Sullivan rose from the bed and padded toward her, weaving his fingers through her hair and forcing her to face him. "What did he do to you?"

"That isn't important."

"It is when you can't let it go, when it intrudes upon what we have together."

"Richard! I am trying to warn you."

"I've listened to your warnings. I promise that I will take them into account. But I won't run from here with my tail between my legs. Too much is at stake." He bent so that she couldn't avoid the iron determination reflected in his eyes. "Damn it, Chelsea, trust me. Trust me enough to see this through. To take care of you—*and* of me. I won't allow him to bring harm to us."

She didn't speak.

"I *will* take care. I *will* be safe. I have people who are assisting me, people loyal to Biddy and her cause. You asked me once to work with you. You chided me once for ignoring my own family. Well, now that I'm helping them, you berate me still. Help me, Chelsea. *Help me.*"

Her nails dug into his wrists.

"Do you trust me so little?" he asked when she still did not answer.

"It's not you I don't trust."

"Then make me understand. Tell me what happened between you and Nigel. Tell me . . . *something.*"

"I have an innate disbelief of perfect things. Invariably there is a flaw, a form of deception." She touched his chest, his ribs. "But I am also a vain creature. I would have you think of me, not as I am, but of someone better. More beautiful, more skilled, more desirable."

"You could never be more beautiful to me."

She smiled shyly, and her expression gleamed with challenge. "Oh?" she drawled.

Pushing him resolutely toward the bed, she waited until he had dropped onto the covers, then retreated. Under his watchful scrutiny, she crossed to the dresser, opening one of the drawers. Even from his vantage point across the room, Sullivan could see that it was filled with silken underthings, lacy chemises, frilly pantalets, garters, stockings, and corsets.

Turning her back to him, she drew several items free. To his infinite consternation and arousal, she slid into a silk dressing gown, then moved to the opposite side of the room. It soon became clear that she intended to clothe herself.

Sitting on the chair several yards away, she gathered one

virginal white silk stocking and inserted her toes into the delicate end, obscuring the creamy flesh beneath, while, inch by inch, she sheathed her foot, her ankle, her calf, exposing the shimmering fabric and elaborate pink embroidered clocking. After smoothing the gossamer hosiery into place, she wrapped a ruffled pink garter around her upper thigh, just below the hem of the stocking, and tied the rose-colored ribbon. Even from where he lay, Sullivan could see the wink and shimmer of beading, the subtle sway of tiny tassels. Elegant thighs.

Then she proceeded to sheath her second leg, just as slowly, just as decadently, just as enticingly. Sullivan's breath came in shallow degrees. Where moments before he would have considered himself satisfied for a time, he felt himself responding.

When she had finished, Chelsea returned to the dresser. She allowed the robe to drip from her shoulders and puddle at her feet. The smooth line of her spine caught a whisker of shadow. The velvety skin of her back, spine, and derriere was bathed in mellow candle glow.

Reaching into the drawer, she withdrew another silk garment, this time rose in color, paler than that decorating her stockings and only a shade darker than her skin. Gathering it over her head, she shimmied into the rustling undergarment, allowing it to settle over her body like an opalescent cloud. The action brought a whiff of the exotic scent that clung to her skin and now tinged his own.

Last of all, she withdrew a tiny wisp of a corset, a mere confection of lace and ribbons and bows. Sullivan had never seen such a creation before. He had heard of them from his brothers—matinee stays, they were called. Proper women were said to wear them beneath their night rails to maintain the illusion of a tiny-waisted figure. But as far as Sullivan could see, the article served no real purpose other than to entice a man into seeing what lay beneath.

When Chelsea faced him, Sullivan swallowed against the tight clutch of desire that had settled in his throat . . . and much farther down. The chemise had been cut to ride low, exposing her shoulders to the tapers' gleam. Except for the way the garment clung to the bastions of her breasts, there would have been nothing to keep it from dropping completely to the floor.

Bending slightly, Chelsea wrapped the corset around her ribcage, affording him a view of her swaying breasts. Straightening, she tugged on the satin ribbon wound through the handmade eyelets marching up the front. The span of her waist grew small, tightening into a rigid drum. Her breasts mounded high and firm and incredibly alluring.

"I used to wear these things under my woolen gowns when I came to fetch you for your lessons, Master Richard. You were so heathenish, so inappropriately garbed, I despaired of ever seeing you properly covered. I thought that nothing could ever be as disturbing to me as your nakedness."

She shot him an indulgent look when he stretched like a preening panther, tucking a fist beneath his head to prop himself up at a better advantage for gawking.

"I've had these unmentionables for years. I bought them whenever I felt blue, tucking them away, never to be worn. But upon arriving at Bellemoore with my new charge, I found myself wanting to wear them. I think I did so because of the way you made me feel." Her voice dropped, becoming husky, enticing. "I often wondered if you knew, if you guessed what I wore beneath those staid, conservative gowns." With one last yank, she tied the ribbon in place. Her bosom pressed against the restrictive lace, the creamy globes quivering with each breath she took. The meager weight of silk coated her hips and her legs in the merest excuse of fabric. Each time she moved, the chemise shifted and swayed, offering peeks of bare flesh and naughty stockings.

"I thought that nothing could ever be as unnerving as the sight of bare skin. But when I saw you today, clothed so completely, I knew I was wrong." Her smile held the temptation of Eve. "I discovered that I'm a woman who loves a mystery. Tonight I wallowed in the pleasure of seeing each layer unpeeled, bit by bit, piece by piece, to expose the treasures hidden beneath."

She leaned one knee on the bed and bent over him, her

bust straining at its bindings, the shaded outlines of her thighs beckoning to him beneath their icing of silk.

"I offer you the same joy of discovery, the same mystery. So that in the future, when you see me dressed in the uniform society dictates I wear, you will never forget what can be found beneath."

She bent for his kiss, a kiss that soon exploded into a flurry of need, an overwhelming passion. At one point, Sullivan realized she had dodged the issue he had been trying to expose. She had still refused to tell him about Nigel. But then he didn't care. He was lost in a maelstrom of white-hot desires.

Later, much later, as he plunged into her eager body, Sullivan admitted she'd been right in her assumptions. He would never forget kissing her nipples through the sheer chemise. He would never forget battling with the strings of her corset. He would never forget drawing the items free to expose what lay beneath.

But the hosiery he refused to remove. He remembered the promise he'd made that day on the moor—that someday, someday soon, he would make love to her while she was wearing nothing more than those stockings.

Sullivan sighed, wearily, happily. For the remainder of his days, he would be unable to forget those silk-clad thighs gripping him, the tasseled garters caressing him, as Chelsea and he became one.

Chapter

21

Nigel rose from his wife's bed and slid into the Turkish dressing gown. He didn't glance behind him, didn't feel so much as a pang of conscience for the bruises he'd left on her pale skin.

Not bothering to don more than that modicum of clothing, he returned to his room. Just as he had suspected, Reginald had returned and propped himself insolently on the bed.

Reggie stared at Nigel over the lip of a snifter of liqueur. "One would think that at your age you would grow less randy, but the opposite seems to be true."

His employer spared him little more than a glance as he stepped to the armoire in the corner, opening the door to reveal the porcelain wash set hidden on a shelf inside. Stripping off the robe, he began to wash with clinical efficiency. "I would hope you haven't been so foolish as to return without some news regarding the errand I gave you."

Reginald balked at the silent threat, taking the time to sniff the brandy's bouquet, then deliberately releasing the air. "Cane has disappeared. However . . ." He trailed into silence.

"What, damn it!"

Reginald's lips quirked in barely suppressed malice. "However, I was able to determine that the stranger who spoke to your wife and the Dowager Sutherland's impostor are one and the same."

Nigel forgot his anger and stared at his assistant in disbelief. "You saw him?"

"At Bellemoore. He was in the garden, speaking to Beatrice Sutherland. He even addressed her as *Grandmama.*"

Nigel toweled himself dry and wrenched open the opposite armoire door, removing a freshly laundered set of underdrawers. As he stepped into the woolen legs and buttoned the front placket, he stared thoughtfully at the opposite wall.

"I have decided to forgive you for your previous outburst, Nigel," Reginald said.

Nigel glared at him but did not respond. Reggie might challenge. He might bully and bother and bicker. But he'd always seen to Nigel's needs.

"Would you like me to kill him?" Reginald asked with bland bluntness.

Deciding to placate his secretary, for the moment at least, Nigel shook his head. "No. Thanks ever so much for the offer, Reggie, but after all she's put me through, I have a deep, abiding craving to see Chelsea Wickersham squirm. Once she's agreed to return to me, I'll take care of him myself."

Reggie sipped at his drink. "And Cane?"

Deep in thought, Nigel stepped into a pair of trousers. When he spoke, his tone was hard. Bitter. "Find him and bring him to me. In chains, if you have to."

"What's the man done, Nigel?" Reggie asked mildly.

Nigel stuffed the tails of his shirt into his breeches, donned woolen stockings and shiny boots, fastened his cuffs, and slipped into a velvet waist and superfine frockcoat. "Never you mind. This is between me and Mr. Cane."

Reginald frowned. His employer had never had any secrets from him before.

Some of Lord Sutherland's snappishness returned. "What re you waiting for, Reggie? I told you to find Cane. *Now.*"

"What are you up to, Nigel?"

"That's my affair."

"You've always confided in me in the past."

"Blast it all! Just do what I say!"

Reggie's lips pursed in anger and irritation, but he comlied nonetheless. Not because Nigel had told him to, but ecause he meant to uncover the reasons behind his employr's uncharacteristic behavior. If the elusive Mr. Cane was at ult, Reginald would take care of him, too.

A tap came at the door. Sullivan was immediately awake. liding from the bed, he spared a glance for his companion nd was relieved to see that she continued to sleep, undisrbed.

Pulling on breeches, socks, boots, and a shirt, he emerged find Greyson waiting anxiously, a taper gripped in his indly fingers.

"A visitor, sir."

"Rupert?"

He shook his head.

"One of Lord Sutherland's men?"

"No, sir. His wife."

Sullivan took the candle. "Where?"

"I showed her into the studio. Away from prying eyes."

"Very good, Greyson."

"Would you like me to come with you, sir?"

"That won't be necessary. I've been expecting Lady utherland for some time now."

As Greyson disappeared down the back stairs, Sullivan urried the opposite way. Opening one of the double doors the studio, he stood in the threshold, seeing the petite oman who waited, her back turned to him.

She stared at the painting of the woman she had betrayed long ago. Her sister. Greyson had provided her with a race of candles. They now sputtered on the desk.

"I loved him, you know."

Sullivan didn't wonder how she knew it was he who had

joined her, but he didn't question her instincts. Despite
that had happened, he felt an affinity with this woma
Perhaps because one so small, so delicate, so beautifu
should not be so inherently strong-willed.

"My intent to seduce your father was not entirely ma
cious. I thought that once Richard Albert had spent a fe
night in my arms, once he'd kissed me, caressed me, love
me, he would no longer care for Julie."

Estella traced her sister's canvas smile, touched th
crinkled lines of laughter fanning from the corners of h
eyes. "I was quite foolish. Quite foolish, and quite smitte
Julie was so innocent in the ways of the world, I was su
that she couldn't possibly be in love with your father. N
really, *truly,* in love as I was."

Night flowed around them like warm India ink, remin
ing Sullivan of the lateness of the hour. For Estella to con
to him this way had been dangerous. For him to agree
meet with her without the benefit of someone to guard h
back had been foolhardy. But somehow he sensed she wou
prove no threat to him, even though she had hurt his fath
immeasurably by falling into league with Nigel's plans.

"Were you in love with him, Estella, or merely infat
ated?"

"Amazingly enough, I love him still."

"What about Nigel?"

She faced him, her chin tipping, a sad mixture of pri
and defiance tainting her expression. "I have become th
consummate actress. In the last thirty years, I have give
him every reason to believe that I worship the ground l
walks upon. He doesn't know how I've strangled beneath h
possessiveness, his jealousy. He doesn't know how muc
I've grown to hate him for what he did to Richard Alber
Not to mention my sister." Her voice dropped. "He doesn
know that the son I bore him is not his own."

Completely turning her back to the portrait, she walke
forward. It was then, as she stepped more completely in
the light, that he saw the bruises on her jaw.

When she noted Sullivan's attention, she met his ga
with a piercing thoroughness that belied her petite frame

"He hit you."

"Mere badges of honor, I assure you. Do not worry overmuch. His actions gave me the courage to leave him, you know. Otherwise, I would not have met with you this evening. I told myself that I wouldn't help you. I told myself I wouldn't even allow myself to remember our brief *tête-à-tête* of this afternoon."

"These changed your mind?" he asked, gesturing to the mottled colors beginning to appear.

"Surprisingly enough, not entirely. This is not the first time he's done such a thing; it wouldn't be the last. No . . . I grew tired of pretending," was her cryptic reply. She reached beneath her cape to withdraw a sheaf of papers. "I believe you asked if I knew anything about the conspiracy to discredit your father. I not only knew about it, but, as a woman scorned, I did nothing to stop it. I thought that if I couldn't have Richard Albert, I would take all he would have given me, the title, family wealth, prestige, and pass them on to the son he never knew he had." She extended the ivory-aged parchments. "Take them."

"Does Cecil know—"

"That you are his half-brother? No."

"You realize that if you do this, he will never stand to inherit. He might be the firstborn of my father, but even if the truth were known, he would be considered little more—"

"Than a by-blow bastard. I know. But in the last thirty years, I have also come to realize that I have more to offer my son than a legacy of deceit. He deserves more. You deserve more."

She hesitated, then reached beneath her cape again. "I trust you, Richard Sutherland. I don't deserve your kindness or your compassion, but you have given them to me freely, nonetheless. So I would like to leave you with two small gifts. The first is yours to use as you will." She withdrew a letter addressed to her husband in her own script. "I have taken the liberty of explaining my actions and the true parentage of my son. If it can aid you and your cause, you may feel free to use it at any time and in any capacity."

Her lips tightened, her chin trembled ever so slightly, but she determinedly pushed away her imminent emotions. "The second is not for you, but for Gelsey . . . no, Chelsea is her name now, I believe." She clutched something hidden in her palm, then opened to reveal a pair of keys tied with a white velvet ribbon. "Tell her that I knew. That I knew and did nothing. I am deeply and most regrettably ashamed." She dangled the keys, waiting for Sullivan to take them. Then she seemed to study those tiny pieces of iron with great remorse. "Tell her that I admire her greatly. She stood up to Nigel—something that until now I haven't had the courage to do."

Without further comment, she hurried from the room in a rustle of skirts.

"Estella," he called quickly.

She stopped but did not turn.

"As I told you before, my father never blamed you."

The air pulsed in silence.

"He should have. I may not have encouraged Nigel to do all that he has done." She shifted to look at him over her shoulder. "But I did nothing to discourage him, either. Until now."

Sullivan waited, listening to the quick clacking of her heels on the marble tile. He heard Greyson's murmured farewell, the creak of the door, the rumble of the carriage. Then the stillness of the evening returned.

Crossing to the desk, Sullivan sank onto the chair and placed the papers on the blotter in front of him. For some time, he didn't bother to read them. The Countess of Lindon had wrapped them in clean paper and secured them with a daub of wax.

His thumb traced the raised pattern on the seal. *Countess.* It was a title that should have belonged to his mother.

Sullivan's eyes lifted to collide with those of the painted visage. Somehow, he had a hard time imagining Julie Perry Sutherland being burdened with such a ponderous prefix to her name. Yet he sensed she would have worn such a responsibility as easily as she'd worn her smile.

But it wasn't to be. Not after fate, in the form of her elder sister, stepped in to change the future.

Rubbing his palms over the smooth, cool paper, Sullivan pondered the irony of his situation. If these were the records he'd asked for, he held the proof he needed to destroy Nigel Sutherland once and for all. The woman who had given it to him had been the same woman who had helped to rob his father of his birthright.

Lifting the packet, Sullivan bent the seal in half, cracking the brittle wax. If Estella had not agreed to help him, he would have continued with his scheme. But he would have lacked one vital piece of evidence. A name. The one name his father had been unable to provide him with. The identity that had remained hidden for decades.

Thirty years ago, Nigel Sutherland had arranged for Richard Albert to be accused of treason. He had manufactured evidence, notified the authorities, then helped to try the case. But it was the original informant, the public official Nigel had bribed and paid to steal the classified documents whom Sullivan sought.

He began to skim the pages, quickly at first, then more slowly, then with growing disbelief. He had asked Estella for one particular shred of information, but she had provided him with more, much more. In his possession, he found evidence linking Nigel to murder, fraud, conspiracy, political bribery, and theft, with dates beginning as early as the turn of the century.

Sullivan's pulse quickened, his mouth grew dry. If he were to give these to the authorities, Nigel Sutherland would not see the light of day save through a prison window. He would be lucky to escape a firing squad. Yet, the one name Sullivan sought continued to elude him.

Damn it, he couldn't see Nigel locked in jail and allow his original accomplice to roam free. Someone had joined with him to frame the Sutherland heir. Someone had been willing to risk death to commit treason. But who? *Who?*

He skimmed the papers, sifting through them, barely registering the horrible acts they outlined, the unspeakable crimes of greed and exploitation.

Then, just when he feared his search had been in vain, he found what he sought near the bottom of the pile. A copy of the stolen papers which had resulted in his father's exile. A scrawled bank draft dated thirty years before.

And finally the name of the traitor he sought.

Reginald Wilde.

Two horsemen brought their mounts to a stop on the hill above the cottage. The house was dark save for a few weak beams of light that seeped through the ground-floor curtains.

"We shouldn't have left Rich—"

"He'll be fine, Gregory. He was sleeping peacefully when we left. The woman at the tavern agreed to nurse him while we were gone."

"Still . . ."

"He wasn't strong enough to come with us, despite his protestations. We need our wits about us. He'll be safer there. Should we be caught, Nigel still won't know of his existence."

Gregory reluctantly conceded.

"You brought the deed?"

"Yes."

"You have the copy of the signet ring like Sully requested?"

"Yes."

"Well, then. We'd best make haste. This is one meeting where I don't intend to miss our entrance."

Nearly an hour had passed since Lady Sutherland had taken her leave. Greyson and Smee hesitated outside the door to the studio.

"What has he been doing in there for so long?"

Greyson assumed an attitude of injured dignity. "I am not in the habit of prying."

"Suppose she hurt him."

Greyson snorted at the unlikelihood of such a preposterous suggestion.

"Perhaps you should rush in without an announcement."

"Nonsense." Greyson girded his courage and tapped on the door. A beat of silence followed. Two. The men fidgeted nervously.

"What is it?"

The gruff reply caused Smee to wilt in obvious relief. Even Greyson's stoic facade cracked.

"It is nearly midnight, sir. You asked me to fetch you once everyone arrived."

Greyson motioned for Smee to return to the kitchen, not wanting the master to think that they hadn't trusted him—or, worse yet, that they'd fussed over his safety like a pair of old hens.

Smee scurried away as fast as his stout legs could carry him. No sooner had he disappeared than the studio door opened.

"They've come?"

"Yes, sir. I was able to round up most of the old staff of Lindon Manor. Just as you requested."

"Very good, Greyson. Follow me."

Sullivan strode through the abutting rooms to the kitchen, his stance as purposeful as a king's. Just as he had hoped, the kitchen was now crowded with men and women alike—short, tall, rich, poor. They served the Sutherlands as cooks and grooms and footmen. There were former servants present as well. Those who either had their services terminated by Nigel Sutherland or had left him of their own volition.

They were a humble lot, most of them struggling to eke out a daily living. All had one quality in common: a fierce determination to see matters put to rights once and for all.

When Richard entered, they stood, en masse, and eyed him with wary suspicion, a suspicion that disappeared as soon as he advanced to the table and joined the other two figures who waited.

The strangers had already attracted a great deal of attention. One was tall and grim with golden brown hair, another a giant with a pronounced limp. Now a third stranger had joined them, claiming to be the long-lost son of Richard Albert Sutherland III.

Sullivan faced the group, his mien hard and purposeful. He did not introduce his brothers yet, but merely plunged headlong into persuading these people to help them.

As he opened his mouth and began to outline his plan, his audience's judgmental attitude softened, then disappeared altogether. How like his grandfather, their original employer, he looked. Not to mention the son—he had Richard Albert's bearing, his command.

Attention bounced from the man claiming to be Richard Sutherland IV to his companions and back again. Soon, a breathless wonder settled over them, a sparkling excitement. There was no disguising those square jaws and rake-hell stances.

Brothers.

Attention slowly returned to Richard Albert Sutherland IV. A respectful hush cloaked their weary shoulders, bolstering them with hope. For as they heard him speak with his father's voice, saw the gleam of his mother's eyes, noted the glitter of the Lindon signet on his finger . . .

They knew they were confronting the true Sutherland heirs.

Chapter
22

Sullivan Arthur Cane Sutherland did not go back to bed. After meeting with his brothers and the townspeople who had agreed to help them, he returned to the bedroom. For long, silent hours, he sat in the chair, watching Chelsea sleep.

He was struck by the ironic similarities of their situations. He had adopted a false name to protect his family. She had adopted a false name to protect herself. Both of them had been caught in a situation not of their own making. But where he had yet to see the consequences of his own actions, Chelsea had made a life for herself. She had cloaked her true beginnings in anonymity and had been willing to risk all she had gained in order to help an old woman.

Sullivan's fingers unconsciously closed over the keys in his pocket, rubbing the intricate designs. To his infinite surprise, now that he knew the unorthodox upbringing Chelsea had been exposed to, he didn't care. The past didn't matter.

He loved her so much. He had never really understood the meaning of that phrase before. He had assumed that he knew what it meant to care for a woman, but he'd been wrong, so utterly wrong. His emotions were heightened, taking on an edge that he had never encountered before. His protectiveness was sharper, his sexual appetite keener. His fear . . .

His fear was a living thing, gripping his heart with icy talons. Never before had he considered the true risks he was taking. By this time tomorrow, his plan would be complete. One way or another. He would have to live with the consequences, or perhaps die trying.

Life had become so precious to him. Because he wanted to spend the rest of his days with this woman. His Chelsea.

Rising, Sullivan crept toward the bed. Bending, he pressed a kiss to the top of her head, inhaled her scent, so womanly, so exotic, then placed a peony on the pillow beside her.

Resolutely, he left the room. By the time the first pink rays began to wriggle beneath the lingering storm clouds, he had joined his brothers in preparation for the upcoming campaign.

A wizened old woman, her body the shape of a wrinkled pear, shuffled through the servants' quarters at Lindon Manor. The Countess of Lindon was a good woman, an honest woman, a charitable woman. Each year, come solstice morn, she allowed the house servants a special treat of an extra hour abed and a cup of tea in their rooms.

Mad Martha, as the gnarled woman had come to be known, was the exception to the rule. Elderly, crabbed, she was basically "out to graze," as the rest of the staff called it. She performed a few odd tasks about the manor, none that really amounted to much. But it was her joy, her pleasure, to prepare the solstice tea.

This particular holiday, Mad Martha was especially pleased with her task. She made two pots. One a mixture of the finest Chinese blend. The other a stronger-tasting Indian variety, with an added mixture of herbs guaranteed to drag a full-grown man to his knees with stomach cramps and intestinal distress.

Cackling in secret glee, she began to make her rounds,

knowing just who remained in favor and who would receive the full brunt of a thirty-year-old wrath.

Come dawn, the majordomo of Lindon Manor took ill. A hearty and healthy man of but forty-five, he experienced sudden overwhelming pains in his gullet and took to his bed. He was soon followed by a cook, three housemaids, a handful of stable boys, and the men known by the rest of the staff as Nigel's personal guards.

With a score of guests and still a week's worth of entertaining, Nigel was forced to do what he could. He went into the village at first light, approached the old gentleman who had formerly held the position of butler, and offered him temporary employment. His proposition bordered on a threat; he was not surprised that the man agreed to his terms.

Upon his return, Nigel discovered that yet another cook had taken ill, as well as three more maids and a hostler. Not wanting such news to spread, Nigel put Estella in charge of hiring more locals. By midmorning, the positions had been filled, and he had the eeriest sensation that he had seen all of these people before. In this very house. In their very same positions.

Such a state was possible, since he had fired at least half of the original staff, and very few of them had moved from Addlebury since. Still, to his knowledge, the townspeople had sworn an oath never to darken his doors again. Nigel was delighted to see that once again they'd been forced to submit to his will.

He was whistling beneath his breath later that same morning when Reginald met him at the bottom of the steps.

"There is a man to see you. A Mr. Wilson."

"Yes, yes. Show him into the study."

Reginald hesitated, then asked stiffly. "May I ask who the gentleman is and what business he has with you?"

Nigel, who had summoned the solicitor posthaste to see if there were any legal possibilities he could employ to retrieve the deed to Lindon Manor, regarded his secretary in sudden irritation. "No, you may not. Just send him in."

"Yes, *sir.*" The last word held a slightly bitter inflection.

Nigel stopped on his way to his study to stare out the windows at the verdant lawns below. The day would be perfect for the solstice celebration. The sun hung in the sky like a pat of butter in a blue sea. The flowers of his wife's rose garden shimmered snow-white amidst a green velvet backdrop.

His lips tilted in a slow, satisfied smile. Yes, it was a beautiful day. In Richard Sutherland's case, it would be a beautiful day to die.

Sullivan Cane looked up from the crudely drawn map of the Lindon Manor floor plan and surveyed the half-dozen people who had intently followed his instructions.

"Any questions?"

One by one, his comrades-in-arms shook their heads. Greyson and Smee, Littleton the baker, Bretmer the blacksmith's apprentice, and Rothel and Lowe, two farmers from the north end of the valley.

"You're sure that Sutherland will not remember you from the village?"

The four locals shook their heads, and Rothel added, "Doubt he'd recognize me own mother, I do, and she served as his nanny fer a time. 'E 'as a way of seein' right through you, 'e does."

"As long as he continues to do so," Sullivan warned. "Very well, gentlemen. Assume your new identities and move into position. Come noon, we will begin."

Bars of sunlight threaded through the *portieres* from the slit of space where they had not been drawn together properly. The greedy warmth spilled onto the floor, heating the air with a humid, cloying warmth and robbing the room of its oxygen.

Stirring in the bed, Chelsea knew she should rise and open the curtains to allow the morning breezes to sift into the room. But she was loath to move when she felt so deliciously weary. So satisfied. After all, she hadn't really had much sleep to speak of.

Her lips tilted in a serene smile. A satisfied smile. She reached out, seeking, stretching across the cool linen sheets in search of the man who had filled her evening hours with such delicious dalliance.

To her dismay, she found no warmth, no dipping of the mattress. But there, upon the pillow, she encountered a velvety petal, a delicate blossom.

Flower. His first word. His first—

Her eyes opened. She grew still. Her heart lurched within her breast as her fingers came away sticky. Wet.

Crimson and white.

"So good of you to finally awaken, my dear."

The dark, silken tones brought a fresh pang of dread, and Chelsea recoiled as she focused on the stains. A scream lodged in her throat. Blood. The snow-white petals were spattered with blood. Swallowing an instinctive cry, she gripped the sheets and dragged the covers to her neck. Slowly, as if she would shatter by moving too quickly, she rolled onto her back.

Nigel sat in the chair opposite. The same chair she had used to draw the delicate underthings onto her body in order to torment the man she loved.

A burning heat flooded her cheeks as she realized the floor was scattered with frothy silk and lace unmentionables. The delicate chemise lay only inches away from the toe of Nigel's boot.

"How lovely you are this morning," Nigel drawled, resting his elbows on the armrests. A red-brown wash covered the knuckles of his right hand. In his left, he held a glinting blade. "How flushed, how eager. How satisfied." The last spat from his lips.

Chelsea couldn't speak. She regarded the man who had broken into her room in horror, sure that he meant to punish her for what she had done. Just as he had punished Jaime.

Richard! She searched the room for evidence of the man she'd come to love so much. What had he done to Richard? Dear sweet heaven, he had threatened to hurt him. Gasping, she strove to wipe away the streaks, sure that it was

279

Richard's blood. Nigel had killed him. Killed him! It was her fault. She had done this to him. She should have forced him to leave.

Nigel clucked in disapproval when he saw her cringe and rub at her skin. "Silly child. I haven't harmed him," he said, reading her thoughts in the uncanny way he'd always had a knack of doing. "Yet."

A shiver racked her frame at that chilling word.

"The man seems to have the instincts of a cat. He must have awakened hours ago. Leaving you alone. All alone."

He surveyed the room in casual disdain. "Pity. I really had anticipated a meeting with the chap, face to face this time." He wiped the knife on the fabric of the chair until the metal sparkled as if newly washed, then tucked it into the top of his boot. "As it is, I feel certain the time will come soon enough." He speared Chelsea with a look that contained a shard of barely concealed malice. "I know that he's planning a confrontation tonight at the Solstice Masquerade. I intend to let him go through with his little charade. Just this once." His lips quirked. "It amuses me. To think that for the next few hours he will plot and plan and maneuver. All to no avail. Because he cannot best me." He rose to his feet and moved toward her, stealthily, like a cat preying upon a bird.

"However. In exchange for my largesse at not killing the man immediately, I will demand a forfeit of you, my dear."

Chelsea shrank back, despising herself for being unable to respond to his threats. She wished she could rail at him, attack him, anything to stop him. But from the moment she'd awakened to find him here, watching her, she'd been flung back into the past. She'd become a shivering child. Impotent against his strength, his cunning, his calculated charm.

He stopped by the side of the bed. Just as he had a hundred times in the past. Just as he did in the nightmares she experienced at least a dozen times a year. His eyes roamed her face, her neck, her bare shoulders.

"My sweet little lovely," he crooned. "My darling one. My precious." Sinking onto the side of the bed, he bracketed her face, leaning over her adoringly. "Come back to me, my pet. Come live with me. We shall have such great times together. I will build you a palace. I'll clothe you in furs, adorn you with jewels."

The familiar promises rolled over her like a murky ocean.

"Be with me, Gelsey. Be my lover."

His weight shifted, and he skimmed the wanton tumble of her hair. Chelsea shuddered beneath the clamminess of blood, the all-too-familiar sweet-copper odor.

In a burst of disgust, she snapped, "Go to bloody hell."

Her unexpected response only made him smile, but a shard of fury flared. "So beautiful. So strong. So fiery."

He touched the fullness of her lips, and she bit her cheek to keep from saying anything more to provoke him as he shifted to touch her ear, follow the line of her jaw.

"I've missed you so, Gelsey. I've pined away for you in utter desolation. I let you know in a thousand different ways that I was thinking of you." The caresses became firmer, harsher. "You've continued to be so mean." His voice took a hard edge. "I never deserved your meanness, Gelsey." His hand curled over the hem of the sheet. "I gave you the world, and what did I receive in return? Nothing."

He tugged at the covering, and though she clasped it in a death grip, he managed to dislodge it enough to expose the smooth upper swells of her breasts.

"I adored you," he continued, his thumb rubbing over the creamy flesh he had disclosed. "I protected you, pampered you. I taught you the arts of seduction—and now you've used what I gave you to tempt that . . . that . . . heathen." His lips twisted. "I never thought you could be so lacking in taste. But then, you've changed over the years, haven't you?" He sighed. "My one mistake was in giving you the time to grow into womanhood. I should have taken you that first day. When you were still awed enough, still naive enough to succumb. But I've never had a taste for awkwardness."

He bent low to press a kiss against her shoulder. "I didn't even care that I would not be the first. After you left, I knew you would probably be seduced by one of those randy employers of yours, but it didn't matter. I've never been overly fond of deflowering virgins. Let some other chap do it." He gripped her upper arms as he levered himself toward her so that his lips could hover above her own. "But I had hoped to be among the first dozen."

He crushed his mouth to hers. Dry, firm, intrusive. He kissed her forcefully, with a barely restrained ferocity, then drew away, searching her features. Reaching out, he retrieved the white rose from where it rested on the opposite pillow. Slowly, tormentingly, he trailed the delicate blossom over her forehead, her face, her neck, her breasts.

"Your savage has gone into town. I have a man who is watching him and knows every move he makes."

His sudden change in topic startled her, wrenching her free from her morass of confusion and disgust.

"At five o'clock this evening, a carriage will arrive at Lookout Point." His grip bit into her flesh. A desperate cruelty snaked into his face. "You will be there. You will come to me of your own volition. You will stay with me until I tell you to go. Otherwise, this eve you will be making love to a corpse."

Dropping the rose onto her chest, he rose and strode to the window. Slipping through the draperies, she heard the scuff of shoes upon stone, the rattle of the metal trellis anchored to the wall, then the scrabble of hooves.

Chelsea took a deep breath, still locked in an icy grip of fear. Rising from her bed, Chelsea threw on her robe and ran to the nursery, hoping that Nigel had been wrong and Richard was merely changing.

But when she opened the door, she saw that Smee and Greyson had been there before her. Now that their master had disclosed his true identity, they had returned the nursery to its pristine order and covered the furniture with huge squares of muslin. They had ostensibly moved Richard's belongings to the only other spare room on the floor, even though Chelsea doubted they were ignorant of the fact of where he had spent the night.

A choked wail split the morning stillness. Chelsea ran into the hall and down the steps.

In the vestibule below, Beatrice huddled on the ground. Alarmed that Nigel has somehow hurt the fragile old woman, Chelsea raced forward. But within a few feet of Biddy, she saw what had caused her cries.

Lying in a puddle of blood lay the crumpled shape of a diminutive cocker spaniel.

Smee and Greyson burst into the room and took stock of the situation. Greyson bent to cover the animal with one of his handkerchiefs while Smee quickly ushered Biddy away. But Chelsea remained.

Wrapping her arms around her waist, Chelsea studied the entryway in growing panic, knowing instinctively that if she did not do as Nigel asked, Richard would not live to see the sun rise on the morrow. Her only chance of protecting the man she loved would be to offer her body to the man she hated. Even then, she knew it wouldn't be enough. She knew that in order for Nigel to allow Richard to go free willingly, she must offer him something more.

She must offer him her complete surrender.

Nigel, Lord Sutherland, seventh Earl of Lindon, slowed his mount, frowning at the sight that greeted him upon his return. One of his coaches had been parked next to the carriage block. Behind it, another, smaller wagon was being loaded with trunks and portmanteaus, boxes, and satchels.

Even as he watched, his wife stepped onto the portico, squinted up at the glowering sky, and tugged on a pair of kid leather gloves.

Tapping his gelding's flanks, Nigel trotted up to her and dismounted. "Dearest?"

"Hello, Nigel." She lifted her cheek for him to kiss, all the while keeping watch on the servants clambering to put the last of the baggage away.

"What's all this?"

"I'm leaving you, dear," she answered, so matter-of-factly, she might have been discussing the unseasonably wet weather they were experiencing for the middle of June.

Nigel chuckled, assuming she was teasing, but her expression remained calm, controlled, and completely serious.

"You needn't worry, Nigel. I haven't made a scene. I've gone about the whole affair quite pragmatically. I put Margot in charge of the final arrangements for the masquerade. I've seen to the decorations, the flowers, and the menu. I've taken care of the last-minute responses to our invitations and prepared places for any unexpected guests to sleep should they decide to stay at the manor after all."

She pointed to a box that lay on the top step. "I'll keep that one with me up front, Manfred," she instructed the driver, then returned her attention to her husband. "Where was I? Oh, yes. Everything has been taken care of. You won't suffer any inconvenience, I assure you."

Nigel still didn't understand her sudden departure. "Has something happened? One of your family taken ill?"

She smiled charmingly at him and patted him on the cheek. "How dear of you to ask. No, nothing like that. I've simply come to a point where I can't bear to remain your wife, Nigel. I know that the news may come as a bit of a shock, and I know I haven't discussed this with you, but . . ." She shrugged. "There it is. In a nutshell."

A slow tension began to build in his gut, a sharp combination of panic, anger, and disbelief. "Estella—"

"I won't make a fuss. As far as the *ton* is concerned, I'll make no announcements. If anyone is to ask, I shall simply tell them that I plan to make an extended visit to London where I intend to live with my son for a time. You do remember him, don't you, Nigel?"

"Of course I remember him, damn it. He's—"

"That's neither here nor there," she interrupted. "Though from the way you ignore him, don't even speak of him, I'm delighted you still remember his name."

The sugar-coated barb stung, just as it had been meant to do.

"Thank you, Manfred. Is that everything?"

"Yes, mum."

"Then let's be going."

Estella lifted on tiptoe to press her lips to Nigel's cheek. "Don't worry, my dear. Things have a way of working out for the best. Especially with you. Like a cat, you always manage to land on your feet." She patted his chest. "See to it that you keep dry in this nasty weather we've been having, and please, please remember to oversee the repairs of that leak we've been experiencing in the upper west attic."

With that, she turned, gathered her skirts, and climbed into the carriage. The footman closed the door and hurried to the wagon which would follow behind.

"Good-bye, dear," she called, leaning through the window and waving one last time. Her lips tilted in her usual smile. The breeze toyed with a lock of rich golden hair. Nigel felt as if she'd plunged a sword into his stomach as the horses jerked at the traces and the entourage rumbled down the lane.

The common room of the inn sweltered in the late-afternoon heat, hugging the smoky air within its stone walls and shutting out the least little breeze that might offer some relief.

Reginald Wilde grimaced, sure that his clothing would soon reek of the same pungent smells but knowing he had no alternative. He had received a mysterious missive. One that had not only piqued his interest but kindled a bit of fear.

Sitting at the far corner table as he'd been told, he ordered a pint of bitter ale, then waited. His timepiece had advanced a quarter-hour before a small, gawky adolescent sank into the chair opposite.

"Well?"

"Are you plannin' t' drink that?"

Reginald shook his head, and the young boy eagerly grasped the mug, drained it of half its contents, then swiped the back of his hand over his lips.

"Your note was barely legible."

The boy grinned. "Right smart idea, wasn't it? Sendin' fer you that way. Jus' likes the gentry is always doin'. 'Ad me sister write it fer me, I did."

"It was a stupid idea. Stupid and foolish. What if someone had intercepted it?"

The boy leaned forward, his blue eyes snapping. "Next time, I'll jus' come up t' the manor house, bold as brass.

They'd all like that, wouldn't they? I'm sure 'is lordship would like a gawk at yer 'ired boy."

Reginald's lips tightened in disapproval. "What is it that's so important you had to see me today? You should be working. That's what I pay you to do—bring me information on the magistrate's activities."

The boy leaned back and grinned. "A man came t' see 'is magistrativeness early this mornin'. 'E came t' talk t' him about you."

Reginald grew still. So still, so cold, so tense. "What did he want?"

"Wouldn't you like t' know?"

Reginald's fist snapped out with the speed of a snake, closing around the boy's collar and yanking him close. "Don't play games with me, boy."

"I don't know! I don't know what they said. I was sent to the stables t' see t' the gent's animal. How's I supposed t' know what was said?"

"If you know so blasted little, then why did you summon me?"

"'Cause I heard 'em say they was goin' to bring you in."

"Bring me in? What in heaven's name for?"

The boy shrugged. "Like I said, I wasn't there when they talked about ye. But I heard a name bein' bandied about—and a crime."

"What name? What crime?"

"Sutherland. Richard Albert Sutherland."

Though his posture remained still and lax, Reginald's skin grew paler. "The crime?"

"Treason."

As if the word itself had mystical powers, the door to the inn burst open, and a giant dressed as a uniformed officer of the law appeared.

Reginald connected with the man's gaze and knew that somehow, someway, his sins had been discovered. Leaping from his seat, he overturned the table, then scrambled through the open window and ran for his horse.

Rupert chortled and removed his hat. Adopting a coarse

country dialect, he crossed toward the far corner booth, saying, "Blimey. What bee bit 'is arse?"

The boy giggled, then stared down at the puddle of ale seeping into the dirty planks of the floor. Sighing, he stood and sauntered toward the giant and the long-haired gentleman who sat in the shadows.

"Well done, Jackie, well done," the man drawled, removing a half-crown and passing it to the urchin. "Now, if you're game, I've got another little something for you to do."

Sutherland. Richard Albert Sutherland III.

Reginald Wilde galloped north, feeling the bitter roiling of disbelief churning in his stomach. Only one man on earth could have exposed such a crime. One man.

Nigel Sutherland.

No. *No!* Nigel wouldn't do that to him. Reginald had given him the best years of his life. He'd slaved for him, stolen for him, even killed for him. Nigel couldn't have asked for more. He couldn't possibly want to be rid of him. Not when Reginald knew so many secrets and had been privy to a host of his more unsavory practices in the past.

But was that his fatal error? Did Nigel intend to be quit of him? Because of what he knew?

Bending low over the animal's neck, he charged toward Lindon Manor. Once there, he jumped from the saddle and ran into the house, ignoring the curious gazes of the guests. Storming into the study, he took a set of keys from the end of his watch chain and unlocked the panels that hid the portrait of Chelsea Wickersham. Swinging the painting aside on its hidden hinges, he exposed the safe hidden behind it. Muttering to himself, he inserted a second key into the lock.

What he found inside made his heart plummet into the pit of his stomach. The chamber was empty.

Empty.

Nigel Sutherland had betrayed him.

* * *

Lady Estella Perry Sutherland, seventh Countess of Lindon, waited until her coach had traveled a good twenty miles away from the estates, then rapped the ceiling with her fan. The conveyance came to a rolling stop, and Manfred bent to the window to take her orders.

"Alter our course to take us to Glasgow, Manfred."

The servant was obviously surprised at the change in directions but did not question the Countess. He, too, had seen the bruises.

As the carriage lurched into the road again, Estella closed her eyes and began to pray. Prayed that her husband would not follow her, that he would not set his bloodhounds on her trail, that he would not remember Cecil was in Paris, not London.

Then, thinking of Richard Sutherland and what he planned to do, she prayed more fervently than ever that justice would prevail. The devil who had once been her husband would receive his just rewards.

Chapter
23

The clock in the vestibule had just finished chiming quarter past four when Chelsea heard hooves on the drive. The pang of relief she experienced was nearly overpowering. She had been so sure Richard wouldn't return in time. That she wouldn't have the opportunity to see him, just once more.

Caring little for propriety or decorum, she burst from the door and ran through the garden, meeting him as he galloped up the lane.

"Richard? Richard!"

He brought the horse to a stop, smiling, but his smile faltered. "What is it? What's wrong?"

"Wrong?" She summoned a contented expression and tried to still the torturous beating of her heart. Her fingers curled around his calf, and she rubbed the muscle there. "I merely missed you, is all."

Leaning down, he caught her behind the coil of braids secured to the nape of her neck. Pulling her on tiptoes, he kissed her soundly. He finally drew back to say, "Then we shall have to do something about that, won't we?" He swung from the saddle and, taking her hand, walked with her into the stables.

Chelsea clung to him, trying to memorize everything about him, his height, the sheen of sunlight on his hair, his clean, masculine scent.

"I suppose I shouldn't have left so abruptly this morn."

Chelsea's grip tightened spasmodically, and she turned to embrace him. "No. No, I didn't mind." Little did he know that had he stayed, his confrontation with Nigel might have come much sooner than anticipated. Remembering the bloodied rose, the lifeless dog, she held him more tightly.

"Chelsea?"

"I barely endured waiting for you to return."

"Had I known, I would not have left at all," he replied indulgently.

"No. I did not mind. Truly." She eased backward and regarded him for long moments, trying to imprint each line, each tone, each plane of his presence into her memory. Then, without saying another word, she took the reins, tying them to the stall support.

"Chelsea, what—"

She stopped his words before he could finish. An urgency filled her. An incredible need. She knew what the days ahead of her would be like. She couldn't fool herself into thinking they would be pleasant. She needed this hour, this moment, to keep her sane. She needed this one memory to help her cope with the future. But there wasn't much time. There wasn't much time!

"Nay, don't speak, Richard. Merely love me. Here. Now. Show me how much you care for me. Prove to me that you will never forget what we've shared. Please."

When he would have questioned her again, she pushed him back until his shoulders pressed against one of the upright beams lining the aisle. "Show me," she commanded, sliding her hands beneath his jacket and stripping it from his back. She quickly followed with his vest, then, with only a thin layer of cambric between them, pressed her body to his, thigh to thigh, chest to chest, and kissed him.

The caress began gently at first, but within seconds passion ignited like an inferno, burning white-hot and out of control. Fingers searched, hips arched. Chelsea responded wholeheartedly, becoming a wildcat furiously bent on absorbing each texture and sensation anew.

Richard fumbled with the fastenings of her gown, managing to expose little more than a strip of bare skin down her chest. He caressed that narrow triangle, delving beneath the cloth until he rubbed one nipple.

She arched against him, gasping, and he bent to take her mouth again. His kiss became bold, rapacious. Tongues dueled and tangled, bodies strained, arms reached.

When he would have drawn back, she clutched at his hair. It had come loose from its leather thong, spilling over her like hot satin and offering her the handhold she needed.

"No . . . don't leave me," she gasped.

"Too fast . . . slow down."

She peered at him wickedly, dragging a caress over his nipples, down the length of his chest, to the top of his trousers. "If you will remember, I told you once: 'One of your first lessons is that a proper gentleman should not keep a lady waiting.'"

Before he knew what she was about, she yanked at the placket of his trousers. Buttons popped and rattled over the cobble floor. Then she plunged down to free him, caress him.

"Damn it, Chelsea," he rasped between clenched teeth. "I can't wait . . . I can't . . ."

She whimpered against him as he reached for the hems of her skirts. To Chelsea, he seemed to take an inordinate amount of time to clutch at the fabric of her gown, lifting, pushing, until the flounces of her chemise and petticoats spilled around his elbows and he encountered the bare skin of her thighs and buttocks beneath.

Then he reversed their positions, her spine against the beam. Grasping her thighs, he took her lips with his own. She could feel him nudging against her most sensitive places as he lifted her, pushed her hips firmly against the support, then surged into her welcoming warmth, hot and powerful. Sleek and strong.

She shuddered, wrapping her legs about him, her arms about his shoulders. Never before had she felt him so deep, so real. She clung to him, savoring it all, the closeness, the passion, the inferno of sensations. When the inner spasms began, she bit into the curve of his neck to stop her cries, knowing that this would be the last time.

The last time . . .

Later, curled up against Richard on the blanket he'd spread over a mound of straw, she rubbed the swell of his chest, the pebbled surface of his nipples.

"My real name is Gelsey O'Rourke and I lived with Nigel for three years," she began softly, not looking at him, not allowing him to speak. "At first, I thought he was my savior, my friend. But I soon discovered he was to be my own private hell . . ."

She told him everything, leaving nothing secret. She spoke of the beautiful house, the clothes, the education. Then she went on to describe how she was trained like a well-kept courtesan—and though Nigel had never taken her himself, she had seen enough, heard enough, to dispel the last vestiges of innocence and ignorance she held. She conveyed the rising horror she felt at knowing he would take her on her sixteenth birthday, Nigel's fondness for liquor and opium, his cruelty to employees and staff. She related all she knew of his crimes and her inability to actually prove that any of them were his doing. Last of all, she talked about Jaime and the painting.

After she had finished, he held her close, so close she nearly believed he could be hers, would be hers, forever.

But time was ticking away. Ruthlessly. Being gobbled up by some greedy god. At long last, she kissed his throat, his breast bone, his navel. One final caress.

He joined the taste of his skin with that of his lips. "Thank you."

"For what?" she asked tremulously.

"For trusting me."

"I will always love you. Never forget. I love you more than life itself."

"Chelsea?"

When he would have questioned her, she said, "Smee and

Greyson will come looking for us if we don't make an appearance soon. I've got to cut some flowers for Biddy." She tried to silently convey all of the adoration that filled her soul. An emotion that, until he had entered her life, she had thought she was incapable of feeling. "Take care of your horse. See if you can't round up your buttons," she teased. "Then we'll talk."

He nodded, and she stood, feeling his eyes follow her each step of the way. At the door, she paused, looking over her shoulder. For all time, she would remember him this way, his hair spilling onto the blanket, his shirt mussed and partially fastened, his trousers only half buttoned and gaping to reveal the golden skin of his hips, a peek of dark hair. Then she walked from the stables.

Out of his life.

The carriage waited for her at the bottom of Lookout Point, just as Nigel had promised. But what Chelsea hadn't anticipated was that he would be there to meet her himself.

He stepped from the carriage, tall, lean, handsome. His smile was welcoming, his manner charming, as he swept his hat from his head, bowed, and extended a posy of delicate white rosebuds tied with a pink ribbon.

"For you."

"Thank you."

"I'm so glad you decided you could come," he said, as if she had appeared for nothing more than an afternoon drive.

She didn't answer, not trusting herself to speak. Her mind was filled with thoughts of the man she had just left—and what he would think of her when he found her gone.

Nigel ushered her into the carriage, then took the seat opposite. "You won't miss him, you know," he stated once they were under way.

Once again, he had known the intent of her thoughts.

The clatter of the hooves was his only reply. He might have forced her to join him in his home, he might even force her to submit to his will, but that was her body. She would never allow him to break her soul.

Sighing, Nigel shifted to sit next to her, caressing her hair, her cheek, her jaw. "Come, my sweet. What's past is past, and you know I won't hold you accountable for all that has occurred."

When she stared at him with barely disguised hatred, a glint of warning appeared. "As long as you are wise and listen to your elders. You must do just exactly what I tell you to do."

Sullivan strode into the house, whistling to himself. But the melody died in his throat when he encountered Smee and Greyson in the kitchen.

He knew his appearance was a little ragged. He knew these men would probably be perturbed since they had supplied his wardrobe. But, in truth, he didn't think it was entirely his fault that several of the buttons to his trousers were now in the palm of his hand.

"Master Richard," Greyson broached, as if picking his way over a battlefield.

"Yes?"

"Miss Chelsea—"

Sullivan waved in the general direction of the garden. "She's gathering flowers, I believe. She said something about an arrangement for Biddy."

"No, sir. I mean, yes, sir, she might have said that, sir, but . . ."

Sullivan frowned. "What is it, man? Speak up."

"She's gone, sir."

"Outside."

"No, sir. She's *gone.*"

The sharp metal shanks he held bit into his palms.

"Where?"

"Well, you see, sir. It all started with the trellis."

"The trellis."

"We noticed that a few of the plants were bruised."

"Bruised?"

"Then Smee was quite sure he heard a horse galloping off."

"A horse."

"But you'd taken one mount, and the other was safely stowed in the stables."

"Greyson—"

"Then there was the dog, sir."

"Greyson, where is all this leading?"

"To that viper, Nigel Sutherland."

The three men started at the weak, elderly voice that had replied. They turned in concert to regard the pale woman standing in the doorway.

"Nigel Sutherland has won," she said wearily. "Once again, he has won."

She swayed, and Sullivan moved to lift her into his arms. "Grandmama?" He suddenly realized how frail she really was. Her body was no more substantial than thistledown. "Damnation," he cursed under his breath, taking her to a chair. He was at a loss for a way to reassure her and restore her strength.

As he settled her into place, Greyson and Smee rushed to find her some smelling salts and a glass of water.

"Leave it be," she ordered, stilling their instinctive ministrations. She turned beseechingly in his direction. "Nigel Sutherland came to the house this morning. Dudley must have seen him and barked in warning, because that man . . ." She sobbed and continued, "Nigel slit the pup's throat."

She pursed her lips to still their trembling, then continued. "I believe he went up to Chelsea's room. I found a rose, a white rose. That was always his calling card to her. A single, white, flawless rose. But this time, the rose was stained with blood. He must have threatened her, made some sort of bargain. Because she has gone to him. In an effort to protect you."

Sullivan growled and sprang to his feet, "No, damn it! We had everything planned, everything taken care of. If she'd only waited, she would have been safe!"

Biddy shook her head. "Nigel gave her no such opportunity. He was one step ahead of us the entire time." Her eyes became bleak. Old. "Now he has taken a hostage."

* * *

Nigel tugged on the bellpull. Waited. Tugged again. Great bloody hell! Where were those servants? He had returned with his prize, sure that Estella would have been there to greet him and her little charade was over, but she was still gone. Gone!

He hadn't thought she would actually do such a thing. Why would she, blast it all! She loved him, she adored him, she worshiped the ground he walked on.

A knock preceded the timid entrance of one of the chambermaids.

"Yes, m'lord."

"Summon Mr. Wilde at once!"

"B-but, 'e isn't 'ere, m'lord."

"Where in the blazes is he?"

She shrugged.

"Very well, then, get one of the others—Blackmore or Derrington."

"They've taken ill, m'lord."

"Ill? Blast it all, don't tell me another batch has come down with this malady."

"I'm afraid so, m'lord."

Nigel waved the girl away and stamped to the window. The rain had begun again, obscuring the garden below in dribbling sheets of moisture. Nigel's rage boiled in him, burned. How dare she? How dare Estella treat him this way? How dare she defy him?

Until Wilde returned, he couldn't afford to make a scene. Once the masquerade was over, he would hunt her down like the vixen she was. Then . . .

Nigel stepped into the bedchamber bordering his own. Quiet, so quiet. The emptiness seemed to drip from the very walls. A bleakness cloaked his heart. His anger drained away.

Estella had gone.

She had really left him.

He gazed at the bed with its brocade coverings and velvet draperies. He had grown so accustomed to joining her here, that even now he expected her to be waiting at the dressing table or in the bed. Delicate, beautiful, ensconced in lace-edged linens and feminine nighttime frippery. Or smiling, seductive, reaching for him as she had the night before.

But she had left him. Left him.

The hollowness that settled into his bones was overwhelming. Unbelievable. Jerking from his maudlin thoughts, Nigel stormed from the room. Using the secret panel, he descended to his study.

To his infinite disgust, he trembled as he pulled the panels away and disclosed the painting. A molten fire kindled in his veins. More than ever, he felt the overwhelming drive to possess this woman. To own her. Break her to his will. Estella might leave him. She might weakly cower in London. But he would have Chelsea. She would match his passion with a blaze all her own.

He heard a whisper of sound behind him and whirled, expecting to find Reginald, his shirt unbuttoned, a snifter of brandy held loosely in his fingers. But it was Chelsea who stood in the threshold leading into the hall.

For several seconds, there was no sound. Then Chelsea's head lifted ever so slightly, her chin holding a rebellious angle. "I never would have taken you for the sentimental type, Nigel," she said, indicating the framed canvas.

"Ahh," he drawled, taking one last look at the portrait, then closing and locking the concealed doors. "Sentiment has little to do with it, my dear. I am merely a connoisseur of fine things."

Tucking the key into his pocket, he joined her, touching her cheek.

She jerked away as if branded, but he caught her chin, holding it in a bruising grip. "Take care, my sweet," he warned. "Take care that you do not anger me into changing my mind. I may not be so lenient with your lover upon reconsideration."

He saw the battle in her, the stark fury, then the emotional struggle as she controlled her normal instincts to fight him and become submissive once again.

"That's better. Much, much better." He stroked her jaw,

her hair. "Run along upstairs like a good girl. A gown is waiting for you in your room. I had Thomas place it on the foot of the bed. Go and dress, pretty yourself for the party. Then tonight, tonight, after the solstice celebration, we shall share the longest day of the year. Together."

Sullivan trotted his horse up to the half-dozen men waiting for him in the lee of the cliff. He surveyed the carefully chosen army, quickly scrutinizing their costumes for the evening.

"Any last-minute questions?"

They shook their heads.

"Good. Just remember that the stakes have increased a bit. If things get dicey, he may try to use Miss Wickersham as a shield. Protect her at all costs."

The men murmured in agreement.

"Very well. Take your places."

His assistants in stealth cantered away, assuming the identities they would play for the evening. Only the Sutherland brothers, Greyson, and Smee remained.

"Smee, Greyson, you know what to do."

The two servants nodded.

"Here is the eviction notice and Estella's letter. Place them in a prominent place where Lord Sutherland is sure to find them."

He extended the items that had been bound together by the white velvet ribbon that held the keys Estella had intended as a gift for Chelsea. Sullivan had never had a chance to give them to her.

Greyson squinted, his brow furrowing as he tugged the ribbon free, and gave the letters to Smee. "My lord, where did you find these?"

"Estella included them with the papers she brought."

"Do you know what we have?" he asked excitedly. "Have you any idea?" He showed them to Smee, Gregory, and Rupert as if they should be aware of their importance. "These are the keys to your grandfather's safe. *Nigel's* safe!"

"I'll be bloody bound," Rupert muttered.

Sullivan's lips lifted in a slow grin. "It seems we have a slight change of plans."

Even Greyson smiled.

From his vantage point in the trees behind them, Reginald Wilde scowled. Damned if he wasn't sure that of the five men below, two of the strangers were Mr. Cane and the elusive Sutherland impostor.

Trap!

Everything in him screamed the word, and he nearly yanked his horse around and galloped into the evening, sure they had been sent by the magistrate to arrest him. But, upon closer look, Reggie thought he recognized one more . . . the giant who . . .

Damn! He'd been taken for a jolly ride in a turnip cart to be sure. He'd be buggered if he didn't think he'd stumbled across a flagrant batch of brigand plots.

"Lord Sutherland?"

Nigel stifled an impatient sigh, holding his arms out so that the manservant who attended him could finish the necessary adjustments to his costume.

"What is it, Thomas?"

"A good portion of your guests have arrived. You asked me to notify you."

"Very well." He waved the man away, but the servant lingered. "What is it?"

"I was asked to deliver this to you." He extended a silver platter holding a single vellum envelope.

Nigel glared at it, surmising it was the written regrets of a guest who would be unable to attend, but when he saw the familiar script, he snatched the missive from the server and tore it open.

My Dearest Nigel . . .

His stomach clenched; bile rose in his throat.

"Get out," he rasped.

The two servants gaped at him.

"Get out!"

They scurried to do his bidding, dodging into the corridor and closing the door just as something crashed against the opposite side and Nigel bellowed, "Get the bloody hell out!"

The first strains of the orchestra beginning to tune their instruments sifted through the open windows into the chamber where Chelsea had been led. She shuddered, gazing about her at the sterile white walls, the cherub-painted ceiling, the rose-and-white damask bedcover. It was the same bedroom she had lived in as an adolescent. Nigel must have kept it like a shrine.

The skittering of a violin rasped across her nerves, and she chafed her arms, remembering how many times she had waited in this same spot for just such an evening to begin, knowing that if she spoke to anyone, begged for help, she would be severely punished.

Chelsea had no doubts that such was the case tonight. Her bond with Nigel was fragile yet. She must pamper him, soothe his ego, and cater to his every need in order to ensure that he would allow Richard to leave England without intervention.

Turning, she stared at her reflection in the full-length mirror, knowing that tonight she would don the most difficult mask she could possibly wear. Tonight she would use all of the skills Lord Sutherland had taught her to make him her slave.

She didn't know if such a thing were possible. But she had to try.

Her spirits were bolstered slightly after witnessing his reaction to her portrait. In that bare, unguarded instant before he had realized she stood behind him, Chelsea had seen that even Nigel Sutherland had a vulnerability. His Achilles heel was the memory of a childish Irish waif who had once been his toy.

Tonight she hoped to rekindle such memories. She hoped to drag him so deeply into the illusion of power that he would not know how much she'd used him until long after Richard was free.

Nigel's choice of costumes for her to wear to the Solstice Masquerade only seemed to enhance her purposes. The gown could barely be called a gown. Fashioned from a single swath of white raw silk, it fell from one shoulder, draping at her breasts and waist, and leaving an indecent amount of her arms and shoulders bare. Fresh rose petals had been sewn strategically over her breasts, down to her hips, her thighs, and from there to the floor-length hem. There were no shoes. Merely a band of gold for her ankle and one for her arm. As she put on the ornaments, the cool metal bit into her skin like shackles. But Chelsea knew that this time, this time, she would be the winner in such a diabolical game.

The door opened, and Nigel appeared. His jaw was rock hard, his features pinched. But when he saw Chelsea, his entire demeanor became enigmatic, hidden behind his ultimate charm.

"How lovely you look. Just like a rose. A pristine rose."

He walked up behind her to clasp her shoulders, forcing her to look at their combined reflection in the mirror. His fingers dug into her skin, then gentled, stroked. He lifted her arm and bent to place a kiss at the tender indentation of her elbow.

Chelsea fought the instinctive revulsion and kept her features carefully blank.

"There's just one tiny problem." He plucked at the pins binding her hair, unraveling the red-gold plaits into a brilliant cascade of curls. Next, he dropped a golden demi-mask over her face and tied the ribbon. "Better. Much, much better." Taking her hand, he settled it into the crook of his arm. "Shall we?"

Chelsea fell docilely into step beside him. They would make a striking couple, she knew. Nigel had dressed to perfection in the role of a Roman emperor. A wreath of laurel surrounded his head. A white brocade toga draped his body, leaving a portion of his calves free. The hems were adorned with gold metallic embroidery, as were the leather sandals on his feet.

The music grew louder as they descended the grand

staircase. As always, Nigel had waited until most of his guests had arrived before appearing. At the threshold to the ballroom, he paused, surveying the glittering scene below.

His guests had risen to the challenge of the ball's theme. The room was filled with every fantastical design imaginable. Costumes had been chosen to represent all manner of heathen elements, from the American Indian to the Aborigine, Africans to Polynesians. There were kings and queens, storybook characters, and period gods and goddesses. Some of the costumes were representational facsimiles, while others were so brief or suggestive, they bordered on the obscene.

The majordomo took his position to the right of the shallow staircase leading down to the dance floor. Tapping his staff on the marble tile three times, he ponderously announced, "Nigel, Lord Sutherland, seventh Earl of Lindon, and his ward, Gelsey O'Rourke."

The assembled crowd turned. In a round of enthusiastic applause, they welcomed their host. Nigel accepted the accolade much like Caesar returning from battle. "Come, my friends . . . laugh, mingle, enjoy the music and wine. Then, upon the stroke of midnight, the first dance will begin. Choose your partners well. For he who selects his mate during the solstice waltz will never be alone again."

His yearly salute was met with a round of exuberant clapping. Nigel signaled for the orchestra to begin. As the strains of a nocturne filled the air, he drew Chelsea into the crush of people.

So began her hell.

Chapter

24

Chelsea became Nigel's pawn, his showpiece. She was paraded in front of his guests like a brood mare. She was forced to converse with his business associates and hang on Nigel's every word.

Soon the evening took on an aura of unreality. The heat of the room became excruciating. The smells of rich food, expensive wine, cologne, and candle smoke were overwhelming. She longed to escape, to rush out into the garden for a gasp of fresh air, but she didn't dare. Not when she knew that Richard would appear soon to stake his claim.

She feared that moment. She knew she would look up to see that he regarded her, not with love, but with disgust. Each time the majordomo tapped his staff, she felt as if the sound went right through her very soul.

"Lady Alice Beaman and her cousin Roland Hall."

"Sir Barton Bartholomew, Baronet of Dorset."

"Edgar, Lord Finney, emissary of His Royal Majesty William IV."

At the last, a hush of respect settled over the company. A smattering of applause followed the portly gentleman who frowned beneath a ponderous mustache and made his way to Nigel's side. He was accompanied by a dour-faced guard.

Chelsea, who had turned upon the man's entrance, gazed at him in confusion. Lord Finney bore a remarkable resemblance to Alby Littleton, the town's baker. But she couldn't be sure . . .

"Sutherland."

"Lord Finney, I am delighted to make your acquaintance. This is indeed an honor to have you with us this evening."

"Doubt it," the man mumbled, staring at Nigel through the lens of his eyepiece. "I have not come for the entertainment but upon official business. However, I see you have guests, so I will hold my questions until a later time"—he paused and added significantly—"when we can speak privately."

"Of course. Enjoy yourself, my lord."

Chelsea saw a tightness edge Nigel's lips. The blaze of emotion she'd seen earlier returned.

"Is anything wrong?"

"No. No, of course not."

The tapping of the majordomo caused them both to start.

"Alice Carter, Addlebury's school mistress."

Nigel's eyes widened, clinging to the woman on the stairs. "What in the—"

It became clear to Chelsea that this woman had not been invited. Her clothing was simple, her demeanor curious. As she stepped into the throng, Nigel's irritation was palpable. Summoning a servant, he said, "That woman is not on the list. See to her dismissal."

The servant bowed in obeisance and made his way toward the majordomo. Before he could reach the man, however, another set of guests arrived, their appearances even more humble than that of Alice Carter.

"Mrs. Jonathan Sike, and her children, Annabelle, Grover, and Laurel."

Another pair arrived. "Mr. and Mrs. Horace Weatherby."

"Mr. and Mrs. Peter Gunge."

"Mrs. Eli Kipper and companion."

Muttering an oath, Nigel began to dodge toward the door, pulling Chelsea along behind him. He had gone less than a few yards when the footman he'd sent to intercept such announcements met him halfway.

Nigel growled and grasped him by the shirtfront. "What in damnation is going on here?"

The servant gasped and held out a vellum card. "They've all been invited, they have. What with your crest on the seal, Carlton said he had to let them in."

Nigel released him so suddenly the man nearly fell. Realizing he was creating a scene, Nigel smiled at his guests, waved for them to continue with their activities, then examined the paper.

It was *his* invitation.

His seal.

Beads of sweat appeared on his forehead, and his grip became viselike.

"Mr. Wilson, solicitor."

He jerked as if someone had clipped him in the jaw. The solicitor nodded to Nigel and descended into the crowd.

"Mr. Rupert Cane."

Cane. Cane?

But the man who appeared was a giant, not the stranger who had stolen his home. This man wore his clothes in a rakish style, giving him the air of a pirate.

"Mr. Gregory Wicket Cane."

That was he! That was the brigand who had forced Nigel to behave so recklessly. Dressed all in black with a dark demi-mask, he appeared to be the thief he was.

Still holding Chelsea's wrist, he plowed through the human sea, his free hand closing over the jeweled hilt of the dagger tucked into the belt girding his waist.

Then, in the seconds before Nigel could make his way to the doorway, a lean, familiar figure stepped into view.

Chelsea stopped, digging in her heels at the sight. As the lone man stopped at the head of the staircase, a hush settled over the room at the formidable power of his presence. Unlike the rest of the guests, he was clothed in elegant black evening togs and a snowy shirt. His cravat had been tied to perfection. But his hair, that long, streaming, black-brown hair, had been left loose and flowing, cascading to his shoulders, clearly proclaiming that this man would be dangerous if crossed.

He scanned the ballroom, immediately settling upon his goal. Chelsea felt a thrill rush through her when their glances connected briefly. Then he looked away, spearing Nigel with a fulminating glare.

The majordomo tapped his staff. The quiet of the room became overpowering. "Richard Albert, Lord Sutherland, the seventh Earl of Lindon."

A furor erupted in the ballroom, but Nigel laughed, dispelling the claim that had been made by saying, "How clever of you to come in costume as one of the mysterious rumors of the long-lost Sutherland heir. Bravo. Bravo!"

There was a titter of laughter about him. His guests returned to their activities, leaving Nigel virtually unnoticed as he confronted his foe for the first time.

"I must congratulate you," he rasped. "You have been much more clever than I would have imagined possible." His grip tightened around Chelsea's bones to an excruciating degree, but outwardly he appeared calm.

Sullivan merely inclined his head, ever watchful, ever ready.

"The added guests were a brilliant touch. The invitations were your doing, I suppose?"

Sullivan held up his left fist to reveal the sparkle of the Sutherland family signet. Chelsea regarded it in surprise. How? She had never returned the ring given to her that first night. That evening, she'd pulled aside the tarpaulin . . .

"The Mr. Canes? Mr. Wilson? Your associates, I believe."

"Not entirely. But I'm sure Mr. Wilson can be persuaded to join me in my cause. Tell me, Lord Sutherland, how is your wife? Your son?"

Nigel's lips grew white around the edges, but he continued. "I have indeed encountered a master." He seemed to struggle for control, then added, "But you should have dressed for the part, don't you think? After all, from what I've heard, you're little more than a savage. You should have come dressed in your true colors."

"Who is to say who is the savage among us, Lord Sutherland?"

Nigel didn't bother to respond to the barely veiled insult. Whipping an arm around Chelsea's waist, he hauled her close to his body. The movement was subtle yet calculated, so that no one but he, Chelsea, and Richard would ever notice the knifepoint digging into her ribs beneath the drape of her gown.

Nigel forced her from the room and into one of the halls.

Chelsea bucked against him, but he hissed, "One word, one scream, and I will kill you first, then your heathen, and feed you both to the wolves."

He dragged her to his study, threw her inside, and locked the door behind them. *Think, think!* It was obvious to him that he was being circled like a rabbit in a hole, but it was also quite clear that Richard Sutherland could not have arranged such a neat little plan. He knew too much—too much! He knew each weakness, each vulnerability: Estella, Cecil, Nigel's willingness to gamble. He had taken Nigel's home and now threatened his titles—not to mention arranging for the presence of a special investigator. The feat would have taken weeks to arrange. Weeks and weeks. Which meant that Richard Sutherland had been fed important information by a traitor within Nigel's own household.

But who? *Who?*

A slight tap on the door caused him to jump.

"Who is it?" he barked, warning Chelsea with a glance not to make a sound.

"Thomas, sir."

"What do you want?"

"Is there a problem, sir? I saw the light beneath the door."

"No, Thomas. Thank you. Please return to our guests. I shall be out shortly."

"Very good, sir." At the squeak of a floorboard, Nigel quickly asked, "Thomas, has Mr. Wilde returned?"

"No, sir. The runner from the magistrate came up to the house a few minutes ago to say Mr. Wilde was detained."

"The magistrate?" Nigel repeated blankly.

"Yes, sir. Jackie's still here if you'd like to talk to the boy."

"No. Thank you, Thomas." More weakly, "No."

Nigel felt a numbing disbelief, a chilling suspicion. Turning, he walked behind the desk to the hidden panels. As h opened them wide, he felt a clutch of disbelief, a jolt o horror. The light of the candles on the far sconces reveale not canvas, not painted linens and velvet skin, but bare wal An iron safe slightly ajar.

Only Reggie had a spare set of keys to the panels, the safe Damn him. *Damn him!* Crying out in rage, Nigel swun open the iron doors.

Gone. Everything was gone. His documents, his diarie his private ledgers. Everything! Inside, there was a singl scrap of paper. Upon lifting it for his examination, one wor in particular seemed to leap from the page: *evicted.*

Reginald Wilde had joined the enemy. Reginald Wild had supplied him with every damning shred of evidenc possible.

That betrayal sliced more deeply than any other.

For the first time in his life, Nigel was running scared. H had to escape. He had to be quit of this place befor Reginald appeared to uncover all of his blackest crimes.

He dodged toward the secret passageway, but as h pressed the hidden latch, the panels refused to give way—a if someone held them from the opposite side. Nigel swore pounding on the wood, thrusting against it with his shoul der, but it would not open.

"The windows," he whispered to himself, but upo reaching them, he saw a pair of men dressed all in black pointing revolvers at him from the other side of the glass.

Grasping Chelsea's arm, he dodged back into the hal intent upon finding some exit, some escape. But he stoppe short when one end of the corridor was blocked by a pair o huge men who generally tended to the mews. The glint o their eyes and the stance of their beefy legs revealed tha Richard Sutherland's treachery had reached as far as hi own servants.

His only avenue was to return to the ballroom. He yanke at Chelsea's arm, but the recalcitrant girl balked each step o the way, screeching and clawing at him like a cornered cat

Whirling to face her, he leveled the knife tip at her throat. "One more sound, one more defiant overture, and I will kill your precious Richard Sutherland this very eve."

The rebellious tilt of her chin remained, but she followed him more meekly. Meanwhile, from the far corners of the house, the various clocks began to chime.

One. Two.

Nigel reentered the crowded ballroom.

Three. Four.

His guests parted and allowed him to pass to the center of the floor.

Five. Six.

The orchestra stilled in midnote. A hush fell over the crowd.

Seven.

The tradition. The solstice waltz. It could prove to be his salvation. No one but the master of the house was to dance during the first refrain. If he could lead Chelsea toward the guillotine windows on the far side of the room, he could escape as soon as the crush of guests began selecting partners.

Eight.

He nodded to the conductor. The lilting refrains of Chopin filled the perfumed air. Tucking the knife back into his belt, Nigel whirled Chelsea into his arms.

Nine.

Slowly, surely, he led her in circles around the space cleared for them by the eager crowd.

Ten.

Chelsea found herself drawn into the dance, whirling, spinning, turning. She felt Nigel's hands grow clammy against her. He was leading her toward the windows. She knew he would try to escape, taking her with him as his hostage.

Eleven.

Then, over her captor's shoulder, she saw him. He strode toward her. His lips moved. He did not say the phrase aloud, but they burned into her soul nevertheless.

"Trust me."

The words speared through her heart, reminding her of the plea he'd once made.

Trust me enough to see this through. To take care of you—and of me.

Nigel never anticipated her intentions. As she twisted free from his grasp, he gaped at her for one fleeting instant, so surprised he didn't even think to reach for the weapon tucked into his belt.

Twelve.

A murmur rose from the crowd as Richard ushered her behind him, using his body as a shield.

"Damn you!" Nigel shouted, whipping the knife free and raising it high.

Women screamed. Guests scrambled toward the exits, but at Richard's softly spoken demand, they stopped, turned.

"I reclaim the Sutherland titles and estates in the name of my grandfather, Richard Albert Sutherland II, whom you murdered, and my father, Richard Albert Sutherland III, whom you disgraced, and in the name of all the true heirs whom you supplanted."

"No," Nigel ground out between clenched teeth. "You lie!"

Two figures stepped forward to flank Richard Sutherland on either side. The men who had come to the party under the name of Cane.

"This needn't be a public trial, Nigel. Drop the knife. We'll go somewhere quiet and—"

"No! I didn't kill them, I tell you. It wasn't me. It—"

"No, Nigel! Don't say anything more." Reginald Wilde burst into the room and lunged down the staircase. "It's a ploy. A ploy, I tell you. These men are impostors. They don't—"

"You!" Nigel spun to face his secretary. "You did this to me. You played me for a fool!"

He lifted the blade high and whipped it down again in a swinging arc.

Reginald leapt out of the way, but not before the metal sliced through his shirt, gashing his arm.

Thrown off-balance, Nigel stumbled beneath the unfamiliar weight of his toga, landing on one knee and an elbow. The weapon bounced out of his grip and skittered across the floor. The two men scrambled for the blade, but it was Reginald who caught it first.

Seeing that his secretary had the weapon, Nigel began to babble. "It was Reggie's idea. Reggie made all of the arrangements. I might have framed your parents, I might have seen to it that they were exiled, but—"

Reginald peered around him in disbelief, seeing the open-mouthed horror of the onlookers, the servants closing in, the trio of strangers who had drawn them both into so neat a trap.

"Reggie was the one who stole the documents."

"Shut up!"

"Reggie was the one who slipped poison into Albert's tea—"

"Shut *up*, I tell you! They don't know anything. They don't know—"

"Reggie was the one who hired those men to hunt you down—"

"Damn you! I was your friend! I protected you! I killed for you! You would throw me to the lions for that? They don't know *anything!*"

"Reggie—"

"They don't—" Biting back his cry, Reginald lunged toward his employer in a blind rage, not really seeing, not really thinking, only knowing that he had to stop him before he said any more, before he revealed their crimes any further.

He had no conscious recognition of drawing the knife back or clasping Nigel's shoulder with his free hand, but then he was stabbing, stabbing, stabbing.

It wasn't until the warm rush of blood bathing his knuckles permeated his consciousness that Reginald realized what he'd done. Crying out in horror, he stared at the crimson river covering him, splattering across his clothes, staining the floor.

His fingers opened. The weapon clattered to the ground.

Staring blankly at his employer, he shuddered in horror.

A huge red blossom spread over Nigel's immaculate toga and ran down in rivulets that covered his bare calves, his shoes.

Nigel blinked at him, his face a perfect mask of surprise and childish pique. "Reggie?" It was a gurgle of sound.

The man wavered, fell, but Reginald rushed to catch him and gently eased him onto the floor. "Nigel?" Cradling his head in his lap, he crooned to him. "Nigel . . . Nigel?" His fingers trembled, leaving trails of scarlet as he touched his employer's face, stroked his cheek. His friend. His soulmate. "Nigel, I didn't mean to hurt you. I only meant to stop you from telling them our secrets. It was a trap, Nigel, a trap." He sobbed, staring up at the sea of faces around him. "He was my friend. My friend . . ."

Crying openly, he bent over the familiar face, the familiar form. "Please forgive me. Please, please, forgive me." Over and over, he rubbed his cheek, his lips. "Please forgive me . . . please. Forgive me . . . forgive me . . . forgive . . ."

A shivering silence descended over the *ton,* an aching astonishment. Never had they seen such a painful tableau of grief and despair. They nearly expected the wounded man to blink, take a quick breath.

But Nigel did not respond. His eyes remained open, bleak, staring into eternity. Reginald, who had lost the only person who had ever shown him a shred of kindness, arched his head back, screaming, "No! *Nooo!"*

Sullivan found Chelsea much later, out in the garden. Someone had given her a cape, and she clutched it around her torso and stared into the gloom. Around her, the white roses from Estella's garden nodded in the moonlight. Pure. Fragrant. Cold.

"Chelsea?"

She made no sign of having heard him, but he knew she was aware of his presence.

"I hated him. But I never would have wished this upon him."

"I know." Sullivan cupped her shoulders and drew her

against him, offering the warmth of his body, the strength of his heart.

"I failed you, Richard. I should have trusted you. I should have told you of Nigel's bargain."

Sullivan experienced a pang of guilt, knowing that he, of all people, was not in a position to cast stones. There were confessions of his own that needed to be made. He could only pray that this woman would find it in her heart to forgive him for a necessary silence.

"We are none of us perfect people," he murmured at last. "We do what we have to do in order to protect the people we love. You did what you thought best."

"I didn't think things through. I reacted on instinct."

"You meant to keep me safe."

"Instead I put you in danger."

"No. Nigel was never a threat to me." He hesitated, wrapping his arms about her more tightly, knowing that he must tell her now, or never. "You see, I was no real threat to him."

She tried to face him, but he kept her still.

"But, Richard, you were the true heir, the—"

"No."

He loosened his grasp enough so that she could shift in his arms and stare at him in confusion.

"I am not the true heir," he admitted, then stepped aside to reveal the two figures silhouetted in stark relief against the brilliance of the candlelit ballroom. "Chelsea Wickersham, I should like to present my brothers to you."

"Brothers?"

"You see, everyone assumed that my father had left only a single son. But he left several."

One of the shapes disengaged from the wall to step forward, and Chelsea watched in wide-eyed disbelief as he moved closer, revealing a face that was familiar to her. A near duplicate of those she had seen in the portrait gallery. An older, leaner version of Richard Albert Sutherland, but with lighter hair and green eyes.

"May I present Gregory Wicket Cane Sutherland." The

man she had known as Richard Sutherland was watching her carefully. "And Rupert Perry Cane Sutherland."

The giant who still remained in the doorway limped forward, smiled at her. "I hope Sully treated you kindly, miss."

"Sully?" She looked at the man who had been her constant companion for weeks, who had tried her patience as a savage and enticed her soul as a gentleman.

The man she had grown to love and adore bowed shallowly at the waist. "Sullivan Arthur Cane Sutherland."

Chelsea gathered her skirts and ran. She didn't know where she was going or what she intended; she only knew she had to get away. Now.

"Chelsea? Chelsea!" Sullivan chased her through the roses, down past the arbor and behind the privet hedge. There, shielded from prying eyes, he grasped her arm and forced her to turn.

"Once again you've made a fool of me, Rich—" She broke off in disgust. "No, not Richard."

"I haven't made a fool of you."

"I thought you had sunk to the depths when you masqueraded as the heathen for so long. But all this time you lied to me, played an elaborate charade, and laughed at me behind your sleeve."

"No." His grip gentled. "I loved you. I love you still. I wanted to tell you the truth, but there were bigger things at stake."

"Such as your blasted fun."

"No, damn it!" He sighed in frustration, then said quickly, "You were willing to believe in me enough to tell me about Nigel. Now let me tell you about my childhood."

His voice became low, urgent. "Nigel meant for my parents to be executed. But through influence at court, they were exiled instead—put aboard a penal ship bound for the depths of hell. But through some act of providence, there was a storm. My father and mother jumped ship and through the grace of God were able to make their way to shore.

"My father and mother nearly died in the attempt. They

were washed ashore—and if not for the help of a pair of Jesuit priests, they surely would have perished. The first few years were a living hell for them. Word of their escape spread rampant in England. Men hunted them like dogs, eager for the rewards offered to find them dead or alive and return them to the officers of the crown. They dreamed of returning to England and proving their innocence, but when my mother became pregnant, they both knew that to confront Nigel would mean putting their child's life in peril. With the crime of treason still hanging over their heads, their only avenue was to make a new life for themselves. So they abandoned all thought of their previous existence. They took a new name and began building a home.

"There were three of us—Gregory, Rupert, and I. My mother died soon after I was born, and my father grew even more bitter, more distant. It wasn't until he was on his deathbed that we even knew of his true identity—that *he* was the infamous Richard Sutherland who had been sought from one end of the continent to the other. By the time we understood the significance of his confession, we discovered that he had sent a messenger to Biddy to tell her where to find him."

Sullivan's lips twisted. "He thought he was doing the right thing. He knew his sons could inherit his title but not his crimes. He thought that we could return in glory and claim the Lindon estates. But he had not counted on his message being intercepted, nor on Nigel's continued cunning. When Nigel discovered that my father was alive and had left a possible heir, he sent assassins to find us. Before we truly understood what was happening, we found ourselves hunted—for no more than the fact that our family had once belonged to the Sutherland clan."

When he saw that Chelsea was listening, he continued more slowly. "Gregory was married at the time. His wife's name was Lydia. She was kind and giving and warm. When Nigel's men were unable to find my father, they found his grave. The villagers told him about our family. Nigel's men tracked us to the coast of Brazil. They set fire to the hut where we were staying with some villagers, and Lydia was killed." His eyes clouded at the memory. His voice grew gruff. "We waited in the jungle and watched, impotent to help her. When the men finally left, we realized that they thought they had destroyed the Sutherland heir.

"Thinking no one would search for us again, we returned to Isla Santiago, the island where our father and mother had first gone to hide from the world. From that moment, we trusted no one. We kept ourselves isolated—even from the natives who lived there.

"Gregory was affected the most by our predicament. He became moody and consumed with guilt. He drank and disappeared for days on end. When another set of English bloodhounds appeared on the island, Rupert and I knew that it was time to discover who was chasing us and why they refused to believe the Sutherland heir was dead."

He touched her cheek. "But it was not Nigel who sent them. It was a sparrow-sweet figure of a grandmother and her lovable servants. Before I could cry 'Nay,' I was swept away to a new country, a new home, and entrusted to the special care of an indomitable British governess."

He paused, hoping that the softening he saw in her stance was real. "I did what I had to do. In order to protect my family. But I never meant to hurt you or Biddy in the process." His voice lowered, became fervent. "I love you. I want to spend the rest of my life with you. If you can bear the fact that I am not a titled lord, I will live with you here. Or, if you'd prefer, I'll take you back to a paradise like none you could ever imagine. You need only agree to surrender your heart to me, as I have surrendered mine to you."

Chelsea thought of all she should say, the anger she should continue to cling to, but none of that seemed important. She was being offered a future. She was being offered hope.

There was time to tell him she was sorry for the way she'd acted. Time to warn him that the portrait was missing and could very well be used to blackmail his family. But as the warm velvet night settled around them, she realized that even if they were to be given a hundred years, there would never be enough hours to love him.

Drawing on tiptoes, she lifted her face for his kiss. A kiss that soon deepened into a flurry of passion. Then he lowered her onto the fragrant grass, opened her cape, and began to pluck the petals from her gown, one by one by one . . .

Two tall masculine forms waited for quite some time on the marble steps leading into the ballroom. When Sullivan and Chelsea did not appear, they considered their best options.

"Do you suppose they're lost?" Gregory asked.

Rupert closed his eyes in a vague, faraway manner as if receiving a vision. "I see . . . I see . . . two figures, entwined, sampling the delicious dalliance of youth and . . ."

Gregory playfully smacked him in the stomach. "It doesn't take the 'sight' to fathom that, you idiot."

Rupert chuckled and rubbed his abdomen. "How long should we give them? An hour?"

One of Gregory's brows lifted in mock disgust.

"Two then?"

"It's the summer solstice, brother mine. I say we give them all the time they could possibly want."

"Meanwhile . . ."

Gregory grinned. "We have a party to host."

"Mmm. I do believe you're right."

"I spied some tender young things. If they haven't fainted dead away, perhaps we could persuade them to dance."

"Capital idea."

The soft sound of a throat being cleared filtered into the darkness, and two masked gentlemen—one stout, one tall —tiptoed forward.

"Excuse me, sirs," Greyson intoned. "Might we trouble you for some advice?"

"What is it, Greyson?"

The elderly butler stepped aside to reveal that his companion was weighted down by the awkward shape of a huge painting.

"We would like your advice as to what to do with this . . . item we took from Nigel's study."

"What is it?"

"A painting."

317

"What is the subject of the painting?"

"Well, it's a trifle . . . delicate to explain."

"Oh?"

The brothers stepped forward in curiosity, but Greyson stopped them. "If you don't mind, I think it best that you not see it."

"Whyever not?"

"It is a portrait."

"Yes . . ."

"Of Miss Wickersham, sir."

"And . . ."

Greyson consulted Smee, Smee consulted Greyson. If Gregory was not mistaken, the two men flushed behind their masks.

"It is a painting of Miss Wickersham . . . *en deshabille.*"

"Really?" Gregory drawled.

"No," Rupert breathed.

Once more, they tried to catch a glimpse, but Greyson slapped a palm to either chest, refusing to let them pass.

"It is a *private* painting. A very . . . *revealing* painting. We would like to know what you think we should do with it."

Rupert and Gregory considered the problem for a moment.

"Rupe?"

"I think you should save it for a wedding present," the gentle giant said. Quirking his brow toward the privet hedge, he added, "I have a feeling that the nuptials will be taking place quite soon. You wouldn't want to be left without some sort of token, now would you?"

"No," Greyson agreed solemnly.

Smee began hopping from foot to foot in utter glee.

A wedding!

How delightful!

Epilogue

Sullivan Arthur Cane Sutherland roused the vicar from a sound sleep just as the first ruby glow of sunrise washed into a clear summer sky. The vicar, grumbling at the imposition, glared at him from beneath his nightcap.

"What?" he demanded cryptically, his disposition far from friendly.

"I need you to perform a wedding."

"Do you have the proper papers?"

"No."

"Then come back when—"

"But I've compromised her, sir. We've shared"—he bent close to whisper—"carnal relations."

The vicar stared at the prospective groom and the bride-to-be. Seeing the grass in their hair and the disheveled condition of their clothing, he ushered them into the chapel, posthaste. If it struck him odd that a tall green-eyed man had come along to serve as best man and another giant as a sort of bride's maid, he did not comment. His only objective was to draw these youngsters away from the very chasm of everlasting hell.

Once the ceremony had been performed, the carriage—

being driven by a grinning Smee and a flushed Greyson—
made one last stop in town before barreling toward
Bellemoore.

Beatrice Sutherland heard the clatter of hooves and the
squeak and groan of tracings the minute the coach topped
the rise.

She had endured a sleepless night, waiting, wondering.
Even when Smee and Greyson had returned in the wee
hours to assure her all was well, whisking a mysterious
package up the stairs, she had not been able to relax. She
needed to see for herself that her family was safe. All of
them. Greyson and Smee. Chelsea. Richard.

Hurrying as fast as her feeble legs could carry her, she
arrived at the mounting block just as the conveyance's
wheels rolled to a stop.

There was a moment of silence. A beat of anticipation.
Then the door opened, and her grandson alighted.

Biddy lifted her hands to her breast to still the beating of
her heart, so relieved was she. "Chelsea? Is she—"

"Safe, Grandmama." He bent to press a kiss to her cheek.
"And, I might add, very, very married."

She cooed in delight. "You've exchanged vows?"

"Yes. Only an hour ago. I hope you're not angry that we
did not come to fetch you."

"Not as long as you're happy, my boy."

"Very happy." The words were Chelsea's. "But we promise to repeat the ceremony again once we have the proper
papers."

"Wonderful. Wonderful!" Biddy would have tugged them
into the house, but the couple balked.

"Grandmama . . ." her grandson began hesitantly. "I
hope you do not mind, but I've brought a few guests back
with me to stay."

"My home is always open, especially to—"

The invitation died as a huge figure appeared in the door
of the carriage. She gaped at the character, seeing something, a glimmer of memory she felt she should grasp.

"Grandmama, I would like to introduce my brother, Rupert Perry Cane Sutherland."

"Brother?" she whispered.

"Older brother, as a matter of fact."

The giant bent to place a kiss on her wrinkled cheek. "I am so pleased to finally meet you, Grandmama."

Dazed, she reached to cover that spot as if the kiss and the man would disappear.

"Older bro—" She could not continue when another man stepped onto the block.

"May I also introduce your eldest grandson, Gregory Wicket Cane Sutherland." Biddy uttered a choked cry. So tall, so lean, with golden brown hair, green eyes, and her husband's smile.

"Grandmama," he murmured, kissing her just as his brothers had done. Then, before she could speak, before she could reach out to ensure they were not phantoms from a feverish brain, he returned to the carriage.

Sullivan continued, "Grandmama, I fear I must confess. I have lied to you all these months. I am not Richard Albert Sutherland IV."

Biddy was so dazed, she barely heard his words.

"My father christened me with your maiden name. Sullivan. Sullivan Arthur Cane Sutherland."

"Oh?" she responded weakly.

"But I should be very pleased to introduce you to your husband's namesake."

Gregory extended a hand into the carriage, and there was a flutter of movement. Biddy took a step forward. Two. Her heart pounded, filling her with a breathless vitality like none she had experienced in years.

"Another son? Your father had another son?"

"No, Grandmama." It was Gregory who answered. "I have a son. As the seventh Earl of Lindon, *I* have an heir."

A childish head poked out of the carriage. Dark curls framed a pale face and eyes as black as midnight. If Biddy had not known any better, she would have thought it was her own son, Richard Albert. Her dearling. Her little one.

Upon seeing her, the boy giggled. With his father's aid, he clambered down the narrow step. He could not have been more than six.

The Sutherland brothers watched the proceedings with pride as Sullivan announced, "This is Richard. Richard Albert Sutherland IV."

"Then *this* is the boy in the portrait I received?" she breathed.

"Yes, Grandmama," Sullivan answered gently.

Biddy's chin trembled, her limbs shook. Kneeling, she extended her arms.

The boy sought his father's gaze in reassurance, tacitly asked his uncles' approval, then stepped forward, shyly considering the woman who waited.

"Gramma-great?" he asked in a near whisper.

Biddy sobbed aloud in joy. "Yes! Yes, my boy. I am your grandma-great. Come. Won't you give me a kiss hello?"

A cool summer breeze sifted through the opened windows of Bellemoore Cottage, filling the corridors with the subtle scent of flowers. The old house creaked and groaned, settling for the night, but to the wizened woman making her way through the halls by the light of a single candle, the sounds had a melodious air to them.

There had been many happy days in her life—her courtship, her wedding, the long-awaited birth of her son—but Biddy honestly couldn't remember being more content than she was at this moment.

Easing open the door next to the scullery, she peered inside the servants' quarters, her lips tilting in a fond smile. Greyson. Smee. What true friends they had proven to be. When everyone else had abandoned her, these two men had stayed by her side. They had never thought her a crazy old woman clinging to pipe dreams but had believed just as strongly as she that one day she would find her grandson.

Shifting, she extended a finger from the rounded ball atop her cane and nudged the black mask draped over Smee's footboard. Yes, they had been good to her. So much more than servants.

Family.

Easing away, she made her way up the back stairs to the guest room. A sliver of light stretched beneath the door. Tiptoeing inside, she found that her grandsons, Rupert and Gregory, had left the candles sputtering in their own wax and wasted to nubs. Uttering an indulgent *tsk,* she limped forward, first drawing the coverlet more firmly over Rupert, the gentle giant, then Gregory, so sober-eyed, so keen. Her hands lingered over the sprawled shapes, absorbing their warmth and vitality, before she blew out the lights and withdrew.

Peeking into the room across the hall, she smiled at the figures entwined on the bed. Unlike most newlyweds, Sullivan and Chelsea had not spent most of their wedding night alone. Upon discovering that Greyson and Smee had secreted the portrait upstairs, Rupert and Gregory had teased the new couple mercilessly, then stormed the bedroom in an effort to see it. Chelsea, red-cheeked, had tried to prevent their actions, but Sullivan, proud of his new wife and her evident beauty, had taken a hammer and nail and hung the picture on the wall opposite the bed.

Biddy breathed a pleased sigh. Over the years, Chelsea had been like a daughter to her, and now that wish had come true. Beatrice remembered the frightened young girl who had come to her for help. What a lovely woman Chelsea had become. Beautiful in form and spirit. Biddy's heart soared to see her finally looking so free, so untroubled. So loved. Sullivan *did* love her. Of that Biddy had no doubt. He would take care of her. He would adore her. Little knowing that in doing so, he had made his grandmother inestimably proud.

Sullivan. His grandfather would have applauded his actions—the way he had remained true to his loyalties and the age-old pull of blood. His efforts had allowed for the safety of his brothers, the revival of his grandmother's hopes, and the restoration of the family name.

Albert also would have approved of the invitation Sullivan had extended for Biddy to join him and his new wife in paradise. Beatrice might be touched with a bit of celebratory fever, but she intended to go. She wasn't so naive as to fool herself into believing she had an abundance of years left on this earth. And before she joined her dear Albert in the hereafter, she intended to live each day to the fullest. As soon as Gregory had put the family affairs in order, they would all go together. Then, after a year or two, when little Richard was ready for more formal schooling, they would return to carry on the Sutherland dynasty.

Retreating, Biddy made her way last of all to the nursery. Opening the door, she felt a tangible pang of joy strike her heart. Toys had been scattered on the floor. Clothing had been dropped here and there by the armoire. The room smelled of powder and chocolate and jam. Fingerprints smeared the panes of glass where a little boy had pressed his nose to the window and looked out over the moors. On the morrow, Biddy would inform Greyson that the spot was not to be washed. Not for some time, at any rate.

"Gramma-great?" A curly head peered sleepily at her from the pillow. Chubby hands clutched a balding toy dog that had once belonged to her own son.

"Yes, my wee handsome one?"

"Will you tell me a story?"

Biddy's throat tightened with unshed tears. Tears for Richard, the man she had married, Richard, the son she had lost, and Richard, the boy she had gained. As well as more, so much more.

"Yes, my little love." Limping forward, she sat on the bed and drew his slender frame into her arms. "Let me tell you a story. A story of brave men, daring deeds, greedy villains, and beautiful maids. Someday, when you are grown, you must promise to tell your own children. Then, one day, your children's children. If you do, we will all live a thousand years and beyond, somewhere . . . in someone's heart."